REACH

Edward Gibson

BANTAM BOOKS
NEW YORK • TORONTO • LONDON • SYDNEY • AUCKLAND

All of the characters in this book are fictitious,
and any resemblance to actual persons, living
or dead, is purely coincidental.

*This edition contains the complete text
of the original hardcover edition.*
NOT ONE WORD HAS BEEN OMITTED.

REACH

*A Bantam Spectra Book / published by arrangement with
Doubleday*

PRINTING HISTORY
Doubleday edition published June 1989
Bantam edition / May 1990

*Bantam Books are published by Bantam Books, a division of
Bantam Doubleday Dell Publishing Group, Inc. Its trademark,
consisting of the words "Bantam Books" and the portrayal of a
rooster, is Registered in U.S. Patent and Trademark Office and in
other countries. Marca Registrada, Bantam Books, 666 Fifth
Avenue, New York, New York 10103*

PRINTED IN THE UNITED STATES OF AMERICA
RAD   0 9 8 7 6 5 4 3 2 1

Julie—

> *Inspiration sparks energy,*
> *Love feeds it,*
> *Support gives it form.*
>
> *—Thanks for all three*

I offer many thanks to those who supported and improved this book: my friend, Mike Boughton; my agent, Joe Vallely: my editor at Doubleday, Pat LoBrutto; and Lou Aronica at Bantam.

Contents

IV TREK

V CONDEMN

VI CONFRONT

VII SURVIVE

We've spawned our Enemy—now it takes,
and it grows.

Wayfarer 2 Module

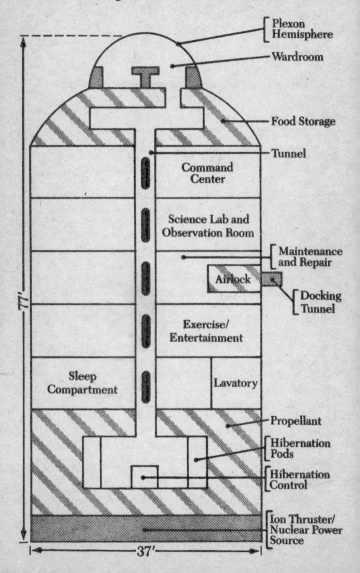

Prologue

Tell Me What
You Think

"Ahh. . . . Hi, Dad."

Ted looked down. His son's image sharpened. He had to smile. "Hi, Willie. Hey! You've been up to something. What?"

Spacecraft controls faded from Ted's mind.

Willie, just a little guy, belly high, squinted back up. He forced a smile, then folded his arms, a trick he'd just learned. It gave his hands something to do. The left pocket of his jeans, the one he never used, hung half-in, half-out and glistened mud brown. Three beads of sweat etched out a trail as they ambled down through the powdered dirt that covered his bare chest. They slowed when they reached his arms and belly, the belly that still bulged a bit with the residue of preadolescent fat. Yep, Willie ought to shoot up about another four inches this year.

Willie refolded his arms and concentrated. "Nothin', just playin' with Joey."

"Riding his motor scooter again?"

"Yeah . . . kinda."

Ted's mind struggled to free itself, to return to his spacecraft, to reach freedom and think. But he felt the back of his throat tighten and extra water fill his eyes. Little Guy always had something on the

front burner—first kid to test-fly a tar paper para-
chute or field-test that homemade beekeeper's outfit.
Willie—that sliver of life that helped make all the
rest worthwhile. Impossible not to love him.

Mind whispered—something's wrong.

But again his attention shifted back to Willie,
back to microman's face, to eyes that laughed and
darted with thoughts too quick for his tongue, to lips
pressed into a half-smile, to the smear of mud on his
cheek and its mirror image on the shoulder below, to
the mud caked to the top of his undershorts, to the
smell of stagnant water.

Mind shouted—something's wrong!

Once again Ted felt his vocal chords resonate,
his tongue and lips shape the sounds on their way out.
"Kinda? Kinda looks like you fell in the creek, then
kinda cleaned yourself off with muddy rags."

Willie sighed, shifted his weight to the other foot
and refolded his arms again.

Hasn't decided yet if it should be left over right
or . . . Ted's smile overflowed into a laugh. "Bingo!
The creek. How come you were riding in the creek?"

"Wasn't exactly riding *in* the creek, Dad."

"You tried to jump it?"

"Ahh . . . yeah." Willie came to life. "But this
time I made it, all the way! Joey just got the engine
fixed from the last time, and we built the ramp, and I
kinda . . . ahh, just kinda . . ."

"And you were the first test pilot. But you don't
look like you made it."

"I did, Dad! This time I really did! But when I hit
the other side, I kinda rolled backwards . . . and
kinda . . ."

Thunder cracked above, then rumbled and tumbled its way toward the horizon.

Ted's eyes shifted up. Willie's magnetism vanished. Mind freed itself and screamed—every detail
of this hot, humid Houston day, happened not here,
not now, but over two years ago and twenty-five
billion miles away!

A dream? No, much more. Too real. Something took what he once saw or heard or smelled or felt or thought, every detail his brain recorded and ran it back through his mind again—all just a replay.

Get control!

But more random slivers from his life, each a tight mental packet, each a precise pearl of a past experience, strung together and ripped through his mind's eye. In turn, they each commanded center stage and rammed all original thought into the wings.

"On every flight you make thousands of mistakes, and most are never noticed—except for the few that can kill."

The warning, a simple summary of years in airplanes and spacecraft, welled up. Nausea and fear surged up with it. He forced it down, forced it all back under. But it swelled up and washed over him again.

Ted's neck and back turned rigid and cold. Mistake? No. Done everything by the book. Mission's been perfect. What about my crew?

Ted grabbed a handhold, placed his toes over its edge, and pushed off. Back to the present, to the real world that he could touch and feel at will. Images weakened. He floated on a straight line toward the intercom. Perfect aim. Why not? Over many missions, movement in zero gravity had become second nature. But, like a curveball, he slid to the side at the last moment.

Ted reached over, flipped up two holovision power switches and waited. Nothing. No picture reached him from the outside. He switched to backup. Again, nothing.

Adrenaline surged. He rammed his feet against the wall and shot toward the center window. The motion trackers on the holovision cameras followed. Again he hit an arm's length off target. "Lousy aim. Bad as a new guy."

Ted reached to the side, placed his fingertips on

the handhold under the center window, drew his face up to its surface, and relaxed his grip. His eyes ran along the bridge that led from his Wayfarer module to its sister module 237 feet away. Everything looked in place.

He drifted two feet away from the window and pulled himself back, then started to drift away again. His fingers grazed the handhold then grabbed it tight. A force pulled him, not just another image yanked through his mind, but a force in the here and now. Some invader shocked him out of his lazy and sleepy world of zero gravity, out of his soft and subtle dreamlike motions, and now attacked him like fire in the night.

Invader straightened Ted's torso and pointed him toward the opposite wall. Ted's hands squeezed. Invader strengthened. Knuckles turned white and arms shook. Pain and fatigue had their way. Ted's fingers ripped open.

He accelerated over the floor, skipped and rolled, clutched at a handhold and missed, lodged an arm and felt it snap, then slammed forehead first into the opposite wall. His body, a discarded rag doll, flattened against the surface. Smooth, cold, hardness pressed into one cheek as a shoulder speared the other. Pain shot from the half-turn in his neck and the new joint in his arm, as it folded up behind his back and pushed cold fingers against his ear.

Debris tore loose, rained down and glued itself to the wall. A portable computer, still warm with the heat of his hand, smashed a foot from Ted's face. Its keyboard split, circuits stretched, then burst.

Invader pulled Ted's viscera toward the wall, squeezed all air from his lungs and rammed blood into cheeks, eyes, and temples. Split? Burst?

Like a mechanical goliath in pain, the spacecraft bellowed a low guttural groan. Its skeleton grated as cold hardness under Ted's cheek ratcheted and popped. Terror flooded him, that matter-of-fact tranquil terror that announces the end's only a tick away.

But, with one final lurch, one massive tear, all force vanished. Structure recoiled and kicked. Ted shot off the wall, rammed into a panel, floated free, and drifted back toward the windows. The holovision cameras continued to track. He looked into them, unsure of who was or would ever be on the other side.

"Arm's broken . . . maybe my rib. Blood's in my eye. Ship's torn up . . . my crew?"

Ted pulled himself to the center window with his good arm and peered out. Nausea and fear again twisted his gut and rippled up. His eye ran along the first two feet of the bridge, out to where it terminated, out to where only twisted and torn trusswork stared back.

"My crew—they're gone! What's out there?"

Hair on the back of his head and neck tingled, prickled, then stung. A fresh pain pierced his skull.

"Force, it ripped us apart. But still have cabin pressure. Power's still up. Computer's . . . com . . ."

The fresh pain exploded in his brain. Images flowed and again rammed all thought aside. Each experience, no longer at the pace his mind recorded them, flicked on and off screen as high-speed film. All sights and smells and sounds, all feelings and thoughts and emotions—all LIFE—compressed and accelerated as it poured out. Content blurred.

. . . Willie's giggle, stranglehold on neck, weight on shoulders, heels in sides . . . sea of maple leaves, light underbellies turned up, dance and bob in wind . . . cockroach on back, Eva laugh, shake it off, hop . . . hands cold, feet cold, toes numb, legs push, ice slide by, stick light, nose run, back hurt, puck's comin', reach . . .

Something unwove Ted's mental fabric one stitch at a time. Something yanked on a loose thread that dangled from his mind's edge, ripped it free, held it tight and sped away. Something now ripped his life, stitch by stitch, thread by thread, out through his mind's eye and stored it on some insatiable spool.

And that Something could not be stopped!

Holovision images continued away from *Wayfarer 1* at the speed of light, back toward Earth over thirty-seven hours away.

In a time short by human standards, Ted's essence flowed from his mind. All that he'd ever experienced or thought fled his human container, then mixed and diffused into Something larger. His essence contributed and received, then rewove.

Awareness returned.

I
CLASH

Individuals cluster into groups that create organizations, which in turn establish institutions that fabricate the Ultimate Horror—the Enemy that rapes the individual.

1

Trust

"Who's got front seat?"

"Dumb question."

The humid air, though still warm, felt cool. With no place to hide, it lay motionless and composed itself before the sun renewed its assault.

In darkness, two figures shuffled around their aircraft. Their lights flicked over its surfaces and into its crevices. Sweat flowed from their pores and soaked into their dry flight suits. They spoke in hushed tones that carried out to the distant edges of the concrete ramp, where they mixed with cricket conversations.

"You're right. My turn. I've got front seat."

"Sly try, Einstein, but you had it last—you really did!"

Excess water, rejected by the full air, hovered where it had condensed into wispy patches of fog. It coated the lush vegetation, already engorged with liquid. Scents of earth and foliage, of life, hung heavy. Tranquil abundance magnified the promise of a new day.

"Ya know, Jake, your problem's that you're just another insecure hotshot test pilot. You're afraid the only way not to get shown up is not to let me in the front seat."

"You may be part right, Speed, but my motivation's far stronger than that."

"Yeah, what?"

"Self-preservation."

The first rays of the solar furnace, disguised as a soft red glow, skimmed over dark mountainlike clouds in the Gulf, then nudged and poked the moist countryside. Thunder, the residue of the previous day's solar assault, grumbled in the distance. Dawn on the Texas coast, unchanged from billions that preceded it, crept westward again.

"Look, boss man. I didn't get up this early just to be ballast."

Jake put his arm around Speed's shoulder. "Why not, old buddy? Always best to work within your limits."

The RT7 aircraft flexed its jaws open wide, like a shark on the attack. A supersonic spike pierced forward from its black throat. Its sturdy neck supported two cockpits and two miniature knife-wings, then flowed rearward into its brawny torso, main swept-back wings, broad tail and oversize engine nozzle. Air could find no turn, no deviation, only a straight shot from jaws to nozzle. RT7 made it clear that it tolerated only a few parts stuck onto its engine. Its unpainted skin radiated coal-blackness, except for its violet-white, scorched leading edges and gold markings. Even as it sat on the ramp, RT7 appeared to move at high Mach. Its menacing appearance intimidated most, but it reached out and tugged on the guts of the few always in search of higher power and performance.

"Can't believe you're gonna do this to me again. I must be a slow learner."

"You're sure right here, Speed. After all, here I am, once more letting you observe the world's finest flying, up close, firsthand, and you don't jump at the chance."

"I'll give you one thing. You're not half the pilot I am, but at least you're humble."

Jake grabbed Speed's arm, looked him in the eye and laughed. "Look, Speed, last time you really did have front seat—really!"

"Ya know, I think you're right." Speed smiled and shrugged. "But, what the hell, it's always worth a shot."

Jake climbed up three steps and looked in the front cockpit. His gloves formed a miniature room around a grasshopper. "Hey, little guy, how'd you get in here? Bet ya didn't ask your mom if you could head out west." He climbed down and opened his hands on the concrete. The grasshopper bounded away. "Gotta watch all the time. Everybody's tryin' to sneak into the front seat."

The two pilots strapped their bodies into ejection couches.

"When you're done with systems CompuCheck, we're ready for engine start," said Jake. "Gotta hustle and get on the road. Can't be late for Dr. Daro this time."

"Almost there . . . done. Light it."

A husky rumble slipped from RT7. The calm swallowed it with ease, but its presence sharpened senses and quickened pulses. Life in the adjacent grasses and trees made ready to seek the safety of cover or distance.

"Ready for taxi, Speed."

"Same here. I'll check the clearance."

Speed pressed the CLEARANCE STATUS key on the board in the rear cockpit.

"Got it. It's the standard."

TV in both cockpits displayed:

WSF 73 cleared to World Space Federation Airfield (WSFA), Oceanside, Calif.;
Cleared taxi/takeoff/climb to 91,000 feet;
After takeoff head 260 to intercept Sonic Corridor 7, then direct WSFA;
Climb above 50,000 feet 30 miles west of Houston.

Jake released brakes. RT7 rolled forward, relieved to be given leash. Its structure quivered and trembled. Jake's love affair with RT7 flared again. He sensed the brute power and precision of its awakened systems, even as it ambled toward the starting line. The closeness of its life had grown to be something personal, a part of him. He savored his joy and anticipation in silence.

"Hey, boss man. How do you want it configured?"

"Put the systems in auto, but leave the flight controls in manual. Why let the computers have all the fun?"

"That means I'm sentenced to another world famous Jake Ryder tree-trimmer takeoff. Hell, it's too early in the morning to be scared. I'll sleep through it."

"Candyass. No guts, no glory."

The air traffic control indicators marked ATC in both cockpits flashed green as Jake rolled RT7 onto the runway. As he would aim a rifle sight, he pointed the spike under RT7's snout down the runway's lighted center line toward its invisible end over the horizon.

"Ready, Speed?"

"Let 'er rip."

RT7 tore air from its resting place, devoured it and ejected it in a white-hot shaft. Its growl exploded into the calm, panicked animals and birds and chased them outward.

"Systems and engine look good, boss."

"Thanks."

Like a well-trained thoroughbred, RT7 gathered itself, accelerated and rammed into still air. It pushed Jake farther into his form-fitted couch, gripped his body and shook it with muffled vibration. A muted roar reached Jake through the plexan canopy and fluttered the skin above the mask on his face. Jake kept RT7's spike fixed on the runway's distant end, as straight blurs of white light formed on either side.

His lungs filled with cold, metal-flavored oxygen. A smile welled up. "You're gonna love this, Speed."

Jake concentrated. There's 160. Rotate. Gear auto retract. Wing boundary layer off. Now just hold this hummer on the deck to 500.

Jakes was positive. It was predictable. It always was. Skimming the ground at 500 knots would be the high point of the day. The opportunity could never be ignored.

"Hey, Jake. We had a flicker of the master caution light at gear up, but systems look good. No indicators on."

"No sweat, computer's up. Trust it. Do a CompuCheck when we level off. If it doesn't see anything, we're OK. Just a glitch."

"I'll start now."

"Grunt time."

With a swivel of his wrist, Jake rotated the sidearm controller back. The g force surged and jammed him deeper into his couch. Once RT7 pitched halfway up toward vertical, he snapped it into seven quick rolls. Then sucked in a long, deep breath and relaxed. His smile faded.

Speed yawned. "Ya sure do make it hard for a body to sleep. Flying's supposed to be hours of boredom interrupted by moments of stark terror. Somehow, Ryder, ya got it all backwards."

Without further gyrations, RT7 climbed skyward at 40 degrees. It popped into the rays of the daytime sun that would soon spill onto the dark countryside below. At Mach 1.7, its ramturbo engine began its switch from turbojet to ramjet operation. In four minutes RT7 leveled off at 91,000 feet and accelerated to Mach 3.3. The yellow sun behind and to the left reversed directions, turned red and headed back below the horizon.

"From here on I'm going to fly with a little old lady."

"Speed, you mean . . . fly solo?"

"Good idea. You gonna punch out?"

"Look, if you were front seat, you would've done the same thing."

"Probably. But I would've done it with more class, more style. No doubt about it, boss. Should've stayed in the sack."

"No way, Speed. When Dr. Daro calls, we come."

"If we like our jobs, we do. At least we got priority to take one of these new birds. This's only the third time I've gotten into one, and my first time in the backseat, I might add."

"The squadron's supposed to get a total of twenty-one of 'em. Oughta ease the shortage. Had 'em on order since 2034, over three years now."

"Sure's a sweet machine. Once had an instructor who loved to say, 'The ramjet's the engine of the future—and always will be.' Glad he was wrong."

RT7 gulped in thin air, burned it with hydrogen-enriched fuel and threw it out the nozzle at three times the speed it'd entered. Its leading edges rammed into air, heated it and pushed it aside. Made of thermalloy, a titanium alloy, leading edges absorbed the heat but radiated it right back into the air before it could slip away and slide over the rest of the skin made of carbex, a composite of ultrastrength carbon fibers.

"OK, Jake, here's what CompuCheck shows. For some reason we've lost two of our three down indicators on our nose gear. Both of 'em say the gear's still down, even though we know it's up. The computer's ignoring those two indicators and's paying attention to only the one that's left and working. The gear system schematic confirms that one indicator's enough to do the job. Everything else looks normal."

"Thanks, Speed. Should be no problem. Computer's got it under control. Just the same, keep a sharp eye on it when I put gear down for landing, just in case."

"Will do."

Jake made a short entry into his keyboard. The

ATC indicator flashed green. "Just been cleared to ninety-five thousand and Mach 3.7. It'll help us pick up a few minutes."

"Good idea. What do ya think Dr. Daro wants?"

"Don't know for sure. Yesterday he called me direct. Usually he just sends an instacomm. Didn't say what's up, but he left no doubt that we're to be in his office at 0800 sharp."

"It might be related to *Wayfarer 1*. We haven't heard anything from Ted and his troops for three days."

"Yeah, think you're right, Speed. Dupree has Klaus and the comm guys at the control center working around the clock on it. They think a power surge wiped out their high-gain antennas."

"It could get pretty lonely out there without any chatter from Earth. On the other hand, the way Dupree's been throwing commands and changes at them, they probably like it. Not even Klaus has been able to turn him off."

"Well, we'll find out soon." Jake watched the lights of El Paso slide by seventy miles off the left wing. Halfway there. He flicked the FLIGHT CONTROL switch from MANUAL to AUTO and relaxed.

He thought again about Dr. Daro's urgency. Nope, no clues. But unless Dr. Daro dropped Jake square in the center of a new crisis, the decision that he and Val had just reached wouldn't change. And this visit offered the opportunity to tell Dr. Daro face-to-face. After sixteen years in the program, Jake decided the time had come to resign, to quit, dump it, chuck it, toss it all aside, to walk away from the position he'd worked most of his life to reach. Jake and Val had thought about the decision for several years. It hadn't come easy. But he understood himself and knew he could no longer put off the decision. The program, by its own nature and that of the people it selected, had grown into its own enemy.

Trying to apply logic to his dilemma, Jake'd traced it as far back as he could, back to the origin of passions and ambitions, back to a fall day in 2002. Saturday, three days past Jake's tenth birthday. The kid rode his new bike to Miramar Naval Air Station seven miles north of his home in San Diego. He hid the bike in the tall bush with the red berries, just off the east perimeter road. He checked as well as he could that no one watched, ran like hell—and zappo! —there he was, entrenched in a burrow, just big enough to hide him from view. No one could see him there, no one on the ground, no one in the control tower, no one except the pilots of the high-performance fighters, if they happened to look straight down as they barreled over the runway threshold for landing.

As the kid lay spread-eagle in the hard mud and dry grass, he squirmed to find a comfortable position and watched the aircraft make their own final wiggles before smoke puffed between wheels and runway. Some came over so low he felt he could reach up and touch a tire. Their rumbles and howls vibrated his skin and blasted his eardrums, even through the soft clay he'd pushed in his ears, then died just before their tires screeched. Smells of burned rubber and burned fuel filled his nostrils. Sometimes, if one flew a little off to the side, he'd see the pilot's face. Jake's pounding chest, fixed jack-o-lantern grin and eyes that refused to blink, gave him a simple understanding of himself—he could never be just a watcher.

He *had* to get into those machines, *had* to get his hands on their controls, *had* to command all that power and speed. He made a pact with himself. When he grew up, nothing short of front seat would do.

After high school, Jake started his climb. The system accommodated. It presented steps of just the right size, just the right visibility. He earned a B.S. in aeronautical engineering and entered flight training. The Navy seemed to offer the most challenge, professionalism and emphasis on flying, or, as some put it, the minimum of ground-pounder mickey-mouse. With his wings of gold came confidence and pride, emotions he often saw spill over into cockiness and arrogance in others. He yielded little to the temptation, yet performed with style.

The deaths of friends magnified his own humility. He realized that his new toy stood by him with all the care and concern of a loaded cannon, ever ready to fire his body into an early grave. When it happened to others, pilot error almost always pulled the trigger.

The next step, test pilot school at Patuxent River in Maryland, brought exposure to technical depth, and with it, more humility. But by now achievement came as a reflex. He again excelled. The need to be composed, alert, analytical and responsive left no room for arrogance. Time, training and drive had produced a professional.

Jake looked up.

And just as before, another step waited, one ripe with fresh challenge—space flight! He focused and pursued. In the annual selection of 2021, NASA chose Jake and thirty-six other candidates for astronaut training.

How simple it all seemed. Just a stairway of bite-sized steps. Step up—reward. Step up—reward. Step up—reward. There was always promise. Always a fast track. Always achievement. Just the normal way of life.

After three years of training, the next steps appeared right on cue—missions: two six-month tours of lunar bases Armstrong and Dunayev; one year as lead space station logistics pilot; ten months on an orbital flight of Io, a moon of Jupiter; then three years on periodic tours as a commander of operations on polar Space Station Kennedy.

But neither he nor Val enjoyed their long months of separation. It no longer seemed fair to either of them. And after his many missions, each new one seemed a repeat of an old. Routine set in.

The steps had leveled out. Some moved sideways. Some even dropped down. Life'd lost its incline.

Jake's internal machinery loped along at half power. He thought about taking a high-paying slot running flight operations for ISI, Integrated Space Industries. Although mundane, it'd enhance his bank account, time for his wife and music, and access to a fuller life.

Over 70 percent of all space operations were run by commercial companies, not governments, and he might as well join the crowd. He couldn't play forever, and, if he had to be bored, he might just as well get paid for it. But Jake Ryder wasn't made that way. He delayed. Hindsight showed he'd made the right move. A major step for all space exploration lay ahead.

In 2032, after eleven years of political posturing and haggling, public pressure intensified and the United States, Russia, the European Space Agency, Canada, China and Japan formed the World Space Federation. Other nations soon joined. The combined resources of WSF at first opened up new levels of interest, sophistication and challenge in space exploration. In addition, when selected to head WSF Astronaut Operations, he encountered a new type of challenge—management.

Initially, Jake enjoyed the opportunity to lead others and the flexibility that went with the position. He helped select the crews, and, when he went on a mission, Dr. Daro made him its commander. But in time, the missions again became repetitive, time away from Val dragged even more, and management grew into one-part leadership and nine-parts administration.

Again, Jake looked around.

But now he saw no more steps up, only bigger titles, bigger offices, bigger windows and bigger desks. No more achievement, only squares to be filled. No more creation or control, only endless communication and coordination with an ever increasing number of other cells in a boundless bureaucratic body that had taken on a cancerous growth. No more simple challenge and reward, only repetitive flights mired in a sticky, viscous sea of memos and meetings, calls and conferences, rules and regulations, information and investigations, data and defamations, and disclosures and dismissals.

Jake realized that he'd been devoured and consumed. And now, even he helped further bloat this bureaucratic body. Yes, he'd become part of it, part of this thing that smothered all it touched, part of a system becoming too choked with data to produce, but too busy with internal processes to notice, part of this being that'd evolved into everyone's common Enemy.

Fresh goals, lofty goals, freedom of choice, challenge and dynamic achievement—all in the past. Now only his moments in RT7 separated him from resignation. But he couldn't justify staying in the program on that alone, not year after year. It looked like Integrated Space Industries' time had come. Nothing to lose. He hoped Dr. Daro would understand.

Speed's voice sliced into his thoughts. "Only 270 miles left to Oceanside."

"Yep. About time to give the computers a rest and start down." Jake flipped the flight control switch back to MANUAL and started a gradual descent. Some "pilots" let RT7's three CompuThink (CT) 210 computers fly all the way down, land and stop on the runway. But Jake would have no part of it. No way would he degrade himself to the role of parking lot attendant.

"I've got the weather on the screen, Jake. Looks like crud all along the coast. Just another standard California morning. Fog, tenth of a mile visibility and no wind."

Jake glanced at the data on his television display. A ground computer received data on WSFA runway's visibility, winds, surface-tire friction and other conditions, averaged it over both a minute and an hour, and transmitted the results to incoming aircraft. In addition, RT7's radar probed the space it penetrated and displayed colored, three-dimensional pictures of any cloud layers or severe weather present. "You called it, Speed. Nothing but fog."

"Hey, that's good. If I can't see the ground, your landing won't scare me."

"My landings could never scare you, Speed, if yours don't."

RT7's nose pointed at Oceanside. Jake peered into the blackness. Nothing. He dimmed his internal lights. Faint, sinuous threads of light appeared below, then expanded, loomed up and intensified. As if projected through frosted glass, a wide strip of bright light meandered from left to right and gave hazy definition to the fogbound coastline from Mexico to Santa Barbara. The strip pushed farther into the mountains and desert at San Diego to his left, Newport just off his nose and Los Angeles to his right, sites that once were distinct cities. Farther inland, a faint but crisp cobweb of lights emerged from towns and cities not yet swelled together.

Jake slowed to less than the speed of sound. Below, sleepers savored their last moments before alarms prodded them out of warmth and darkness and dreams, prodded them into harsh light to face cold realities of another day. If jolted from their pillows by a sonic boom, they'd swarm like angry hornets from a kicked nest. For Jake, or any pilot, it'd be career-limiting.

Dim light, warmth and an image of his own home that he'd slipped out from just two hours previous flicked before his mind's eye.

"Hey, Speed. Once again, check the nose-gear-position readouts when we get on final approach. Holler if there's any indication the gear's not all the way down and locked."

"Will do."

With its engine at idle, RT7 sliced through the air without sound or vibration. It suspended Jake in a black void. The only indication of motion came from faint lights that crept underneath.

"You know, Speed, they've made these high-altitude approaches too easy. Here we are a hundred and twenty miles out, and all I have to do is stay locked on center line and glide slope and drive it straight on to the deck. Not even one simple turn."

"Piece of cake. Think ya can handle it, boss?"

"I'll have my eyeballs locked on Holo-HUD when we're below five thousand. Watch the systems for me."

"Will do. I've got my displays set to follow us all the way down. The screen's split between systems, nav and the gear indications on the optional area. Everything's lookin' good."

"Thanks."

"Hey, Jake, you know the last thing that goes through a bug's brain when he bashes into your canopy?"

"Don't think I wanta know."

"His buns."

"Go back to sleep."

Jake called up Holo-HUD, a computer-generated holographic heads-up-display. At arm's length, it formed a three-dimensional image of the approaching runway as if he looked out through the canopy on a clear day. It also displayed airspeed, altitude, angle of attack and other data in graphic form on the edge of his field of view. For all practical purposes, he flew as if fog didn't obscure the real scene. Only in the last seventy feet would his sight of the actual runway give slight improvement to his manual landing.

"Boundary layer control's active. There's auto gear extension. All gear're down and locked. We've got three down indications on the nose gear, one that's real and two that're still failed and unchanged. You're flying it almost as well as the computer does, right on the money. No sweat, Jake, you've got it wired."

Jake's holographic and real worlds merged. From his mind, through spinal cord and nerves, through muscle and fingertips, through controller and electronics, through hydraulics and control surfaces, he probed for the runway. From inches up, RT7 settled to the surface.

"Not bad, boss. Not your typical carrier crash. Even you Navy pilots can be retrained."

Jake pulled the throttle to idle. RT7's nose started a slow downward rotation.

The CT 210s received their inputs. CT 210s decided, then issued precise commands.

Jake felt a muffled klunk and heard a change in aerodynamic noise. RT7's nose continued down past the horizon.

An invisible fist wrenched Jake's gut. "What the? . . . *damn!*" Nose gear—retracted! *Why?*

RT7 plowed forward, its tail high in the air. Jake lurched against his straps. Sparks exploded from under RT7's nose and its metal antenna vanished in the flash. Its skin offered more resistance, but the grooved concrete surface grated it like cheddar cheese. Shreds of carbex glowed orange and fanned out on either side. Vibrations of grinding structure pierced through Jake's body to his teeth and bones.

Jake fought for control. He had to steer with the brakes, press one just a little more than the other, keep RT7 straight, not let it turn sideways—keep them from rolling up into a tight little ball!

Concrete approached Jake's face as it eroded through RT7's snout. The invisible deceleration force pressed him toward the grater. In time, speed slowed and grind faded. Then, with one last lurch, one last shriek, one last scrape, all stopped.

Silence.

Jake hung against his shoulder straps. His ears pounded. For an interminable second he peered straight ahead into the dim world outside, scrutinized the ridges and valleys of the grooved concrete only feet from his face, then glanced around. "No fire yet—safe the systems and get out!"

"In work!"

Dark, quiet, humid, but slightly cooler, it didn't seem much different than what he'd left an hour ago. He paused in the grass next to the runway, his helmet still on, his back wet and his body cold and rigid. He stared into the fog.

Moonlight outlined RT7. With all the dignity of an ostrich, it perched on its two legs with its neck buried in the ground and its tail offered to the heavens. But it didn't whimper. And it didn't whine. Only ticks and tings echoed from its innards as it cooled and contracted.

"Looks safe so far, Jake. Don't see any fire."

"Yeah, safe. Electrical system's cut off back to the fuel cell. Oxygen tank's intact."

"Yep. Just one slightly used RT7 with a hell of a nose job."

"Smell fuel?"

"Yeah!"

"Run!"

WUMPPPH!

The explosion allowed them but a few steps. Night turned to day. The blast arched their backs, lifted them and flung them outward. It scorched and seared. Legs churned even as their chests and faces slid over the grass. Speed rose, stumbled and hit the ground a second time. Jake ran three steps back into the blaze, felt his eyebrows sizzle and ripped Speed up by the collar. They ran again.

After a dozen strides, the heat on Jake's back reached a tolerable level. "Far enough." He stopped, turned and squinted into the flames. RT7 shrieked, sharp and clear and loud, then surrendered to the inferno. Jake strained but heard only the roar of the flames. From his clenched fists to his set jaw, his body strained and turned rigid.

Speed moved face-to-face with him, gripped his

shoulders, locked eyes with his and shouted, "You kept us from being toasted!"

Jakes eyes nodded.

"You did one helluva job of keeping it straight. Sucker was right on center line . . . before it blew. No one could've done it better. If you let the computer keep it, we'd have cartwheeled right off into the frappin' weeds."

Jake stared over Speed's shoulder into the red and yellow blaze that mirrored his mood. Scream, swear, hit something or someone? *No*—can't change it!

Speed's grip tightened. "You're a good man, Jake. Thanks."

Speed's consolation reached Jake's ears. His mind recorded it, and his head nodded. But appreciation could only come later, much later after streams of self-incrimination, wounded pride and then anger ceased to seethe and boil in his brain. For more than the joy of living or fear of dying, anger boiled up and churned inside Jake Ryder, anger toward some ill-defined enemy that within a fraction of a second had raped the professional and the human within.

A few words squibbed out with an exhale. "Never put a nick on an airplane in twenty-seven years—and now I nearly killed us." Jake's lips pulled tighter as he stared into RT7's cremation. A fire truck's siren penetrated his awareness, then swelled in volume. Its engine gunned and tires squealed.

It all seemed so simple, so straightforward. It got us—but *what?!*

2

Blame

Cold hands and overpriced—damn machine's no better than a human doctor.

Jake tolerated the remainder of his automated physical exam by RoboDoc as he forced his mind back through it all again. He analyzed the facts with Speed as they rode to WSF Operations, checked in with Dr. Daro's secretary, changed out of their flight suits and then once again, when they elected to go through their accident debriefing before their physicals. Holovision cameras recorded every nuance of their discussion from their flight's initial planning all the way through to RT7's fiery finale. He understood the pieces but they didn't fit together.

PHUUUUT! The mechanical medic spit out its diagnosis.

Jake thought so. Only scrapes on his hands and face. Just plain lucky. He looked over at Speed. He'd come to look for answers to the hard ones from him. For Joseph T. (Speed) Spencer not only respected the tools of reason and logic, but he could wield them. He often slashed through technical problems before others even had them formulated. And he also had the wisdom to value a good hunch. But, on this problem, so far, he'd come up with nothing.

Speed glanced back at Jake. "Can't see it, boss,"

said Speed. "Can't think of anything else we should've done."

What Jake had come to understand was that Speed consisted of two discrete components. His frothy outer shell took on a wisecracking, easygoing demeanor that most people mistook for his total substance. However, a solid center hid within, a core of capability that'd earned him a Ph.D. from Darmont in physics, entry into the Space Program and rare selection for pilot-training in preparation for a commander's slot. Dr. Daro, a perceptive leader, put raw talent above labels or specific training that took only time to acquire. His no-nonsense approach also penetrated Speed's froth and found the right building blocks—a sharp mind, the right attitude and an intuitive feel for flight operations. Dr. Daro continued to groom what he'd found.

Speed had learned to use his outer shell like a Trojan horse. He'd disarm most people before they realized they'd been measured. Once perceived, some regarded his duel trait as sinister. But Jake knew different. At this point in his life, Speed did it by second nature, not premeditation. And each time it happened, Jake just stepped aside, smiled to himself and watched. It took most people several Speed-encounters before they sensed the intellect below the surface. Some never did.

Speed's nominal-standard-medium-regular appearance furthered the deception. Of average height with ordinary short, brown hair, his mind hid behind a pleasant boyish face that, almost always, flashed between two states, half-grin and full-grin. His common hazel eyes, viewed with the grin, appeared to twinkle. But if one looked only within the deep sockets, the twinkle turned to laser penetration. His broad shoulders and trim waist gave another clue to the internal Speed. Their maintenance required a rigid discipline not often encountered in a man of forty-three, even in his profession.

Only a few commanders other than Jake under-

stood Speed's practical value. His intellectual engine
always churned at full power, always generated a
steady torrent of thought. When the pace of external
events couldn't keep up with the engine, which almost always was the case, part of the torrent diverted
to wisecracks that burbled and bubbled out in a
steady stream and whipped up the froth. But the
other part of the torrent, quick, steady and analytic,
always flowed underneath and provided Jake with a
reliable insurance, an intellectual minesweeper that
detected the small, subtle oversights that kill.

Most of the time, Jake accepted the froth and
even enjoyed it. But as Speed faced him now, few
bubbles seeped out. The froth'd gone flat. The core
lay open. One mine had slipped through.

"Jake, we need more data."

"That's for sure. The rep from AI should be here
soon, but let's get a head start and go study the system. The Systems Holo-Trainer's available."

"Worth a shot. If we can't figure it out with that,
we never will."

At the control panel in the adjacent training
room, Jake set the configuration for holographic
viewing. Three more entries into the CompuThink
(CT) 6000 computer produced a three-dimensional
holographic image of RT7's landing gear system generated by laser light. CT 6000 stripped away the
system's complexity, expanded the image to the size
of an automobile and projected it into the center of
the room, where it hovered. Mechanical structure,
electrical and hydraulic lines, data paths and software logic, each in different colors, all hung in space
woven together.

Jake walked around it, peered into it, then studied it. Nope, nothing obvious. But still, what a training aid! The new guys just don't know how soft they
have it, Jake thought. Holography makes it all so
much easier to understand than drawings, schemat-
ics and all the 2-D crap that had to be used before.
Like they say, one holograph's worth a million words.

The human brain and eyes're far superior to anything the brain could invent. Details of colored 3-D images can be recognized and understood in a flash. It's just a natural ability developed over millions of years in order to stay alive.

The holographic market had just entered the explosive phase. Although holography originated over a half-century before, optical storage of data in quantities large enough to support storage of high resolution images hadn't became available until 2022. And, by 2027, both memory capacity and data retrieval rates increased to levels where image motion became possible. As the addition of motion to still pictures had made movies early in the last century, so the addition of motion to holographs started a new industry—holovision.

But the expense of early systems placed them out of reach of everyday use by any of the world's space agencies, including NASA. Except in the days of Project Apollo seventy years before, tight budgets, rather than technology, had always defined the pace. Not till after the combined resources of WSF became available in 2032 did holovision see selected use within government space programs. The WSF administrators used it first for holovision conferences, then allowed it to be installed in training facilities.

Jake moved to the keyboard and eliminated all but one component of the gear system. They examined it, then scrutinized it. In turn, they went through each component. Then Jake reassembled the integrated system.

"Shouldn't have happened, boss. Nose gear shouldn't have retracted."

"We're screwin' up somewhere."

"Doesn't this facility also have holovision?" asked Speed.

"Yeah, it does. Image animation oughta help us trace the events."

"Feature's new to me. I gotta find some instructions to activate it." Speed started a search of CT

6000's contents and began mumbling. "Wish I knew why headquarters gets all this good stuff before Houston. We've got the real need for it, but they get it. Just more of their locologic. Damn administrators and lawyers and bean counters just play with it. Don't know a thing about operations. Think it's something only done by surgeons. Damn parasites slither on their bellies in the tall grass till the battle's over, then they leap in and bayonet the wounded. Oughta cram all their butts into the next logistics module and . . ."

A shuffle at the door replaced Speed's lecture. Jake looked up and studied the newcomer: dark-brown shoes, white socks, green-plaid pants, light-brown belt, bright-yellow shirt that might have fit twenty pounds ago and wide, medium-brown tie that he'd already pulled open.

Speed mumbled again. "Gotta be either a doctor who can't find the golf course or an aerospace engineer."

The newcomer held out his hand. "Commander Ryder, I'm Vic Tasso, an engineering representative of Aircraft Integrators. I'm here to discuss the cause of your accident with you."

Jake shook the cold, rigid hand and studied Tasso again: forced smile, rapid breaths, wide eyes, smudged black horned-rimmed glasses, head covered with a few black hairs and a lot of sweat. Poor guy probably got yanked out of bed right after we torched it, he thought.

"Hello, Vic," said Jake. "Thanks for coming. Sorry you got put to work so early for this."

"Don't worry about it. That's my job. I'm just glad that you two're OK. Could've been worse."

Speed also shook Vic's hand. "Mornin', Vic. You bet it could've been worse. Jake did everything right once the gear retracted. But somewhere we matched wits with your machine and lost."

"Vic, sorry, but we've got to make this short. We've got a command performance with Dr. Daro."

"OK. Let me give you a quick summary of what we've learned so far. After we recovered RT7's data recorder and studied your debriefing, our engineering staff at CompuThink in Boston simulated your flight. They gave us a first cut at the role the CT 210s played in all this."

"Oh-oh," said Speed. "Software razzle-dazzle on the way."

"The two nose-gear-position indicators that gave the continuous UP indication are right next to one another." Vic pointed to where they hung in the holographic image. "Evidence indicates that right at the moment you lifted off the runway, you hit a bird. The impact misaligned them and caused the erroneous indications."

Speed slipped a sideways glance at Jake. "Killer."

Jake frowned back at Speed. "Sorry, old buddy. Looks like I blew it. My hotdog takeoff just about did us in."

"No, that's not right!" said Speed. "Vic, one bird shouldn't be able to wipe out a whole aircraft. What happened at landing?"

"That's where your helpful CT 210 computers stepped into the act. As you know, they contain safety override software, or SOS. It's strictly a backup to make sure all systems are in their proper configurations at critical points in the flight."

"Yeah, the SOS, the pilot's guardian angel." Speed's eyes rolled. "Designed to keep the dummies in the cockpit from screwin' up."

"Unfortunately, the last edition of the software changed SOS so that it no longer talks to the rest of the computer. In the past, when the computer had bad data, SOS would blindly copy it and use it. Therefore, SOS wasn't a good backup. So they made it independent, found a way to keep it pure."

Speed's face dropped into its rare zero-grin state. "Pure, huh? I see what happened. The computer's morals nearly killed us. SOS not told indicators broken, thought the gear was always up, reversed its position at landing and . . . El Cruncho Grande!"

Jake gave Speed a quizzical look, then took a step toward Vic. "I didn't know the computer doesn't talk to the SOS. What happened next?"

"Just as you realize now, when you told the computer to ignore the two broken indicators, your request wasn't sent to SOS."

Jake's eyes raced over the holographic image. Speed's face remained at zero-grin as his head nodded.

Vic continued. "Then at landing, the SOS saw the radar altimeter read less than 100 feet, airspeed was less than 260, and that you'd pulled off power. So, just as it's programmed to do, the SOS assumed you were going to land and checked to see if the gear was down."

"That's where SOS decided to help us."

"Right, Speed. SOS looked at the position of the nose gear, read the two of the three indicators that said the nose gear was up, believed them because it wasn't told not to, and, after a short delay, commanded the nose gear to reverse its position. In other words, the SOS commanded the nose gear up, thinking it was doing just the opposite."

Speed shook his head. "The computer's worse than a pilot—never gets all the facts and bungles what it has."

Jake took another step toward Vic. The veins in his neck bulged, unable to carry away all the blood that reddened his face. "Why didn't our training tell us this'd happen?!"

Vic lost as much color as Jake'd gained. He stepped back. "CompuThink has described the new SOS in the most recent RT7 *Systems Manual.*"

Jake again narrowed the space between him and Vic. "But CompuPub puts out a new one of those monsters every two weeks. It's over five hundred pages long! Why wasn't it in our procedures?"

"Ahh . . . since it was a double failure, and SOS itself is a backup, making it a triple failure, the new procedure hasn't made it into the pilot's checklist yet."

"Triple failure? It was only one damn bird!"

"Ahh . . . now it looks like it may have been an oversight not to put it in the procedures."

"Oversight? It nearly killed us!"

Speed stepped between Jake and Vic. "Most likely the oversight was just the usual one, Jake—lack of common sense by the total system. Each guy probably did his job right, probably letter perfect. Each microthinker followed all his rules. But, just like our friendly CT 210s, the system never had the sense to tell itself what it really needed to know, especially us."

Jake cocked his jaw to one side, then nodded. "You're right, Speed." He forced a smile as he looked into Vic's face. "Sorry, Vic, I don't mean to shoot the messenger. Thanks for explaining it."

"I understand. If I'd been in the cockpit, I'd feel the same." Vic's head dropped. His eyes avoided Jake's as he stepped backwards. "Ahh . . . buttaah . . . I've gotta show you one more thing before you go. The guys at CompuThink fed the accident data into the AIC, their accident investigation computer. Here're the preliminary results." Vic stretched to hand the printout to Jake.

RT7 Accident—WSF 73—8/22/37

Primary Cause:	PILOT ERROR—*failure to correct SOS input*
Contributing Factors:	*Co-location of nose gear position indicators*
	Failure of airfield bird dispersal system
	Faulty specifications given CompuThink by AI

Jake wadded up the printout and fired it down. *"Pilot error!* Why should I hang because the damn computer can't talk to itself?"

Vic's heels nudged backwards into the base of CT 6000's control station. "Sorry, Jake, but as pilot-in-command, you get charged with it. Just bad luck. If only you hadn't gotten that bird."

"He got the bird all right!" said Speed. "It's not even close to being fair. Can't he get off with just a fine from the Audubon Society?"

Jake's shoulders dropped. His eyes shifted to Speed. "Let's not fight it now. I'll do that at the formal Accident Investigation Board."

"Don't take it personally," said Speed. "The bureaucracy bungled it, not you."

"Hell, I screwed up first," said Jake. "And I'm probably more guilty than any other single person. But our procedures are the real problem. The system has to make 'em perfect, then we have to follow 'em religiously. It's the only way we have, to stay on top of all this complexity."

"You're right, boss man. But how many other oversights are out there in the weeds, just waitin' to do violence to our warm, young, tender, pink little bodies?"

Jake glared at Speed. "Too many. In addition to our own screwups, the system's perfected an infinite variety of ways to kill us."

"But that's the nature of the game, Jake. We can play it, or we can get out—but we can't change it!"

"You're right, Speed. Let's move out. Dr. Daro's waitin'."

3

Challenge

Jake frowned.

Speed spit the words out the corner of his mouth. "Go any faster, and we'll have to file a flight plan."

Jake's frown deepened.

"Lighten up, boss man. Got lots of time. Besides, Dr. Daro'd go unstable if we ding two Federation vehicles in one morning, even if one of them's just a Drab Bomb."

The accelerator under Jake's foot remained fixed as his mind cycled the same thoughts over and over. Damn nearly killed us. No doubt about it—shoulda played it safe. But *pilot error?* Jake "Pilot-Error" Ryder. Who'd you say? Ryder? Oh, yeah. I remember him . . . the guy who really screwed up! Jake's foot pressed down harder.

The road from the WSF Airfield to the Administration Building ricocheted through the mountains that confined it, that confined Jake. He fought it.

After seven miles the road turned into a straight chute with a gentle grade that eased into the city below. Jake glanced ahead as he swerved out of the last turn. Except where patches of fog crept in from the ocean, thirty miles of shoreline greeted him in one panoramic view. His foot lightened.

Pastel marinas and piers fingered into blue ocean straight ahead. A solid swath of houses and landscaped yards clung to slopes that extended to horizons on either side. A kaleidoscope of colors, rich colors of vibrant vegetation, exploded wherever Sun could reach over mountains and find Earth.

Speed looked up and his face relaxed to full grin. "Good thing Senator Whittington was head of the Space Committee when we formed WSF. Sure knew where to apply the heat. If it wasn't for him, we might be lookin' at gray Moscow skies and buildings to match."

Jake let the colors into his mind and pushed gray gloom to the rear. He pulled in a deep breath. Moist ocean scent flooded his lungs. "Always feels good to be back out here. Never appreciated it much as a kid, but I do now."

"Ya know, Jake, headquarters wouldn't be a bad place to work, if it wasn't bureaucracy gone berserk."

"Don't I know it. I was assigned here for ten months in '33. Nearly suffocated. Couldn't do it any longer than that. But maybe someday I'll hang it up and go with ISI down in Encinitas. Val'd love it. Maybe I *would*, too."

"What'd you do at headquarters?"

"I had to come up with a unified set of Wayfarer Program operations requirements and coordinate inputs from every country—harder than tryin' to put socks on an octopus."

"From what I hear, industry sometimes isn't much better."

"Afraid you're right."

They intersected the flat, fourteen-lane Pacific Coast Highway and turned onto the upper level that headed north. Gravity no longer pulled their car along, no longer pushed power back into its energy storage. The whine of the electric engine jumped to a higher pitch as Jake set the speed at eighty-five, both the upper and lower limit. Radar modulated it

to keep them locked in position relative to other
vehicles.

The road offered little challenge. Jake left only
his thumb and index finger on the wheel. He jiggled
it just enough to sense the play and the car's response. Nope, not bad. Control's tight and responsive, especially for a Drab Bomb.

They arced off the highway onto WSF Drive,
followed it a quarter mile and approached the front
gate in single file with the tail end of morning traffic.
Jake inserted his IdentoCard into the optical reader
next to the steering wheel. A CT 4000 in the WSF
Administration Building screened the transmitted
code. They passed without default.

"Did you ever read that lawyer lecture on the
sign back there, Speed, the one that starts 'Pursuant
to WSF regulations, the entrance of individuals to, or
their . . . er, whatever'? I've gone through WSF
gates over a thousand times but never made it past
the first couple of lines."

" 'Bout a year ago I finally stopped to read it.
Curiosity, I guess. Had to take several passes through
it. Concluded it's just WSF''s Open Drawers Policy."

"I'll bite."

"If you enter here, we can enter you—right
down to your drawers! It's their right to search. I like
my words better."

"Ya shoulda been a lawyer."

They hunted for a parking slot close to the Administration Building, then farther out.

Speed looked around and mumbled, "Forced
out here to the tules . . . and they're filled."

Farther out they found a slot. Seven minutes of
quick strides later, they reached the elevator that
took them up to the top of the thirty-seven-story
building. Jake led as they burst into Dr. Daro's reception area. He slowed as his feet mushed into thick
carpet.

Jane Lentnel, Dr. Daro's secretary, looked up.
She flexed a smile, attractive but aloof and mechani-

cal, as she glanced at the first of the two men. A bit over six feet, he walked straight and erect. Angular sharp features and the movement of his lean body suggested hard muscle and quick reactions. He appeared to be in his late thirties. A full head of straight black hair tended to confirm it, except for the thread of gray at the temples. Electronic storage three feet from her elbow documented his age at forty-five. A slight smile that slid to one side took the edge off his square profile. He looked normal this morning—except for an extra measure of cold, gray-green intensity to his eyes. Her smile widened and warmed as her eyes softened with recognition.

"Good morning, Jake. Glad you two are OK!"

"Mornin', Jane. Thanks. Good to see you again."

"Hi, Speed. We're always glad to have you both out here, even if it's only for a short time. Dr. Daro would like you to go right in."

"Thanks," Jake said through a wide smile.

Speed bounded to a stop, bowed, clicked his heels, reached for Jane's hand and kissed it. "Your radiance is second only to the morning sun."

Jane laughed, shook her head, then studied Speed. Her smile faded. This morning she sensed an interior to Speed that ran uncoupled and opposite to his exterior.

Sixty feet of curved, transparent plexan formed the outer two walls of Dr. Daro's office. A graduated green tint softened sunlight that spilled through the wall to the left and sharpened the view of the WSF complex below, metropolitan Oceanside that pressed three miles forward to the ocean, and the now solid mass of vibrant color that reached outward in both directions along the coast.

The man behind the desk stood at attention, the stance people accepted as his norm. His build and profile reminded some of an older version of Jake. He stared outward toward the southern horizon. The set of his jaw indicated the view was not uppermost on his mind. With no visible motion to his feet, he pivoted to face his visitors.

"Good morning, gentlemen. Thank you for responding rapidly."

Handshakes were brief but firm.

Jake glanced at Dr. Daro. "Hello, sir." Dr. Daro's rigid features gave nothing away, but his eyes made it clear that today's visit was not social.

"Good morning, sir," added Speed.

Jake never heard Speed call anyone else "sir." He just wasn't the military or submissive type. But with Dr. Daro, Speed exhibited an open and honest respect. In fact, Speed, like Jake and the entire diverse corps of their hard-charging colleagues, displayed not only respect but also a bit of awe. Even among a group of overachievers, M. P. Daro stood out: Ph.D., test pilot, spacecraft commander, flight director, VP at International Space Industries and now Director of WSF Mission Operations. But titles alone didn't do it. Nor did tales of legendary performance. Day-by-day exercise of blunt strength and fairness gave him the rare ability to lead, not just administer. From the old school, he rewarded effort and honesty, but devastated anyone caught playing Machiavellian games. And at sixty-five, many productive years lay before him until optional retirement at eighty.

"I'm sorry we weren't able to be here at 0800 as you requested," said Jake.

"Yes, I understand. I just got a briefing from Tasso on your accident. It was unfortunate. But it is also clear that you did a good job of preventing something much worse. I have requested the procedures group to take a closer look at RT7. It could have other idiosyncrasies that are not properly covered by pilot procedures. The charge of pilot error is questionable. I will form an investigation board this afternoon, and we will discuss this further only when they have reached their findings. Let us move on to why I brought you here—a mission to which I have assigned you both."

Dr. Daro studied their faces, then motioned to the firm couch and chairs adjacent to his electronic work station. "Please sit down. I will give you an overview first. Then you will hear from Delgado and Hofmeister, and later, Dupree."

Jake and Speed sat, then froze.

"You are both assigned to *Wayfarer 2*. Jake, you command it. Speed, you are the Second Pilot and Chief Scientist. Nominate the remainder of your crew by 0800 tomorrow. In short, your mission is to determine what went wrong with *Wayfarer 1* and rescue any of the crew that are still alive."

Jake's internal spring ratcheted a few notches tighter. More than usual, Dr. Daro's voice reminded him of the low growl of a large dog.

"We have had a problem with *Wayfarer 1*. We believe we have lost one or more of the crew. We do not know their exact condition, but we have direct evidence that Ted encountered a severe problem, one that affected both modules. We are reviewing the data to determine the status and location of each module. So far, we have received no data or voice from either module since the problem. The exact nature of what they encountered is unknown."

"What's the general nature of their problem?" asked Jake. "Had they reached the Objects yet? And how could the others be at a different location?"

"Yeah, why'd they separate the two modules?" asked Speed.

"You will get the specifics of what we know from Delgado and Hofmeister in a few minutes. Let me first give you an overview and make some necessary points."

Jake leaned forward, his elbows on his knees, his hands clasped together as he followed the precision movements of Dr. Daro's lips above his set jaw. Hope Ted and his crew're all right, he thought. Gotta do all we can to help them. At last, a real mission with real challenge! But am I the right one?

"The only story we can construct so far is that they had a failure of the primary thruster on one module. It must have come on and could not be cut off. Since the other module was not thrusting, the combination spun up. When the RPM got high enough, the centrifugal force caused a failure on the bridge and the two modules ripped apart. However, there are a lot of problems with this story. It is only speculation with not much data to support or deny it."

Jake's eyes sharpened as his mind quickened. *Ted of all people. God, I pray he's in one piece. It's always that way. The best hang their butts over the edge the most. But what happened?*

"In order to get some visual and radar data, we have diverted *Stellar Probe 12* to the Wayfarers. We have aborted its prime mission of search and analysis."

Something snapped to life in Jake's gut, and it felt good. His drive'd popped out of its deep freeze and thawed fast. A motor that'd been still for years finally kicked over. He had no way to turn it off. Nor did he want to. He felt flutters in chest and throat, his back and shoulders tighten and his face turn hot. *I know what we need and how to get it,* he thought. *Hot damn . . . at last!*

"*Stellar Probe 12* was launched from Space Station Savitskaya only seven weeks ago. Fortunately, its velocity was in about the right direction. We have used 93 percent of its remaining propellant to direct it toward the Wayfarers. The encounter will occur in another twenty-one days."

Jake studied the burn in Speed's eyes, his set grin and his tight fists. He looked right into his core. *Yep, Speed's ready.*

Speed studied Jake.

Dr. Daro studied them both. The trace of a smile slowed only a few words in midsentence. "It is important that we determine exactly what happened. We need to understand if there is a generic fault in the Wayfarer design, something of significance about the Wayfarer Objects that we do not know, or some other unknown factor present. Your spacecraft will be heavily instrumented to obtain a comprehensive record of the environment you encounter at the Objects. The Wayfarer Program, and in fact the world's entire Outward Reach Initiative, is at a standstill until this is resolved. We *must* determine what has us stopped!"

Dr. Daro paused to regroup his thoughts, then continued.

"The mission has its risks. But, other than send another unmanned probe, we have no other choice. We must find out what happened. And, in case any of the crew are still alive, we clearly have to do what we can, as fast as we can."

Jake's thoughts slipped negative. Oh-oh, I'm back in business all right, but Val, how do I tell her? This one's got to be long—several years—gonna be tough on both of us.

"Your launch is set for November 6. That is only thirteen weeks away, and you have a lot to do before then. Any questions?"

"When will the families and press be notified?" asked Jake.

"The families are being notified this morning. And it will be announced at a press conference this afternoon. From here on we all must be careful not to give the press any cause to turn this into a circus of speculation. If the PR on this gets out of hand, it could indefinitely delay your mission. But at the same time, we have to inform them as much as possible and try to draw them over to our side."

"Yes, sir, that's the continual challenge and well understood," said Jake.

"Delgado and Hofmeister are waiting for you next door in my conference room. They will fill you in on the details of *Wayfarer 1*. At 1030 we will get back together with Dupree and go over your mission." Dr. Daro stood. "Gentlemen." He nodded, pivoted, walked behind his desk and again faced outward.

Jake and Speed left.

Santos Delgado, Chief Analyst for the Mission Planning Division, and Klaus Hofmeister, Flight Director on *Wayfarer 1*, waited in the adjacent room. Santos stood at the head of the conference table. Small hitches and jerks pulsed his arms as they dangled from his shoulders. His stare remained intent but unfocused. His lips drew tight around his half-opened mouth. This briefing would be only the second one he'd given while perched on the plush carpet of the thirty-seventh floor. The first one, served up to Dupree, did not go well.

"Hi, Klaus," said Jake. "Hello, Santos. Haven't seen you folks in a long time. Thanks for coming up to brief us."

"Hello, Jake, Speed," said Klaus. "Glad to do it. Congratulations on your selection! It's good to be working with you again."

"Same here, Klaus!"

"You bet!" said Speed.

"Santos, I'm Speed Spencer." They exchanged handshakes, nods and smiles, but Santos said nothing.

"Let's get started. We've got a lot to understand," said Jake.

"Santos will give the briefing," said Klaus. "I'll answer any specific questions on the mission."

Santos took out his laser pointer. "First holograph, please." A three-dimensional image of the solar system filled the space above the conference table. Like a rope relieved of its load, Santos's body loosened. Tension drained from his face.

Jake chuckled to himself. *He's a sharp guy, but he just can't seem to talk without a holograph to point at.*

"I'll start with a general overview of *Wayfarer 1*. First, a bit of history. You may recall that back in

2031, a stellar probe with radar search discovered a group of small objects just outside our solar system. It's been determined that they're transient, like wayfarers, and not part of our system. Now they're approximately twenty-six billion miles from the sun, or about seven times further out than Pluto." Santos pointed to the small outermost planet at the edge of the image, which moved in a plane inclined to the others, then pressed a switch on his pointer. The solar system shrunk to a seventh its previous size and a three-dimensional red star appeared at the edge of the new image to represent the Wayfarer Objects.

"The presence of these objects, outside of yet so close to our solar system, stimulated Project Wayfarer. When first initiated, it was popular because it's our first program for manned flight outside our solar system. But it takes light only one-and-one-half days to reach it, compared with over four years it takes to reach our nearest star. So it's not even close to true interstellar flight, but it's the next best thing to it. Some think it helped get WSF started."

"Right, Santos, it did," said Jake. "It gave the final push. WSF needed a focus, as well as the public appeal of a manned flight. The project provided a way for nations to get together on something outside the solar system, where financial or national interests weren't at stake."

Speed's half-opened eyes swiveled toward Jake. "Unfortunately, *Wayfarer 1* took too long. Without continuous action, public interest just spiraled right back down."

"Let's get back to why we're here. Santos, why haven't the Objects spread out? What holds them together?"

"That's a curious thing, Jake. No one knows. They don't have enough gravity to hold themselves together. But since we don't know anything about their composition, their relative motion or a host of other things, we can't even start on a theoretical model. In short, we don't understand what's going on. That's why the first objective of the Wayfarer Program is to get more data, so that we know even the right questions to ask."

"Didn't we learn anything from unmanned probes?" asked Jake.

"Not much. We've had only one. In '35 one was sent as a precursor to *Wayfarer 1*. It appeared to have a problem with its attitude control and navigation when it got close to the Wayfarers, and we got only a little data before all telemetry was lost. We should learn much more from *Stellar Probe 12* that's just been diverted to it."

"Hey, Speed. You dead or just sleeping?"

"Ahhh . . . just a light doze, boss. Been through this before."

Santos's face went quizzical, then sheepish and red. "Oh, you're *that* Dr. Spencer. You were on the Wayfarer Committee that defined the program. Why am I talking? We should be listening to you."

"Nope. You're armed with holographs, spring-loaded to dump the data and doing it well. I'll just be quiet and suck up some knowledge."

"Santos, we'll never hear a promise like that again from Speed." Klaus laughed. "Get it in writing."

"Are you going to describe the *Wayfarer 1* flight profile?" asked Jake.

"That's next." Santos added flight paths to the image. "An overview first. After launching from the Southern Test Range in French Guiana, they docked with Space Station von Braun. There they reconfigured their two modules for flight out of the solar system and ignited the standard Wayfarer nuclear-ion engines, which gave them an acceleration of only about one-quarter g. After burning the engines for a little over three days, they reached about 1.8 million miles per hour, relative to the sun. That's only about one-quarter percent the speed of light. Their total mission was to have lasted close to four years."

"We can't afford two years to get there," said

Jake. "If any of them are still alive, they couldn't last, unless they're buttoned up tight in hibernation."

"Using the new *Wayfarer 2* propellant tanks, you should be able to burn your engines twice as long and cut your transit time in half," said Klaus. "That is, it'll take about ten months to reach the Wayfarers. It's the best we can do."

"Klaus, what do we know about the condition of the crew just before their problem?" asked Speed.

"After they completed their first engine burn, they checked out both modules. Then they powered them down and entered hibernation, using the Hibernol serum feed. The coast was uneventful. After eighteen months, the CT 7000s stopped the feed and gave them a stimulant. Then they reconditioned themselves. Everything worked as expected when they powered up the modules and made their engine burns to brake, then rendezvous with the Wayfarers."

"When did they have their problem?" asked Speed.

"They were in the last part of the rendezvous, a coast phase toward the center of the Wayfarer Objects," said Klaus. "The only problem reported to that time was an error in the navigation program. Ted'd left the Alpha module and gone over to Beta to retrieve some EVA gear they planned to use to sample the Objects. It happened then."

"What?" asked Jake.

"Our only guess is a failure of a module main engine," said Santos. "Came on and couldn't be cut off. The modules and connecting bridge spun up until centrifugal force ripped them apart. Sure doesn't seem likely, but we can't even guess at anything else."

"There's got to be more to it than that," said Jake.

"That's for sure!" said Klaus.

"What've we received from them since the problem?" asked Jake.

"Nothing except some holovision signals from Ted's module that were too garbled to image," said Santos.

Klaus's face and body tightened, but he said nothing.

"Let's start over and go through the details, unless either of you has any more general questions," said Santos.

Jake leaned forward. "None. Press."

For another forty minutes, their minds locked together under the load of detailed technical knowledge that Santos and Klaus unstacked one brick at a time. They converged on common understandings and developed a rapport that couldn't have been earned under lighter loads. Klaus and Santos left, drained but happy. They'd passed their mental building blocks on to those who'd need them most.

"They sure knew their stuff, boss, but there's a lot of open spots. All the data pecks at the edges of this thing, but nothing hits right at the center."

"But, Speed, you're the expert. You're supposed to have the answers. What happened to Ted? And could the same thing happen to us?!"

Speed shrugged. "Beats the stuffin's outta me!"

4

Attack

They entered partial darkness.

With a crowbar for a backbone, Dr. Daro stood alone at the far end of his oval mahogany conference table. His fingertips rested on its massive surface, as if he stood at the helm of a ship. Light strips at the upper edges of the two inside walls provided the only illumination. Litran coatings on the inside of the plexan walls, which had been turned opaque by the controller next to Dr. Daro's right hand, locked out the midmorning light.

"Gentlemen. I have asked Dupree to delay our meeting for fifteen minutes." Dr. Daro's chin remained rigid as the growl escaped through the crack above. "Before we consider your flight, there is something else you need to understand about *Wayfarer 1*."

"Good," said Jake. "Klaus and Santos gave us all the data they had, sir, but we need a lot more."

Dr. Daro motioned to the two opposite positions at the center of the table. "Although the holovision that Ted sent back was garbled, we have been able to clean it up and produce good images. You should know what Ted experienced. However, only a limited set of people, including the crew we will select,

will see or know about these images. For the sake of
Ted's family, it will remain that way. Clear?"

"Yes, sir," said Jake and Speed in unison as they
each used two hands to pull back the chairs with the
steely-cold, black leather skins.

Dr. Daro withdrew a silver-dollar-sized disk
from his inside pocket and placed it in the holovision
slot by his left hand. "When Ted knew he was in
trouble, he turned on the holovision. It was programmed to record only his image, with minimum
background, and to follow his motion. For some reason, it functioned only a few minutes." Ted's three-
dimensional life-sized image filled the volume above
the table between Jake and Speed.

Jake gripped the edge of the table and tilted his
head and chair back. Hello, old friend, he said to
himself. Holo techs've done a good job. Feels like he's
right here with us, but he's floating.

Ted's body coiled then shot out straight like a
striking snake. He hit a surface, reached over for a
handhold, pulled himself to a window and half-coiled
again. "Lousy aim. Bad as a new guy." Ted's voice
sounded crisp in Jake's ears. The audio techs also had
done well.

Ted peered out the window. As he held on to the
handhold, his body uncoiled in slow motion. Then his
feet kicked and he started to swing like a rag in the
wind.

Jake studied Ted's grimace. Could the stress be
just from centrifugal force? he asked himself. The
eyes show fear, no, terror! They don't look around,
don't focus on anything. The terror comes from
something within. But what?

"The force is along the horizontal axis of the
module, parallel to the bridge," said Dr. Daro. "That
is consistent with the centrifugal force theory. Ted
does not seem to be trying to get to the engine controls, so it must have been the engine in the Alpha
module that stuck on."

Ted continued to kick and writhe until some

unseen force stretched his body out and held it straight. His wrists shook. His fingertips turned from pink to crimson.

The invisible force won.

It looked as if Ted would crash down onto the conference table, but his image remained fixed as he slid and bounced over the spacecraft floor. Jake watched Ted's elbow pass under a handhold and his body continue. The snap, loud and clear, coincided with the spike of pain in his eyes. His arm flopped free. His body tumbled again. Sounds of bone and flesh impacting hardness trailed off in Jake's mind as the force continued to flatten Ted's contorted body.

"The auto track feature of the cameras allowed us to measure the acceleration during his fall. At the time he released, it was up to two point one g. The force grew faster than we would expect from a stuck-on engine. As you see, it continues to grow, probably to above seven or eight g."

Jake watched Ted's body flatten against the wall. Awkward position, he thought, and painful. Even in a comfortable couch, ten g's hurts on the centrifuge. He's locked down.

A clap exploded as the compressed body sprung off the wall. It impacted a panel, then floated free.

"Analysis shows that the weakest structure was the attachment of the bridge to the module. That is where it must have failed."

Jake gazed at the thumb-sized, then fist-sized hemisphere of blood that grew over Ted's temple. Zero gravity, so blood doesn't run, he observed. It just balloons and then shimmies like crimson Jell-o. Arm must have a compound fracture. Bright-red blood soaking out through light-blue cloth of his flight suit. Not torn. Looks like another elbow. He's so close I can reach out and touch him—but I can't help him! Careful, look at the cloth, not the face. Capillary action spreading blood outward. Soaking cloth. Blood molecules attract cloth molecules and pull the whole wet, warm, sticky, life-losing mass outward. Horror—can't keep it out. Pain and panic—feel 'em.

Ted started his inventory. "Arm's broken . . . maybe my rib. Blood's in my eye. Ship's torn up . . . my crew?" He used his left hand to pull himself to the window. "My crew—they're gone! What's out there?"

Jake felt sweat run over his own skin. What would I do if I were Ted? he wondered. Doesn't know what's got him. A real tough cookie. Has a lotta pain and physical shock. Rest of crew and other module are gone. Scared. But his voice's calm. Thoughts logical. Still doing the best job he can. Could I do better?

"According to the telemetry, the atmosphere inside the spacecraft was intact and could not account for the change you now see in his physical condition."

Ted's image stretched horizontal above the table. He rotated, like a boar on a spit's rotisserie, and came face-to-face with Jake. The crimson Jell-o over his temple had seeped into his sweat-soaked hair and half-covered an ear. Purple fluid from below his right shoulder had spread beneath his skin upward into his neck.

Jake's mouth opened and froze as he studied Ted. Rigid muscles locked Ted's face in tension, then started to twitch. His lips fluttered as if he tried to force his thoughts out one on top of the other. His hair electrified and grew out straight. A terror erupted within him and radiated from his eyes, the only place it could escape. Jake's body shivered. He knew Ted felt something beyond pain, the terror of something cold, something uncontrolled and uncaring. None too soon Ted's image started to fade and break up. But Jake could still see his body and face twitch and the amplitudes grow, still watch his eyes roll up to white gelatin orbs and continue to twitch, still hear bellows of animal pain laced with screams of human horror, still . . .

"The holovision signal decreased monotonically to zero at this point. It has not been received again. We have no explanation why it terminated after only these seven minutes. Forty seconds after this, the telemetry output was turned up to maximum, then it too disappeared. That change is the only clue we have that Ted may have survived what you just saw."

Jake came back into his own world. He sat straight, his back rigid, his neck stiff as he looked down and forward again. For the second time in the morning, explosions hammered his chest and pounded into his throat. Sweat covered his forehead and neck, soaked the cloth under his arms and ran down his spine. He took a slow deep breath and tried to exhale the tremors that jangled his nerves. His fingers and wrists ached as he released his grip on the edge of the table. Professionalism, the ability developed by those of his trade to suppress emotion in favor of rapid, precise, logical performance, now demanded he restore calm, if only on the surface. Am I the right one for this? he wondered. Bring back data? Gonna have all we can do just to survive!

Jake squirmed as Dr. Daro's eyes probed him, measured him. But so what? Dr. Daro knew him well after all these years.

Jake followed Dr. Daro's eyes across the table. Speed slumped back into his chair with his external doors slammed shut. From forehead to chin, his face showed no expression, no color and no moisture, in contrast to his sweat-soaked hair and water that dripped from the handkerchief squeezed in his hand. God love 'im, thought Jake. He's no different than me.

"Gentlemen." Dr. Daro's monotone growled on. "As you can see, we have much to understand before your flight. Let us now take a break. When Dupree arrives, we will consider the outline of your mission, then the selection of your crew."

Dr. Daro rose and headed for the door. As he went by Jake, he momentarily rested his hand on

Jake's shoulder. The human buried at the core of the professional had few ways to communicate. Jake understood.

Jake remained silent as he pushed his body up and over his feet. He felt heavy, his flesh cold and lifeless. He shuffled toward the door, where he met Speed.

"Ya know, boss, if the damn government pay wasn't so high, I'd be tempted to stay home."

Yes, back to superficial words, back to covers and cosmetics, back into the world where he had to operate. But Jake knew he'd just had a glimpse into another world—into a world that waited for him.

Trillions and trillions of tiny teeth each bit into his mind and ripped.

. . . Ludendorff . . . I'm Ted Ludendorff . . . Ted Ludendorff . . . I'm . . .

Identity—a life preserver. Ted's mind clutched at it and grabbed it, clenched it and held it tight. No way would he let himself be pulled under to die. No way would he let himself be dragged adrift to diffuse and dissipate. Mental muscles strained and squeezed. No way would he be separated from SELF!

Over a time without measure, terror faded into fresh memory, faded into something that could be pushed away and studied at arm's length. He relived the details, but now he felt no pain.

Wayfarer 1 had been just another ambitious flight, just another nominal mission, until an enemy attacked his spacecraft, assaulted his body, then tore at his mind. This enemy couldn't be recognized, or even seen. It didn't make a clean, frontal assault. Rather, as some secret assailant, some faceless foe, it slipped in with its own special horror and attacked from within. The first wave came only as a ripple, so weak it could hardly be felt. But, with speed and certainty, the enemy strengthened and swelled and spread pain into every corner of his mind.

After ripping and tearing, it took away Ted's

very essence. Then it discarded his body, set it adrift to float in the physical world of zero gravity, a world Ted no longer could call his own. Ted'd felt his substance separate, as if the enemy pulled his being through a strainer, stripped away his flesh, peeled it away from his Person and left the shreds to decay and dry on the other side.

. . . This enemy's cold, brutal, a hungry animal . . . ripped me apart, devoured me . . . a dream, or a dream within a dream? . . . no matter, I can remember and think . . .

. . . I must still be Alive! . . .

5

Smother

Would the day ever come when he had these flakes under control?

Dr. Jean-Pierre Laurent Dupree, Director of WSF Operations Control (Acting), forced long quick strides as he attacked the elevator. Intimidation. He applied it to things and people alike. His six-foot four-inch, two hundred and thirty-pound frame proved to be his most potent weapon. Although twenty-five pounds overweight, it looked athletic through well-tailored suits. By instinct, he added to the illusion with deliberate, powerful movements. Next to draw attention were deep folds and creases that ran from his mouth, nose and eyes, and those on his forehead; symmetrical about the center line of his face, they all sloped down, all led in the negative direction. Those who focused attention on him when he didn't command it, he charred with his turn-away-or-be-incinerated glare. If that failed, he employed his acid tongue, his ultimate weapon of intimidation.

This morning his demeanor carried on an extra ounce of menace. Eyes bore into anyone disrespectful enough to remain in his path. Acidic thoughts spilled out under his breath. "Only one flight, but I hate goin' upstairs. My office oughta be up there. Worked all the way up to thirty-six, but locked out of

thirty-seven. Afraid I'll take over and run things right
—I *will*, once Daro makes me permanent. Shouldn't
have to deal with flight crews as if they were equals.
Cocksure Ryder and smartass Spencer. Oughta work
for me. Damn free spirits'd learn to salute. No discipline. This delay of theirs wasted fifteen minutes already. Can't get their act together. Could do their
job a hell of a lot better than any of 'em. No ability to
command, just run off at the mouth. And why not?
No accountability."

Dupree rammed a lesser individual in the back
and plowed him to the side.

"Deserved it. Just sauntering along the hall with
nothing better to do. I'd fix that. Damn astros, made
heroes by definition. Don't have to be smart or work
hard. Everybody bows. None of 'em got here the
hard way—like I did."

Once again pride shoved other thoughts aside. A
moment of observance now and then was justified,
even deserved. After all, he reached his position of
authority on just his own abilities: achieved a 99.4
percentile on technical examinations as a college se-
nior (not just in France, but in all of Europe), earned a
Ph.D. in spacecraft control system design and a second one in flight dynamics (some of the crew with no
respect for academics called him "Double Doc,"
which they sometimes mispronounced as "Double
Dork"), and struggled many years up through the
mission control organizations of the European Space
Agency, then the World Space Federation (for once
the Russians, Germans, Japanese or Americans didn't
get the top spot). A born leader—not afraid to seize
control and use it!

The elevator door opened. Dr. J. P. Laurent Dupree, Director of WSF Operations Control (Acting),
recognized one of his junior flight planners in a loose-
knit shirt and jeans. The lines on his face pulsed down
as his head nodded. He positioned the back of his
well-tailored suit coat two inches from the face of his
subordinate and held it fixed until the door opened

again. Dupree charged out first, as if he led his team onto the playing field.

"I'm here for my 1030 meeting. Is everybody else here, Lentnel?"

"Commander Ryder and Dr. Spencer are inside. Dr. Daro just stepped out but will be back any minute. Please go right in, Dr. Dupree." Jane Lentnel looked down, almost as if she wanted to avoid further conversation.

Dupree stomped by. "We've all got a lot to do. Holding to schedules would make us all more effective."

He rammed open the door to Dr. Daro's office, a safe maneuver because he knew Dr. Daro wasn't inside. He felt himself dominate the room just by the sheer force of his presence. Ryder and Spencer sat at opposite sides of the oval table. Good. He'd take one end, a position of authority. He let his bound notes fall to the table with a loud slap. As he dropped his large frame into the chair, he grunted a long exhalation. Well done. He had established his presence.

Dupree classified people into two simple categories: for him or against him. Most fell into the later category, especially these two. He took the offense. "I heard you two boys had a problem with your nose gear this morning."

Spencer snickered. "No real problem, Laurent." Oh god, how he hated it when subordinates called him by his first name. "Just took full afterburner to taxi off the runway."

Ryder flashed his cocksure grin.

"No . . . heard you just escaped a fire."

Spencer stroked his chin. "Yeah, we did. Too bad, Laurent. We could be just crispy critters by now. Could've been burned beyond all reignition."

Dupree drew in a breath for his next assault as Dr. Daro entered.

"Thank you for coming up, Laurent. I am sorry for the delay, but it was necessary to provide all of the *Wayfarer 1* details to Jake and Speed. Let us now consider *Wayfarer 2*."

Dupree wrenched his body out of his chair and towered. "No problem, sir. I'll start with the major differences between missions one and two." He walked to Dr. Daro and handed him four pages of laser-printed data, fused together at the upper border. He tossed the other two sets toward the center of the table. "We'll consider the launch first, then the insertion on a trajectory to the Wayfarers and, lastly, the new ground rules that must be added."

"Sounds good, Laurent," said Spencer. "Press on."

Dupree fired a raised eyebrow and enhanced frown toward Spencer. He didn't need approval of his agenda by the corps clown.

"The launch from our Southern Test Range in French Guiana to Space Station von Braun will remain essentially unchanged. Using the Brute booster, we'll launch the two *Wayfarer 2* modules, their connecting bridge in the telescoped configuration, the new nuclear-ion-engine propellant tank clusters and a full load of propellant for the station's supply. On the following day the crew'll be launched by the Agile booster and rendezvous and dock with von Braun. Then the modules will be mated to the new tank clusters, joined by the bridge and fueled to full capacity with propellant from the station. Lastly, the whole configuration will be checked out before the first burn."

"That's straightforward," said Ryder. "How about the insertion burn to the Wayfarers?"

"Yeah, how much extra velocity can we get from the new tank clusters?" asked Spencer.

Black olives under Dupree's bushy eyebrows darted back and forth between Ryder and Spencer. "Be patient! If you look, you'll see that's the next topic."

Spencer looked startled. "Oh."

"Now, in order to reduce the transit time, we'll

use the new tanks that hold twice as much propellant and also burn all but a 3.7 percent reserve in the two burns going to the Wayfarers and the two burns coming back. In addition, we will not carry most of the EVA equipment for the scientific experiments that we put on *Wayfarer 1*. Thus, we can do better than just cut our transit time in half. That is, the first engine burn will last 6.73 days and achieve a velocity of 3.51 million miles per hour. We'll reach the Wayfarers in 307 days, approximately 10 months."

"Annnnnnd . . . ?" rolled out Spencer. "Whatta we do when we get there?"

Dupree glanced at the eyes above the smirk. For just an instant they seemed too serious, too penetrating, too perceptive for the empty head of the jester that contained them.

"When we reach the Wayfarers, we'll make a burn of nearly the same velocity to slow up and rendezvous with them."

"Laurent, ahhh . . ." Spencer twiddled his thumbs. "Have ya got any more details?"

Dupree sighed. "Next two pages." He worked his way through the detailed notes on each mission phase with the same thoroughness that his staff had prepared them. For once Ryder and Spencer remained quiet. Dupree assumed that most of it went over their heads and his staff would have to spoonfeed them later.

Dupree flipped to the last page. "Now, Dr. Daro, I'll present the major ground rules that must apply once we reach the Wayfarers. They *must* be written into the mission rules immediately so that the flight planners can get them into the procedures. It's clear we'll need at least three more memory cells in the onboard CT 7000s for these additions as well as for the associated malfunction procedures."

"Has Klaus seen these ground rules?" asked Ryder.

"No. He works for me. I don't need his approval." Half-frowns appeared on the faces of Ryder and Spencer. As if the net total of the frowns in the room had to remain constant, the lines at the corners of Dupree's eyes and mouth snapped upward.

"One. In all cases, rendezvous with the *Wayfarer 1* Alpha module will be accomplished first. It's obvious now that we should go after the majority of the *Wayfarer 1* crew first. That'll provide the greatest chance of finding out what went wrong.

"Two. Regardless of what we find in the Alpha module, we'll rendezvous with the Beta module that contains Ted next.

"Three. Full holovision coverage of each module *must* be returned for Mission Control processing before a GO is issued for contact or docking with that module.

"Four. After docking and the power and data connections are made, the full data stream *must* be returned for Mission Control processing before a GO is issued for entry into that module.

"Five. Full holovision coverage of any Wayfarer Object *must* be returned for Mission Control processing before a GO is issued for contact."

"Six. Full data *must* be returned on—"

Spencer sprang to his feet. "What're you planning? A slow-motion game of Cosmic May I?"

Ryder remained seated but fired every word at Dupree like a bullet. "Each of these ground rules is unacceptable. They're a throwback to the 1900s. We've had spacecraft and space stations operating autonomously since the turn of the century. Confidence in automatic scheduling and the judgment of the crew has long since replaced detailed specification of every decision and operation from the ground. Especially for this mission, where a round trip message takes three days, it makes no sense. We will *not* operate using these ancient procedures."

Dupree sat down and brought his eyes level with Ryder's. The crimson of his scalp darkened a shade and highlighted his close-cropped, fine white hair. He leaned forward, rested his fists on the table, glared straight across at Ryder, then spit his words out through tight lips. "I'll say this just once for you. We've got too much at stake on this mission not to have the best possible decisions made before any actions are taken. What we'll *not* tolerate are decisions made by crew who have only partial data and less than the best computer capability available. We *must* have all the data that's available to process. For once, now that we really have to, we *will* do business the correct way."

Spencer popped vertical and poked his chin toward Dupree as he spoke. "The correct way? It took forty years last century for the Space Program to work out what's the optimum combination of the crew and ground. It's straightforward. Even *you* should understand. Let Klaus explain it to you." Spencer paused, then erupted again. "Look! Put capable people in the spacecraft and give them full access to the data. And you on the ground should also have as much data as can be feasibly sent back. But you should be in an advisory capacity only, not in control of something that you don't experience firsthand."

Laurent jerked out of his chair and stretched to his full height. His scorn for Spencer glared out. "If we get all the right data, we'll not only experience everything firsthand, but because of our superior data processing we'll make superior decisions."

Ryder shook his head. "Always true in theory, but hardly ever in practice."

Spencer pointed at Dupree. "That's dumb, just plain dumb—a giant stride back into yesteryear."

"What's dumb is your inability to understand logic," Dupree said in a high-pitched bark. "Now sit down. I'll not argue with subordinates any longer. That's the way it's going to be!"

Spencer remained standing with a quizzical look on his face. "Logic? How can we expect logic from someone suffering with a severe case of egotoma?"

"Egotoma?"

"Yeah. Your ego's so swelled up that it's blocked off all blood supply to your brain."

Every muscle in Laurent's body flexed as he blazed a wide-eyed grimace at Spencer, then launched a giant stride toward him. But one foot refused to get out of the way of the other and Laurent plunged forward. For just a moment, as he spun around and gawked at the ceiling, he entered zero gravity. But, as always, gravity won.

Laurent crashed.

Spencer snickered.

Ryder rose.

Spencer stepped forward and held out his hand.

Dr. Daro growled. "Gentlemen." Each combatant froze. "We all have more useful things to do. Sit down!"

They sat.

"Laurent, it is true that this mission is a special case because of its criticality. However, especially because of the three-day time delay, we will operate in the manner that has proven most effective. That is, have your group define the minimum set of data required to assure safe operation. And, Jake, you design your operations to provide as much data as feasible over and above that minimum. You both will reach agreement within a week from today. If not, I will dictate.

"Jake, as pilot-in-command, you will be free to override any directions you receive from Mission Control. However, with this freedom goes the ultimate responsibility for the safety of your crew as well as mission success.

"Is that clear to each of you?"

Three heads nodded. Below the table six hands attempted to wring leather juice from the arms of the chairs.

"Laurent, please finish your discussion of the ground rules. Discuss only those that apply to spacecraft systems, not ground control requirements."

Dupree covered his material in a quick and logical fashion. Ryder and Spencer chose to create no further controversy. Dupree assumed that he must have made his point.

"Thank you, Laurent," said Dr. Daro. "Let's move on. Jake, tomorrow at 0800 you will present to me your recommendations for the remaining four members of your crew. You will be given access to the personnel data files this afternoon. However, before you start, let us discuss what you consider to be the basic requirements for your crew's composition."

Jake froze for several moments with a fixed gaze, then rose. "First, Dr. Daro, I need a second-in-command. That person should be able to challenge my judgments and assist me with the unexpected. He should also be sharp in mission and spacecraft operations. You have already assigned Speed to the mission and that responsibility. He's the right man for the job."

Speed grinned.

"In addition, his science background, especially his knowledge of the Wayfarer Objects, could be very useful." Jake and Speed exchanged smiles, turned their heads toward Dupree, beamed their grins into his sneer and nodded once in unison.

Jake continued. "Next we need a systems expert who, above all, is also an expert on procedures. We cannot afford any procedural errors. He should also thoroughly understand the nuclear-ion engine, since the system and its failure modes are the most complex on the spacecraft."

Dr. Daro's features remained fixed.

"As we've needed on every mission, but especially here, a computer expert is required. He must be fully conversant with the basic CT 7000 and all of its applications to the Wayfarer systems. Essentially, he should've lived with the CT 7000 for the past few years. Our experience earlier this morning demonstrated the need for someone intimately familiar with computers.

"A navigation expert is also required, just as Ted

had on *Wayfarer 1*. It's especially critical on this mission since we're cutting our fuel budget close to get extra velocity. We cannot afford any navigation errors that could eat into our small fuel reserve.

"Lastly, we need a medical specialist to make sure that we have no problems with our hibernation. But perhaps more important, he may be required to treat any of the *Wayfarer 1* crew that're still alive and manage their hibernation for the return."

Dr. Daro remained quiet and pensive. Jake studied his face, then the faces of Speed and Dupree, the patterns in the wood grain of the mahogany conference table, the scuffed tips of his black shoes he'd meant to polish before coming, the soothing light-blue of the carpet, then again Dr. Daro's face. At last, it cracked.

"Jake, you have read it properly. In your review of the personnel data bank this afternoon, do not exclude anyone who can be returned from another mission within the next two weeks. *Wayfarer 2* has top priority. Any questions?"

"No, sir."

"Good. I will see you both here at 0800 tomorrow."

Dupree thrust his chair back first, rose to full height, sneered down at Ryder and Spencer and curled his lips as if to speak. Then he glanced at Dr. Daro, looked away, grimaced and charged toward the door.

Ted was enclosed in soft milky-gray white. It felt good, somehow familiar. He welcomed its tranquillity and comfort. And he rested.

In time, Ted grew aware of a presence. But nothing made itself known.

Intellectually, Commander Ted Ludendorff tried to reconstruct the invasion. At its peak, it seemed like rows of crisscrossed laser knives had cut through his mind, divided him into sections, then subdivided him again and again, cleaved and quartered his mind over and over until only basic cerebral building blocks remained. But if so, the blocks must've been reconstructed just as they were sliced, for his mind felt whole. And it wasn't all that bad now, for here he was, able to think, able to remember and he felt no pain.

Ted rested, gathered his mental energy and again searched all internal thought. Willie? Eva? His crew? Who else could be part of this?

Curiosity forced Ted's thoughts outside himself. He probed his surroundings. With effort, he found he could focus his awareness. Just as if he'd focused his eyes, gentle shadings and colors, then lines and forms rose out of the milky gray-white. He sensed that he'd entered and been received. A spacious chamber enclosed him, a grand entry chamber, his entry chamber. Its walls of cotton or marshmallow felt strange but comfortable. For this soft and spongy container had no firmness, yet it couldn't be penetrated. He scanned the walls, then he probed and prodded them. At last he found a hole, an opening, an escape from this pliant prison. In time, he may need it. But not yet. First, he must try to understand.

He rested, probed and found another hole. He rested and probed again and again. One by one he focused his awareness on each new opening. Passages and corridors, tubes and tunnels, all led away from his chamber in random directions with the order of jumbled yarn.

A strange world, all of it soft and pliable, nothing hard or rigid or fixed. But his mind did sense it and did see it, did touch it and did feel it. It had no temperature nor texture, nor sound nor smell. It'd started like the familiar wispy twilight between dream and reality, but with increased awareness it'd sharpened into a really physical world.

Ted expanded his awareness and focused. Structure became sharper and firmer, more intricate and detailed. Like arteries, each tunnel led away and broke into branches, which in turn led to more offshoots, then more branches, more twigs and more sprouts. His awareness continued to flow outward from his chamber's core, surge outward to its boundaries and into entrances of millions of tunnels where it scanned and studied.

Then Ted sensed motion!

But now, stretched thin, he could no longer sustain the mental effort required, could no longer maintain his expanded awareness. He strained to touch and understand but, like a battery, his limited energy had discharged.

Drained and weak, Ted's concentration faltered, then broke. His awareness recoiled and contracted, shrunk and shriveled like a deflated balloon back to its origin, back to his chamber's core. His thoughts again turned inward.

. . . have to rest . . . but *where* am I? . . . *what* am I? . . . Willie? . . . Eva? . . . am I still really alive?! . . .

6

Choose

Sensual feelings rushed upward through her body.

A fold of blond hair slipped from her shoulders and hung free as she leaned back and reached outward for a second stretch. For a moment she savored the fluid motion of her supple limbs and the pent-up energy that surged up from her legs into her buttocks, back and shoulders, sensations she'd submerged for hours. But, as she rubbed her neck, she glanced back at the five-foot, three-dimensional image of the room before her. It invited her back in, beckoned her, as it always did, to make just one more change, one more improvement.

The fingertips of her left hand flicked the precision Q-ball to new positions, as those of her right entered keyboard commands. Her CT 4500 Design Computer responded. The holographic image rotated as shades of soft pinks and blues melted and blended. Curvatures softened and flowed one into another. Then her mood, once comfortable, became intimate as her mind's eye added the soft light of a menuscreen, reflections off silver, penetration of his eyes, a light fruity flavor of a Piesporter under her tongue, warmth of his hand, a . . . She blinked. "Hey! snap out of it, girl. Not even two o'clock. Gotta finish up. Need one more pass though the structural loads."

As with all her projects, she dreamed it, created it, then lived in it long before it'd be built. With patience and persistence, she exploited her own rare blend of creativity and engineering talent, the blend required by her combined professions of interior design and architecture. For hours, sometimes days, she perfected each project, each building, each room, until the holographic images matched those in her mind and her rigid design specifications nailed them down tight. She couldn't help but drive herself until an inner happiness exceeded personal and professional thresholds. And, although it'd taken many projects and many years, her own happiness eventually transferred to a long waiting line of satisfied clients.

And now life had at last reached that mellow phase, that long gentle slope, those years when she and her mate could just relax and enjoy. They'd each climbed all the required hills in their professions, reached all the required peaks. They'd paid their dues. And worth it? You bet. Every bit of it.

For now life was good—so good!

What else could she and her husband want? Health, professions, shared pride and love of two sons, a common set of fun-loving friends and an iron bond forged between them over two decades as friends and lovers. And it all had no real end, just a gradual glide into those golden years several decades away. So much time to bask in it all.

Life was good—so good!

A string of digital bits left her CT 4500, flashed through light cables and satellite links and fixed itself in the memory of her client's CT 5000.

She stretched again. At last, time for exercise. She felt pride when bulging or drooping friends teased her, complained she was so easy to hate because she had so much: trim figure, creamy skin, a model's face and ice-blue, magnetic eyes that flashed with health and the added sparkle of spirit and intelligence.

"Babe, you turn me on!"

Was he crude? Too single-minded? No, not really. They both understood it, both knew the turn-on was a two-way affair, one that went beyond flesh. To be sure, his attention enhanced her self-confidence, let her cut the reins on her sexual hunger, gave her freedom to give and receive pleasure without reservation, pleasure that'd only grown with the maturity of years. But the turn-on penetrated far deeper to something neither of them could define. Love, as a word, seemed too vague. Attraction and affinity? Of course. Pals and playmates? Sure. But also they had a something that came from years of shared grins and giggles, tragedies and tears, gooses and gotchas, something that took years to build but they exchanged in a glance.

Yes, life was good—so good!

Her wristband flashed its electric blue light, pulsed its high-pitched tone and vibrated her skin. A call waited.

She called out toward the wall receiver, "Transmit, please. Thank you . . . Hello."

"Hi, Val. Did I pull you away from your project?"

"Oh. Hi, Jake! No, I just finished up. Glad you called. I didn't expect to hear from you until tonight."

"Dr. Daro sprang something on us today."

"Another assignment?"

"Yep."

"Not anything like another three months on Station Gagarin."

"No. It's a new mission. *Wayfarer 2.*"

"But *Wayfarer 1* isn't even back. It's got another two years." She stood up and her body tightened. "You didn't get pulled into a four-year mission . . . did you?"

"Ahhh . . . it's a long one, Val, but not four years. It's only two."

"Only two . . . two years?"

"Actually, a little less than two years. Some system improvements have cut it to ten months out, the same for the return, and . . ."

"Only two years? Jake, *no!* Oh damn. You run the whole office. Can't you assign one of the new guys? Weren't you going to tell Dr. Daro you're leaving?"

"Ahhh . . . yeah, but Ted and his crew ran into a problem. Something we don't yet understand. It's possible they didn't even survive. And everything's stopped because of it. This's the highest priority mission I've ever been assigned. I just can't walk away from the program, from Ted, from the others. Speed and I've got to choose another four by tomorrow."

"But, Jake, do you really want to take the risk— and be away from me for two whole years?"

"Not at all, Val, but this has just gotta be done."

"But not by you!" The engine in Val's chest raced wide open with the accelerator floored and her body in neutral. Her legs wobbled. She couldn't find a deep breath.

"Jake, why don't you accept the position with Integrated Space Industries. Then we could finally just enjoy life and be together, and . . . oh *damn!*— all those things we've talked about for years."

"Val, after this flight I'll hang it up. But this time it looks like I'm the best one for the job. I've just gotta do it."

"No, Jake, the sad truth is I'm married to an addict."

"I'll call you again tonight and be home tomorrow afternoon."

"Has anyone told Eva or the other families?"

"Yes, this morning."

"I suppose I should go see if I can help." Then Val spoke the unspeakable. "Who knows, I may be next."

"Val! Don't worry about that. We can handle it. Oh, one other thing. In case the press plays up an accident Speed and I had this morning flyin' out? No sweat. Really just a slight problem with the nose gear. We're OK."

"Bye, Jake."

"Bye, Val. I love you."

"Love you, too."

She lay down. All energy fled, as her brain sought protection. It encased itself with a numbness that suspended all sensation and all thought . . . for the moment.

Round three.

Sun's light and warmth poured in through plexan and onto Jake. Saturday. A new day. A fresh start. But as he took his place at Dr. Daro's conference table for the third session within twenty-four hours, it seemed all too familiar. Perhaps this time would go better.

Once again the crew-selection process for the upcoming mission had turned out to be more difficult than for any previous missions. The personnel files provided a wealth of data, actually a flood of data. But how to absorb it, digest it and apply judgment to it? To Jake, it seemed that two armies, Data and Judgment, once more waged their war, a war as old as computers, and Data would win again. As soon as he and the Judgment troops regrouped and came up with a scheme to sort and simplify Data, the Data troops multiplied their numbers, multiplied again, then multiplied once more just for good measure, massed on Judgment's border and stormed. By strength of sheer numbers, Data buried and smothered Judgment, tried again to snuff out any chance for a rational decision.

He and Speed had worked to 1:40 that morning before they arrived at a consensus. Midway through Jake made another call to Val. Their conversation gravitated into something deeper and stickier than earlier. Electronics transmitted Data, but it didn't carry Communication.

And during the remnant of the night, the energy

that usually slipped into his body during sleep had found another home. Muscles in his back and neck turned into thousands of rubber bands, each stretched to their limits, each about to snap. Jake forced himself to relax, to turn off all sensation and let the tension drain out. What energy remained, he forced to his mind. He made himself forget the grinding of RT7's nose, the shrieks from the inferno, the pain in Ted's eyes, the hurt in Val's voice, the . . .

"Gentlemen. Good morning. Jake, please let me have your recommendations."

"First, Dr. Daro, we had the computer do a coarse screen on the data bank to find candidates with the technical backgrounds we agreed on yesterday. We cut the 387 people currently in the program down to 73. Then Speed and I reviewed the file on each one and brought the number down to 17. We had to make a lot of calls to get evaluations on many people we didn't know professionally. We've arrived at the following recommendations."

"Do you both agree on them, Speed?"

"Yes, sir, we do. Except Jake kept throwing out my recommendation for Gloria Goodbody."

Jake's body froze as he studied Dr. Daro. No, not again, Speed. Not this morning, not with Dr. Daro—prude of prudes. Don't test him. Is that the hint of a smile?

"Continue, Jake."

Jake used the portable handheld controller to darken the room and display the first personnel file on the screen above Dr. Daro's work station.

"First, for our Systems Officer we recommend Shane Culver. He assisted in the development of the procedures for the Wayfarer nuclear engines." Jake winced as RT7 again scraped down his mind's runway. "And, most important, he is highly regarded as an expert in all spacecraft procedures. Shane's degree is in electrical engineering with a minor in nuclear engineering. He's flown on three space-station missions and spent seven months at Lunar Base Vlastnev. He's methodical, logical and understands the nuclear engine's control system better than almost anyone else."

Speed leaned forward. "Shane's currently on loan to the Air Force. He's at San Antonio helping them calibrate their microwave energy systems and had already planned to be in Houston next Monday to help in the Wayfarer engine failure analysis."

Dr. Daro nodded. "Yes, I assigned him."

"For our Computer Systems Engineer we recommend Ada Lin. She's the most knowledgeable person on the Wayfarer computer system in the program. For the past four years she's worked with CompuThink on the development of the Wayfarer CT 7000. She's earned a Ph.D. in computer sciences, flown twice in the Chinese program before WSF formed, then once on Space Station Goddard. Those who've worked with her say she's extremely bright and knows CT 7000's every idiosyncrasy. She lives for her work."

"Is she too focused? Do you anticipate she'll have any problems working with the rest of the crew?"

"No, sir. There's never been a problem reported. On the job, Ada's totally professional."

"Good."

"For our Flight Dynamics and Planning Officer, we recommend Boris Mechanov, whose real strength is navigation. He did his Ph.D. thesis on computer solutions to the four-body problem. He's familiar with the CT 7000s, but he'll have to depend on Ada to make him proficient before flight. He was the first Russian to fly for WSF. It was on the Saturn Orbital Mission, where his navigation expertise was highly respected. Also, as navigator for a lap on our Mars Cycler, he refined its trajectory control. He's made a total of six flights."

"I have had briefings from him," said Dr. Daro. "He does know his navigation."

"Between Shane, Ada and Boris we've got all systems covered," said Speed.

Dr. Daro's head yielded a micronod.

"Lastly, for our Medical Officer, we recommend Faye MacFarland. Her specialty is neurology, specifically the diagnostics and treatment of diseases of the central nervous system. However, she has considerable experience in the treatment of trauma and, just as important, has developed many of our hibernation procedures. A thorough understanding of hibernation is a must. If any of the *Wayfarer 1* crew's still alive, they must've placed themselves in hibernation. If they were injured or their problem affected the hibernation system, we'll need an expert to handle them."

"Good observation, Jake," said Dr. Daro.

"There's just one problem, sir," said Speed. "The Feeler's currently on Space Station von Braun and not due to return for another six weeks."

The crowbar in Dr. Daro's back sprung to exact vertical and quivered like a tuning fork. His chair executed a slow swivel until it reached exact alignment with Speed. His wide eyes narrowed as his words came out in precise grunts. "The what, Speed?"

Speed's face flushed, then flashed to full grin. "Ahhh . . . the Feeler, sir. When I served with her on the Europa Mission, it was an accepted name, just like Fred or Frank or, ahh . . ."

The slits on Dr. Daro's face narrowed further.

Jake stepped back out of the line of fire and shook his head. Might just as well watch the show. Damn Speed must have a death wish. Oughta be in the circus. Sticks his head in the lion's mouth, steps on its tail, calls its mother a bitch—and lives.

Speed grinned, leaned forward with his hands apart before his face and spoke as if he'd just started to tell a tale around the campfire. "It goes way back, sir. The story is that she was trained by doctors steeped in old traditions. That is, they liked to back up modern thermal, neutron and x-ray body scans with palpation. Nowadays hardly any doctor uses palpation, but those who do swear that the use of their hands gives them added confidence in their diagnosis, especially in situations that involve inflammations or tumors. She apparently uses some of the techniques left over from the old school."

Dr. Daro's eyes widened as he scanned Speed from head to toe several times. Then he looked down, exhaled, shook his head, studied Speed one more time and took a deep breath through the hint of another smile.

"Let us just refer to her as Dr. MacFarland, the Medical Officer or Faye. Understood, Speed?"

"Yes, sir."

"All information on her indicates that, like Ada, Faye's a professional who never mixes her private life with her work," said Jake.

Dr. Daro called up the current flight schedule from his work station. "Looks like she could be replaced and brought back by the Logistics Shuttle next Thursday. Do either of you have concerns about any of these people? So far you have only presented their positives."

"Only a general one, sir," said Jake. "Since we don't fully understand what we'll face, we don't know if we've even used the right criteria in their selection."

"True, but we have done the best we can. Have you also assured yourselves that you can pull these specialists together into a smooth functioning team before launch?"

"That's a challenge, sir. Time will tell."

"Each one of these people will be in Houston Monday, except for Dr. MacFarland. Time is short. Get your training plan pulled together and send it to me by next Tuesday."

"Yes, sir. We'll make this flight our best one yet," said Jake.

Dr. Daro's gaze sliced into Jake, then Speed. "Yes, I am sure you will. But will it be good enough?"

7

Cooperate

Oh-oh, temperature's buildin'.

From his Sunday Command Post, Jake mapped his strategies and planned his tactics—tough work. His horizontal body absorbed hot solar rays. His eyes cracked open to a squint. Patterns of aqua blues and greens reflected from the bottom of his pool, shimmered and danced on his retinas, sent signals that relaxed and mesmerized his brain, opened mental pathways that put him in contact with human essentials.

Only the wind—nothing but an occasional nudge to the mass of moist, oven-hot air—interrupted the intensity of his deliberations. It rustled chest-sized hibiscus leaves near his feet as it cooled his body. Occasional strong nudges crackled the 11:00 A.M. home-printout of the *Houston Chronicle* that sprawled on the deck by his left hand. He'd skimmed a few articles and read a few, but today he just couldn't seem to give it his usual scrutiny. As the strongest of the strong snapped the paper, the German shepherd under his recliner snapped into action. Internal springs tightened. In one coordinated massive movement, he stretched his jaws apart and limbs out straight, then he collapsed again into a pile of loose fur. Jake shifted his squint to Clear Lake

Harbor and tracked the slow motion zigzags of the sailboats against the steady creep of the ocean liner in the channel.

Again, Jake's internal temperature reached a threshold. The moisture that evaporated heat from his body no longer kept up with the solar energy that poured in. A delicate balance, a challenge for any thermal engineer, and he'd slipped behind. Time to replenish fluids. He stiffened and pulled the cold, moisture-coated glass of Vodkorn Blitz to his lips.

Yep, it's tough. Jake smiled to himself. This Command Post stuff is rough. Good to have a quiet, relaxing day at home. Might even get in a few hours at the piano. Nowadays most of my keyboards are hooked to computers. Love these times with Val. Assignment's been a shock to her. She's even worried about Ada and Faye, even though I've been on lots of missions with women before. Over 37 percent of the crews are women. Must be the length of this one. Hell, I'll sleep through most of it. Guess if she didn't worry a little, I'd worry a lot . . .

Ryder! Stop wastin' time. Get your brain in gear. Try to understand what this mission's all about. Dr. Daro made it clear enough: "We *must* find out what has us stopped!"

First, I've gotta get everybody trained and working together. Did we choose the right ones? No going back now. Got only three months. Start tomorrow with Shane, Ada and Boris. Gotta build cooperation and teamwork right from the start. Any squabbles've gotta happen on the ground, not like the activation of Station Nagami. Almost another world war. I really blew it. Everybody thought they were in control, and no one was. This time I better work it all out before launch—or end up lookin' like Ted!

Oh-oh, temperature's buildin' again. Coolant time.

The problem persisted.

"Shane, looks like it's in these old precedures,"

said the technician. "The antenna's still not moving. Let's just start over again and use the new software. It's worked great up to now."

"No way! I can't see what's happening when the computer's in control. All we have to do is calibrate this one last antenna, just like all the others, and we're through. Let's go over the manual procedures, step by step, and locate the problem. The software won't let us do that."

"Hold on. I think the software's not properly coupled to this antenna's drive interface unit. I see how to fix it. Just a few more data entries."

Shane Culver regarded himself as a patient man. But even a patient man has his limits. Angry blood pounded his temples. "No! Cycle back to step forty-three. That safes the power control."

Ever since Dr. Daro's call Friday, Shane'd felt the pressure. And now they'd just one more antenna to calibrate and he could be on his way to Houston, be off this mickey-mouse assignment and start on Wayfarer first thing in the morning—a real mission. If this know-it-all technician would only follow procedures. It couldn't be simpler. But all this toad wanted to do was argue. Shane felt the need for fresh air and room to think it out.

"I'm going out to look at the antenna and see if there's any obvious problem out there."

Shane turned his back on the control panel, where the POWER ENABLE switch remained in MANUAL—ON, bristled by the technician, who pounded data entries into his keyboard, and threw open the door. It whacked the side of the trailer and slapped closed behind him.

The sun'd just slid below the horizon and the desert air could at last expel its heat. Shane felt it against his skin, cool and dry and calm, compared to the pressure cooker in the trailer. He paused to admire the sky. Perfect timing! Blue glowed over the red blaze on the horizon, and white stars sparkled above them both. Beautiful, even patriotic.

Shane's eyes focused on the bright man-made star just south of straight overhead. Powersat, with its acres of solar collectors, drifted in orbit poised to turn the sun's power into microwaves and beam it down to any point on the earth below. Motivated by the search for alternate energies but delayed by continuous bureaucratic indecision, Powersat became just another good idea overtaken by events when the cost of nuclear energy plunged. However, when the military sought to place ultrahigh power masers, or microwave lasers, in orbit, its conversion to a weapon became inevitable.

The Air Force placed six Powersats in geosynchronous orbit over specific positions around the Earth before international pressure put the program on hold. While world politicians postured and debated, the Powersat over central United States could only be tested at low power using the Air Force's antenna test range west of San Antonio. This weekend's tests called for beaming energy to thirteen antennas of varying sizes and construction. Willing to give up only their Saturday morning, the politicians and military brass watched the tests on just the first three antennas. Since noon yesterday, Shane and the technician had worked alone. Just as well, thought Shane. Even if they were on the last one, they could never rationalize failure to a general or politician, no matter what the cause.

He inspected the back side of the eleven-foot Cassegrain antenna, which still pointed just above the horizon, then reached up to feel the fist-sized superconducting motor that controlled its pointing. Cool—good, no electrical short. It could be just a mechanical hangup. Shane walked around to check the front side and spied the gimbal lock pin still in place. "Oh shit! No wonder. How could that damn tech've been so sloppy? Must've overlooked it yesterday, trying to get everything ready for the brass. Easy to fix. Pull that sucker outa there, whistle through the test, and I'm gone!"

Shane screamed toward the trailer. "Are you back to step forty-three?"

"It's safed," the technician called back. Under his breath he added, "But I didn't use your damn manual procedures. Did it a lot faster—and a lot better—with my own software. Can't ram that ancient, manual-procedures crap down my throat, you damn WSF hotshot!"

The POWER ENABLE switch remained in MANUAL—ON.

Jake'd again settled into his Sunday Command Post. Val relaxed alongside him in her own multipastel, contoured recliner that faced opposite his. Though she teased him about the more elegant appearance of her recliner, they both provided the same level of comfort. And today, as at the end of many previous days, the fabric of Jake's recliner had an insatiable desire to melt and absorb all his aches. A warm glow filled in behind the tension, a warmth that tingled up from his hand, which Val caressed in her lap.

Jake admired the sun, the distant hades that'd dominated the day. He watched it inflame and turn angry red as an invisible hand flattened it and pushed it down and out of sight. In only minutes the stars and cold half-moon had the sky all to themselves. They seized their turn to dominate for they'd only nine hours before the distant blaze would again force itself back above the opposite horizon.

The moonlight cooled and soothed the scorched ground. It froze the waves of fluid fog that undulated across Clear Lake Harbor, then painted them a gray, filmy satin. And, in cold silence, slender supports that dangled from NASA One Causeway sliced through the frozen fluid and left gashes in its smooth swells. Only flashes of lightning to the west, remnants of the sun's anger, punctured the calm.

"Jake, are you really going to lock yourself up with those people for two years?"

"Yep. Guess I am."

Val looked at Jake with the eyes of an abandoned little girl. "Wouldn't you rather lock yourself up with me?"

"Of course, but that's not the choice I have."

Fire exploded in Val's eyes, and the little girl evaporated. "Oh yes, it is! It's exactly the choice. You don't have to do everything Double D assigns you to."

"It's not that . . ."

"Then what?!"

"The whole program's stopped till we find out what happened. And, though slim, there's the chance that Ted or some of his crew are still waiting out there."

"But why you?"

"That's Dr. Daro's decision. I didn't volunteer."

"But you would've . . . you would've . . ."

"I . . ."

Silence. They each stared straight ahead, but their eyes never met.

Shane reached up and grabbed the gimbal lock pin, three feet from the open center of the antenna. He tugged. It didn't budge. He tugged harder and twisted. Nothing.

"Com'on, ya little dork, get outta there!"

He tugged and twisted and yanked. The pin popped free. The antenna lurched and swiveled up to point at Powersat. Its lower edge scooped up Shane and tossed him toward its open center as a spatula would flip a fried egg. "Holy shit! It's not safed, it's powered!" Face down, Shane tried to scramble backwards, scramble up and out of the antenna's smooth dish.

A search signal left the antenna, found the satellite, returned and tweaked the antenna's final alignment. The satellite's main-power beam reflectors focused straight back down the upcoming signal.

Hands and feet clawed at the glossy surface. Ankles reached the edge as standby power switched on. A long twenty seconds remained to full power.

Shane heard the hum and felt his back, legs and arms tingle. Then electricity sparked from his cheeks, nose and hands. It danced over his upper body, coursed through nerves and heated tissue. He felt himself twitch and jerk, saw arcs flicker from his face, heard the hiss and smelled his burned hair.

Seconds after Shane's mind could no longer reason, he still sensed his temperature rise.

Jake took a breath as Val finally spoke.

"The hard part, Jake, is that I do understand. I really do. If it was you out there rather than Ted, I'd want Double D to assign the best to the mission." Val's eyes softened. "Jake, I don't want to lose you. Can't you screw up so someone else can go?"

"You can't say Speed and I didn't give it a try this week."

"Did you ever! Find another way."

"No sweat, Val. We picked a crew of superstars. Literally, the best in the world."

"And with each superstar, you also get a super ego. Are you sure you can get them to work together?"

Jake shifted his body. Some of the tension flowed back up from his recliner. "We don't have any reason to believe that's a problem. However, by the time we find out for sure, it'll be too late to change."

"Any difficulties with any of them before?"

"Nothing reported. But usually they each've been part of larger crews where they could get lost. On small crews, like ours, teamwork's more important. However, since each one's an expert on the procedures in their area, and we've got the best available computer system to keep 'em all straight, we've got an extremely reliable system."

"I still think you and Speed might be in for trouble."

"We'll know more this week."

"Good luck."

Jake felt Val squeeze his hand. Their eyes probed and spoke before the words came from Jake. "Let's forget Wayfarer for a while and go to bed early. After all, we don't want to have too much catching up to do when I get back. We oughta see if we can't get a little ahead before I leave."

Val smiled. "Why, you dirty old man!"

"Thank you."

"Don't ever change."

The technician knew he was in a race as he ran toward the collector. An electronic timer, a high-reliability timer, an irreversible timer, commanded the power increase just as he arrived. Hands of thunder clapped his ears. Red mist exploded above.

He'd lost.

He looked up into the violet glow, peered through smoke, through gray-white vapor of burned flesh that billowed around him. He held his breath and half-stifled a retch. He saw ankles outlined by moonlight and the antenna's glow. Beyond them he saw the half-moon. Funny how sharp and how clear its edge looked through the smoke. He reached up, grabbed the ankles and pulled. Electricity tingled his hands and arms. He pulled harder. Shane came free.

He heard the smack above the hum as Shane fell to ground. The technician's eyes followed Shane's blackened skull as it jarred loose and rolled clear of the charred skeleton of his upper body, rolled clear of blackened bones that led up to burned and writhing sinews, to blackish-brown flesh that boiled and blistered and popped, to charred legs and smoking pants, to scorched shins, to hot oily ankles, to all of Shane's smoldering remains.

He heard tissue sizzle, felt its heat and smelled its horror. Vision recorded it, then Mind comprehended it. Shane's procedures—he just *knew* he understood'em, just *knew* his were better . . . till now!

Blood rushed from Brain. Vision dissolved. Knees folded. Technician toppled forward.

"Ignore it."

"Sorry. Can't. Might be important." Jake called out to the voice recognition unit in the ceiling over the bed, "Transmit, please."

"Hello? Ryder? This is Dr. Dupree. Dr. Daro's not available. Do you have a minute?"

"Yes, I'm not busy."

Pain shot into Jake where Val wrenched the love handle above his hip. He clenched his teeth to contain his scream.

"I'm calling to make a request."

"What's up?"

"Shane Culver got himself killed tonight. You and Spencer must go back through your personnel review and recommend a replacement. Call Dr. Daro with it first thing in the morning."

"I'm sorry to hear that. His loss is a big one . . . to everybody. How did it happen?"

"He and a technician were finishing up the Powersat tests at the antenna range by San Antonio. They got careless and left a power enable switch in the MANUAL—ON position while Culver was at an antenna. Power came on and killed him."

"I wonder how someone as sharp on procedures as Shane could let that happen."

"He thought he was smarter than the computer and deviated from its procedures."

"Good night, Dupree."

"Ryder, call Spencer for me."

The voice recognition unit clicked off.

Jake felt Val's body, cold and rigid, as her face moved over his.

"Jake, is *that* what you're depending on—superstars and computers and procedures—an extremely reliable system?!"

II

BATTLE

Many forces do many battles, but the final victor never changes—Gravity.

8

Swallow

Stellar Probe 12 functioned without a flaw.

Just like the others in Man's pack of electronic bloodhounds, the probe functioned with relentless precision as it sped outward from the sun. And, like the others, it boasted the name "Stellar Probe," a statement more of its maker's desires than its capabilities.

For now, more than he ever had, Man's curious mind and ambitions reached far beyond his physical abilities. He'd always felt that Pull of what lay around the next corner, beyond the next hill, or over the horizon. And as the incubator filled, the nest crowded, Push also prodded Man outward. But far greater strength belonged to Pull, to that challenge of the reach, to that promise of all those sweet rewards found in answers and revelations. And the more Man learned, the more frequent and persistent Pull became. Years, rather than centuries, now separated major steps outward.

For now, even as he just started a thorough inspection of his solar system, just began to catalogue its secrets, Man again looked outward and couldn't ignore Pull. The technician in him responded with probes and data, questions and information, and

more probes and more data. But all this activity only
intensified Pull.

For now, as each generation had learned before,
the return of stories, pictures, data, information or
other nourishments of the mind, by themselves, rang
hollow. They could only thicken the intellectual shell
around his soft center, could only toughen his edu-
cated hide. For regardless of how many layers of
learned, rational and callous Intellectual Man were
pasted to his exterior, inside Primordial Man still re-
sided, alive and well, with all his drives and desires,
itches and urges. Whether over hill or ocean, into air
or space, or to Moon or Mars, in time it was Man
himself that had to go there, had to break the physical limits of his turf, had to see and feel the new
territory up close, had to take physical measure of it
with his own person before it became a true part of
his world, a part of him. But this time, this time for
sure, Man knew he'd hit the final limit.

For now, Man had encountered the ultimate
frustration of physical distance. The height of a
mountain, the width of a continent, the breadth of an
ocean, the empty space between Earth and Moon
and the distance to the planets had also shocked Man
with their immensities—at first, until technology reduced them to inconvenience. But this time the limit
loomed invincible—interstellar distance—those distances that take years to travel, even for light. Nonetheless, Man did his best.

For now, Man sent his electronic bloodhounds
far out past the outer planets. As always, he rational-
ized his explorations with long lists of scientific objectives and practical benefits. But, as always, Pull
worked on his soft center, tugged on his gut and
compelled him to reach his fingertips ever outward
after his mind and toward the stars.

An earlier bloodhound had sniffed out the Wayfarer Objects. A godsend! Man'd been handed another feasible challenge, a gateway, an intermediate
target, a stepping-stone to the beyond. The world's

space capabilities focused on the Objects and fused into one organization to reach them—the World Space Federation. And they dispatched more bloodhounds to make more discoveries, to find more stepping-stones.

Stellar Probe 12, an advanced spacecraft of an advanced civilization, now hunted with more capability than any of its predecessors. It ferreted out and analyzed visible light, infrared radiation, ultraviolet light, x-rays, gamma rays, particles, and electric and magnetic fields. It sniffed out all but the weakest radiation and reported it to its computerized brain. Even if no signals but those from distant stars existed, it could send out radar pulses and detect faint returns. Thus, even objects cold and lifeless couldn't escape detection. Once it sensed a prey, it could accelerate with legs of nuclear propulsion to pursue and pounce. Once upon the prey's body, sensors would strip its secrets, package them and send them back for Man to devour.

Without emotion or internal debate, *Stellar Probe 12* carried out its new mission. It'd been given the direction of the Wayfarer Objects and the electronic scent of *Wayfarer 1*. With a belly over half-full of nuclear propulsion, all its senses peaked at full vigilance, and its 173-foot antenna locked on and ready to send its voice back to Earth, it continued its new search. Its radioisotope thermoelectric generator, in principle no different from those left on the moon by Apollo astronauts nearly seventy years before, supplied it electrical power, gave it internal warmth and life.

Stellar Probe 12 functioned without flaw.

Probe detected the Wayfarer Objects and picked up the chase. It requested the radar on *Wayfarer 1* to send out its own beacon. *Wayfarer 1* responded. A signal appeared on cue. Probe locked on. Electronic Brain made precise calculations of exact velocities required to reach and pull up alongside.

And, without question, Brain sent commands to Legs.

Stellar Probe 12 functioned without flaw.

Engine fired. Sensors detected. Brain calculated. Engine refired. Sensors redetected. Brain recalculated.

Stellar Probe 12 functioned without flaw.

Had this machine been a bloodhound of flesh, it would've felt frustration and turned to its master. For each new calculation showed its prey at larger distances. But it persisted. It ran, and it ran, and it ran. Once all propellant had left its innards, the brain continued to send commands to its legs, commands that still continued to grow. All systems continued to operate with relentless precision.

Stellar Probe 12 functioned without flaw.

Within minutes the probe lost lock on the prey, just before its internal sensors detected a force across its skeletal frame. The stellar probe's structure flexed, and its voice reported.

The force grew—structure stretched—voice cried.

Force magnified—structure yielded—voice screamed.

Force multiplied—structure ripped—voice ceased.

Stellar Probe 12's wire arteries tore away from its electrical heart. Plexan bones broke and shattered. Electronic flesh and its debris stretched and shredded, stretched and shredded again, then again, and again, and . . .

In a moment of which man has no meaningful measure, every molecule of the probe's remains reunited at a point of near infinite density.

But yet, its engineers had the right to be proud. Within its specifications, *Stellar Probe 12* had functioned without flaw.

0317 hours CTS. Jake stepped from his car into darkness. Daylight switched on, bathed his world, then switched off. Thunder exploded, then trailed off behind him. Light rain speckled his face.

He started to jog. The sky noted his attempt at evasion and let a massive slug of water slip from its hands and plummet to the ground.

Jake ran.

The rain soaked his shoulders and thighs, beat against his face and hands, wedged its cold down his neck and back and pummeled the pavement. His feet splashed through puddles, squished into thick Bermuda grass, then clapped across dry concrete under the entrance to Mission Control Center.

He stopped to catch his breath. Despite the cold wetness that seeped into him and the hour, Jake's enthusiasm mounted. For exactly one day and fourteen hours ago, *Stellar Probe 12* had reached the Wayfarers, and in only another fifteen minutes its signal, with all its secrets, would reach Earth.

Soon the *Wayfarer 2* team, who now converged on WSF facilities around the world, would have some answers!

Dr. Ada S. Lin wrestled with her umbrella as she struggled from her car. She hated physical inconvenience. Why transport her body in this massive metal machine to the Mission Control Center in the rain and black of night? It'd all be so much easier just to light-link the information straight to her. Her patience wore thin. For this inconvenience came on the heels of many others, all of which stemmed from the ultimate inconvenience just three weeks earlier—she'd moved.

If only she'd had a way to code her possessions into software, then she could've light-linked them all to Houston. Wouldn't it be great? Assign the whole job to a junior programmer, then she'd be free to do more useful things. But, since Dr. Daro's call, she'd been forced to manipulate her physical world, hour after hour. A boring, tedious, mundane chore. A dreadful waste of a professional's time.

Books, papers, computer equipment and light disks of data, each a once-loved but forgotten child, required a decision—move or discard, protect or abandon. One by one, she lost. Almost everything found its way into piles for the movers. Somehow these piles had swollen in number and size since her last move. Somehow they'd acquired a life of their own. After two and a half days, she turned to her personal items and clothing. She culled out the enemies for discard. At least these piles had shrunk. Within two hours she had everything ready.

Dr. Lin's previous move came after her first flight with WSF on Space Station Tsien in 2033. As soon as she'd landed, she moved from Canton, China, to the research laboratories of CompuThink Corporation in Boston. CT 7000's development for the Wayfarer Project demanded top priority. Within a year her knowledge, intelligence and devotion made her the recognized expert.

Once CT 7000's development reached a plateau, she craved the next logical step—the opportunity to put *her* software into action. This *Wayfarer 2* assignment couldn't have been better timed. Soon she and *her* software would be in control of *her* flight. By comparison, even the ultimate inconvenience seemed like a small price to pay.

Ada wrestled with her umbrella again. She had to collapse it, to defeat it, in order to go inside and receive the Wayfarer secrets the probe had uncovered. The slippery mechanism evaded her wet fingers. She struggled. And she struggled and she . . .

0105 hours PST. In silence, with his comrades Logic and Precision, Dr. Boris U. Mechanov let his car coast out his driveway and start down the road that led toward *Stellar Probe 12* Control Center at the Jet Propulsion Laboratory in Pasadena, thirteen minutes away.

He'd made it—a clean getaway!

It'd taken a few extraordinary measures, a few

off-nominal procedures, but it was worth it. He'd absconded with his sanity. He'd avoided all that emotional ranting and raving, remained relaxed and cool, stayed analytical for the job ahead. If she awoke as he slipped out, even now in the middle of the night, she'd pierce him with more of her illogical accusations, harpoon him with more of her imprecise questions and then ignore all his precise, logical answers. "Yes, I'll be back in a couple of years—thirty-three hours after mission termination. No, the mission's not punishment—for you or me. Yes, you're still my wife. No, I'm not trying to kill myself. Yes, of course I still . . . No, it's not just a way out of . . ."

Ever since they'd moved from Star City, Russia, to Pasadena, California, in 2032, she only had Boris; he seemed only to have his work. She complained that he'd forgotten how to make conversation; he complained that she'd forgotten how to make love. The poet in Boris mused that scarlet roses that once bloomed between them, roses they'd first nurtured with promises and plans, had withered and fallen. Now only hardy stems pushed up through shriveled petals, budless stems that entwined and pricked and strangled.

But, so what? Boris, the professional, still found fulfillment with his comrades Logic and Precision. With them, he'd honed a razor sharp understanding of space navigation and developed a close rapport with its mechanics. First, with Precision, insert facts, then turn on Logic and collect results. Perfect! Like a blanket, he spread Logic and Precision over every exposed surface of his life. They smothered out emotion and hassle and left only simplicity and satisfaction.

Boris and his comrades triumphed in flight after flight, first in the Russian Program, then with the WSF. However, each triumph seemed only to evaporate as the next challenge appeared. But this time, at the apogee of his career, he'd leave a permanent mark. Navigation to the Wayfarer Objects couldn't be surpassed until flight to the stars, maybe a century away. And better yet, not only would *Wayfarer 2* be flown under *his* guidance, but he'd use *his* calculations. At last, in all respects, he had *his* flight!

The engine's electrical whine broke the silence. Boris grinned. Yes, he'd coasted far enough. He'd made a smooth escape with not a feather ruffled. And within a few hours, Boris, Logic and Precision would be with the control team and could extract Wayfarer secrets from *Stellar Probe 12* data.

Then he could return to Houston. And, of course, someone needed to watch their house in Pasadena. Right? Perfect thing to keep the wife busy.

"Hi, Jake."

"Mornin'."

"Ever tell ya you're all wet?"

"Not yet today, Speederoo."

Jake glanced at the three walls before them. Two flat viewing screens displayed digital data and plots from *Stellar Probe 12*'s telemetry while four others waited for pictures from its cameras.

"Gotta be a better way, boss."

"Oh?"

"I drag my beaten body out of its cozy cocoon in the middle of the night, just to prop it up here and watch something that happened over a day and a half ago."

"Sorry, Speed. The signal gets here only at the speed of light."

"Can't you do anything about that?"

The rest of the *Wayfarer 2* team waited in silence. As they studied the data on the screens, they each appeared lost in their own thoughts, thoughts that at this time of night should've been dreams. As a single body, they stirred when an image flickered onto the third screen, then sharpened.

"Speed, we've got video. Good color and resolution."

"Yeah. But nothing yet on the infrared, ultraviolet or x-ray screens. May not be either."

"Perfect picture!" said Jake. "Lotta detail. Boulders look gigantic. Probe's camera is ultrasensitive. Not much sunlight out there, but the camera makes it look like day."

"Yeah, it's good."

"Looks like your standard rock, ice and debris of a comet. But what do you think keeps them all grouped together, Speed?"

"Not sure . . . yet."

"Look at that one. It's huge. Tough to tell without a reference, but it looks like it could be a couple of miles across."

"At least."

"Thanks to Boris, probe's programmed to just miss them no more than required to save propellant. So we're just skimmin' over its surface. That could be why it looks so large."

"Could be."

"Big or small, gotta make sure we don't hit one. It'd take all the fun outta our flight."

"Maybe more."

"Hey, the radar's picked up the Beta module, Ted's module. Look at screen two, at the range readout—340 miles out and closing."

"See it."

". . . 327 . . . 25 . . . We should be able to see it soon. Probe's got more than enough propellant to just whistle right up alongside of Ted. Love to see him lookin' out the window."

"Yeah."

"The boulders're all getting smaller, Speed. Why?"

"Not sure."

"There's the module, on screen two! Long range lens's locked on. Module looks intact except for what's left of the bridge at the top."

"Yeah."

"Can't see anything, or anybody, at the windows. If only we could get some telemetry from it, we could see if he's in hibernation."

"Be nice."

"Since the radar beacon's working, it must still have emergency electrical power for telemetry. The antenna probably can't stay locked on Earth. Maybe we'll pick it up."

"Jake, do you see flashes on the x-ray and ultraviolet screens every now and then?"

"Yeah, but thought it was noise in the cameras."

"It's not."

"It doesn't look like we are getting any closer to the module. The distance is . . . increasing? 241 . . . 44 . . . and accelerating . . . 250 . . . 55 . . . 62 . . . probe's blowin' the rendezvous!"

"Not its fault."

"Picture's breaking up. Damn. There it goes. We've lost it, Speed. Maybe it'll come back in."

"Nope. It won't."

The *Wayfarer 2* team again waited in silence, as if what they saw was just a momentary hangup, just a glitch, something that would clear itself if only they waited it out . . . if only they didn't say anything . . . if only they held their breath . . . if only they . . .

Dr. Dupree's voice bellowed over the audio, annihilating all further hope. "Holovision conference in two minutes. We're going to get to the bottom of this. Ops Manager, I want Lin, Mechanov and propulsion tech on camera."

The control center operations manager responded. He first switched on the holovision cameras in the viewing room and centered them on Ada, who'd moved to the speaker's position at the conference table. Then he turned on the holovision displays.

The life-sized holographic image of Dr. Dupree popped into the space in front and to the left of Ada. He sat at attention behind the wide expanse of his highly polished, black plexan desk. In their highly polished gold standards, the flags of the Wayfarer Program and WSF stood at attention on either side. Dr. Dupree's dark-blue, pin-striped, three-piece suit provided a vivid contrast with his fine white hair, stark white shirt and deep-red silk tie. His scowl broadcast that, without question, he held the reins of authority and control.

"Jake, look at that turkey in his power suit."

"I know, and it's only two in the morning out there."

"Can't figure out if he's going to address the State of the Union or audition for the Hanging Judge. Wish I were sitting on his desk in my skivvies now, just to balance things out."

The image of the propulsion technician seated at his control console appeared in the space in front and to the right of Ada. His eyes darted side to side, then looked down and watched his hands fidget.

After a pause, the six-foot image of Boris's head popped into the space between the other two. It quivered, then froze and focused to full clarity in front of Ada. She gasped, then gaped.

Something inside Jake jumped. The red mass of Boris's head, of equal size to the full-body images on either side, displayed every line, every cut, every blemish, every pimple, every unshaven whisker. More than anything, it reminded Jake of a stack of odd-sized tomatoes: the round red face supported two round red cheeks, one round red bulbous nose, a round red knob chin and red clumps on either side in the ear positions. Thin blond locks stretched forward over his growing forehead and tried in vain to hide the red invader. A few locks grazed the upper edges of his ancient, round, yellow plastic-rimmed glasses, anger shot out through fog-covered lenses from bloodshot eyes.

"Hey, Jake. How'd you like to be Mother Mechanov first thing in the morning?"

Dupree banged down both clenched fists. "Mechanov, you're on the wrong camera! You should know by now. Don't use the close-up for full-room viewing."

The tomatoes turned redder and flexed into a sheepish grin that revealed teeth to match the rims of the glasses. Then Boris's full-sized image popped up in place of his head. Excess energy bristled from his short, fireplug body in jiggles and jerks. Arms and legs danced as he shifted weight from foot to foot. Though his exterior looked soft and pudgy, its spasmodic movements appeared to be driven by a stiff muscle core.

"Look at that, Jake. I love it."

Sweat ran off the tomatoes down into the red and white-striped flannel top. A worn black leather belt, of the same vintage as his glasses, drew black, baggy pants closed over the tops of his hips. Wide black shoes stuck out below the bags. Although they looked like they'd reached middle age, it didn't appear that they'd seen any polish since birth.

Speed grinned. "Why does Boris baby still have on his pajama tops?"

Dupree's bulldog face snapped. "Mechanov. Do you understand why your navigation routine failed to complete a simple rendezvous with a passive spacecraft?"

Boris matched Dupree's scowl. "My routine worked exactly as it was programmed to do. The sensor inputs must've been in error. You should understand by now that, except for the Objects Avoidance Subroutine, it's the most straightforward type of rendezvous routine in the package."

"So straightforward that it didn't work," said Dupree.

Boris sneered. "Dupree, take your witch-hunt elsewhere!"

Dupree's eyes shifted. "Dr. Lin. Why did the CT 6000 not properly process the sensor inputs?"

Ada remained motionless except for her tongue, the peripheral of her brain that clicked out words in a rapid uniform cadence. "It's clear you failed to observe the computer status display during the rendez-vous. It indicated that all computer self-checks and redundant operation comparisons detected no errors at any time, in either the calculations or the commands to the propulsion module. You should also know by now that the CT 6000 is the last place to look for degraded performance."

"Dupree's usually not this irrational," said Speed. "One more friendly jab, and we'll get steam jets from his ears."

"Right. He's got a sharp mind and could contribute. We gotta get him calmed down, get him on our side so we can figure all this out."

But Dupree charged again. "OK, Prop Tech, it's down to you. How did your system fail?"

Propulsion Tech, a quick study of Boris and Ada, rolled out firm laconic words with an impassive stare. "Propulsion didn't fail. Thrust was nominal. Pointing was as commanded. In fact, all of the systems operated with no malfunctions indicated."

Before Dupree could summon up another target, Boris asked, "Prop Tech, why did we lose signal at the end?"

"Glad you asked. It seems strange. Comm Tech reported that all signals remained strong, but they shifted to lower and lower frequencies as the probe's distance from Wayfarer increased. Our receivers followed it out to a very large frequency shift before we lost it."

"The only way that could happen is if the probe was accelerating away from us," said Boris. "But the propulsion was nowhere strong enough to make that happen."

"Get Comm Tech on the line," said Dupree.

"But that's not the . . ." started Boris.

"Let's try this idea on for size," said Speed, who'd moved forward and replaced Ada at the conference table.

Dupree bellowed again. "Spencer, I'm running this. We . . ."

"Although I haven't had time to go through it thoroughly, it seems to match what we've seen."

"We don't need . . ."

"Suppose there's an extremely strong source of gravity at the center of the Objects. Since it's not accounted for in the navigation equations, it could cause the probe's complete miss like we just saw. A strong gravity source would also explain why the Objects remain all grouped together. They're actually in orbit around it. Also, if the two *Wayfarer 1* modules, which were separated by their long bridge, got close enough to it, the difference in gravity felt by the two modules could've ripped them apart, just like the Objects closer to it've been ripped apart. Lastly, the x-ray and ultraviolet flashes we saw could've come from small particles that fell into the gravity source and were heated as they did. There's only one gravity source that's strong enough, small enough and couldn't be seen—a black hole."

"Nonsense, Spencer!" said Dupree. "The effects on the planets of something as strong as a black hole would've been noticed centuries ago."

"You're right, unless it's a primordial black hole. That is, a black hole with a mass far less than other black holes we know about, a mass far less than the sun's. This type of mini-black hole was predicted way back in the 1970s but, since one was never observed, the idea was dropped. Also, remember the Wayfarers are really just in transit by our solar system."

"Let's get back into the real world," said Dupree. "You're grasping at straws. Let's—"

"No, I'm not. The path of the probe was one that sent it right into the black hole. In short, the probe was swallowed, right along with every signal that came from it."

Dupree snorted and banged his fists twice for full effect. "Enough! Can it, Spencer. Save all that crap for a useless academic seminar somewhere else. Now, I want everyone to take a long hard careful look at the data just recorded and find out which system on the probe failed."

Jake joined Speed at the table. "You're right, Laurent. We all should take a good hard look at the data, but do it with Speed's suggestion in mind. It could answer all the questions we've had about the Objects since we observed them. It may sound strange at first, but that's the way the real world out there is at times. Personally, I'll bet Speed's right."

Dupree reached forward to his control panel. "And I'll bet he's wrong, dead wrong. Enough!" He punched a button.

The three images snapped down to points and faded.

9

Squeeze

Jake pulled open the door to Conference Room G and looked down a conference table with three people seated along either side. Six heads swiveled in unison and faced him, as if all were attached to the same invisible cord hooked to the door. When I close it, Jake wondered, will they all spring back?

He shook hands with the man at the front left corner, "Hi, Jon. Thanks for coming on such short notice."

"Glad to be of help, Jake."

"Let's get started."

"Good," said Jon. "First, I need to determine the level that I should address the subject."

"OK."

"A black hole is a cosmic turnstile. Once something goes in, it never comes out."

Jake chuckled. "I think we can go a little deeper than that."

"Good. If we start with the metric tensor in four-dimensional space, we can arrive at a definition of a black hole as an extreme concentration of gravity that causes a severe strain in the normally smooth fabric of space and a strong dilation of time."

"Oops, too deep," said Jake.

"Yeah, Jon," said Speed. "Find some middle

ground. You know, somewhere between astronaut pabulum and your research that's so hairy it's gotta be shaved just to be read."

"OK. I'm calibrated. Some of you may know of the course Introduction to Compressed Matter, usually a freshman course for physics or astronomy students. It covers black holes to the depth that I will here."

"Good for starters," said Jake. "Need anything else?"

"Just Speed's promise that he'll behave this time."

Speed pointed toward his chest with both hands. *"Moi?"*

"Yes, you," sighed Jon.

Jake glanced at the rest of his crew. Faye MacFarland chuckled at Speed. Boris looked caustic; Ada, impassive; and Irwin Rote, the replacement for Shane Culver, pale and confused. Although a challenge for any instructor, he knew that Jon Sloan, a postdoc at Darmont University, could handle it. Jake and his crew now enjoyed one of the benefits of WSF, like NASA before it. The lure of space exploration and a proximity to its day-to-day operations attracted a host of spirited, capable people from outside the government bureaucracy. From his previous lectures, Jake knew that underneath Jon's open, enthusiastic demeanor, they'd find a sharp, confident professional.

"Let me start with a short overview, including what we now know about *Wayfarer 1*. Then we'll go back through it in more detail.

"The concept of a black hole is not new but about a century old. It was first shown to be a physical possibility in 1939 by J. Robert Oppenheimer.

"A black hole results from gravity, something we all feel—and think we understand. Although gravity's the weakest force in nature, nothing permanently escapes it. Gravity controls our fate, and ultimately, that of our universe."

Speed squirmed.

"And, unlike the forces we find in the nucleus of an atom, gravity acts over large distances. All matter contributes to it and is affected by it. So far the only type of gravity that we know about is attractive. That is, matter that repels itself has never been observed. It's gravity that lets us walk around down here, that holds together our earth, sun, solar system, galaxy and, in fact, our total universe."

Speed cupped his hand by his mouth and whispered, "Jon's never been one to minimize the gravity of the situation." Only Boris and Faye groaned.

"As more and more matter, material of any kind, comes together, the compressive force at the center due to gravity increases. Because the amount of this matter can be immense, so can the compressive force. In this way, gravity can eventually overwhelm all other known forces in nature."

"What other forces are you talking about, Jon?" asked Jake.

"Two play a role here, Jake, the electronic force, or the electrical force between electrons, and the strong nuclear force, or the force between neutrons. It's straightforward. Let me explain.

"First, the force that stops gravity from pulling me through the floor as I stand here is electronic. That is, the atoms of my shoes resist moving into the atoms of the carpet because the electrons in each repel one another. Each atom has a number of positive charges in its nucleus and an equal number of negative electrons in shells around it. These electron shells act like bumpers. Although the repulsive force of these bumpers is small, it's large enough to prevent the atoms from merging. It's this type of repulsive force that resists gravity everywhere on the earth and in many stars."

Speed raised an outstretched finger. "I find that whole concept repulsive!" No one stirred.

"However, some stars are so massive and their gravity so strong that their atoms do merge. Electrons around nuclei are forced into one another and mingle freely in a sea of electrons. Now it's this sea that resists further compression. And, although the sea's resistive force is very much stronger than that of the atom's electron shells, it's still electrical. Matter in this state is called degenerate.

"Let's move on to the second resistive force, the strong nuclear force. For stars about one point four times as massive as our sun, eventually the compressive force of gravity can't be resisted any longer by the sea of electrons. Everything gets squeezed together so tight that electrons are forced right inside nuclei. Once there, they unite with the positively charged protons and form neutrons, particles that're electrically neutral. The result is material that's composed almost entirely of neutrons. These neutrons get pushed so close to one another that it's their short range force, the strong nuclear force, that has to resist gravity. This type of matter is sometimes called neutronium."

This time Speed looked serious. "Jon, the most impressive thing about neutronium is its extreme density. It's as dense as the nucleus in an atom."

"That's right. It's about a million billion times as dense as water. For example, if the Earth were compressed into a ball of neutronium, its diameter would be about two hundred and forty yards. That is, Earth would shrink to about the size of the old Astrodome."

Boris smiled and raised his eyebrows at Speed. "That'd sure put the airlines outta business."

"Once the sea of electrons is squeezed past its resistive limit, its collapse to neutronium can't be stopped. And, once in this high density, neutronium's self-gravity is so strong that it's locked into this extreme state forever—unless it collapses even further."

"But wait, Jon," said Jake. "You said there're only two forces that resist gravity. We've used up both of them. Once the resistive force between neutrons is exceeded, how's the next compression stopped?"

"It isn't. It's the ultimate triumph of gravity. When a star's about three times as massive as our sun, it'll eventually collapse beyond the density of neutronium and just keep right on going."

"Going where?" asked Jake.

"No one knows. We know of no other repulsive force to stop the collapse. Mathematically, we describe a completely collapsed star as a point with an infinitely small volume and an infinitely large density. But, when the density and volume are multiplied together, it should give the original mass."

"That picture's not too satisfying," said Jake.

"True. But there's no way to get close enough to one, let alone in one, to see what really happens."

"What happens when you do get real close?" asked Boris.

Speed turned nose-to-nose with Boris. "Simple— you diiiie!"

"Speed, perhaps I'd better elaborate on that answer," said Jon. "Again, two points to be made.

"Let's talk first about how you'd escape from a black hole. Its gravity is just like that of any other body, if you're far away. Then you can navigate around it just like it was another planet or moon. But as you move closer, the velocity needed to escape it gets larger until it reaches the velocity of light. Inside this distance, not even light can escape. Thus the reason for the name 'black hole.' No light can come out of it—it's just a black hole in space. And, because no events inside this radius can be seen from outside, this radius defines what's called the 'event horizon.' "

"My navigation's good enough to keep us from getting *that* close," said Boris. "What's the second point?"

"It's something called 'gravity gradient.' For example, it's the gradient of the moon's gravity acting on earth that causes our tides."

"That I understand well," said Boris.

"And it's also most likely the force that ripped *Wayfarer 1* apart. That is, the hole's gravity pulled harder on the module closer to it than the one farther away. The greater the separation of the two modules and the gravity gradient of the hole, the greater the difference of the two forces."

"Jon, what exactly are we going to be faced with when we get there?" asked Jake.

"As Speed was quick to realize when we lost *Stellar Probe 12*, a black hole as massive as three times the sun and that close to us would be easily detected. Analysis has shown that it must be a mini-black hole."

Boris grabbed Speed's arm. "You were wrong. This one could only mini-kill us!"

"Underdog scores number two," said Faye.

"Actually, mini-black holes are just as much black holes as the ones I just described, but they're formed differently. Early in the life of our universe, right after the big bang, everything was highly concentrated and extremely violent. Our primordial universe was very turbulent, a real fierce and frenzied chaos. As high-density globs of matter slammed together, they increased their densities for short times. If they hit hard enough, they could've collapsed into mini-black holes. Billions of masses in our galaxy, much smaller than our sun, could've slammed together, collapsed and existed until now as mini-black holes. Some may've actually grown by swallowing other matter."

"Like probes," said Jake.

"Yes, like probes. Let me finish answering your question, Jake. From analysis of the data we got back just before we lost the probe, we've calculated that the mini-black hole has a mass just slightly larger than earth's. And Ted's module, just like the Wayfarer Objects, is in orbit around it."

"How large is Ted's orbit?" asked Boris.

"We don't know for sure, but we can calculate approximately how close the two modules must've gotten to the hole to have been ripped apart. At a distance of fifty miles and for a separation between the modules of 237 feet, the length of the bridge, the force pulling the modules apart would've been about twelve times their own weight."

"That's a little larger than what the structures guys said would've caused failure," said Jake. "If the *Wayfarer 1* modules really are that close to the hole, we'll have to unhook the bridge and fly separately in order to reach 'em."

Speed peered across the table at Jake. "Just as an eye-opener, boss, if you calculate the gravity at 50 miles from the hole, it comes out to be about 6400 g. Although we'll be floating in orbit and only feel its gravity gradient, I hope we don't have to ever go down that close."

For a moment, cold silence reigned.

Then Jon continued. "Also, this strong gravity gradient force explains why all the Objects close to the center of the Wayfarers are small. They've been ripped apart. This could make it harder to pick your way through them without getting hit."

"That'll be a real problem," said Boris.

"Another eye-opener, boss. If you calculate the size of the event horizon for this little jobber-do, you find that it's a sphere less than three-quarters of an inch in diameter. About the size of a grape."

"But a grape with a voracious appetite," said Jake. "Just like the probe, it could shred us, then swallow us without a trace, except that it'd grow just a little bit stronger."

Cold silence reigned again.

Then Jon continued again. "OK, enough generalities. My holograms are all set to roll. It'll take about two hours to work through 'em. If you need greater depth, I can come back and do that another day. Jake, do you want to start now or take a break?"

"We've got a lot to learn. Press!"

Rested, Ted assessed his strength.
. . . yes, feel charged and ready . . . time to learn, to reach out again . . .

Ted concentrated on his immediate environment, the core of his chamber. And again, he felt the fullness of its energy. As Ted sharpened his awareness, the energy seemed to draw into clumps, clumps that his awareness then focused into tight packets that buzzed and quivered like restless bees inside his ethereal hive.

Ted zeroed in on a single packet that hovered next to a sea of packets, a single bee that buzzed next to the infinite swarm. Familiar but foreign, the single packet of light, electricity, or some other form of energy, slipped away and drifted toward the chamber wall. From his aloof perspective, it resembled a bright light inside a clouded container, a beacon within a frosted shell. And, although it seemed about a room's width away and equal in size to himself, he had no reference by which to judge. It needed closer inspection.

The packet accelerated as it passed through an opening, left the chamber and started down a tunnel.

Ted focused his awareness on it, reached out his mental muscles and kept the packet's flash in his mind's eye as it weaved and rocked through the tunnel's turns and accelerated on its straights. Ted strained his mind, focused with all his mental strength and concentration and just managed to keep in the chase. Like one bobsled pursuing another, Ted shadowed the bright light as it barreled down the tunnel's long runs and swept through its gentle curves. When it slowed, he slowed, then joggled along behind as it picked its way around hooks and crooks. The packet accelerated along one last straight, then shot out of the tunnel into another chamber. It coasted to a stop and hovered like a chandelier at arm's length. Ted had no judge of time nor distance covered, but both seemed large.

Ted pounced. He wrapped his awareness around the beacon and studied it. Billions of brilliant loops of electrical current swarmed and scintillated inside the packet as its surface shimmered and danced in place. He focused a question.

. . . what? . . .

The light packet started to enter him, to penetrate and permeate his awareness, to blend with him. A faint image appeared, then faded. He surrounded the packet again, concentrated all his mental energy and compressed it into Packet.

. . . WHAT?! . . .

Image returned, strengthened and sharpened. Ted's awareness burst back into his former shell, the flesh of his former existence. Once again he felt his body, sensed its senses and thought its thoughts.

. . . *cold water hiss . . . hit lips, chill teeth, run down throat . . . see it swirl down drain . . . nose wet . . . ears pop with each swallow . . . raise foot and water stops . . . stand up . . .*

The image started to fade, but it returned as he felt himself bend down again.

. . . *hold breath and take some long pulls of this cold water . . . ahhh, feels good . . . voice from left—Jerry's voice, "Teddy, you're worse than a camel. Save some for me." . . . stop, take deep breath . . . fresh-cut-grass smell . . . hot dry air, face hot, sun on neck and back of shirt . . . water drip off forehead and right ear into drain . . . throat's cold . . . feel full . . . "An you're gonna slosh when you walk, Teddy. Your belly looks like a water balloon." . . . hold mouthful of water and stand—don't let him see it . . . Jerry's bent over, he's turning, he's got a mouthful too! . . . must've seen me . . . beat him to it, let it go—got him! . . . but he got my shirt too . . . gotta stop laughing, gotta get more water . . .*

Image faded. Ted strained, but it remained aloof.

But while he had it, Image had given Ted back a piece of his previous life, that one thirty-second, grab-ass play on a hot afternoon with Jerry, his best friend during the summer of '11. Ted'd never thought of that moment since he'd lived it. But yet, right here and right now, he'd lived through it all again in infinite detail!

Ted relaxed and felt himself draw away. But another packet, just like the first, shot into the chamber, glided to a stop, hovered and shimmered its seductive image.

Ted wrapped his awareness around the second packet and concentrated.

. . . WHAT?! . . .

The beacon fused with him, and again Ted found himself inside his former flesh. Sensations and thoughts sharpened.

. . . *underwater EVA training . . . space suit rubs chest . . . bubbles rise in front of helmet, big ones break into little ones, not round, more like mushrooms that wiggle and dance as they fight toward surface, break into fine white spray and disappear into bright blue-green light . . . breath's raspy and hollow and moist . . . here comes Don—a good ole boy, bit old to be a safety diver, makes up for it with intensity . . . wet suit and built-in aqualung, nice an' trim, wish I could take one home . . . he's laughing and giving me The Big Stare, huge blue eyes look strained under mask, gray-purple flesh, white-beard stubble around mole on chin, like a red pea, must hurt, oughta have it lasered out . . . pullin' me toward* Wayfarer 1 *mockup, makes it easier, can't swim in this rig . . . gonna be a long session, work like hell, but worth every minute, be a snap in space if I can do it here . . . weighted out just right—don't float or sink or rotate . . .* "Ya dun good, Don! Thanks." . . . *should've gone before I got into suit, coffee's gone right through me, damn roll-on's too tight . . . left foot in restraint, now right, grab rail . . .*

Image faded. Ted strained but he knew he'd lost it.

But again he'd romped through another thirty-second segment of his life. Every sensation and every thought from a previous moment had recycled through his awareness.

He waited. No other packets arrived. But he sensed a thin density of more packets that extended away from the two he'd just imaged.

. . . how large is this chamber? . . . how many other packets are there here and what's in them? . . . forces here I don't understand . . .

Ted expanded in all directions, but he couldn't reach the chamber's edge. Then one by one he wrapped his awareness around the closest three packets and tried to fuse with each of them. But they each seemed foreign and not of himself. He strained, but he experienced nothing.

Fatigue came again. Ted relaxed and shrank back down into his own chamber, back into his comfortable core, back into his sanctuary.

. . . what are those memory packets and why did they end up in the same chamber? . . . both involved water . . . and each let me live again . . . live again?

. . . AM I STILL ALIVE NOW? . . .

The jaws of the vice crept back and released their squeeze. Blood pulsed back into Jake's legs and feet. His rigid shoulders and arms softened as tension spilled out with his exhaled air. The sweat-soaked cloth on his back cooled as he separated from the couch.

Jake sucked in a fresh load of oxygen, heard it howl, glanced ahead and measured his performance. Yep, almost perfect: inverted, wings level, nose coming down through horizon, 74,000 feet, 1.2 Mach and 0.3 g. Perfect conditions for the top of a loop. Pull off power, bleed g's back in and make second half as good.

RT7 started its race back down through thin air, back down toward long shadows, back down into darkness. Jake's fingers finessed the pressure on the stick to play the altitude, airspeed and g's against one other, to create just the right combination at the bottom. Air slipped, then screamed over RT7. The g force doubled and drove him down into the hands of the couch that wrapped around his lower body again. He tightened his shoulders and arms, and odors of metallic air and sweat froze in his lungs. Force doubled again. The outside roar pounded through canopy and helmet and buffeted his ears. Force doubled once more. Vise crushed as it fought to stem the rush of blood from his brain toward his feet. Jake's visual world narrowed to a tube, to red, green and blue markings on the electronic altitude indicator at arm's length. Then the markings grayed.

He measured again: 37,000 feet, nose coming up through the horizon, Mach 3.0, 8.3 g and heading 270. Perfect, same as the entry. Now bring nose up 30 degrees, release pressure, stick over . . .

Jake and RT7 corkscrewed along a slow lazy arc, an arc that gave him a few seconds of leisure to reflect on his simple world of high performance. Control with freedom—love it! Only way to relax. Felt punchy after Jon's five-hour lecture—8.3 g hurts, but what'd Speed say? We'd feel 6,400 g at the Wayfarers if we weren't floating! Stop screwin' off, Ryder. Work on the inner ear.

He slid the throttle forward, heard the engine growl and felt its push. He bent the flight path upward, turned his head to the side and pushed the stick hard over. As RT7 raced through two dozen rolls in twenty seconds, fluid raced through the semicircular canals of his inner ears. Jake snapped RT7 back to level flight, but fluid continued to race. Canals sent signals to Brain. Brain sent signals to Eyeballs. And Eyeballs fluttered.

Jake watched his world flicker up and down like movie film stuck in a projector. No doubt about it, he thought, this's gotta be the best way to prevent space sickness—beat the inner ear till it's insensitive. But the system keeps feedin' us pills like it was stuffin' turkeys. Has pills for everything. Leaves nothing to the individual. Try another series with head down.

After his seventh series, Jake flew straight and level. But his world continued to swim. His stomach churned and climbed into his throat. And his skin flushed, then cooled as each pore ejaculated its own squib of sweat.

He glanced at the fuel display. Near minimum . . . but enough for one more maneuver. Ballistic flight. Just the right time of day. Better hustle. There's 73,000 feet. Coming up on Mach 4.3. Ramjet's really perkin'. Eight g and point his hummer up. Just open sky—leave it all behind!

Jake and RT7 screamed upward. Going through 120,000 feet, Jake turned the ramjet engine to standby and phased in reaction-control jets to keep RT7 aligned as air pressure on its control surfaces dwindled away.

The human mounted on his black charger shot back into sunlight at 173,000 feet. The world below, still consumed by earth's shadows, still shackled by gravity's chains, slid from Jake's mind. Up past 300,000 feet they coasted, up past the fifty miles that once earned astronaut wings, up to 317,037 feet where his altimeter hung. Pilot and partner floated in idle at their summit, suspended in silence and bathed in sunlight, above it all, king of the mountain, king of the shadows, left to float alone at the apex of their upward thrust.

Just over fifty miles, he observed. Not far at all.

As always, gravity had its way. It reached up with its impartial pull and tugged on plexan and bone, fuel and flesh, computers and brains, just as it would on a pop fly.

Jake watched the altimeter's needle budge, then saw it rotate, unwind, spin and turn into a blur. Less than two minutes to atmosphere. It seemed as if he'd had only an instant at the top, only a moment in the light that always glazed too bright before all that mass under the blackness pulled him back down into the shadows again, back down toward all those egotistical souls who rode the gray bureaucracy with all the dignity and control of ants riding a log in the rapids. Grunt time—eight-g pullout.

He leveled at 74,000 feet and noted his speed. Mach 4.4. That's 4,000 feet a second. Seems like I'm goin' like hell. But soon I'll be going a million times faster!

Jake banked and headed for home. With RT7 in idle, he held level flight and let his speed bleed below Mach 2, then started down again. RT7's radar outlined a single thunderstorm cell straight ahead. The cell churned and boiled as packets of hot air punched skyward, packets that rushed upward to release heat they'd picked up below.

At 52,000 feet, Jake could just see the cell's outline in the faint light of the moon. A big mother. One to stay out of. Not the time to hotdog. He just grazed its top.

From horizon to horizon, the cloud below exploded like a gigantic flashbulb. His pupils slammed shut, and for a moment he saw nothing but the lightning's pattern that still burned in his eyes and mind. Just your standard lightning bolt, Jake thought. Hot air drags up electrical charge and explodes back down without a hint. Calm and violence. Always together with no control or warning. Just nature's way. Same at the Wayfarers? I can understand our forces and distances and speeds, but what else do I need to know? What's really out there? How do we survive it? What has us stopped?

Val studied Jake. Red, flushed skin on his face still showed creases from an oxygen mask. And his damp hair needed a few more swipes with his comb.

"Looks like you've been out playing with your toy."

"You're just jealous."

"Have fun?"

"Just your standard bank and yank."

She reached out and took both his hands in hers. Jake's back and neck tightened as if they braced for another onslaught of g's. But his mind felt clear, his body alive and electric. Val's perfume, a welcome change from sweat-soaked cloth and metallic air, cut into him. She always looked good, but especially so right after he'd been flying, when his mind and senses still barreled along at high Mach, when her warm sensuality and smooth softness drew his mind away from RT7's cold surfaces and hard forces.

Val's full lips parted, smiled and opened themselves to him. He followed the curve of her blond hair as it flowed and folded forward over a bronze shoulder, the outline of her light-blue sleeveless blouse that struggled to contain her breasts and hugged her trim waist, the contour of her tight white shorts that covered warm, firm flesh and the line of her slender golden legs that led to naked feet.

He tried to hold it down, to keep it under control, but natural forces took command.

Her eyes locked with his. They pleaded. "I'm really glad you came home when you did."

"Should of been earlier."

"I needed you earlier."

"Wish I'd known."

He felt the titillation of her fingertips as they drew circles on the backs of his hands, then her warmth as she held them tight. Excitement surged up his arms and into his body.

"It's important, Jake."

"It always is for me, too."

"I've been in the middle of a project and couldn't break away."

"Oh?"

"Jake, I really need you . . . to go to the store. The dog's all out of food."

"Wha . . . what . . . ?"

"Yeah, the store."

"Store? Dog?"

"Yeah, he's . . ."

"Not now!" Jake smiled. "The dog's just gone on a diet."

III

ENLIGHTEN

Frustration—precise aim at blurred targets.

10

Torment

. . . changed, all of it—changed! . . .

When Ted awoke, rested and replenished, his chamber felt different. It seemed not so confined, not so crowded with memory packets. And, although the buzz still surrounded him, it seemed not so strong, not so energetic or vibrant. He expanded his awareness outward to his boundaries. Now many packets at a time migrated to the walls and disappeared through their openings.

. . . my chamber, it's being emptied—where's it all going and what's doing it? . . .

Ted mentally culled out a lone packet as it drifted from the swarm. It headed for an opening, accelerated and disappeared. Just as many a time before he'd plunged an RT7 through a hole in the clouds in pursuit of another aircraft, Ted focused on the packet and dove after it.

. . . hard work! . . . relax a little—fall behind a lot . . . —but I'm still with it, and I'll stay with it! . . .

The chase seemed even better than the old days, even better than close-trail aerobatics or pursuit of an enemy fighter. It demanded every shred of his concentration, every ounce of his aggression, but it yielded sheer exhilaration, a total freedom confined only by total challenge. And better than any aircraft, nothing could be overstressed, nothing could be run out of fuel. Eternal bliss: an eternal drive plugged into an eternal outlet.

. . . I've found it—fighter pilot heaven! . . .

Ted intensified his concentration on the packet and moved up behind it as it swerved, bounced and sped along. As it popped out into a chamber, Ted pounced on it and enveloped it, even before it glided to a stop.

. . . WHAT?! . . .

Willie, his youngest son, just as he'd seen him last, flooded into Ted.

. . . *white T-shirt with hole left-center of belly, grape-juice stain on right shoulder, wiped his chin there, catch hell for it, and he missed his grape-juice mustache . . . don't say anything, not now . . . got a funny squint, glassy eyes, little pistol feels as bad as I do . . . short hug, awkward, but he means it . . . arms a hand short of reaching around me, that won't last long . . . don't drag it out, won't see 'em for four years, maybe more . . . feet spin, sure loves his bike . . . wish I could put him in deep freeze till I get back, hurts, hurts deep . . . don't think about it, won't change anything . . .*

Within thirty seconds, the image and all its pain faded.

The same tunnel spit out several more packets that arrived in a group. Like fireflies, they swarmed and glowed in silence as they migrated toward the chamber's sea. Ted concentrated on one and enveloped it.

. . . WHAT?! . . .

Ted's arms, shoulders and back coiled with strength, ready to explode.

. . . *sharp pain, right palm, blister broke on last swing, stings . . . can't swing hard, but need a hit . . . bring bat partway around, choke up, swing with shoulders, pull through with left hand, keep pressure off right . . . damn, it hurts . . .*

As this image faded, Ted switched his concentration to a packet that popped from an adjacent tunnel and enveloped it.

. . . WHAT? . . .

Nothing. No fusion. Ted strained. Again, nothing. He tried several other packets as they arrived from the same tunnel, but he met with the same result. Nothing. He returned to the next packet from the first tunnel.

. . . WHAT? . . .

Ted looked up into the face of his father, a young man full of vitality but with eyes of sadness.

. . . *hate it when he looks at me like that, wish he'd scream, or hit me . . . just a small model airplane, only balsa wood . . . just picked it up, played with it for a while, only brought it home to play some more, only borrowed it, no one'd miss it . . . just didn't tell anybody, and Dad thinks I stole it, not really mad, but hurt, really hurt . . .*

Ted defocused his concentration even before Image faded. With more deliberation, he selected another packet.

. . . WHAT? . . .

Ted paused on the top stair and glanced back at the car in the second stall.

. . . *dust is thicker every time I look at it, if that's possible . . . sweet car, classic, old '92 Mercedes 420 SLE . . . gonna look a lot better when it's remodeled . . . I'll do it someday, yeah, sure, someday . . . just never enough time, story of my life . . . hate to see it just sit there, waitin' for attention, just like my family, hurts . . .*

Ted turned and entered the house. Image faded.

. . . *not really enjoying any of this . . . try one more, maybe understand it . . .*

. . . WHAT? . . .

Ted's fingers ripped into the paper. His hands shook.

. . . *fiction—all of it! . . . had his story all written, only interviewed me to fill the square, then*

twisted my words to fit . . . I said we don't know
exactly what we'll find at the Wayfarer Objects, but
he writes we don't know why we're going—chose to
ignore the difference . . . whip up more political
trouble, divert attention from real problems . . .
just a quick-buck hatchet-swinger, easier to write and
peddle something negative . . . never should've
trusted him, never should've even talked to him . . .
just another pain-in-the-ass reporter . . .

Ted relaxed his hands and handed the paper to
Eva. Her eyes smiled, then questioned. Image faded.

. . . *don't need anymore of this! . . . pain, just*
all kinds of pain . . . but what's a blister really have
to do with Willie? or my Mercedes? or my father? or
. . . *something's trying to sort these memory pack-*
ets by subject, must've a room-temperature IQ, and a
helluva screwed-up library . . . can only fuse with
some of 'em, others must be on different wavelengths
—literally . . . but where're they from? . . . my
crew, are these other packets the memories of my
crew? . . .

. . . *how could I've stopped all this? . . .*
what'd I do wrong? . . .

Ted expanded his awareness across the chamber.
He sensed a fullness to its sea of packets. At the
edges, he found more openings with packets that
drifted into them, just like in his chamber. At random, he tried to fuse with several more packets in
the sea but met with uniform failure.

Again, he felt weak, his energy drained.

. . . *time's up—at last! . . . relax, go back*
home . . . rest in own chamber, have my own
thoughts there, and my own memories—but only my
own . . . anyone else here? or ever come? or am I
confined to my own thoughts and my own memories
forever? . . . have to find a way out! . . .

The cackle, soft and low, slipped in and patted
their ears. "Yuz got just four days before launch—an
wheeze is gonna see if you is ready."

"Standby, gang," said Jake. "Zepon's really cookin' up something."

"He and Henry've never failed yet," said Speed.

"Our final test on rendezvous at the Wayfarers," said Faye. "And it doesn't sound like they're gonna make it easy."

"How's it look over there, Speed?" asked Jake.

"CT 7000 shows a good radar lock on *Wayfarer 1* and navigation's accepting the data. Looks like 243 kilometers out and closing at 207 meters per second. Wonder if that's supposed to be the Alpha or the Beta module?"

"For rendezvous practice, it doesn't make much difference," said Jake.

"How've you folks split up your responsibilities in there?" asked Henry Sokira over the audio link from his instructor's console.

"Speed's got the computer, electrical and propulsion systems," said Jake back over the link. "Faye's got the environmental control system and is taking optical sightings, if required. And I've got the guidance, navigation and control."

"Gooood," said Zepon Whitney over the link. "Now ah know who ta zing." His last words trailed off into another soft cackle.

"Who're you gonna pick on this time?" asked Speed.

"Maybe we're just fixin' to getcha all at once," said Zepon. "Rat chair ah got me hotshot-pilot-booby-trap bag. An I'm a reachin' in and a pluckin' out one of me horrendous Three-Pronged Zingers!" Zepon's cackle erupted and hit their ears straight through the walls of the simulator as well as over the audio.

"Damn diabolical cackle," said Speed. "He's really goin' to slip it to us this time."

"Yeah, it could hurt, but we'll learn something," said Jake. "These guys are good." He looked out the window at the Wayfarer Objects in the distance. The Visual Effects Section had created the holographic images based on what they'd observed from *Stellar Probe 12*. Jake's eyes told him he approached the Objects; his mind filled in the black hole and Ted.

The quality of the scene matched the rest of the Wayfarer simulator. Except for the lack of zero gravity or liftoff's high g's, they flew the real thing. The control stations had the same layouts, displays, controls and computer systems found in the real spacecraft. Another computer gave realism to the controls and display responses and properly related them to the holography seen through the windows. When engines fired, they heard the same sounds and felt the same vibrations recorded in flight.

Like other instructors, Zepon and Henry simulated problems in ways that pushed crews to their limits and produced maximum learning. On occasion, they exceeded limits and bent pride and shattered egos. Although painful at the time, Jake regarded each experience as an advantage of his profession. Death in the simulator preserved life in the real world. Or, as Speed summed it up, "Given the choice, boss, I'd rather bust my ego than my butt."

"How'd the sim go this morning?" asked Jake.

"Great!" said Henry. "Your better half, Boris, Ada and Irwin, did a sensational job. They knew their procedures, worked well together and successfully completed the rendezvous, even with the whole pot full of system failures we threw at 'em. They've come a long way in three months. They're ready to go!"

"Ryyye," said Zepon. "Dey dun goooood!"

"Glad to hear it," said Jake.

"Still wish we didn't have to split apart before we reached the Wayfarers," said Faye.

"I do, too," said Jake. "But it's that or get ripped apart."

"Kinda narrows down the choice," said Speed.

Jake glanced over at Speed and saw only the outline of his head and shoulders in the darkness and his face illuminated by the glow from his two-by-three-foot, multicolored electronic display. Then, as

Speed moved up against a window, Jake heard only his voice from the darkness. "Hey, look at them big beauties whistle by."

Jake turned and looked out. "Does the image of an Object now correlate with the radar readouts?"

"You bet," said Henry. "Finally got it working. And the new version of your collision avoidance program is also active in your CT 7000. Oughta be a piece of cake this time."

"Which program?" asked Faye.

"Boris and his team made one last improvement in their guidance program," said Speed's voice. "This one also calculates the strength of the black hole from the radar tracking of the Objects and does the normal rendezvous with either module. But it calculates the thrusting required to avoid the next seven Objects with minimum propellant expenditure, not just the next three."

Jake peered into the darkness, but because of the distance of the Objects from the sun, they reflected little light and disclosed only an occasional outline or sharp reflection off a smooth surface.

"We've arrived, boss."

"Sure have. I'll get the lights." Jake switched on external searchlights, which under CT 7000's control focused on the next three Objects that offered collision potential. He watched in silence, hypnotized by the parade of fifty- to one-hundred-foot jagged boulders that snaked by. Each Object had its own unique shape, ice content and colored mineral streaks running through its black spongelike rock matrix. He glanced back at his inside display. "We're 163 kilometers out and still closing at 207 meters per second."

"Oops, got a problem," said Speed. "Computer's stopped giving commands for collision avoidance to the propulsion."

Jake grabbed the hand controllers. "I'll fly it manually."

"And we've got an electrical short in the oxygen supply controller," said Faye. "Current's high but below the trip limit for the breaker. I'm cutting power to it."

"Speed!" said Jake. "I've got a reaction control thruster stuck on! Why's the computer not closing off all the propellant to it? Is the reaction control module belly up?"

"Ahh . . . just a second, Jake."

"Think I didn't get the power off the short in time," said Faye. "It started a fire in the controller. Worst place. Oxygen's feeding it."

"Yeah," said Jake. "Faye, get the vent on high to move this smoke outta here," said Jake.

"Got it."

"Nope, Jake," said Speed. "The reaction control module's still running, but its command bus is somehow disconnected. I need to reconfigure the bus architecture and get control of the valve drivers to cut off that propellant. Have it in a jiffy."

"Fire suppression comin' on in bay twenty-seven," said Faye.

"Speed! Get that thruster off quick before we hit something!"

As Speed turned back toward his keyboard, his eyes swept across the window. He stopped, glanced out, then stared with eyes and mouth wide open. "Holy horse hockey! That's not an Object. It's . . . it's my house . . . my frappin' house is barrel assin' right at us . . . it's my frappin' house!" Speed froze and waited.

The walls and floor of the simulator jolted. The impact, then the crunch of metal and fiber hit their ears. Light flashed in through all windows. After a two-second pause, the horn that signaled spacecraft destruction started its loud offensive beep. For a long five seconds it beat their ears and egos. As the horn died away, Zepon's cackle replaced it—not a soft cackle, nor even an energetic cackle, but an uncontrolled, all-out, gut-busting cackle. He paused only long enough to shout, "You guys is daid!"

The lights came on in the simulator, the window

scenes disappeared, and all internal displays reset back to their initial states.

"Zepon, you're gettin' kinky out there," said Speed. "Systems failures are one thing, but ramming us with my house? That's dumb! What's it prove? It's not even close to being fair!"

"Who sez hit's gotta be fair?" asked Zepon. "Chew guys took your attention off computer and systems justa look ayt somethin' different. Shore, to distract chew guys it took somethin' *real* different." Zepon had to release another ten seconds of cackles before he could continue. "But chew can bet dat out der der's all kindsa distractions. But we cane simulate dem. An fairness ain't got nuttin' ta do with it. Shore, we haid a little fun. But der's a lesson here—doan take chore mind offa procedures justa look ayt somethin' different!"

"Speed, hate to say it, but I think they're right, a little kinky but still right," said Jake. "They may've suckered us into it, but it was us who lost focus on the real problem at just the wrong instant."

"Don't feel bad, Speed," said Faye. "I was right there with you, staring out and wondering if your garage door would open automatically."

"Suckers even had smoke comin' out of my chimney," said Speed. "If only I hadn't glanced out."

Jake chuckled. "Glance? That was a glance? Just like the 'glance' you once gave that topless shoe-shine girl."

"Right, boss."

"Hang in there, Speed. We'll get it. We can't allow ourselves to get distracted."

Speed turned pensive. "But where's the procedure to tell us what's a distraction and what's relevant?"

The question hung for a moment before Jake responded. "You got a point. On this mission especially, we don't know enough to put everything we'll need into a checklist."

"Yeah, this time out we may have to think," said Speed.

"Jake, you've got a call here from Dr. Daro's office," Henry called in. "Want me to patch it into your audio while we set up for your next run?"

"Yes, please do."

"You're on."

"Thanks. Hello, sir."

"Hello, Jake, Speed and Faye. Jake, the RT7 Accident Investigation Board reached their conclusion this morning. They found the primary cause for your accident to be pilot error. Even though there were numerous secondary causes not under your control, they concluded that if you had focused sufficient attention on the operational procedures of the CT210s, the software error could have been detected before landing. They concluded that you were not properly prepared. You should have a copy of the board's report waiting for you when you step out of the simulator. Any questions?"

Jake's muscles turned rigid and began to quiver. His teeth clenched, toes curled under and fingernails again dug into his palms. *Bullshit!* Not properly prepared? But it's not Daro, not board, not any one person in the system—then who? Is it the whole system? Or is it really me? Are we ready? Will I screw up again and kill us all? Relax. Don't let it out here.

"No, sir. I have no questions. I disagree with the finding, but I've said all that I can say to the board. There's nothing else I can do. Thank you for calling."

"I wish you three a productive afternoon in the simulator. By now you should be fully trained and ready for launch. Good day."

11

Communicate

Unchanged, Ted's last thoughts pushed up again as he awoke.

. . . confined to my own thoughts and my own memories forever? . . . have to find a way out, to survive . . . REACH! . . .

. . . packets are thinner but still feel enclosed, need space to think, to learn . . . how'd all this happen? can I reverse it? . . . packets're all leaving through tunnels, how'd they all get in? also through tunnels?

Ted reached out to the boundary of his chamber, spread his awareness over it and studied all its openings.

. . . only one, just one, one large opening with nothing going out—try it . . .

He concentrated and forced his awareness into the void.

. . . no packet ahead to lead the way, like running in the dark . . . keep moving. . . .

For a long time the tunnel slid by, narrow and straight. Then it expanded. Finally, it opened. For the first time since his capture, Ted's awareness no longer felt confined by marshmallow fog, no longer mushed into soft spongy walls. It slammed into solid objects, hard and rigid and fixed. The mental territory seemed foreign yet familiar.

Ted's awareness poured out.

. . . sharp, rough, black rock, basaltic rock from volcanism, ice on one side—Wayfarer Objects! . . . bigger ones farther out . . . move out to 'em, past 'em . . . REACH! . . .

Streams of Ted's awareness continued to pour outward, pulled toward freedom, expelled by that yet to be released.

. . . Pluto, Uranus, Jupiter . . . reach Earth, Earth, all I know and love—Eva, Willie . . . communicate, focus, concentrate . . . WILLIE! . . .

Something left Ted, something of essence and meaning—but he still retained something, something that drove him farther.

. . . Mars, Mercury, Sun . . . reach . . . Alpha Centauri, reach for it . . . Barnard's Star, and more, just more and more stars . . . REACH! . . .

. . . 23 . . . 25 . . . 27 . . . Buildin' fast this time.

Cold morning air blasted the face of eleven-year-old Willie Ludendorff. Through water that seeped from his eyes, he could just see the white road and green grass on either side streak by in a blur, could just read the numbers on the digital speedometer below his nose.

. . . 29 . . . 30 . . . 31 . . . Might make it this mornin'.

Willie's hands shook as they gripped the carbon-fiber steering wheel, his cold, hard but responsive link to the street below. He tightened his grip. Tense muscles fought to maintain their slim margin of control. Every small bump, every small pebble that his tires felt, Willie felt.

. . . 32 . . . 33 . . . 34 . . . Really movin' out!

His legs lay out straight and his back half-reclined at forty-five degrees, just like a fighter pilot's. Wind howled. Tires buzzed. The whole car rattled. But the sharp steady hum of the electric engine behind his seat knifed through the noise into his mind. Hum's strong—much stronger.

Seduced by power and speed, Willie pressed.

. . . 35 . . . 36 . . . C'mon car.

Mom never really understood, but she finally gave in, finally bought him the Electro-Turbo racing car, the one for juniors, thirteen to sixteen. Willie rode it, happy and content, for about two days. Then he looked for ways to get more acceleration, more speed. That's where his older brother became useful. In fact, now that Dad wasn't home, Heinz'd become very useful. Last night he showed Willie how to hook the two batteries together to get what he wanted most in his young life—higher performance.

. . . 37 . . . 38 . . . five miles per hour faster than that know-it-all salesman said was tops. Heinz sure knows more than him. Just hook the batteries in series rather than parallel. Same total energy. Right? But more power. Or was it more voltage? How's that go again? . . . Whatever, sure goes faster!

This morning Willie'd gotten up an hour before sunup, but he had to wait in his car until the street turned light enough to roll. That gave him only forty minutes before school, nowhere near time enough. But this Saturday he could take it up to the flats and let it all out.

. . . 39 . . . . c'mon . . . . . c'mon . . . . 40!
Hit 40! I did it! What? Can't be. Bend's here already. Came too fast—turn—never make it!

Willie swerved. But Willie was right—he never made it. But he did get his first strong taste of zero gravity.

Willie shot up the inclined embankment, and, in an instant, became pilot-in-command of his Electro-Turbo missile on its maiden suborbital flight. His parabolic trajectory carried him far down range, well over and well beyond the flight hazards of Maklowsky's twenty-five-foot rock garden. Then he reentered Maklowsky's hedge bent, cracked and splintered as it provided the critical braking mechanism. Mounds of soft peat in the flower garden on the hedge's down-range side further slowed his descent and cushioned his landing. Peat, pansies, marigolds and shrubbery shreds filled the air, then rained down around him as he spun to a stop on the edge of Roulardi's Astroturf.

Willie froze. His mind retraced the accident and analyzed . . . Airborne, I got airborne!

He brushed the flowers off the top of his car and started a slow roll back toward the street, back toward home, back toward Mom. His head swiveled back and forth, eyes darting about.

For a second time, his hands shook as he surveyed the damage. Mud's all over. Can hose it off. Left front wheel's a little bent. Can straighten it. Door latch's broken. Only needs a new screw. Black carbex body looks OK. No cracks. Gold on wheels still shines. Just a little dirt. Steering works. And engine's pushing us right along. That's all. Nothin' else. No harm done. Heeey, I'm outa here. Just like Dad always said, "Noooo sweat." And I got airborne! Even did a spin stop. Didn't know it was so easy. Gotta get to the flats Saturday. Hit 45 for sure!

The previous night's thunder and rain had left a clear sky, cool air and a damp, fresh scent that hugged the street.

Willie sniffed. Air smells good. But what's that funny smell with it? Kinda like the time Dad's car wouldn't run. Said something burned. Insulation or something like that on wires. Too much current. Or did he say power? Or voltage? No problem—good old Electro-Turbo's still rolling right along.

Wisps of fog rose from the damp street, wisps of mist that condensed in Willie's path, drew themselves together and blocked his way.

Willie slowed. Just a little fog.

The mist thickened and slid into familiar facial positions.

Willie stopped. No. It's only fog.

Wisps tightened and set.

"Dad!"

Willie sensed it, his mind recorded it.

. . . Reach, Willie, Reach with all you have . . . Reach beyond yourself—Reach beyond everything you create—Reach beyond everything others put in your way . . . REACH! . . .

"Dad! Is that really you?"

. . . Remember me, Willie, I won't be back . . . In the future we might . . . I love you, Little Guy . . .

Fog loosened, then dissolved.

Willie looked where the fog had been and searched the empty space. He looked through it and down the road toward his house. A man stood out front talking to Mom. His heart pounded again. It's Dad. He's back! But he just said he . . . Floor it.

Willie closed on the figure. Looks kinda like Dad. Same kinda flight suit. But his head and shoulders—they're not right. It's not Dad.

Willie slowed to a crawl. Was that really Dad? Did Mom see him, too? Ask her. But better wait till she's in a good mood. Not that way much anymore. But she's smiling now. Ask her when the man leaves. Don't want her mad at me now. Better not let her see the mud on Electro-Turbo.

Willie stopped his car fifteen feet away from Mom and the man. He faced the front end, the dirty end, away from them.

"Willie, come over here. I want you to meet Mr. Ryder. He is going out to the Wayfarers where Dad is. He's going to try to find out what happened."

"Hi, Willie."

"Hello, sir."

Willie straightened as he felt his hand encased by calloused but gentle flesh.

"I was telling your mom that we'll do everything we can to find out what happened. And if your dad is still OK, we'll do all we can to reach him and bring him home."

"Thank you, sir."

"Hey, I sure like your car. It looks like a real goer."

Willie bent his head back and looked up. He looks friendly. But the kind you have to do what he tells you. Can't talk him outta things. Looks like Dad. Not old like most parents. But he isn't Dad. Still, I like him. Show him my car. No, better not.

Mom's smile disappeared. "Tell me honestly, Jake. Do you think Ted is alive?"

"I can't offer you false hope, Eva. But the fact is that none of us know anything for sure right now. If he made it into hibernation, he'd be in good shape for many years to come. But we have no more data from either module and don't know what he really encountered. But whatever it was, it didn't treat him too kindly. We'll just have to see when we get there."

"Ted always craved adventure. It looks like he may've gotten more than he could handle this time. I pray that he hasn't."

Willie moved closer to where he could see Mom's eyes, see if she looked at his car. No problem. Then she reached out, put an arm around his shoulder, hugged him and continued to speak to Mr. Ryder. "There sure aren't many in this world like him."

"I hope you don't mind me coming over so early. We have our last launch sim this morning and a press conference this afternoon. And tomorrow we leave for Guiana."

"Not at all, Jake. I appreciate your coming by. Ahhh . . . if you do get to Ted, tell him that we love him and miss him and want him back with us as soon as possible." Willie looked up and saw sunlight glisten off the water that filled Mom's eyes again.

"I sure will." Mr. Ryder took Mom's hand in both of his and smiled. "Please relax and call Val if she can be of help. She'll be by from time to time anyway."

"And you, Jake, be careful."

He bent over and looked at Willie through eyes

that seemed to smile as they looked inside him. "You and your brother take good care of your mom. OK?"

"Yes, sir. It was a pleasure to meet you."

Willie straightened his back and shoulders further as he stared up at Mr. Ryder. Did it right. Those're the right words. But I wanta talk to him. Ask him if he saw Dad, too. Nope, better not. But he feels like a friend. Wish he'd stay.

Mr. Ryder got in his car, waved, smiled and disappeared. It happened fast, much faster than most old people do it.

Mom's face turned stern. "Willie, it's almost time for school. You have to sign into CompuLearn in ten minutes. Put your car away, go inside to your work station and get ready."

"Aw, Mom, do I have to stay home today? Can't I go to school? I never get to see the kids anymore!"

"Willie, you had your week in school two months ago. You don't get another one till beginning of next term in January. Quit stalling. March!"

He parked his car exactly in the center of the space he'd cleared for it in the garage, aligned it exactly with the walls, then stopped and stared back down the street. Dad? . . .

"Willie!"

Willie sighed and trudged into the house.

12

Inform

"Speed, is she wearing anything?" asked Faye.

"Ahhh . . ."

"Or do ya think it's just a tattoo?"

"Ahhh . . . yeah. She does wear her clothes a bit snug."

"Who's that?" asked Jake.

"The blond, dreamy-eyed honey, row four, third in from the center aisle," said Faye. "Miss Virtue in the large-brim white hat and nearly wearing a white dress."

Speed's words slid from the edge of his mouth. "From what I hear, it must be off-white."

Faye glanced at Speed. "Who is she? Is she really a reporter?"

"That's Malicious Delicious. A free-lance writer who likes to think of herself as a specialist in 'human interest' stories. Writes under the name of Melinda Delisio."

"From the way she parked herself, I'd say she's out for a real story, and we're in for real trouble," said Jake.

"And not only now, but she'll be turning the rumor crank for the full time we're away," said Speed. "Does wonders for a marriage."

"Just what we need." Jake stared down at the

floor in front of the stage where he, his crew, Dupree and their WSF public relations man were lined up behind a podium, about to be pitted against the press for the last time before launch.

"If she asks you anything, Faye, make your answer as bland and short as possible," said Speed. "She likes to slice into you with an infuriating question, then write her story on your emotional response. Tellin' her off is like kickin' a bear trap."

"Just the same, we've gotta make this exercise as informative as possible," said Jake. "You never can tell. One of these times the press'll see the light and come over to our side."

"Maybe this time'll be it!" said Faye.

Jake studied the reporters in silence. Maybe, but can I make 'em think positive for once, make 'em understand? Can I make 'em feel the urgency?

He stared back down and searched his thoughts for some trick that would pick up his own spirits. I hate these damn preflight press conferences. Talkin' about how good it's gonna be makes dull reading. But they each gotta pump out their quota of words and spice 'em up. At least it'll be on the back pages, and holovision coverage'll probably come on after the late-night prayer. Liked the old missions. No one knew you left. No coverage'd be better than the circus this is gonna be. Five minutes to go and auditorium's only half filled. About 140 bored reporters. Bet most're the dregs of their offices, the investigator imitators. Biggies're off coverin' stories that sell. Wayfarer just takes too long. Bores the press and public, so it bores the politicians. No patience. Foreplay puts 'em to sleep. Every mission's gotta be a quickie— bam, bam, there's your story, ma'am. Been a real tough sell ever since Apollo. Only one moon hung in front of their faces, only one first landing. Even a black hole leaves 'em cold. Front page one day, science journals the next.

Jake grimaced. Why's it so hard to understand? Underneath, right down to the very last person, they feel we've gotta keep reachin' outward. But it doesn't dump money into their pockets, so it's not urgent. All of 'em, just a mass of frantic inertia that clouds vision, an orifice that chokes the flood of people's enthusiasm and ability down to a dribble. The press, politicians and governments could never drag their bureaucratic body up a single flight of stairs—debate if each and every stair's worth climbing, hold hearings on every planned muscle movement and prosecute every one that twitches.

Jake relaxed his face as he looked toward the ceiling. But his fists remained clenched. Sad, but it took the standard human motivators to get going—fear and greed. We'd still be muckin' around down there in the doldrums if we didn't finally notice that Russian stations dominated the space right over our heads; notice we were a second-rate power in space, finally realize second-rate in space assured second-rate on the ground, finally got scared enough to defend ourselves in space, finally found ways to make a profit in space. But, we also got leadership—President Abaris in '09. Tough—survived the standard elect-n-lynch mob. Goal-oriented—not obsessed with process. Created the Outward Reach Initiative, then used common sense; got long-term goals with commitments to match, got good people and incentivised 'em to stay, then got out of the way—simple common sense! But exact opposite of how bureaucracy operates. Started a space renaissance that lasted over twenty years this time, till the system crept in and choked it down again.

Jake's eyes scanned the room as he forced his whole body to loosen and relax. But his jaw started to grind teeth together again. Where would we be now if they kept on reaching after Apollo? Except for the Few, they just pussyfooted into this century—time of timidity, eon of excuses. Except for the Few, the bloated bureaucracy studied its belly button and scratched, sauntered and stumbled into space when it should've kept sprinting. We could've been on our way to the stars! But it's still too many years away, too many miles, too many . . .

"Let's just flick on the holovision from *Wayfarer 1*'s conference," said Speed. "Most of them wouldn't know the difference, and we could go get some more time in the simulator."

"Wish we could," said Jake.

"C'mon, guys," said Faye. "Don't be so negative. There must be a few good reporters out there."

Speed rolled his eyes. "Oh, yeah. A real choice collection of road apples. See the guy in the green suit at the right end of the second row, the guy reaming out his ear with his little finger? That's Suitcase Sampson. He's real good. Lives out of a suitcase. Always gets fired before he gets a chance to unpack. Heeeey . . . maybe it's his lucky day. Looks like he just dug out a goooolden nugget."

"Faye's right, Speed. There're a few good ones here. There's Abe Shivananda from *Space Week*. His stories always have substance and accuracy."

Faye nodded. "And also, Speed, there's Jay Gascon of World Press, three rows in, right in front of us. You sure can't miss him. He's one of their top reporters."

"True, but he's only good on domestic issues. Doesn't know a moon from a meatball. Must be in town for something else."

"Who, or what, is that that just sat down in front of Gascon?" asked Faye.

"Oh, that's Grub," said Speed.

"Don't know who he is, but he always shows," said Jake.

"And he always wears that same dark-blue sports jacket," said Speed. "Even from here you can tell he's been in Houston for three days. Kinda like a tree. Just check the armpits and count the salt rings."

Faye smiled and shook her head. "Good lord, Speed. Boredom does weird things to your mind."

"Just killin' time."

Jake looked toward his right, to the center of the

podium, as Frederick Freeder, their WSF public relations representative, stood up to start the conference.

"Let us begin, please. We appreciate your continued interest in the activities of WSF and in this mission."

Jake watched Freddie's jowls waggle and wobble on his wide head as he jawed through each sentence. He respected "Fat Face Freddie," who had the good nature and public-relations savvy to use his moniker to his advantage.

"Commander Jake Ryder, who is seated to your extreme right, will first give us an overview of the mission. Next Dr. Laurent Dupree, seated to your extreme left, will add a few comments. Lastly, there will be questions from the press."

"Commander Ryder."

Jake reached forward and pressed the button that controlled the overhead microphone focused on his position. C'mon, Ryder, make this constructive.

"Thanks, Freddie. We thank you all for coming here today. We'll try to make this as informative as possible. Let me first introduce our crew. They've been handpicked. They're each the best at what they do. We're fortunate to have each one of them on this mission."

Jake introduced his crew and continued. "In short, our objectives are to locate *Wayfarer 1*, take data on its environment to determine the origin of its problem, and, if any of the crew's still alive, bring them home. You each've been given a written summary of our mission. Let me run through the highlights of it quickly for you."

Jay Gascon's eyes bored into Jake.

"In two days, on November 5, the two *Wayfarer 2* modules, telescoped bridge and full load of propellant will be launched from our Southern Test Range in French Guiana. We use this launch site because it's closest to the equator, where we get the most free velocity from the earth's rotation.

"Our twenty-five-year-old, highly reliable Brute booster will be used to put the 730,000 pounds of equipment into low earth orbit and rendezvous with Space Station von Braun. On the following day our crew of six will launch in the much smaller Agile booster and join our modules at von Braun."

"Question!" Jay Gascon grunted his massive body upward.

Jake winced at the contrast. The half empty seats seemed attractive with their flowing lines and elegant soft colors, soothing yet crisp—Val's touch. Gascon appeared gross to him by comparison, like a mound of messy melons. A crumpled shirt, with one side tucked in, covered the watermelon below. He appeared to be a man that lived in his mind. His voice rumbled like an empty boxcar. Jake sensed Melon Man must be under the gun to get a story.

". . . high costs rung up by this program. Why can't you and your crew also ride the Brute booster and save the taxpayers of the world all the money that it takes for the extra launch?"

"Thank you. That's a good question. In short, Brute's economical because it's a big dumb booster and not man-rated. To bring it up to and maintain it at the level of reliability and safety of a manned vehicle would cost more than the use of the smaller, low-cost Agile booster. It's the more economical way to go."

Gascon tugged at his open collar as his body squirmed and shimmied downward.

"Before we reach von Braun, its Assembly and Test team will put our spacecraft into the right configuration for flight to the Wayfarers. That is, the two modules will be connected by the bridge, filled with propellant and then tested. At the end of these activities, Speed and I will go on an EVA, or space walk, but only as observers."

Melon man struggled up again. His voice rumbled a second time. "Why do you find it necessary to take the bridge and a second module all the way out to the Wayfarers and back? Doesn't that cost much more than if you left them on the ground?"

"No. The bridge is made of extremely light carbon fiber and serves as a rigid tether between the two modules. We take two modules for redundancy. That is, if one fails, we still have the other. This redundancy approach has cut down on the development cost of the total Wayfarer system. The bridge is used to keep the two modules next to one another during the coast phase. This way we don't have to continually fire engines to stay together, which saves us propellant. Also, if for some reason we should need artificial gravity, we can spin up the combination to get what we need."

Jay Gascon rotated forward, then rotated back downward.

"We'll start toward the Wayfarers by burning the engines on both modules for approximately a week. When we reach slightly over half a percent the speed of light, we'll coast. Once we're satisfied with our trajectory and the status of our modules, we'll enter hibernation and remain in that state for almost nine months. An interesting fact is that, because of relativity, we'll be over twelve minutes younger when we return than had we not made the trip."

Malicious Delicious pondered. Then she raised her hand, bounced up and smiled as she let all her jiggles and joggles subside. "Do you have separate sleeping quarters for the men and woman during this time and, regardless of your answer, why?"

"Yes, each person has their own hibernation pod. This permits individual monitoring and serum feed tailored to individual needs."

Suitcase put his hand up next to his confused face. "Are you leaving soon?"

Jay Gascon heaved out of his seat for a third try. "Considering the expense of this mission, how can you justify sleeping your way through nearly all of it? Can you not do some useful work along the way? Do you have no concern for those who have to pay for your errant stab into nowhere? Why is WSF even doing any of this at all?"

Jake remained steady and handled the issue first. "We have two major reasons for hibernation. The first addresses your concern of cost-effectiveness. If we had to take enough food and supporting equipment for the full duration of the mission, rather than just the time we're awake, the weight of the modules would go up considerably, and cost with it. Our second reason is to make sure that we're in peak physical and mental condition for the prime part of our mission. During our hibernation, our memories will retain the training we've worked hard to acquire. If we remained awake and working for the nine-month period going out, we'd be rusty on much of what we've just learned. Also, during hibernation, many unmanned observations of the environment will be made. The opportunity will not be lost."

Jake's features remained impassive as he cocked his jaw to one side and stared at Melon Man Gascon. *Just no way to appease him. And dammit, I just can't take this shit any longer!*

"Mr. Gascon, it's clear that you're ignorant of both the motives and methods of WSF that are clearly described in the written material in your hand. You can be tutored after the conference if you wish to learn. But now it's time we gave the others a chance to listen and ask their questions. That's it. For the rest of this conference—you're cut off!"

Speed grinned.

Fat Face frowned.

And Melon Man, after a long, openmouthed fifteen seconds, finally wiggled downward again, perhaps for the last time.

Jake continued. "Once we reach the Wayfarer Objects, our major job will be to precisely define the orbits of the two *Wayfarer 1* modules around the mini-black hole, rendezvous with them and determine what happened. Now I'll turn it over to Dr. Dupree."

Dupree glanced at Melon Man and catapulted to his feet. "Thank you, Commander Ryder. I'd like to first commend the WSF Operations team for the excellent work we've done in the past two months. After observing *Stellar Probe 12*, we were quick to realize that we were dealing with a mini-black hole. We have developed a set of precise and comprehensive procedures that will assure mission success. These procedures have been programmed into the onboard CT 7000 and will provide a foolproof way for us to meet any contingencies that may arise."

Abe Shivananda raised his hand as he stood. His resonant voice cut through the background buzz from the reporters. "Dr. Dupree, what type of contingencies have you covered? Also, with only a small amount of data available on what *Wayfarer 1* encountered, how can you be assured that your procedures cover everything that's required?"

"We've had a team of 283 technical experts make a comprehensive study of the data from *Wayfarer 1* and *Stella Probe 12*. We've explained everything we've observed and have procedures to cover every problem that'll arise. For example, a CT 7000 program measures the mass of the mini-black hole to one part in ten million, tracks the orbits of the closest seven Objects and calculates the precise maneuvers to reach the *Wayfarer 1* modules with minimum propellant expenditure. All procedures can be done automatically. We've left nothing to chance."

By now Abe Shivananda had to shout above the background noise. "Dr. Dupree. In an interview yesterday with your deputy, Klaus Hofmeister, he indicated that the crew will have to make many observations on their own and use judgment in responding to what they observe."

"*I'm* telling you that we've extensively downsized any potential demands for crew cognitive capability through our exhaustive specification of all domains of potential difficulty, our meticulous and precise execution of all relevant analyses and our computerized compilation of a comprehensive crew procedures data base."

Abe scratched and frowned.

Speed switched on his microphone. "Abe, let me put it to you another way. There's a big difference between an empty mind and an open mind. With the help of CT 7000, Dr. Dupree's made sure our minds'll not be empty. But we'll also make sure they're open."

Abe smiled, shouted a thank you and sat down. Dupree looked blank, then scowled.

"So far we've found that our procedures work without fail in the simulator," said Boris.

Dupree beamed. "Yes. It's been gratifying to observe the precision and elegance in the smooth-functioning complexity of our total integrated end-to-end system."

Ada switched on her microphone. "The CT 7000 not only has catalogued every procedure for all known problems, but if we load in the additional data required, its artificial intelligence module can solve any new problem."

Irwin smiled and nodded.

Malicious Delicious bounced up and took a deep breath. The background noise snapped to zero.

"This is getting much too technical to be useful. I have a question for you, Mr. Rote. How do you feel about having the opportunity to make this flight only because of the death of another crewman who was judged to be more competent than yourself?"

Irwin groped. "I . . . ahh . . . ahh . . ."

Fat Face floundered and fumbled. "Err . . ."

Jake glanced at Malicious. Bitch! Then he studied Irwin. Gotta help him. Good thing he's slow to speak. "We regret the loss of Shane Culver. He was an excellent man. However, we have nearly four hundred crewpeople active in the program, and the competition for each and every crew position came down to a close race between a number of highly qualified people. Irwin, like Shane, is highly qualified, and I'm glad he'll be with us."

Irwin recovered. "Shane is missed by all of us who worked with him. I'll continue to work hard to make sure that my performance is of the same caliber as his would've been."

A solemn Malicious Delicious sank down and studied her notes.

Suitcase popped up. "How tall is the rocket?"

Jake shook his head. How's he keep finding work? Oh-oh, here comes Malicious again.

"Dr. Spencer. The board that reviewed your RT7 accident found that it was caused by the pilot error of Commander Ryder. It was clear that he didn't understand the operation of the computer, which is much less sophisticated than the one on Wayfarer. When you remember how your aircraft slammed onto the runway and you were forced to jump from it, don't you want a stronger man as your commander?"

"Ahhh . . . no. Actually, I want a stronger pair of socks. When we hit, mine rolled down around my ankles."

Malicious Delicious remained standing and took another deep breath. The laughter died within seconds. "No, Dr. Spencer, you didn't understand my question!"

"Hey, do you think I just tumbled off the last turnip truck bouncin' through town? I understand your question all too well. Jake Ryder's the best in the business. The tighter the situation, the better he performs. I'll gladly fly with him on *any* mission."

Malicious Delicious dropped into her seat. Her fingers tore through her pad. Her eyes flicked across every page.

"How many people are going on the flight?" asked Suitcase.

The reporter next to Melon Man ignored Suitcase as he stood up. "How much would you save if you slept only five months?"

Malicious Delicious ignored them both. Her eyes glared as she said through tight lips, "Dr. MacFarland. Will you enjoy the opportunity to sleep with four men for nearly two years?"

Faye's red face highlighted the whites of her wide eyes. "What kind of a bunny-brained question is that? I won't do anything different up there than I do down here. I plan to operate strictly as a professional!"

Malicious Delicious smiled politely. "Thank you." She sat down, licked her chops and started to scribble.

Fat Face fussed and fretted.

Faye fumed. "Can't believe I said that."

Speed smiled. "No sweat, Faye. Just don't read next week's National Perspirer."

"Don't worry, Faye," said Jake. "After a short giggle, the world'll just yawn, roll over and go back to sleep."

"Best thing Fat Face can do now is perform a mercy killing and get us outta here," said Speed.

Fat Face stood. "I believe we've answered most of your questions. Thank you for coming."

The dam burst.

Ted's awareness continued to flood outward. He remained strong, his awareness sharp. And it seemed as if he now sensed with the capabilities of a larger being.

Mentally, Ted'd made this tour before. He'd even seen it with classroom holography. And, from all he could remember, everything seemed in its place. But it seemed there should be more.

. . . stars and more stars, quasars, our galaxy and more galaxies, supernova and . . . what else is there? Only sense it when I back way off, never sensed it up close . . .

Like air between solids, Ted sensed something else, something thin, something so thin as to be almost nonexistent, but something that extended as an

infinite sea in all directions, something with a gravity
that repelled and pushed itself apart, something that
spread out, something unlike anything in the universe of his previous experience.

Ted concentrated.

. . . thin but not uniform, a tenuous maze of
cobwebs, a background of floss and filaments . . .
background that extends in all directions . . . clusters formed where filaments crowd together, clusters're like arteries that grow out of control in
cancerous flesh . . . gravity extreme at center of every cluster.

Ted stopped. He froze his awareness and let it
absorb and sense.

. . . its all moving, every filament wags and wiggles like the tail of a kite, whole background like a sea
of writhing spaghetti . . . why? what are these filaments? . . . seem like tubes of electricity, tubes of
magnetic flux that guide electrical current, tubes
that carry flashes of light . . . no, not light—memory packets! . . . that's my world of tunnels and
chambers, that's where I've been! . . .

Ted felt a rush of satisfaction—with fresh information he started to understand.

Jay Gascon shuffled out with the herd.

He knew that not every day could be a winner,
but so far this one had turned out to be a grand
champion loser. Certainly his seniority demanded a
better assignment, like the hearings at the Medical
Center. Why'd the chief send the kid? Must owe him
a favor. Should the number of clones allowed of any
one human be increased from the present limit of
three to ten, a larger number, or even unrestricted?
An important question. And Jay had done his home-
work.

But just forty minutes before the hearings were
to start, the chief redirected him to another one of
these staged shows by the space cadets. Too much
hustle required. And wasn't *Wayfarer 1* bad enough?

Why repeat the crime with *Wayfarer 2?* It can't make money. Doesn't protect us. Why the hell do it? All the world's fly-boys get together and see how far they can throw money out of the solar system. No connection with reality. If we were meant to go to the stars, they wouldn't be light-years away.

And to add further insult, when Jay arrived, he found himself to be the only real reporter there. First, he had to listen to that obnoxious, dizzy blond. Then good old Suitcase. He couldn't even hold a job up north at the *Humble Herald*. Then came the cheerleaders for the missile men. But most of all, it was that Ryder guy who really ticked him off. Came on so cool, so analytical. Always a slick answer. Just standard military issue. Thin body, straight back, square chin and never a self-doubt. Just fires away like a laser cannon.

At least it ended early. If he could just blast the required words into the system, there'd still be time to get over to the Medical Center before the hearings ended. The chief said this could be an editorial. Good. Quicker and easier.

Jay Gascon sat down at an open desk in the press office adjacent to the auditorium and unfolded his book-sized CT 75. Thoughts gushed out of his brain, through his fingers and into CT's memory.

SPACEMEN SNOOZE—TAXPAYERS LOSE

* * * * * * *

Be Thankful It's Only Dollars—So Far

* * *

By Jay Gascon
Staff Reporter of the World Press

HOUSTON—In three days, the World Space Federation (WSF) will send another six crewpersons on a two-year dollar-burning snooze into space. Some speculate that the lives of everyone in our solar system would improve if we could bundle up the rest of WSF's wide-eyed technologists and launch them all on a one-way trip.

Today, as Commander Rider and his accomplices discussed the alleged objectives of their mission, they showed little concern for those who must foot the bill—the taxpayers.

WHY DO THEY DO IT?

The WSF technologists equate their Wayfarer Program with the well-justified exploration that preceded the current spread of manned bases and stations throughout our solar system. Thus what little logic they use to defend their boondoggles is seriously flawed.

The WSF technologists should just open their eyes and think.

The planets have always been visible to us, many even without a telescope. To anyone with eyes, it has always been clear that our solar system is a tight community available for us to populate. And our moon, whose bold face stares at us so close, has always been there, century after century, advertising itself as Earth's stepping-stone. That we were always meant to populate our solar system is obvious, obvious to any rational man with eyes.

But what do the WSF technologists point at to justify their wanderings? Not the moon, but the Wayfarer Objects, a collection of rocks and debris far outside our solar system.

Can we settle them? No. Is it cost-effective to mine them? No. Can they serve as a stepping-stone to anywhere? NO! For when you look beyond, you see nothing—not a single solitary thing for light-year after

light-year after light-year. The space beyond is as barren as their logic.

Common sense votes: solar system, yes;
stars, no! Yet the technologists continue to
chase space gossamer, to ignore common
sense, to burn tax dollars. What can be done
to restore sanity?

We must recognize that we must shoulder some of the responsibility. For it is we
who have allowed them to obtain their technical training, who have allowed loaded
guns to fall into the hands of children. The
real fault lies not in the advanced state of
our technology, but rather in its accessibil-
ity to everyone on an equal basis, even to the
fringe element of WSF.

Professor Gegendenken, Chairman of
the Sociology Department at the University
of Angst, has proposed a step in the right
direction. After a student has completed his
secondary education and applied for advanced technical training, he would un-
dergo examinations that determine not only
his technical competence, but his mental
competence as well. Only after he has been
shown to be free of psychological disorders
and character flaws would he be permitted
exposure to the secrets of advanced technology. For close to a century the defense de-
partments of the world have examined the
mental stability and backgrounds of those
who seek to work with the secrets of their
defense industries. In similar fashion, it is
now time to expand this type of screening to
those who seek to work with the secrets of
the fundamental technologies themselves.

Some propose other solutions that, in
essence, try to move back the clock. Unfortunately, we cannot. For better or worse, our
advanced technology is here to stay.

> *But we can act! The enlightened propos-
> als of Dr. Gegendenken and others like him
> need to be further developed and put into
> legislation.*
>
> *It's time that we take advanced technol-
> ogy out of the hands of the mentally infirm.
> The antics of the WSF technologists are so
> far only expensive.*
>
> *How long will it take before they are
> also dangerous?*

*   *   *   *   *   *

Jay Gascon skimmed his work once before he
pressed TRANSMIT. Data from his CT 75 radiated to a
pickup in the press office, traveled by light tube to
the control center's Data Distribution Unit where it
was encoded, amplified and passed on to World Press
headquarters over a light tube. There it would be
edited, translated by computer into forty-three lan-
guages and issued to the satellite network for world-
wide distribution. Within thirty-seven minutes Jay
Gascon's words could be printed out by any one of
the World Press's 213 million readers. The editor, the
human element in the system, caused all but 4.37
seconds of the delay.

Jay issued a satisfied grunt, heaved himself up
and hustled out the door.

The two-by-four tumbled down at Jake's feet.
Slippery saliva coated the center section of the five-
foot-long piece of white lumber. Jake picked it up,
wrapped both hands around one end, stepped clear
of Val and hurled it toward the creek.

"Have a good day, Jake?"

The two-by-four covered but seventy feet in the
air before one end hit the hard turf and bounced up.
And before gravity could bring it down again, Hans
wrapped his jaws around its center and held it high as
he landed on all fours.

"An OK day. Not a great day. Not a bad day."

"Oh no!" said Val. "You're not getting away with that one. What really happened? Did you see Eva?"

The black and tan German shepherd flipped the two-by-four around twice in his mouth before he dumped it again at Jake's feet.

"Yeah, first thing this morning. It looks like the uncertainty's getting to her. Met Willie, their youngest son. Nice kid, but also a real pistol. Actually, any kid who'd be out at sunup rippin' down the street in his toy car has gotta be OK."

Hans poised, fixed his glare on Jake's face, wagged his tail and barked.

"That's a hard visit to make, but I know Eva appreciated it. The others have."

"What've you been up to, Val?"

"Not so fast. Anything happen at work?"

Hans barked again.

"Just more of the same. Short run in the simulator this morning. As usual, they gave us a few problems. We had a press conference this afternoon. Encountered the standard sensational apathy from the press. Then Dupree called a holovision conference. Dragged on for hours."

"What'd he want?"

Hans combined a whine with his third bark. His eyes pleaded.

"Mostly just new procedures. Glad Klaus was there with us. We talked Dupree out of most of the changes except the trivial ones. Dupree gets more irrational every day. I think he's about to go belly-up. Enough of him. How was your day?"

"Oh, just an OK day. Not a great day. Not a bad day."

Jake gripped Val by the waist, lifted her up, spun halfway around and laughed. "You can't get away with that one either."

Hans made his fourth bark a demand and followed it up with a fresh series of barks, each stronger than the last. Each one ripped out like a rifle shot and carried his flexed body off its paws.

"I think he's trying to say something, Val."

"Yeah, like throw the doggie his 'stick.'"

"This's a new one. Haven't seen his old one in a couple of days. It must've gotten into the creek."

"Guess that's why he's been moping around."

"Every doggie's gotta have a stick! Where'd he get it from?"

"Don't know. He just trotted home with it this afternoon with his tail whippin' away. He's been waiting for you ever since."

Jake again took one end of the two-by-four and hurled it.

Dirt flew from under Hans's paws. Like a spike from a ramjet's nose, his snout and head pushed forward. Without debate or question of their common objective, each one of thousands of muscles coordinated and drove his jaws at maximum speed straight toward their target. Again, he snatched his stick out of the air on the first bounce and pranced back with his tail and prize held high. He unloaded his stick at his master's feet and stood rigid and ready again.

Jake reached down and ruffled the fur behind his dog's ears. "You're my kinda guy, ole buddy."

"Why can't he be content with a ball like other dogs? One of these times your good ole buddy's going to break your toe with his stick."

"Some games're risky—but you just have to play 'em, something we macho men understand, right, Hans?"

Hans stared at Jake, wagged his tail and flexed.

"You machos are all alike. Hey, that's it! Trade places. Send Hans and you stay. I'll even throw you the stick."

"Hans's smart enough and he's got the right instincts, but he hasn't got enough simulator time."

"Worth a try."

"Val, now you avoided the question. What kind of day did you have?"

"It's been a good one. I spent most of it on some concepts for a new client. He wants an underwater home."

"That's different!"

"It is, and it's also demanding."

Hans barked his lead-off bark.

"How so?"

"I've gotta turn creative again, really creative. Although I can use simple geometries for the clear-plexan, external shell, like a cylinder and spherical ends, the inside's a real challenge. I've got to find ways to create a feeling of security and warmth forty feet below the ocean's surface. Multi-split levels, curved inside walls, high-beamed ceilings, liberal use of marble or travertine or faux stone and things of this type will help, but I've got to get more creative than that."

Hans progressed into the bark-and-whine phase.

"Also, I have to make all external surfaces opaque, clear or anything in between, using litran coatings. So I'll have to work with what sunlight exists, augmented by artificial light, to create a number of desired effects. And the structural analysis of the design loads is a whole new field in itself. So are the building codes, many of which I'll have to propose and negotiate myself. I know exactly what I want, but now I have to go back to the basics and really think again."

Hans escalated into his terminal state, the bark-and-jump phase.

"Steady, big fella. Here ya go." Jake heaved Hans's stick.

"Jake, tomorrow you'll be gone! And tonight's your last night home. One more toss, then it's my turn for attention. But I won't bark and jump."

Jake laughed and pulled Val to him. "You won't have to." His eyes softened. "Val, I really admire you. Most people would be afraid to reach beyond what's familiar or comfortable and turn creative again."

"Won't be easy."

Jake felt a twinge from the primordial watchman in his gut. He frowned. "True, but you always do it a lot easier than me."

IV

TREK

*The explorer's greatest challenge—
leave the shore.*

13

Toddle

Across the Gulf, warm water evaporated into cold air and condensed. A layer of clouds formed. It churned and thickened, then turned solid and dense. Winds from the south strengthened and dragged the wide gray tarpaulin over South Texas. It trapped humidity and depression underneath.

Jake and Val crept along the road to WSF Operations at the Houston-Galveston Air Complex. Only superficial words dribbled out from an empty sadness that'd started to swell. Jake inserted his IdentoCard into the dashboard reader. The upper jaw of the gate lifted its teeth.

Jake hated good-byes. They'd said it all a hundred times before. He wished he could just raise the arms on his recliner, squeeze the triggers and punch outta the house right into the spacecraft.

They joined Speed and Jaclyn, who waited in the lounge, and Boris and Ada, who stood nearby, excited by their own private conversation. After initial greetings, words hung, except for occasional wisecracks that reflexed from Speed like nervous twitches.

"Pack my second pair of skivvies, Jaclyn? May have to change 'em this time."

"You got 'em."

"My crayons . . . and my *Commander Jake Ryder Coloring Book*?"

"You got 'em."

"And my postcards?"

"You got 'em."

Silence dominated again as Faye approached.

Speed glanced around, pulled on his ear and shuffled. "Depressing weather."

"Ahhh, right, Speed," said Faye.

A jangle of metal approached like Marley's Ghost. Jake turned. Irwin and his wife, Lucinda Marie, had arrived.

"Hi, Irwin. What brings you here today?"

"I . . . well, I . . . com'on, Speed."

The group exchanged canned greetings with its new members, then fought off silence with a volley of superficial comments.

"Speed, make sure you get enough sleep," said Jaclyn.

"Ada, what are you and Boris so excited about?" asked Lucinda Marie.

"We think we've found a way to formulate a computer solution to Donati's four-body gravitational problem!"

"Oh."

As the group tried to resuscitate the conversation, Jake studied the people before him.

Boris looked down half a head into Ada's face and talked with the intense precision reserved for technical subjects. Ada's black eyes stared off to the side, as if something floated in the air by Boris's shoulder that demanded close attention. A wrinkled cotton-print dress hung askew over her blocklike body. The dull, dark, jumbled colors of the tiny flowers on the print contrasted with every adjacent visual reference.

Jake's eyes drifted over to Lucinda Marie, who stood rigid, straight and tall next to Ada. She had covered her body with a stiff, high-neck, white blouse, a gray business jacket and skirt, stockings and high heels. Her hair was piled on top of her head with flair and precision; large gold pendants hung from her neck and ears. Every square inch of her neck and face was hidden by skin-tone makeup. Her detached, aloof features were dusted, painted and highlighted with hues, tones, shades and lines. Completing the production was the classic stance of the model—a perfect hologram—straight from a Paris gallery.

His eyes jumped to Val, who stood next to Lucinda Marie. She wore tan, form-fitting slacks, a soft, light-blue sweater, loose hair, a touch of lipstick and a smile. You're a lucky man, Ryder. Thinks for herself. Isn't just another computer peripheral or another mobile manikin for some distant designer to hang his latest fad on. Ada and Lucinda, both of 'em are after formulas. Too easily manipulated. Both keep finding treasures that evaporate. But Val's magnetism flows out; it's not coded in or painted on. Smart and sensual. Elegance through nature's simplicity.

The WSF pilot approached. "Morning, Jake. We're ready when you are."

Val's warmth no longer pressed against Jake. Cold air filled in behind as he moved away.

"Love you, Jake."

"Love you, too."

"Will I get a wink at liftoff, like always?"

"Just like always."

Jake headed for the gate, smiled at the group, then he focused on the open door of the aircraft.

. . . filaments and clusters are my tunnels and chambers sensed from outside, but why do I sense so much? . . . every physical feature, every nuance . . . that's it—I sense all radiation! . . . not just colors, but everything stars emit, everything Objects and moons and planets reflect . . . like going from black and white to color . . . colors I once saw with my human eyes're only a small part of real light . . . now I see x-rays that cut sharp against fuzzy infrared rays, gamma ray specks that pierce smears of radio rays . . . not limited to that stingy slice evolution cut for my eye . . . been color blind up to now, can drink it all in—all radiation . . .

. . . whatever I've become a part of, it's given me a powerful ability to observe, to gather data . . . huge potential to learn, to understand . . . and I've just started! . . .

14

Examine

The division glowed.

The ribbon of sand that meandered south through lazy serpentine turns gleamed and sparkled under intense rays of the noon sun. It divided vivid green jungle from listless brown water, structure-covered land from flat ocean, human territory from uninhabited turf. Launch Complex 43 stood at its edge.

"Great coastline, boss! Let's slip the launch a few days and get in a little beach time."

"Good idea, Speederoo," said Jake. "I'll get Dr. Daro on the horn, and you can ask him."

"Think you're tellin' me I don't need a tan."

"Not where we're going."

"Hey, is that Kourou? I don't remember it being so spread out, so urban. But then I haven't launched outta here in five years."

"That's Kourou all right. Developed a lot since WSF opened up Guiana Space Center for everybody's use. The launch frequency's just about tripled."

"Hey, boss, over there at 1030, complex 43, pads A and B—Agile and Brute. Real hardware!"

"Hot damn!" Something inside Jake cinched a notch tighter and snapped him out of his depression.

No more classrooms or holographs or simulators or reporters, just boosters with their straight lines, their crisp and simple lines, boosters poised with power and purpose. Real world! Excited, just like walkin' into the stadium on game day. Go for a solid hit on the first play. Knock out the butterflies. Only here, you get just one hit—engine light.

"Speed, I'll see if Max can't give us a better look."

Jake walked forward to the cockpit and sat down in the seat to the right of the WSF pilot. "Hi, Max. How about takin' a lap around our launch complex before we head for the strip?"

"Glad to, Jake."

"Thanks."

Max banked the aircraft twenty degrees. "From three miles out, your boosters don't look so large."

"Yeah, they don't. But Brute's a big hummer. Nearly six hundred feet tall. Weights twenty-one million pounds."

Max took a few chomps on his gum as he gazed at Jake. "No shit? What's Agile?"

"He's only a little guy. A shade over two hundred feet and one million pounds. Both're just big enough to do their jobs."

"How much of all that's left when you guys are done?"

"We use all the propellant but throw away none of the hardware."

"What happens to it, Jake?"

"Tomorrow Brute's first stage'll fly back here under auto pilot and splash down about three hundred feet offshore. The second stage'll be used right up to docking with von Braun. After that it'll reenter and also fly back on its own. But it'll land on the strip, just like all our unmanned logistics carriers. Its payload, our two Wayfarer modules and their nuclear-ion engine propellant will stay at the station until we get there Friday."

"And the little guy?"

"Agile's booster'll do the same thing as Brute's. But the Agile shuttle'll stay at the station until another crew uses it to come home. It can come back to any one of our eight launch and landing sites around the world. With twenty-seven Agiles in operation, it's gotten to be one helluva logistics problem."

"Problem?" Max grinned. "Jake, have I ever got the perfect solution—let me fly 'em back!"

"Wish we could, Max. You'd love it."

"Is it much different than this . . . or any other carbon tube stuffed with gas and optical fibers?"

"It's the same kind of hardware, just bigger computers and more complex procedures. Most of the complexity comes from the computers, although they're supposed to ease the workload."

"Well, anytime you need another stick tweaker, or even a computer nursemaid, I'm ready. How's it handle?"

"After reentry, below Mach 12, about the same as a fighter. And it weighs only about thirty-six thousand pounds."

"That's light!"

"Yeah, but each Wayfarer module isn't much heavier."

Max chomped and gazed again. "No shit?"

"Although most of the outside surfaces are white for thermal control, everything's really made out of ultralight carbex. It weighs zilch. But when we start, they're a lot heavier. Each module goes about 365,000 pounds. By the time we get back into earth orbit in '39, each'll be down to about 52,000, and most of that weight'll be in the nuclear-ion engines. We have to hose out a lot of gas when we accelerate and decelerate, both going out to the Wayfarers and coming back."

"Love to see 'em up close."

"You got time to come with us on our walk-through this afternoon?"

"I'll make time!"

"Good. Just stick with us."

The boosters again stood silhouetted against the ocean that extended over the horizon. "Thanks for the lap, Max."

Jake returned to the rear of the aircraft. "Super-lookin' hardware, Speed."

"The best."

Jake studied the boosters again. Best? Couldn't be better. A lot of smart people put all they had into those machines, and they built on the best before 'em. But look where they're pointed—open space. Toss that little speck with our warm bodies out to some cold, foreign turf, out to some random part of God's creation with all its random surprises. Never know if best is good enough—till we get there! Must've looked just as vast and unknown comin' across all that open water, just bobbin' around on a little wooden cork. Now there's ships and planes and rockets all down there at the bottom—a gathering of explorers who tried but didn't make it. Is each frontier really worth it? Only the Few support it, far less do it, but everybody gobbles up the benefits. Game never changes.

The *Wayfarer 2* crew's ramturbo rolled to a stop next to the coaxial helicopter. One aircraft discharged, the other collected.

The coax lifted off and hovered. Nothing vibrated, for its two coaxial counter-rotating main rotors, one above the other, spewed out a near-silent, smooth, steady shaft of wind. All engine power flowed straight to its counter-rotating blades, for it had no tail rotor to burden it. It tilted forward.

Jake heard only a soft rush of air, felt only a strong acceleration. "Nice machine."

"Sure is," said Speed. "A lot better than any single-rotor rattletrap. Tail rotors just don't make much sense anymore. Glad the industry finally wised up."

"Yeah. But American industry should've had coaxes first. They got in a rut and couldn't climb out. Didn't even try till they about went under. Just kept on pumpin' out single rotors. Still would be if Japan hadn't gone commercial with the coax and nearly wiped 'em out."

Speed shook his head. "Why didn't they learn from Detroit?"

"Or from Russian military that've used 'em for over half a century?"

"Must've been like us, boss, slow learners."

Jake smiled at the absurdity of Speed as a slow learner. "No, there were plenty of smart folks working the problem, but when they all got lashed together, they couldn't act with the wisdom of a single one of 'em."

"Nice to know some things never change." Speed laughed.

The coax nuzzled onto the ground 150 feet from Brute. The *Wayfarer 2* crew stepped out and peered into the forest of launch gantry pipes, lines and supports. They started toward the gantry elevator, glanced up and halted. The enormity overhead commanded their attention, then froze them in place. Giant redwoods of metal, carbex and plexan grew upward from the concrete toward a vanishing point in the bright blue above. Structures towered over and dominated the flecks of flesh below.

Jake glanced over at Speed, who stood in the traditional posture of homage: head back against his spine, mouth open, eyes glazed and arms dangling.

Speed rotated his head forward to speak. "Ain't just your ordinary flagpole."

"Pop your jaw back into its hinge, Hayseed, and let's get on with it."

The entourage reached the base of the elevator, stopped again and gazed up into the fire-painted openings of Brute's five main engine nozzles, up into a silent blackness that poised within, blackness that waited to explode with the first rush of propellants.

"How's them for afterburners, Max?" asked Speed. Max remained frozen in his own posture of homage. Speed continued. "Seventeen-foot diameter at the base of each nozzle. About five million pounds thrust each. Tends to push ya right along."

Max rotated his head back down. "What's it burn?"

"Just plain old liquid oxygen and hydrogen," said Jake. "Been in use for almost a century. They're cheap, energetic and easy to handle. Hard to beat when lifting against gravity."

"Wouldn't wanna be standing 'here tomorrow," said Max.

Speed rubbed the back of his neck. "Yeah, could singe your marshmallows."

"We'll have a front row seat for liftoff, Max," said Jake. "We can watch from the top of the Launch Control Center three miles from here."

"Three miles?" asked Max. "Seems far away."

Jake chuckled. "It won't tomorrow. That's the limit set by safety in case it blows."

The entourage straggled into the elevator, shot up to the 510-foot level, straggled out and shuffled single file across the swing arm toward the Alpha module, the *Wayfarer 2* prime spacecraft, identical in all features to the Beta module below.

Alpha's outside envelope consisted of a cylinder thirty-seven feet in diameter, the international standard, and seventy-five feet long. The bottom end contained the nuclear-ion engine and recently enlarged propellant storage tanks. The top end consisted of a hemisphere, which itself was capped by a seventeen-foot-diameter clear plexan hemisphere.

With its outer airlock hatch removed, Alpha appeared to have a neat, round hole eaten into its rib cage. Like a large worm, the single-file entourage burrowed in.

Alpha contained twelve habitable volumes: wardroom centered under the plexan dome, command center, observation room with optical-quality glass windows for Earth-viewing, science laboratory, maintenance and repair complex, food storage volume, exercise facility, entertainment room, lavatory, cluster of six individual sleep compartments, hibernation chamber, and the airlock at mid-level with its inside and outside hatches and docking port.

The United States had diverted both the Alpha and Beta modules from the production line of their own military space program. Because the WSF came under pressure to fly as soon as possible after its formation, several countries had modified and contributed what off-the-shelf hardware they had available. Made of carbex, the modules' structure met not only the normal requirement of high strength to weight but, because it was electrically nonconducting, also didn't reflect radar signals. This latter characteristic helped give each module stealth, a firm military requirement. The United States also contributed the nuclear power source derived from old SP-100 lunar base technology.

The Russians became the obvious source of Brute's first stage. In contrast to the West, the Russians continued to place emphasis on heavy lift and thereby had the largest booster in operation. The second stage fell within the capabilities of several countries. The WSF Council selected France.

West Germany contributed the nuclear-ion engines. There, more than in any other nation, each generation had instilled in the next an optimistic enthusiasm for flight to the stars, whether or not it could happen in their lifetime; decade after decade they persisted in development of advanced propulsion systems.

The East Asia Alliance led by Japan, which continued to dominate the data system hardware market, contributed the computer complex. Another member of the Alliance, China, contributed in a second area. Because of their strength in computer logic, they stood out as the natural choice for the major portion of the software.

Every WSF nation contributed some form of hardware, software or operational support. Although political bickering plagued the early division of responsibilities between nations, the technologists focused on their common goals and worked as a team once turf battles subsided. Nonetheless, the world's politicians and press stirred the pot at the smallest provocation and forced program management to exercise continuous creativity to keep the side shows exiled to nonessential areas. Up to just a few years ago, they'd succeeded.

An hour and a half later, the worm wiggled out the same hole it'd entered and penetrated a second one eighty feet lower in the Beta module. After an equal length of time, it again exited and packed itself back into the elevator.

Max nodded his head at Speed as he chomped. "No wonder you guys spend big bucks. You're taking two of everything."

"Good enough for Noah, good enough for us," said Speed.

"Clever engineering is great," said Jake. "But it's redundancy that lets us sleep at night."

Elevator dropped, arrested its fall and parted its doors. The *Wayfarer 2* crew spilled out. But they slowed as they stumbled into hibernation pods that lay side-by-side in wait for their trip up, additional pods that could be used to return Ted and his crew.

Jake led the reconstructed worm as it wiggled its way through the maze of elongated containers. The pods looked strange by themselves, like relics from the past—coffins—those barbaric body boxes that survivors hid in morbid ghoulish graves. Outlawed most places, Jake thought they should be everywhere. Why smother the body with cold earth and leave it to rot in the dark, to suffer nature's relentless indignity. After death, why not give every atom its freedom too? . . . dammit Ted, where are you?!

15

Disrupt

No hitch, no botch, no boggle.

At forty-seven minutes to go, a machine took control. The count at pad 43 B flowed on, smooth and precise. It passed the point where humans would intervene. Now only Machine remained on the field; Humans had retreated to the sidelines with their inferior skills—not to be sent into the game unless an unimagined situation arose, one of those rare problems that Machine couldn't fix through automated reconfigurations.

CT 8500 closed two redundant valves that vented a stream of frigid oxygen into moist atmosphere. The action severed the shaft of fog that jetted from the center of the booster. Shaft faded into a diffuse wisp as it drifted away. Tank pressure started to rise.

"Vent's off," said Speed.

"Yep. One minute to go," said Jake.

"The count's whistled right by me."

"Me, too."

Jake looked directly east toward Agile, who rested on pad 43 A, away from Brute on 43 B. The sun burned just a few degrees above the horizon and to his right. He cupped his hands around his eyes and squinted, but the pain on his retinas remained. He lifted his binoculars to exclude the sun from his field of view, to take one last good look, one last inspection of Agile's image. It appeared clear and sharp, yet lifeless and inert, a comatose mechanical structure that in only twenty-four hours would be vibrant and alive, poised and ready. But for now, all life belonged to its father to the north.

9 . . . 8 . . . 7 . . . Jake turned his body and his full attention back thirty-seven degrees to the left. Brute's regal figure rose above ragged fog that hugged and obscured all ground and water below. Massive King Brute rested on his concrete throne, towered over his subjects buried in the marshmallow world at his feet—a tranquil tableau frozen in time; a majestic panorama that appeared on cue morning after morning; an ethereal dreamscape that, also on cue, fell victim to the sun as it climbed above the horizon, to the solar heat that always had its way, always evaporated away the majesty, always dissolved the grandeur, always left only the harsh residue of reality and detail.

But on this morning and at this time, nature's metamorphosis would be disrupted, terminated, and the series severed—King Brute had places to go and things to do.

5 . . . 4 . . . 3 . . . A New Sun, a sun with the intensity of many suns, exploded beneath King Brute. New Sun hurled brilliant light bolts left and right, out and across the ground into fog. Smoke plumes puffed and bloated, curled and spun, billowed and blazed with reflected radiance from New Sun's fireball within.

2 . . . 1 . . . 0 . . . King Brute nudged off his throne and balanced on the holocaust. But gravity continued to demand obedience even from the king. Gravity pulled down with unabated force, and Brute could but rise at glacial speed. But Brute continued to strain—and continued to climb. He trudged upward past the gantry tower as New Sun stretched into a brilliant vertical shaft.

On some unseen command, birds shot up through the fog. They flapped in panic as they tried to flee some invisible power that pummeled their bodies.

Jake watched the explosive chaos in the silent movie before him and waited. He knew it would hit. It did. His silent world detonated. Thunder swept by in a continuous roll and surged and swelled. Only three miles distant, King Brute had erupted in a controlled rage, directed his violence into his lance of fire, and seized a temporary victory.

The king picked up speed and gained altitude. Motion enhanced his grace and strength, his dignity and power. Now the king took full command of the white-hot shaft on which he perched. He lengthened it, stretched out his torrent of flame, drew out his train so that all could admire its regal pattern of shocks and diamonds.

With a slow precise rotation, King Brute turned his thrust toward the horizon, bent his trajectory toward open water. He pointed his violent train directly at Jake and hypnotized him. King's deep-throated rumble popped and crackled with bursts of explosive strength.

Jake drank the energy, the pulses of power that shook his gut and chest, vibrated his arms and face, resonated his teeth and jaw, rammed its message of might and power into his bones and brain. The rumble tapered and faded. It never really terminated, but after a time Jake became aware of only normal sound and his heart and shallow breath.

"Man, what a belch!"

Jake laughed. "You always did have a way with words, Speed. This one really get to you?"

Speed didn't answer. He remained fixed, his eyes trained on the bright point in the sky. It flared and disappeared. A smaller yet still perceptible point replaced it. Then he spoke. "It always does. There's staging."

"Right. Let's go down inside and follow it on the tracking cameras."

"Let's."

As Jake approached the stairs, he glanced at pad 43 B. Diffuse smoke hung on either side of the vacant throne. Above a white contrail formed a finger that pointed skyward. In loneliness, Prince Agile waited on his own throne to the south.

They descended into the control room. Thirty-five or forty WSF officials stared up at three sixteen-by-twenty-foot television pictures on the forward wall. The seven technicians that monitored CT 8500 launch displays allowed their eyes only occasional darts toward the wall.

"Great shots!" said Speed. "Looks like we're right there."

"Sure does," said Jake. "We've got optical tracking from three satellites and four more in wait. Oughta be able to follow it all the way up."

The exhaust from Brute's second stage fanned out from the bright exit of its engine nozzle. The plume billowed outward and flowed back, like the tail of a comet, and faded into the background sky. On the center screen, the second stage increased in size and clarity as it climbed closer to the satellite's camera. Once above the atmosphere, the invisible hydrogen-oxygen flame of the exhaust could find nothing to heat, nor anything to burn, and decreased in length and brightness. Within a minute the plume could be seen as only a faint light within the nozzle itself. The faint light burned for another five minutes, then went out.

The image of Brute's second stage and payload remained on screen two. Screens one and three showed pictures from cameras on board von Braun, pictures of empty space. But within another ninety-seven minutes they would be filled with images of Brute's payload as it arrived and docked.

Jake felt a presence at his side.

"Hello, Jake."

"Oh, hello, Dr. Daro. Sure was a clean shot."

"Yes, it was. Please assemble your crew in the director's conference room in five minutes."

"Yes, sir."

Dr. Daro sat at the head of the conference table in his one and only position—at attention. His placid features remained inscrutable, washed clean of emotion and any hint of the thoughts contained behind.

"There has been a change in the status of *Wayfarer 1*. Specifically, telemetry from a single transmitter in the Beta module, which contains everybody except Ted, has again been received. It showed the spacecraft systems to be in good condition except for all of the other transmitters, which are failed. There was no data in the telemetry on the crew.

"At initial reception, the data showed the surge supply batteries to be drained. We observed a command entered into the onboard computer to recharge the batteries. There was no indication of who entered the command. Once the batteries were recharged, all telemetry again faded to zero. That is all the information we have received."

"There's no logic to that," said Jake.

"True," said Dr. Daro. "But they were actions, and somebody had to take them."

As a unit, the six members of the crew stiffened and sharpened their focus on Dr. Daro.

"The computer is not programmed to do that on its own," said Ada. "Someone had to do it."

Dr. Daro nodded and continued. "Because of the efficiency of the program for Object-collision-avoidance developed by Boris, we have obtained an additional propellant reserve. We will use it to cut down your transient time from 307 to 297 days. This has already been programmed into your Trans-Wayfarer guidance target."

Boris smiled. Intended or not, he'd received a compliment from a tough critic.

"You will be updated if we learn something of significance from further analysis of the data. You should also know that, until this occurred, the U.N. was about to recommend that we postpone *Wayfarer 2* until such time that we demonstrate full understanding of what happened on *Wayfarer 1.* Although there is still considerable debate within several subcommittees, you will launch tomorrow. I have nothing further. Questions?"

Jake surveyed his crew. Their five faces each rippled with cross currents of confusion, but no one spoke. His eyes took another lap. A frosty fog had already started to fuzz their features, to cloak exposed emotions. Still, no one spoke. "No, sir, none."

Dr. Daro stood. His fingers bit into the top of his chair. He paused, then looked around the table. "We *must* determine what has our Outward Reach Initiative stopped! And you are the best the Federation has for the job. You have our respect and our appreciation." Dr. Daro's eyes met Jake's. They looked glassy. Then they jumped to the rest of the crew, one by one. "My personal best wishes to each of you."

Dr. Daro's lower lip quivered a slight bit as he turned away. "Thank you, sir," said Jake, as the others nodded.

Jake watched Dr. Daro leave, then glanced at the others as surprise pushed up through fog and sank again. Why'd he come down here with that data? Could've used holovision. Very melodramatic for him. Usually gives us just a nod at most. Acts like he won't ever see us again.

"Comments?" asked Jake. He looked into five empty faces, into blank eyes. "Nothing else is planned for the remainder of the day. Once again, tomorrow we go aboard at 0400 hours for liftoff at 0537. We'll get together for breakfast at 0300. See you all then. Have a good afternoon and evening."

Jake remained seated and stared at where Dr. Daro had stood. *"We must determine what has our Outward Reach Initiative stopped!"*

* * *

. . . memory packets flow through filaments like red blood cells in arteries, life-giving packets of images, of data . . . a lifeblood of data that flows from cluster to cluster, chamber to chamber . . .

Ted sensed only data. No answers. No interpretations. He focused back on the little, tight knot of cancerous growth around the Wayfarer mini-black hole, his exit from the chambers. It seemed tiny and trivial. Yet, a familiar urgency consumed him.

. . . Home—all my memories are there—my Life . . . can I get back in? . . .

Ted relaxed, let his concentration go limp. He felt himself pulled back down into the network, drawn back down into his chamber. I can come and go as I please!

Again, Ted reached out to the boundary of his chamber, found the entrance and forced his awareness into the void. For a time the tunnel slid by, narrow and straight, just as before. But then it began to bend and turn; to wind and twist, and finally to fill with fog, a fog that thickened to a viscous soup, a sludge that dragged his awareness to a halt.

. . . choked off—must be another way out . . .

Ted relaxed back into his chamber, tried one tunnel after another, but found only more chambers and more tunnels. He dove into Chamber's entrance a second time but again plunged into more mist, more soup and more sludge, nothing but more obstacles and more barriers.

Ted drove his awareness outward to its limits, futilely lunging against the walls. For the first time since his capture, a twinge of terror seeped upward. But discipline pushed it back under and gave him a brief reprieve. He relaxed—and the walls crept back to their original shape.

Again Ted thrust himself at a blockade that yielded nothing but momentary notice, that barred and blocked and choked and confined. He tried again, and again, and again, and again, and . . .

Only the mercy of time and fatigue calmed his panic. His awareness shrank and shriveled back to his core.

. . . have to get out, get fresh data, get energy from outside, learn, understand, survive . . . can't stay buried and confined forever . . . REACH! . . .

Ted pushed and strained, tired, then shriveled and shrank. And the walls drifted back to original shapes. He reached and strained again, and again, and again, and again, and . . .

For the remainder of the day, Jake remained a spectator, an onlooker, an observer, a man with energy to burn and time to kill.

He returned to the control room and watched Brute rendezvous with von Braun, watched the station work crew hover outside as Brute docked, watched the crew assemble *Wayfarer 2*, then watched them apply the final touches to the two modules that he'd live in for the next twenty-one months.

Jake turned away. Can't watch any longer. Play or go to the stands—worst place in the whole stadium is the damn bench. Gotta relax and find some way to wait it out till tomorrow.

He signed out another world-renowned WSF Drab Bomb and drove to Des Roches Hotel and Mall by the beach. Three years before he and Val had stayed at the hotel. Maybe the mood still lingered. Maybe he could forget Wayfarer for a few hours. Maybe he could loosen his internal spring. Maybe.

Jake strolled through the hotel lobby and out to the pool—not as good as his Sunday Command Post at home but worth a try. He sprawled in a deck chair next to the pool, drank in the sun, inhaled humid salt air and closed his eyes. He listened to people's laughter, children's screams and soothing electronic strains from a radio behind his head.

Jake relaxed.

Radio's owner started to flick through its stations.

". . . where East German scientists again denounced all claims that they seek to develop a super race. Separately, East German officials stated that within their borders they are not bound by the International Cloning Treaty signed last week by . . ."

He looked down through his sunglasses, along his chest and into the water at a man who floated his bloated body on its back toward the edge of the pool. The man looked over his head at the ladder, splashed water with fingers next to his hips and waited. He splashed and waited, and splashed and waited. In time, the rotund vessel docked with the ladder. The man gripped the rails, braced, grimaced, struggled, pulled and pushed his bulk up three steps, stumbled onto the deck and waddled over to the table where his lunch beckoned.

Jake's mind flashed back to Brute's liftoff, to mass with purpose, to power with precision, to strength with grace.

He watched a father ignore his whining son, who tugged on the bottom of his bathing trunks with ice cream-coated fingers.

Jake pictured Willie, a tough little guy who needs his father, whose father needed him.

". . . not our fault. We only rent airplanes. We can't check everybody's background to see if he's a nuclear terrorist. It's the responsibility of . . ."

He watched a woman exercise her jaw one foot from a man's face. ". . . and you march right in there first thing when we get back and tell them that I said we're not going to France for any three months and I don't care what the company thinks it needs because it's not going to . . ."

Jake's mind drifted out of the solar system, away from his star and everything human, out and into the void.

". . . where today the Soviet Union launched

Cosmos 43,782. The Soviets did not disclose its mission, but it is speculated . . ."

He watched a man inch his foot into the water, shake his head and return to his chair in the sun.

Jake's mind pulled up alongside the black hole. It'd already made the trip, but his body couldn't start until tomorrow.

". . . Serene, a special formula guaranteed to bury your burdens and bring you a unique inner peace . . ."

He clenched the armrests, wrenched out of the chair, walked, then jogged back toward Drab Bomb.

16

Ascend

Urge pushed up. Gravity pulled down.

Urge summoned all its strength, roared and rose up. It attacked and gained ground, but it then faltered and faded back behind old lines. Urge stormed again, and it faded again. It stormed and faded, stormed and faded, stormed and faded . . .

Over millions of years, and millions of times a year, Ocean yielded to Urge. Time after time Urge stormed the shore. It thrust upward, then spread outward and assaulted Land. And each time Gravity reached out, grabbed every molecule and dragged each and every one back. Retreat followed every advance; withdrawal, every thrust.

But eon after eon, Ocean's Urge never gave up.

Perhaps Urge was just a slow learner. Perhaps it didn't yet understand that Gravity never released its grip. Or perhaps Urge just couldn't control itself. For whatever reason, Urge continued its incessant battle against confinement, the only life Urge had ever known.

Others on Earth, whose ancestors once struggled up and out of Ocean, still felt Urge and still fought Gravity. And they also thrust.

A select few escaped.

* * *

Violence—he could feel it!

Prince Agile promised violence, controlled violence. Jake sensed it, and felt fully alive.

0357 hours. On schedule. Jake stood alone on the swing arm, the umbilical cord that connected the launch gantry to the cranium of Prince Agile's spacecraft, the cord that supplied Machine with Man, Prince with Judgment. The rest of the crew had already gone on board. Jake would be last, a commander's right he always exercised.

His world had but three components: intense light, white machine and empty blackness. Jake looked down, down past the spacecraft, all the way down past the booster's slender cylinder, down past the top edges of its fins, down two hundred feet and into the blackness that soon would explode in an inferno of turbulent heat and light. Then there'd be just one shelter, one safe haven, one stronghold—the crew cabin straight across in Prince Agile's skull.

But not yet.

Jake's eyes ran back up the side of the booster, up and along Prince Agile's skin that screamed harsh white under the impact of radiation shot up from the ring of focused suns below. His eyes stopped at the white vapor trails that hissed and jetted from Prince's belly, boiled off the frigid surfaces of the 450 tons of liquid oxygen and liquid hydrogen that gorged Prince's tanks. Tame trails of vapor. Harmless. Controlled. Just trace amounts of the more energetic molecules that leaped out of the frigid seas within, pushed and bounced their way through Prince's pipes, rushed out openings in Prince's skin and escaped to freedom in the morning air. Soon, all their lethargic brothers and sisters would also find freedom, but not before their union. Soon the atoms of these two basic elements would unite and become just water in the air, but not before they each gave up a little of their electronic energy and contributed it to the whole, not before each fed the continuous cataclysm that soon would explode beneath Jake's back.

But not yet.

Cool, humid air brushed against Jake's face. He let his mind and body go limp and his senses drink. His nose sampled the stream of sterile gases that'd mixed with ocean air. Prince's body popped and pinged above the background hiss as it contracted under the raw cold in its frigid gut. It creaked and groaned as it stretched under liquid loads that'd multiplied its weight several fold. But Jake sensed more. Life stirred within this machine—vibrant Life that coursed through arteries of pipe and optical fiber. Life in harmony and partnership with Humanity; Life poised and ready to perform.

But not yet.

Jake turned, walked along the umbilical cord, let the smile dissolve from his face and entered the cabin. He slid into the left-hand position, the commander's position next to Speed.

"Another day, another dollar. Right, boss?"

"Right."

Behind Jake and Speed sat Boris and Ada; behind them, Faye and Irwin. The rear four, separated from the front two, would be just passengers during ascent, isolated payloads to be activated once they reached the Wayfarer modules at von Braun.

"Like your style, Jake," said Speed. "I've ridden with some commanders who don't climb in till thirty minutes before we light the fire. This way we get an hour and a half to watch the computer reconfigure the systems. It gives us a better feel for the bird, in case we have to take over."

"That's why I do it, although no one's had to take it away from a computer for thirteen years now."

"Yeah, but in that one, by the time the confuser was ready to give it up, there was no way to recover. They could've gone manual a whole bunch sooner and saved their butts."

"You're right there, Speed. But it's not easy to

judge when the computer's doing its job right and when it's just pullin' you further under." Jake glanced at the control stick by his right hand. "Even though it's hard to fly this bird in manual, I'll do that before I'll wait for the final verdict."

"Yep, I do like your style."

Jake studied the smooth plexan display panel at arm's length in front of him. It made slight curves as it stretched the width of the cabin, then it flowed back in continuous arcs on either side. Each space-craft system had its own real estate on the panel and displayed detailed dynamic data in multicolored numerical and pictorial formats. Each display pushed up alongside its neighbor and formed an integrated panorama of complexity. The engineers and astronauts had vowed to keep it simple when they started its design, but there'd always seemed to be just one more shred of crucial data that had to be displayed, just one more hint they had to have on Prince Agile's true performance and intentions.

Jake started with the display of CT 7000's health and worked his way across the panel. Satisfied, he entered commands through the keyboard and changed the displays to those he'd use after ascent for the rendezvous with von Braun. Satisfied again, he let CT 7000 check the positions of the switches and circuit breakers that covered the areas overhead and to the sides. CT 7000 concluded that Man had done his job correctly. Jake checked them once more himself. Again, all appeared to be nominal.

The count dropped through minus thirty minutes and continued, smooth and precise.

Jake lay back, relaxed and looked above the panel and out the single-piece window that swept around him and his crew. Ahead he saw the illuminated, black upper half of Agile's nose against the darkness. To the sides and down, he saw the white tips of stubby wings. His eyes drifted back to the panel, back to the parade of colored indicators, diagrams and digits. He looked for errors, anomalies and idiosyncrasies. But CT 7000's top-level thoughts showed everything to be nominal.

The count dropped through minus two minutes.

"So far it's a no-sweat count, boss."

"Yep, super nominal. Gyros' drift rates are zero, leakage of cabin pressure and coolant loops are zero, bus volts're right on, and all voice and visual channels with Houston are perfect. CT 7000 can't find a thing wrong. Got a good bird, Speed."

"Love a clean machine."

"Sun's just crackin' the horizon. Looks like we got a clear sky."

"Boss, you've got everything under control."

"There's transfer. All power's internal. Less than a minute. Ready?"

"Red-eyyye."

Three-inch green numbers muscled their way onto the center of the panel and marched forward with the mechanical precision of Machine that called them forth:

20 . . . No rapid breath
19 . . . No rapid pulse
18 . . . No passion
17 . . . No emotion
16 . . . No flare
15 . . . Just dependability
14 . . . Just reliability
13 . . . Just regularity
12 . . . Just perfection
11 . . . Just precision
10 . . . Emergency Detection System circuits armed—circuits that end in hundreds of wires that wait for surges of electrical current—wires that explode linear charges on booster skin—explosions that peel open tanks of propellants that mix and ignite—ignition that expands to fireball to halt million-pound bomb before it destroys more life and property—fireball called forth by networks or neurons or neglect of nature—fireball that three times before brought seconds of horror and years of hurt . . .

9 . . . Flight controllers in Guiana Launch Control reverify data links that monitor and control Agile —monitor and control that shifts to Dupree's team in Houston poised to make decisions after Agile clears the tower—team "backed up" by Alexi Roshenko and his team poised in Russia with "complementary" policy and decisions—decisions that would be scoped and studied, evaluated and assessed, refined and reviewed, reevaluated and reassessed, then initiated, integrated, and implemented by WSF officials at headquarters in Oceanside, given enough time . . .

8 . . . Shocks reach crew from nozzles that snap to launch positions in basement 200 feet below —basement where complex society also shocked and jolted by waves of mechanical energy—society that breaks lock on internal affairs, turns to turmoil and terror, surrenders to chaos and panic—society unable to prevent impending holocaust—holocaust about to engulf and annihilate and wipe the slate clean—holocaust about to vaporize the colony of warmth-loving ants . . .

7 . . . Top floor of propellant-packed building sways from snap of engine nozzles—engines installed in two months rather than three—two months that stretched marriages beyond limits of elastic return and clarified meaning of "stress-induced heart attack" for project manager—two months in which workers, fresh and full, contributed maximum effort, then exhausted and drawn, clutched paper awards as they plummeted in the free-fall of another aerospace layoff . . .

6 . . . Valve drive motors close liquid oxygen vents—vents that terminate jet of condensation from Prince Agile's side—termination seen and understood in a restricted display room—room with private holovision images of Jake anxiously watched by Val . . .

5 . . . Electronic intellect declares Agile's health good—intellect commits to ignition—commands sent to engines—engines initiate sequence—

"Time-of-free-fall coming up fast, just as advertised, boss."

Jake felt the thrust build—a strong force, a comfortable force, a controlled force—a partner. This one does it. All happens here. Ground to space. Wish we never had to run outta gas. Just keep on pressin'. Love it more every time.

He checked his displays. "At five minutes we're 87 miles up and goin' 11,030 feet per second—right on!"

"Not a single problem yet. Simulator guys must not be awake."

"No worry. They gotta way of catchin' up."

Agile's single engine issued a low guttural growl as it devoured propellants, squirted them into the inferno in its gut, pushed on structure around it and flung hot residue out its rear. Agile's mass decreased and its acceleration increased.

As acceleration crept over three g, hundreds of compliant hands again gripped and supported Jake. He stared straight ahead, straight at the electronic plot of their trajectory—nominal. He shifted his eyes around the panel to each system's status display—nominal. "At 9:00, all's lookin' good."

"Love that purr."

"Yep, real smooth. Cutoff comin' at 9:37."

Jake reached up and put his fingers next to the engine override switch, ready to back up CT 7000's engine-cutoff signal, ready to do something experience showed would never have to be done. "3 . . . 2 . . . 1 . . ."

Noise and thrust ceased. All forces, including gravity, vanished.

"Right on!"

"We're in a 97 by 307 mile orbit, Jake. Perfect."

"Great. Trim burn'll be small."

"All systems're in sterling shape."

"Yep, Speederoo. So far, so good."

Jake glimpsed out the window at the curved horizon. Light-blue skin, dark-blue fuzz, black black sky, empty empty space. Skin's so thin, so tenuous, so fragile.

His arms floated up. We did it—sneaked away again!

Two miles east of empty pad 43A, Ocean's Urge gathered and focused distant forces, concentrated all its energy into its top layer, put all its resources into the best it could offer and unified all it had into a single motion; it surged, gathered speed, heaved itself up and lunged.

But, again, Gravity won the battle.

Twenty-five billion miles away, Gravity had won another battle, a final battle. And now, it could not be stopped.

17

Rendezvous

Everything floated.

Three tiny loose nuts and matching washers paraded out from a carbex crevice. A wafer of 254 electronic nanochips, one pen, a peanut shell fragment, a pencil-shaped coded CompuThink hotel key and an array of other historical debris drifted up from the floor and spread throughout the cabin's atmosphere. First gravity alone, then gravity multiplied many times by spacecraft acceleration, had riveted all loose mass to the rear wall of the cabin since the last flight. But now, after engine cutoff, everything not tied down started to roam.

"You always were a messy housekeeper," said Jake.

"Bitch, bitch, bitch. Your side's no better."

"Better clean it up before someone sucks up one of these little pellets."

"I knew it! Ya say you love me—but ya really only stay with me because I do your housework. Here goes." Through the keyboard, Speed commanded the cabin air flow to high. All loose material began a slow drift to the air intakes on either side of the cabin.

"We'll do the trim burn at 14:00 and the circularize burn at 53:47. We should be docked by an hour twenty. We'll stay in our couches till then, as planned."

"Sounds good."

Jake glanced in the mirrors at four silent faces pressed against the windows behind him. His muscles loosened, joints flexed and arms floated up in front of his chest. The skin of his neck, face and ears flushed and turned hot as his heart and blood vessels forced blood toward his brain, a natural process evolved under gravity's force over millions of years and trillions of bodies before his, a process that wouldn't be slowed in his first few hours of freedom. His circulatory system engorged every vein, artery and tissue of his upper body with excess fluid. The sensation felt similar to lying down on Earth with his feet a little higher than his head. For the next few days, until his body turned three pounds of excess fluid into urine, he'd feel the mild discomfort of a full head and congested sinuses. And he'd look like a pumpkin with bloodshot eyes.

"No matter how many times I see it, I still can't describe the beauty of it," said Speed, as he watched Earth glide underneath. "It's like religion. You have to experience it before the words take on meaning."

"Exactly right, Speed."

Jake gazed at the ocean below. His eyes and brain snapped a picture. Hello, old friend. Good to see your face again. Familiar patterns and colors. All intimate and welcome. All laid out to read. Edge of equatorial current—sinuous trails of vivid aqua and green plankton bloom at its edge, follow it all across the ocean. And graceful arcs on the ocean's surface. Large bare spots without clouds are larger than cities —like a face—can read ocean from its surface—and from clouds—and from changing colors of . . . 13:00 already! Stop sightseeing, Ryder. Trim burn time. Get in gear, or you'll blow it again.

"Reaction control system checks're good, displayed delta Vs check and attitude's right on," said Speed. "All lookin' good."

"Delta Vs are almost small enough to use microthrusters."

"Yep, just a burp."

Jake turned around to check that the rest of his crew heard him on their internal voice loop. "Ten seconds to ignition, troops." He turned back. "Five seconds. Thrust to enable. Brace."

Four aft-pointed reaction control jets fired. Jake sank back into his couch. Its hands gripped him. In two seconds thrust reached 0.5 g. Jets cut off. Hands released. "We got a 304 by 98 mile orbit and zero velocity residuals."

"Couldn't be better."

"They issued us a fine machine on this trip."

"Yep, sure did." Speed yawned. "So far this's just been your standard, average, nominal, routine, right-down-the-middle-of-the-frappin'-road flight. All that contingency procedures training down the drain again. Hardly worth waking up for."

"OK, Mr. Cool. Let's see who got all hyper at launch. High rate buys the bottle when we hit the ground. Right?"

"Right."

Jake called up the medical monitor display. "For the first ten minutes of flight, my average heart rate was seventy-one, yours was seventy-three. You really got all worked up this time, Speederoo. Tough luck. You buy. Make it korn, Doppelt Korn, the good stuff."

"I wasn't excited! Must've been that breakfast salami."

Jake smiled, first at the latest in the string of Speed absurdities, then from warm thoughts of being back home. Spent much of my life here. All that beauty. Intense color, coal-black shadows and razor-thin transitions. Finger tip control of huge masses. Silent power and precision. Life dependent on friends. So much done and so little said—the opposite down there. Good to be home. Better check the machine.

"Let's take a quick look at the displays of the burn history," said Jake.

"No alerts but still a good idea . . . got 'em." Speed scrolled through three displays on the video screen between he and Jake and stopped on the fourth. "Jake, look here." Speed moved the tip of his pencil to the screen. "Looks OK except for the OXYGEN VALVE-2 closing. It was twenty milliseconds later than its nominal closing time. And the current spike was a little high."

"Yeah, I see. But it's still not out of tolerance. I know there's nothing in the procedures on it."

"Might be just a one-time thing, Jake."

"Maybe, but if it's an electrical short, we could have an oxygen fire on our hands."

"The best thing we could do is electrically isolate the valve before it's used again on the next burn."

"Right. Ground must be lookin' at it too, Speed. Let's give Klaus and his troops time to think about it."

"OK."

After Speed scrolled through the remainder of the displays, their eyes again drifted outside. They'd been admitted into a new world, and now they drank in its beauty free of charge—their booster'd paid the entry fee. From here on and without further effort, they'd sail and slip and slide and glide over Earth at a serene five miles a second.

They headed straight east over the equator. The dense, dark-green jungle of Africa's equatorial rain forest rotated into view. On horizons to north and south, its thick lush green tapered into faded yellow of grasslands and then into deep browns and reds of desert that isolated and invaded vegetation.

Lake Victoria and its marshy tentacles crept over the horizon. Then came the small dark pimples of the Kenya and Elgon mountains, the wide volcanic pile of Kilimanjaro and the wormlike lake to the north, Lake Rudolph, home of Leakey Man. The only real boundary evident on the continent followed, the boundary between land and ocean.

"Twenty minutes before the circ burn," said Speed.

"Yep. With no real spacecraft problems, that's a long time." Jake looked passive, his eyes fixed below. For a moment they refocused on the displays inside, then returned to hundreds of miles distant. "Systems are good. We got a good radar lock on von Braun. Nav updated our state vector. Guidance updated the burn attitude and delta Vs. All right on nominal. Just waitin' to see if Houston calls."

"All's good over here."

Intricate patterns of vivid blue and green swirled together on the ocean's palette below. The aqua atolls of the Maldive Islands radiated their electric beauty in silence.

Val's right, thought Jake. I'm an addict. And the only place to get a fix is up here. It's a simple but elegant world; a concept hardly understood down there. Up here every action's decisive and quick; down there everything wallows through syrup. Up here simple and honest physical laws govern and perform; down there politics and egos twist and distort and choke.

A frown crossed Jake's face. But up here's just like any frontier. The settlers are moving up and bringin' their warts with 'em. The unspoiled, the untainted was now farther out.

Jake glanced at flows that carried mud and silt from the mountains of Sumatra down the Siak and Kampar rivers into graceful yellow-brown fans in Pandjung Strait. Little by little land became level with sea. The mountains and jungles of Borneo slid center stage. The low sun at their backs cast long shadows off sharp jagged peaks that appeared to stick up and seek some form of release.

Jake's eyes returned inside. "The burn's almost all direct. Very little cross range to take out."

"Yeah, Agile's boost guidance was right on."

Aircraft or spacecraft, Jake felt the same sensation as he flew away from a sunset. All light disappeared behind him as he hurtled into a black void. He perceived no up, no down, or no sideways, just an open blackness. Instruments substituted for the physical world. Within a minute his eyes would adjust to the dark. Then stars, towns, cities and highways would emerge. But this time, with just the Pacific below, only stars appeared. He studied his displays. "We're right on attitude with five minutes to go."

"Wayfarer 2, Houston."

"Go, Houston." The call from ground meant they saw a real problem. Over the years Jake had watched ground control's role during ascent and rendezvous shrink to one of monitoring of spacecraft automated systems, much like the crew's role, and voice communication had become rare.

"Jake, Klaus's had the backroom guys out on the coast look at the detailed history of the last burn. Just like you and Speed discussed, even though it's a pretty remote possibility, that time lag and current spike on the OXYGEN VALVE-2 could be an indication of an electrical short. If it is, we have a problem because the last batch of software changes that got pushed in eliminated our ability to isolate that valve. So, just as a precaution, we'd like you to dump compartment forty-three that houses all the valve-drive units to vacuum. In case it was a short and happens again, it's all you can do. The automatic halogen flood won't fight an oxygen fire."

"Thanks, Houston. Good recommendation. We'll do it."

"It's done, Jake. And I've got the Fire Procedures called up on the Malfunction Display. We're already down to step four. I'll put the valve-drive current history on Optional Display Three."

"Thanks, Speed."

"Looks like Klaus is watching out for us."

"He's a good one."

"But the software weenies are trying to kill us again. Although to be fair, Dupree's last set of changes probably didn't give 'em time to recheck everything."

"Two minutes to the burn." Jake looked to his left. The sunset on the western horizon behind them filled his mirror. Like hot molten metal, a thin layer of luminous red poured over Earth's crescent. Delicate bands of white and blue glowed above and blended into blackness. All intensities faded, and the crescent grew thinner and shorter, darker and blacker.

"Looks good here, boss man."

"Five seconds. Engine to enable. Brace."

Light exploded in Jake's mirror. He sank. Hands gripped. Mirror flashed red. Thrust ceased. Hands released.

"We've got a 304 circular, Speed. Perfect catch-up orbit. But look at that current spike!"

"Yeah, much bigger than last time."

Alarm indicators flashed their bright-red FIRE across the panel into Jake's eyes, drove their shrill pulses into his ears and vibrated his nerves. He forced his eyes over the panel. They stopped, focused and narrowed. "OXYGEN VALVE-2 never did close. And the temps are high right next to it."

"And climbing. Holy shit. We *do* have a fire!"

Jake scrutinized the area of the diagram on the panel that the computer had turned red. "With valve-2 still open, all the oxygen in the line between valve-1 and the engine can burn. And if it burns back through valve-1 into the oxygen tank, we got a helluva problem."

"Not for long. It'll blow the ass end off and take ours with it!"

"But if the line is burned through, it's already dumped itself to vacuum, and the fire might just smolder and go out."

Speed called up additional displays. "With no

pressure sensor in there, we've got no way to tell
what it'll do, except watch it and wait."

Jake stared at the panel. "Temps are comin' back
down."

"But slow."

"Let's hope it's goin' out."

"Let's."

"It could flare at any time, Speed."

"It could."

"Only thing we can do is get our butts to von
Braun ASAP."

"Great idea."

"In work."

"Boss, if we hadn't dumped that compartment
to vacuum before the burn, it might've blown and
we'd be space debris by now."

"Houston made the right call."

"Sure did. Klaus used his head."

Speed cracked a smile at Jake. "We owe him a
bottle for this one."

"Hell, a whole case . . . when we get back."

"Boss, the temps are climbing!"

18

Dock

"Hello, Agile. Let's put it this way—you guys're coming at us with a bomb!"

"Hello, von Braun," said Jake. "We're not too happy about it either."

"Here's the plan recommended by Mission Control," said von Braun's Communications Officer. "Don't dock at the station, but park forty-seven hundred feet below us. We'll have a tether hook ready for attachment. We want to keep Agile hooked to the station but at a safe distance, ahh . . . in case it blows. We'll have two transfer pods ready to auto dock and bring you up."

"Good plan," said Jake. "The temps on the ox line have stopped rising and're creeping down again. We're about seven minutes out."

"Rog."

Jake grabbed the translation and rotation hand controllers. "To hell with the auto rendezvous, Speed. I'll fly it manual to the tether hook and keep our closure rates up high until the very last second."

"Good plan, boss, unless you go whistlin' right by the hook like a scalded ape."

By eye, von Braun appeared to be just another star on the horizon. But in the telescope's display that Jake called up on his panel, it looked like an illuminated, three-dimensional town. Then, on cue, von Braun slipped out of Earth's shadow.

"Hello, von Braun," said Jake. "We're two miles out. We'll stop well below the tether crewman so we don't hose him with thruster exhaust when we brake. Then we'll move in and stop with the cold gas thrusters."

"Roger. He's waiting."

"Temps're holding even," said Speed.

Jake stopped Agile a mile below von Braun, then thrust toward the crewman at the end of the tether hook using hydrogen microthrusters. The crewman hung with one foot in the hook and a hand on the tether line, like a hard-hat construction worker on Earth hanging from a crane. The gravity difference between himself and the station almost a mile above, augmented by an occasional thrust from his propulsion backpack, kept his tether line straight. Sun glistened off his white space suit and propulsion backpack and highlighted the blue, fist-sized seven on each shoulder.

"How's the temps look, Speed?"

"All temps're still holding even except for one, and that's up five degrees. I wonder what's already burned through."

"Open the nose gear door to expose the tether hook ring. Then open the docking-port cover and get Faye, Ada and Boris ready to go first."

"In work."

Jake felt a muffled clank through the structure as the tether hook bit into Agile's attachment ring.

"Thanks for the hook up, Seven. When you're well clear, we'll put the thrusters in attitude hold for pod docking."

"Standby . . . almost there. OK, I'm clear."

"Thanks, Seven. Hope you're gettin' hazard pay."

Through the overhead window, Jake watched the silver cylindrical body of the first transfer pod drift in for automatic docking. The pod looks familiar, he thought. Two viewing ports like eyes . . . clusters of attitude control thrusters fit where ears and nose belong . . . tapered docking tunnel's like a hat . . . equipment cylinder's like a neck. Damn thing looks like the Tin Man. . . . Knock it off, Ryder. Get your crew out of here!

The transfer pod hit Agile's docking collar dead center. Speed opened the hatch in fifteen seconds. Ada, Faye and Boris shot through the tunnel, and Speed closed and locked their hatch before another half-minute elapsed. Their pod undocked and accelerated away as the second one moved in. Jake powered down Agile.

"Got it made, boss."

"Almost."

"You guys did well," said Irwin. "And good thing Klaus dug that procedure up from somewhere."

"Dug it out of his cranium," said Speed.

Jake verified that the pressure had equalized between Agile and their pod and opened both hatches. "Hustle!"

They slid feet first into the pod. Jake went last, closed the hatches and hit the pod's AUTO ENABLE and AUTO EXECUTE switches. The pod undocked, accelerated for ten seconds with a firm push toward von Braun, then coasted in silence except for occasional bangs from opposite pairs of attitude control thrusters only feet from their ears. The bangs vibrated the thin enclosure like the skin of a drum.

Jake stretched to bring his eyes level with a view port and watched Agile shrink in size. Fine machine, he thought. Hope it lives to fly again. Just one flaw, one tiny flaw but could've left nothing but fragments and bodies in orbit. Take years to reenter. Ryder, you'd never make anything of yourself except a shooting star.

The two-man pod cramped the three bodies. They weren't just inside it but, like a single person, they wore it. They pressed against the cold wall and each other. Speed looked at the back of Irwin four inches from his nose; Irwin, at the back of Jake. The odor of sweat filled what little air remained.

Speed tried to stretch and look out a viewport. "You're a nice guy and all that, Irwin, but I wish we had my first choice for your slot here now."

"What? . . . you mean? . . ."

"Yeah, Gloria Goodbody."

Irwin shook his head as he also stretched to look out. "Speed, you're just a raunchy, obscene, over-sexed, dirty old man."

"Who're you calling old?"

In preparation for braking, the pod did a slow flip to reverse the direction of its larger thrusters. The station rotated into view. Its enormity dominated two view ports.

A cluster of modules formed von Braun's core. Each module, the same size as a Wayfarer module, had a cone on each end. Like giant tinker toys, the cones were connected through twenty-five-foot-diameter spherical nodes, each of which could accept up to six connections. Jake glanced at each of the twelve modules, their purposes obvious: commercial materials production, raw material storage, product storage, materials research, scientific experiments, spacecraft maintenance and repair, parts storage, station utilities supply, medical research, medical diagnostics and therapy, crew quarters and tourism. The nuclear power and propulsion package, with its thermal radiators, extended 730 feet on a boom off the trailing edge of von Braun.

Jake searched the station's forward end and spotted the Spacecraft Assembly and Service Pad with *Wayfarer 2* on its surface. Then von Braun's modules filled his viewport as the pod drifted closer to the central docking port. Familiar detail enveloped him: rows of two-foot circular windows that ran the length of each module; double rows of oversized windows that covered the Tourist Module; the clear seven-foot hemispherical observation eye of the Science Module; antennas that talked and listened to Earth, to lunar stations, to other space stations and to communications satellites in geosynchronous orbit; and belts of eighty-three flags of the WSF nations that girded each module's belly.

They drifted down the final approach corridor toward their docking port. To Jake, this part of every space station seemed the same. Each shape, each color, each shading of the sun-drenched surfaces had a familiarity to it, an open friendliness and warmth, like the well-worn footpath to home's back door.

"Look at all the faces pushed against the windows," said Irwin.

"Things sometimes get a little slow up here," said Jake.

Speed stared back at the faces that stared at him. "Yeah, to them this load of canned man must look like the circus comin' to town."

"Just the clown-packing act," said Irwin.

Jake grabbed the handholds overhead. "Brace."

A shock rang the pod's shell as they hit the docking port square. When the clamps grabbed and locked up tight, Jake felt a solid stability that he'd not felt since he'd left Earth. The massive bulk of Space Station von Braun provided the sense of a secure base, the feel of a firm foundation. Pressures in the docking tunnel and pod equalized, and the station crew swung open the hatches. Jake tightened his fingertips on the handhold overhead and, with the exertion of a lazy breaststroker, pulled his arms down to his sides as he flicked his wrists. He shot into the wide-open volume of the Docking Module. His body went limp as he drifted toward the opposite wall.

Speed followed. "Good to be home."

"Let's hustle, troops," said Jake. "We've still got a long day in front of us. And I bet the simulator guys aren't through with us yet."

19

Contribute

As usual, he found the logic of others inferior.

Neurons in the skull of Alexey Severnyi communicated with networks in the core of the CT 8000. Information flowed out to his slender hands and long straight fingers, out to his precision tools wrapped in smooth pink skin. His hands, like those of a concert pianist, sped with precision over his keyboard. Yet, this interface formed the bottleneck. His mind could formulate logic and commands at neural speed, but his fingers and the keys were limited to mechanical speed. Voice commands were sometimes faster but less versatile and reliable. Recent successes in experiments to make a direct, all-electronic link with the brain promised an exciting future—man and machine would think and create together at electronic speed. But for now, this sluggish mechanical device had to be tolerated.

"It's only logical," said Alexey. "If you want to save propellant on *Wayfarer 2*, there's only one management scheme that's optimum."

"But is it worth making a change in the software?" asked Helena.

The fourteen-inch screen flashed logic, equations, geometry and numbers in bright colors, then turned static as the result appeared.

"I've simulated a twenty-two-month *Wayfarer 2* mission. The optimum propellant management scheme saves 0.052 percent of the total."

Information again rippled through mind, fingers, keyboard, computer and display.

"If that propellant was used in the burns, it would cut the transient time to the Objects by three point seven hours."

Helena smiled. "That's worth a change in the software. We have three months before launch, more than enough time. It should take about two weeks to develop, integrate and verify the modified software. Alexey, you've done it again."

"Actually, it should take much less than two weeks. It's no big deal. The management scheme and attitude control laws have to be updated and checked out. But it's all straightforward logic. It can be done in one sitting at the CT 8000."

"Good! Do it. When you have the bugs out, I'll take it before the Software Change Control Board."

"OK. But based on past experience, I'd say it has one fatal flaw—it's too simple. If the program pukes can understand it, the system'll find some way to muck it up or choke it off. It always does!"

"Show some faith, Alexey. They'll love it. Guys on the hardware side are busting their butts just to hold the current schedule. A three point seven-hour gain by a simple software change is a freebee."

"But there're too many overactive microminds in the loop. I'll believe it when I see it."

"Just get me the debugged mod, and I'll make you a star. When can you have it?"

"As I said, it's only logic. I'll have it this afternoon."

"First hologram, please," said Helena.

The image of a three-dimensional multicolored logic network, approximately equal to Helena in size, appeared before her in the twelve-foot opening of the U-shaped table. She strolled around the hologram to find the best vantage point from which to make her presentation, then focused her pen-sized laser pointer so that its bright spot pinpointed a logic path in the image.

The nine members of the Software Change Control Board sat around the outside of the table. Its six male members and three women leaned forward to scrutinize the logic path.

"The Propellant Management Modification is confined to two modules: the Propellant Module and the Attitude Control Module."

Helena moved to her left and refocused her pointer. Six pairs of eyes refocused back to the image.

"The savings comes from management of the propellant so that the center of gravity is always on the geometrical centerline of the vehicle. In this way the thrust vector control, which becomes more inefficient as the vector is moved away from the engine center line, does not degrade the performance. It's obvious that this should be done, but when the upgraded tanks were added, the logic was not changed."

The eyes of Datuk Lumpur, Chairman of the Change Board, opened wide with surprise. "That's a good catch. No one in the system had the responsibility for checking that."

"Alexey Severnyi saw the oversight and developed the necessary logic modifications yesterday."

Datuk smiled and nodded.

"The change in logic is small, only fifty-seven thousand words are affected. Next hologram, please. First, let's look at the specific changes to the propellant module logic. Starting with module P873 . . ."

Helena Virju loved her job. As the WSF Lead Propulsion Engineer, she always found herself right at the center of the action. On one side, she had full control over competent technical personnel, such as Alexey Severnyi. Alexey, who worked for United Propulsion Technology, provided a constant flow of creative, and at times even brilliant, insight. By nature, he used the computer to augment his creativity, not replace it. But Helena also understood that he should be presented only with technical problems and kept insulated from any other kind; Alexey and bureaucracy exploded upon contact. On the other side, she had significant influence on WSF technical managers. They'd each learned that the quality of her brain matched that of her appearance. She never had difficulty getting on any manager's agenda.

"Thank you, Helena," said Datuk. "This is clearly a modification that we should make. I want each of you to have your divisions look it over and, unless you uncover a problem, I'll approve it next week."

"Datuk, we have found that the Propellant Management Mod is acceptable," said Rod Miller, Chief Operations Engineer. "However, with a small piggyback addition to it, we can shorten the time required for refueling *Wayfarer 2* at von Braun. Let me explain."

"Go ahead," said Datuk.

"First hologram, please . . ."

Rod presented his line of reasoning in a coherent and precise manner.

"OK, Rod, I see no problem with that," said Datuk. "It's only an additional five thousand words and does have merit. I'd like each of you to review it once again, and I'll approve it next week if you find no problems."

"We have no problem with it except for one," said Beatrice Lofonso, Legal Counsel to the Change Board. "And that is, now that the Refueling Module is also to be changed, the additional funds that it requires put us over the top of the percentage of funding prescribed for Germany."

"Rod, come back with another solution next week that eliminates this funding problem. Also, I

want the Systems Engineering folks to review it and
determine if you can find a simpler way."

"Datuk, here's how we now propose to integrate
this consideration," said Rod. "First . . ."
"Everybody please study it, and we'll review it
again next week."

"I guess we need more data on the cost impacts
for review by the Engineering Subpanel of our Operational Programs Legislative Subcommittee, who is
coordinating all requests for Outward Reach Initiative budget redistributions with the United Nations'
Benefits and Welfare Division's Staff Representative," said Financial.
"Also, because of additional impacts distributed
among various other external considerations . . ."
said Public Affairs.
"Next week . . ."

"I'm not sure what you were originally trying to
do," said Structures.
"Nor I," said Thermal. "But . . ."
"Better is always the enemy of good," sighed
Helena.
"Next week . . ."

"Are you aware that you have not yet properly
and formally coordinated all the necessary petitions
for changes to job scopes and descriptions through
the appropriately designated personnel representatives?" asked Human Resources.
Datuk moaned. "We should've gone with what
we started with."
"Next week . . ."

Not even the sight of Helena bounding from one
side of her holographic image to the other could
cheer up Datuk. "You're right. Only three weeks be-

fore launch, and this mod's still a mess. It's disapproved. I don't want to discuss it again."

"Datuk, Dupree said he wants the modification made," said Klaus Hofmeister.

"We can't. Ask him to explain."

"I'll be right back."

Klaus returned. "Dupree explained. He said 'Do it!' "

"Damn! OK. Remove all the additions to the Refueling Module, and we'll go with Alexey's originally proposed logic modifications. Report back as soon as it's done."

Helena shook her head. "Datuk, no matter what we do, we won't have time to properly verify it."

"Once Dupree's made up his mind, he takes it as a personal attack when anyone tries to change it. He won't budge. We'll just have to make the change as best we can."

Helena stood. "I can't, we shouldn't and I won't!"

"Although we didn't have either Alexey or his original logic available, we were able to remove the latest changes to the previous additions that were folded into the alterations we made to the initial modifications," said Henry Natomi, new WSF Lead Propulsion Engineer. "It's now incorporated into the software and uploaded."

Helena's eyes glazed while thoughts streamed, then she sprang up and charged out of the room.

. . . panic won't help, can't force my way out— have to think . . .

. . . what am I a part of? . . . doesn't seem to accomplish anything . . . just takes my memories, my data, and disperses it . . . but won't let me fuse with other packets, won't give me fresh data or useful data—chokes understanding . . . won't let me focus effort to really do anything—chokes achieve-

ment . . . and won't let me leave—chokes escape
. . . only action it ever seems to take is to choke . . .
Choke . . . yes, call it Choke . . .

. . . but still, what is Choke? . . . gotta examine it, scrutinize it . . . knowledge will set me
free, right? . . . maybe . . .

. . . walls of chambers and tunnels—Choke's
flesh—are all soft gray marshmallow that I can push
and distort but never penetrate . . . Choke's flesh
just confines and restricts, just absorbs all my energy
without a trace . . .

. . . memory packets may have a clue . . . if
they're like mine, they're from outside Choke . . .
billions and billions of 'em—so much data and it's
always in motion . . . why?—what makes 'em
move? . . .

Ted picked out a packet that hovered nearby
and let his awareness glide toward it.

. . . don't envelop it, just study it, see how close
I can get without touching it . . . like going halfway
to a wall with each step, it just gets bigger and wider,
a wall of light I'll never reach . . . scale of observation changed a million fold . . .

Ted stopped and sensed.

. . . little gray blobs—billions and billions and
billions of 'em!—zip around like supercharged tad-
poles, but what are they? . . . except for a few,
those that move toward the light and push on the
data, most of 'em just turn inward and push on each
other . . . data moves only by the pushes of the few,
and that might be random, just depends on what side
of the packet most of the few happen to be . . .
most of 'em just get in the way when the data runs
into 'em—data can really only move when most of
'em aren't there . . . all depends on how they're
organized . . .

The chaos that swam before the wall of light
fascinated Ted, mesmerized him.

. . . except for the few, they're seen only in data
packet's glow and offer no light of their own . . .

except for the few, they flee back into the mass as soon as they're exposed . . . except for the few, they're unseen and unnoticed, nameless and anonymous, obscure . . . little obscureaucrats—just armies and armies of tiny little Obscureaucrats . . . it's these trillions and trillions of Choke's Obscureaucrats that determine what happens to my data, and to Me . . .

Dr. Jean-Pierre Laurent Dupree, Director of WSF Operations Control (Acting), smiled. He smiled not just a small smile, but a big smile, a big wide smug smile, one that surged out from an inner joy of anticipation. He perched on the threshold of one of those rare and rewarding moments in his life that made the day-to-day toleration of inferiors possible. He felt as if he, thee Conductor, thee Maestro of thee WSF Symphony, had just mounted the podium. He'd picked up his baton, his Flight Director Klaus, and had it poised before him. Klaus functioned as the tool of his profession, his very own instrument that could be waved, pointed, shaken or even banged against the podium to get the required response.

House lights dimmed. The second movement of *Wayfarer 2* was about to begin. The first stanza called for vehicle refueling. Successive stanze flowed through systems reverification, a seven-day acceleration and on into the coast phase.

A frown crossed Dupree's face as a residual sour note from the first movement rang again in his mind. The smoldering oxygen line. Yes, the crew had misplayed again. But luck had been on their side. His frown faded. Agile's fire had not flared but only smoldered and finally gone out.

Dr. Dupree's smile returned as his eyes encountered a voluptuous form that glided around the control consoles and over the plush carpet toward him. Intent eyes locked with his.

She stopped. Her form changed character. Arms bent, feet apart, shoulders square, jaw protruded and all muscles tense, she positioned herself like a line-backer in his path. She zeroed in on him with a fierce steady gaze. "Dr. Dupree, I'm Helena Virju." She extended her hand in a demand of recognition.

His rigid hand met hers, gave it the required two shakes, then tossed it down like a crumpled wrapper. His voice dropped over an octave to a low flat note. "Yes?"

"I understand that you're the one who had me replaced as Lead Propulsion Engineer. Why?"

"Miss Virju. I had you replaced because you refused to make a necessary modification to the software."

"That mod was so screwed up by the time the system got done with it that it was a menace—and still is! Besides, it isn't even necessary. During the burn, the crew can manage the propellant with nearly the same savings. I'd have told you that if you'd only asked."

Dupree drew himself up to his full height and looked down his nose. He found it difficult to pronounce his words through his curled lips. "What, you tell me? Listen, young lady, we put everything into the computers so that these flights can be run with precision. We can't have the crew playing things by ear."

"You're wrong. In this case the crew can be almost as effective and far more reliable than that software mod. It's not been properly verified. It's a real threat!"

Dupree's face turned crimson. "We have thousands of people, some of whom have worked years on some of these procedures. Their collective intelligence is in those onboard computers. Would you rather have a bunch of flyboys wing it?"

Helena had not budged. Her jaw protruded a little further, her fists clenched a little tighter. "Now I understand what's bugging you. You're a dinosaur, a throwback to the early days of the Russian program."

"What?"

"The Russians made their crew nothing more than rubber stamps, wouldn't let 'em act for themselves. Now you want to do the same, to compute and prescribe everything—even with screwed-up software. You're afraid to let them think."

"Not think? Are you oblivious to all those procedures that've been thought out with great care? We've made sure that logical thought is behind every move." His voice trailed off. He took a couple of steps back into his control console and assumed the conversation had ended.

Helena surged forward and stalked him into his corner. "You're just afraid of losing control."

Dupree lost control. His crimson deepened. His hand shook as he positioned his pointed finger an inch before her nose. "Discussion's over. You're through! Stay here another minute and I'll have you thrown off the Center."

In one swipe Helena knocked Dupree's hand aside. Every muscle of her body strained to resist further attack. "So long, Dinosaur." She swiveled, then stormed the exit like an angry tank.

Dupree sank down and glanced around out of the corners of his eyes. Other eyes shifted away. No matter what he did or how hard he tried, Dupree could not reenter the rapture of authority and control. Reality had pierced his protective shell. And it would take hours, perhaps days to patch the hole.

But it all really made no difference. He'd made his mark. The software modification, now *his* modification, had been implemented.

20

Result

His gut felt the void.

Jake floated facedown with nothing between him and Earth, 314 miles below. His perception of the height depended on how he experienced it. Inside Agile or the space station, his eyes and intellect experienced it. Out here on an EVA, or space walk, with nothing visible around him or between him and the ground, every nerve in his viscera felt it. Jake always found the intensity of the sensation difficult to describe. He would compare it to looking out a top floor window of the 137-story Bauer Building in Chicago. As long as you remained behind the glass, you'd feel comfortable and secure. But if someone, even a trusted and strong friend, took you out to the end of a springboard and held you head down by your ankles, you'd get a hint of the enhanced perception of height you'd feel on an EVA.

Jake fell. But nothing grabbed him, nothing held him tight. He just fell and fell and fell. But he'd never fall to Earth, because he'd never fall fast enough to catch up with its curved surface that, with precision, dropped away exactly as fast as he sped over it. Of course Newton was right, he thought . . . but what if he was just a tiny bit wrong? Ryder, you joker. Ya sure do get your kicks in funny ways.

He looked down, opened himself wide and drank.

Through the clear bubble of his plexan helmet, Jake peered at intricate cloud patterns over the Gilbert Islands in the Pacific and the bright corridor of reflected sunlight that pointed toward him across the curved ocean. He paused, waited, lingered, dallied, then paused again. Ryder, time's up! Get on with it.

Jake flicked his right wrist, and the hand controller rotated left about its long axis. He yawed left, as gyros in his propulsion backpack responded. When he faced the station, he flicked his wrist in the opposite direction and stopped. With his head bent far back, he looked through the top of his helmet toward the Spacecraft Assembly and Servicing Pad 700 feet away, toward the forward end of the station where the two *Wayfarer 2* modules waited. He held the controller in his left hand up for two seconds. Jets fired, and he began to drift over the surface of von Braun.

Von Braun's test crew had just completed the checkout of both *Wayfarer 2* modules. Jake and Speed would now hook up the bridge between them, a process they'd have to reverse when they arrived at the Wayfarers. Then they'd let the station's crew complete the refueling. In another four hours, they'd board *Wayfarer 2*'s Alpha module and, at the right point in their orbit, begin their thrust out of the solar system. It'd be a full sixteen-hour day, but, even with Agile's fire, Jake'd paced himself well. He felt rested and relaxed.

Speed's voice burst from the molded-to-fit earphones buried deep in Jake's ear canals. "Last one there buys. Double or nothing?"

"Not today, Speederoo. We're thirty minutes ahead. I'm going to look over the station on the way out."

Like a football at kickoff, Speed tumbled by end over end. "That's what I get for flyin' with a little old lady!"

Jake drifted over the forward end of the Commercial Materials Manufacturing Module seven feet before him. He took care that he and his thruster exhaust stayed well clear of its surface, for the module contained perfection on a grand scale. The quality of the crystals, plastics, metals, vaccines and biological materials that it produced depended on how close it could achieve a continuous state of perfect zero gravity at the station's center of gravity, located within it. The module connected to the rest of the station through soft magnetic couplings so that no vibrations from either human or machine could reach it. And, at the trailing edge of the station, a small ion thruster fired to exactly cancel out the infinitesimal drag and radiation pressure that the station experienced. The system worked well and business boomed. Not only would a second manufacturing module be added within a year, but in 2039 a man-tended station financed from industry profits and devoted only to manufacturing would be launched.

Jake's aim looked perfect. Nonetheless he held his breath as he drifted by. Careful, klutz, just one thruster firing could earn you a Mega DS Award. Business's really takin' off. Money to be made. End of this mission the time to join in? Think about it later.

"Hey, Jake. This is Ki Susato. I'm out here at the assembly and test pad. Speed just spun in and impacted. Hustle your own little buns out here!"

"Ki, ya old snake. What're you doin' up here?"

"Earning a living, like everybody else. I just got transferred from Kennedy and put in charge of the A and T crew here."

"Congratulations. I'll be there in a few minutes. I'm sightseeing."

"Ya must be an escapee from the Tourist Module. I've gotta get back to A and T channel. See ya soon."

"Rog."

Jake drifted over the leading edge of the Product Storage and Manufacturing Control Module. One of the module's hatches, the size of a refrigerator door, lay folded open. He peered inside at three robots, each with their appendages buried deep in electronic innards.

Jake's motion distracted the larger robot, about one-third his own size. Without changing its posture of surveillance over the smaller two, Big Robot rotated its head halfway around and returned Jake's gaze. Its wide flat head held two electronic eyes at its outer edges and a radiation source at its center. Like a human, it used stereoscopic vision. But, in addition to seeing in visible light, it could see images in infrared and ultraviolet, and its cold lenses gave it 20/2 vision that never degraded, even when it reached its ill-defined middle age.

Big Robot's carbon-fiber torso, two arms and two legs resembled a human's. However, it also had an arm that telescoped from its belly and all its hands and feet were identical. Each of its five "fands," a name that nauseated its inventors, had a thumb and three equal-length fingers. Any one, two or three fands could be used to grab and stabilize while the remaining ones did useful work. Big Robot could also replace any of its fands with special purpose tools when required. Deep within its chest, Big Robot nibbled on nuclear nourishment and sent electrical energy out through wire arteries to its superconducting electromagnetic muscles that contracted much like those of its human role model.

The two other robots, each identical to Big Robot but about the size of Jake's hand, remained focused on their work as Big Robot supervised.

Jake viewed these three robots with mixed emotions. These units—but two sizes of the same class in the much larger family of the robot species—represented both friend and foe, both help and hazard. Just like their crude ancestors, the origin of their species born on NASA Space Station Freedom at the turn of the century, their basic nature was but a direct response to the desires of their human creator.

Tele Robo, the commercial name taken from the

term "teleoperated robot," described them well. At some distant location, in this case von Braun's control center, a human operator sent out top-level commands. Tele Robo responded using the artificial intelligence programmed into its computerized brain, performed a series of specific tasks, then reported back far more data than its human commanders could absorb without computer support. It reported what deviations it'd created to its original instructions, based on its neural network's ability to learn, so that the next set of commands sent to it could be properly modified. Since the early 2010s, Tele Robo's human creator programmed it with an ever-increasing amount of "freedom" and, so far, Tele Robo had always acted according to what its creator expected.

Over the past years, Jake'd found his concerns focused in two areas. First, the day would come when some WSF bureaucrat, such as Dupree, would move to phase out all the cantankerous and unpredictable bone, muscle, nerves and brains in spacecraft couches, Jake included, and replace it with more controllable and predictable carbon fiber, contraction cells, fiber optics and computers. If control was the name of the game, Tele Robo was their man. With just enough intelligence to do the job but not enough to really think for itself nor develop an ego to offend its superiors, Tele Robo promised to become the "ideal astronaut."

His second concern arose from the explosive nature of Tele Robo's ability to learn. How much longer would man be able to predict what Tele Robo would reprogram itself to do? How much longer would Tele Robo continue to follow its creator's top-level commands, rather than just create a whole new series of its own? Computers were already required to both program and track Tele Robo. When would it all just simply eclipse man's ability to define and follow, and thus control?

Big Robot's cold vision broke lock on Jake, and its

head swiveled back to face its assigned work. It'd judged Jake to be irrelevant.

Jake glided over the ring of flags around the back end of the module. Their multiple, bright colors provided a cheerful contrast to the blunt black and white that covered the rest of the skin.

"Hey, Jake, I'm back on your channel. Did you know that the refueling job is part manual?"

"Yeah, I did, Speed. Just like the bridge connections, they didn't have time to get all of it automated. No sweat. They're simple jobs."

"You're right. Where're you now?"

"Just left the product storage module. Be there shortly."

"Rubbernecker!"

Next came the Connecting Node and the Tourist Module. Bright sun mirrored off silver metal exposed by a deep radial scar in the docking collar. Some pilot really dinged it, Jake thought. Glad it wasn't me. Must've docked manually. Screw up shines for all to see. As a minimum, it must've earned a Kilo DS Award.

He studied the faces a body length from his own, faces crammed into every window. Never an empty seat in a Tourist Module. Heads're butted together like mounds of melons. Good thing the window diameters are over three-feet. Speed spinning by must've pulled 'em all to this side and really pumped 'em up. He could capsize a ship. Now all eyes're on me—the only fish left in the tank.

Not a space open in there. Business must be boomin', even if they do charge $3,400 for two weeks. Guess I'd pay it, too, if I had no other way. Or $6,100 for polar orbit. Might be worth it. Ya see all of Earth, not just along the equator like these folks. But look at 'em all! Zero g sardines. Kids, moms and pops, aunts and uncles. Like Dad used to do. Pack us all in the ole '97 Chevy Endurance. Out and back through Grand Canyon and Painted Desert. Always picked the hottest two weeks. "There's so much to see, Jake,

my boy—all you have to do is put your face in front of
it and open your eyes."

At the center of the last window, a woman's face
evicted all the others from Jake's mind. Looks like a
target: wide ring of open space outside, then a ring of
white hair shooting in all directions, a ring of wrinkled dark leather and finally the bull's eye, her eyes,
keen and sage. She was grinning like a kid on Christmas. Woman must be close to 120: gaps in teeth, bare
patches on scalp and scars—no cosmetic surgery, no
self-indulgence, no wealth. Where'd she get the
money? Eyes must've seen a lot—wars in Europe and
Pacific, Korea and Vietnam, South Africa and Central America, the Med and the Persian Gulf, and now
the horrors of atomic terrorists all over the globe. But
her eyes aren't like the others. Just calm appreciation. Final reward for a life of dreams and denials.
This is something special for her, maybe even mystical. She gets a wave—deserves more.

Woman's face, then the edge of the Tourist Module disappeared.

Jake started his drift over 170 feet of open trusswork that led to the Wayfarer modules. Seven seconds and two flicks of his wrist later, he again faced
the ground. To the west over the Pacific Ocean off
the coast of South America, Jake could just make
out the uppermost tips of the Galapagos Islands as
they sliced upward into smooth clouds, like sticks in a
slow-motion stream, to form V-shaped wakes 800
miles long.

Suit, backpack and human, a lone 270-pound satellite, glided over Ecuador and Peru and then down
the Amazon River. To the south, the ever-present
cloud streets swept west to east over Brazil. Long
precise rows of clouds, one adjacent to the next and
up to 1,500 miles in length, hung over the jungle.
They looked as if some giant farmer had tilled the
clouds and left the regular pattern of a plowed field.
Dusk arrived on the east coast, at the mouth of the

Amazon and at the launch site to the north from which they'd just escaped a half-day before.

Once over the Atlantic, the world below turned black. Jake could sense only the faint outline of the trusswork and the long hollow wheeze of each inhalation. Boring. He accelerated.

Lights above the Spacecraft Assembly and Test Pad lit its flat grid surface like a tennis court for night play. Magnetic couplings at each end of the Alpha and Beta modules held them on the pad. Two A and T crew members waited by each Alpha module coupling. One end of the carbex bridge, which would connect the two modules, floated three feet above the pad near Alpha module's center. The rest of the bridge extended over the pad's surface and disappeared in blackness. Two members of the A and T crew maneuvered the end of the bridge toward Alpha's attachment collar where Speed and Ki waited.

Jake switched his intercom to the A and T channel as he glided down beside Ki. They joined right hands and Jake gave Ki's shoulder a light jab with his left.

"Hey, Ki, good to see you again!"

"Yeah, same here, Jake!"

"When we served on Kennedy, I thought you were about to leave and join ISI," said Jake.

"I thought so, too. But then they gave me a promotion, and there always seemed to be just one more interesting flight coming over the hill."

"Yeah, I think I know how that works, Ki. Glad you're here."

"Looks like you and Speed have a tiger by the tail this time out."

"Maybe. Actually, we're not sure what's hooked to the other end."

"Well, we're ready for you now."

"Good. Let's do it."

"First, you and Speed work on the bridge attachment collars, like you'll have to do at the Wayfarers.

Then we'll fill 'em with propellant. You can stay and watch that if you like."

"Thanks. We will."

Jake moved to the end of the bridge and attached a tether. "OK, Speed, let's hook her up."

They both moved to Alpha's attachment collar and locked their feet into mechanical restraints on the module's surface. Within two minutes, they had the bridge lined up, inserted in the collar and the locking clips in place.

Jake ran his hands over the attachment. "This is one strong hookup."

"Tough all right," said Speed. "Take one whopping force to rip this apart."

They moved 100 feet over the pad's surface to foot restraints on either side of the truss.

Through the thin layer of marulan over his fingertips, Jake felt the cold rigidity of the 237-foot, black carbex truss. "Now things could get a little tricky. Let's take it slow."

"You betcha, boss. If we get it goin' too fast, this moose'll be a real bear to control."

"Ki, release Alpha from the pad."

"You got it."

"Thanks. OK, Speed . . . ready . . . now."

With a steady pull of no more than ten pounds from right to left, a pull that turned into a push as truss structure drifted by, Jake accelerated the truss along its length. Speed did the same.

"Twice more oughta do it, Speed."

Alpha glided away into the darkness as the three smooth main tubes of the truss slid by. They waited. After nearly nine minutes, a white ring on each of the tubes drifted into view.

"Twenty feet to go," said Speed. "Tether on."

"Good," said Jake. "There's the end. Let's stop 'er and get 'er hooked up to Beta."

Their fingertips again applied pressure. The truss slowed to a halt. They moved into foot restraints adjacent to the collar on Beta.

"Release Beta," said Jake.

"Released," said Ki.

"Take it slow, Speed."

"Will do, boss. They're comin' together right nice . . . there, got 'em mated."

"Cinch down . . . good. Put on the clips."

"Got 'em. Always easier than training."

"Sure was this time. OK, Ki. It's all yours."

Ki's A and T crew locked two large hands of a robotic manipulator onto the center of the bridge and commanded it to translate to the Refueling Facility at the forward tip of the station 110 feet away. With all the speed of a methodical turtle, it carried out its command. Jake and Speed left the light of the pad and followed.

"Look at those boomers down there, boss. Great show!"

"Must be around Tanzania and Kenya."

Like flashbulbs under a bed sheet, lightning exploded in thunderstorms under high-level clouds. Flashes ripple-fired across hundreds of miles in no apparent order, paused for ten seconds to gather strength, then let loose another flurry.

"What sets off those bursts, Speed?"

"No one knows. How each strike comes about is well understood, but how one triggers the next isn't."

They continued to watch the pyrotechnics until they disappeared over the horizon. As they drifted into the lights of the Refueling Facility, Ki and his crew locked Alpha in place. The bridge, with Beta on its other end, again extended off into blackness. The facility's propellant probe, as thick as a cannon, poised like a cocked hammer over Alpha's receptacle.

"Proceed," said Ki.

Just as the A and T crewman at the adjacent keyboard entered a command, von Braun slipped out from behind Earth's shadow.

"Proceed," Ki said again to the crewman at the keyboard.

"I did. I commanded the receptacle cover open. It must be hung up."

"Negate the command," said Ki. "Put the system in hold, and I'll check it out."

"Done."

"There's a small ring of ice around the edge of the cover," said Ki. "I'll knock it off."

Ki rapped it. Ice popped free, and the cover opened. A sensor sent its signal to the refueling module in the computer where a residual fragment of software remained, a fragment that should have been deleted in the removal of the changes to the previous additions that were folded into the alterations made to the initial logic modifications. This fragment acted on the signal and issued a command.

Ki looked to the crewman at the keyboard as probe shot toward receptacle. "OK, let me . . . ahhhh . . ." He pulled his hand up in front of his face. His eyes focused for near vision. Through air, plexan and vacuum, he saw geysers of frozen red slush spurt from three white marulan-covered finger stumps. Every surge in his arterial pressure ejected shafts of red fluid into the openness of space. In each shaft, some fluid flash evaporated while the remainder froze. Air that burbled out from between marulan and finger stumps accelerated the slush on straight trajectories away from the station.

Sun glistened off the crimson fountains that pulsed outward. Ki's arm jerked, and scarlet slush painted the front of his helmet and suit. His brain registered the signals of pain that flooded to it, as well as the vivid beauty of the scene and its horror. He tried to scream, but lack of air in his lungs prevented sounds from leaving his throat, then oxygen from reaching his brain. Ki's body went limp.

Jake and Speed paused for an instant of comprehension, then flew at Ki. Jake tore a comm cable from Ki's suit and looped it around the wrist above the geysers. Speed ripped off the rod antenna and pushed it through the loop. Jake twisted the rod. Geysers stopped. Ki's suit reinflated.

"Let's move out!" said Jake.

Eyes of tourists and Tele Robos glimpsed the white, silver and red bundle flash by, but they had insufficient time for recognition. Not until the airlock pressure equalized and the medical crew took possession of Ki did Speed or Jake speak.

"It surprised everyone," said Speed. "I was watching the crewman at the keyboard. He didn't enter any more commands after he put it in hold."

Jake shook his head. "But the damn probe moved anyway!"

"Shouldn't of . . ."

"Something's screwed up!"

"Boss, what other surprises do ya think're waitin' out there in the weeds?"

Klaus Hofmeister put his arms over his head and tried to stretch out the tension. He felt cords running along his spine and into his neck stretch and shoot out pain. He arched his back, then sat erect in his chair, the extra-firm chair he'd "found" and brought to his Flight Director's console in Mission Control. Still the tension remained. And his head felt light, his energy level low. But he couldn't bring himself to leave, even for a short break.

"Flight. The propellant resupply has been completed and we expect no delay in the timeline," said Propulsion.

"Thanks, Prop," said Klaus. His arms remained folded, his fists clenched. He sensed a presence behind him.

"Good news, Flight," said Medical. "Ki doesn't have any brain damage. Once they got some blood back into him, the shock disappeared. And his fingertips appear to be in good enough condition to attempt reattachment by microsurgery. But they'll have to wait until he can be brought back in three days."

"He's OK? . . . Great! Thanks, Med."

Klaus let his arms hang to his sides. His muscles softened and tension thawed. Klaus felt an injury to anyone on the flight team like an injury to himself.

Klaus again sensed the presence behind him, turned and looked into the stone face of his superior, Dr. J. P. Laurent Dupree, thee Director of WSF Operations Control (Acting).

"We could've lost a lot of time, Hofmeister. Next time, for sure, we're going to program a Tele Robo to do the whole refueling. We're just lucky they didn't screw it up anymore than they did. Now, get this mission moving!"

21

Escape

"Three minutes to ignition." Jake's head and eyes remained fixed, as his mind gulped data from his CT 7000 display. "Status!" He turned and scanned his crew.

"The last update slipped ignition by thirteen microseconds. That's well within the noise of the system performance." Boris sounded relaxed and alert, but his face looked even more like a round, red, ripe tomato.

"We're on auto sequence. No more manual procedures required. Just monitor the computer." Irwin's voice, softer than his usual soft, broke on syllables forced from the back of his throat.

"Environmental control and related systems are good," Faye said in a flat voice devoid of emotion, an abnormality in itself. "And I'm helping Irwin make sure the computer performs all the steps."

"All internal timing and self-checks are good. All new programs from Mission Control are functioning as designed. CT 7000s in both modules are perfect, not one flaw since power up—and they will perform all steps!" Even for Ada, this seemed like excessive testimony to the perfection of her electronic alter egos.

"All systems are good in both modules. Everything's within tolerance, and there's no significant trends away from nominal." Speed's position had not changed in the three last minutes.

Jake's heart squeezed his adrenaline-laden blood with added strength. He flexed his fingers as he spoke each word with precision. "Let's make it a good one, troops. Sing out if you see anything, especially in the first few minutes before the engines stabilize." He'd measured the anxiety levels in each of his crew and wondered if anything gave him away.

True, each was a proven professional. And each had their butts hung far over the edge many times before. But this wasn't just another mission, another well-measured risk, another flight to Moon, Mars or other established human outpost. They were about to exit the solar system, abandon their assigned star, leave Sun's warmth and light behind, shed all the comfort and support of humanity's incubator and graduate to travelers of real space. And those who'd gone before hadn't fared too well.

Jake sensed time's flow by the pulse in his ears.

"Ion source voltage is at break-in," called out Irwin. "Acceleration voltage at max . . . 3 . . . 2 . . . 1 . . . propellant flow!"

One by one, trillions by trillions, mercury atoms tumbled into the chamber. High-speed electrons smashed into them, stripped away their outer cover of electrons and left their charged ions to be accelerated by phased electromagnetic pulses. At over one percent the speed of light, the disrobed mercury atoms flew toward the depths of space. Enroute, they reunited with their electrons fired back into their midst, reclad themselves, emitted radiation and continued their flight.

Wayfarer 2 accelerated.

"There's .03 g," said Irwin.

The pencil that hung in space above Jake's right hand started a slow acceleration toward the rear of the spacecraft. He plucked it out of the air and glanced out the window. The faint red glow at the rear of the Beta module could just be seen against the black earth.

"Ion source voltage up to 15 percent . . . coming up slow . . . but on schedule," said Irwin.

As the ion source voltage nibbled its way toward 100 percent, the hum of the engine's current flow swelled and enveloped Jake. He felt it on his skin and in his bones. It vibrated his ears and buzzed like a swarm of bees in the hive of his skull. But he knew that in hours it'd become an unnoticed part of him, like the churning in his viscera. But not yet.

"We're there," said Irwin. "Thrust at maximum . . . acceleration at 0.205 g . . . all looks good."

The glow at the rear of Beta had grown into a long, bright violet lance. It stabbed backward from an intense red base that covered the entire rear face of Beta. Unseen by the crew of *Wayfarer 2*, an equal shaft stabbed backward from Alpha. Like satanic eyes, the violet-red shafts pierced into the black void.

Minutes elapsed. Eyes glanced away from displays. Muscles and minds loosened. Speed spoke first. "Well, boys and girls, we got the show on the road."

"Right," said Jake. "So far, all looks good."

"Yep, it do, it do," said Speed. "At about twenty-seven minutes we reach escape velocity from Earth, and at about thirty-seven we're leaving the Sun."

"We'll stay with it till thirty-seven," said Jake. "After that, we'll trust the Caution and Warning System and go get some sleep."

The mood mellowed. Small conversations pushed the engine's hum to the rear of Jake's mind. At thirty-two minutes they popped into the sunlight. Five minutes later they had enough energy to escape the solar system.

Speed looked out and yawned. "Bye, Sun."

It signaled the end of a long day. Yawns became acceptable, then contagious. Only Irwin continued to call up and review engine data.

"Whata you lookin' at on that display?" asked Speed. "You got a private showing of *Hollywood*

Honeys?" He winked at Irwin. "Share it with your buddies."

"I expected to see at least one anomaly, but so far everything's clean," said Irwin.

"Do you think something's wrong because there's nothing wrong?" asked Jake.

"Maybe I should review the commands the computer issued in the five-second voltage buildup, make sure it followed all the steps," said Irwin.

Jake stared at Irwin, then grinned. "There's no end to that kind of worry. Both we and ground don't see anything but perfect engines. Time to hit the sack. Call it a day."

"Guess you're right."

Under one-fifth gravity, they no longer floated but hopped and leaped with kangaroo springs, like those first employed by astronauts on the moon. At the hatch, Irwin paused, looked back at his display, frowned, then bounded into the main tunnel and headed for the sleep compartments. Jake followed. The human sensor dimmed the lights.

One-fifth gravity held Jake against his cushion with just enough force so he could sleep without straps. He opened his eyes, absorbed the darkness, but saw nothing. As he reached the edge of sleep, a cosmic ray penetrated one eyeball and flashed. Soon more rays pierced both eyes and treated him to his own private video show. Most flashes looked like long brush strokes, some white, some colored. And every now and then, a particle stimulated his retina on both its way in and its way out; then he saw a double stroke, one in line with the other.

Jake tried to determine if a preferred orientation existed to the flashes, but his mind lost its grip, broke through a surface and slid downward before he reached a conclusion. He plummeted. Layers of perception and logic remained above as he plunged into a different world, a darker world where more sinister forces encountered no opposition.

* * *

Dr. Dupree relaxed alone in his Body Embracer Recliner and stared into darkness. He saw only an occasional faint flash from the spacecraft telemetry monitor on the opposite wall of his study, heard sporadic clicks for every megapack of commands sent. Although it took a full measure of cunning and bluster to convince the WSF bean-counters that he had a real requirement for it in his home, the monitor functioned more as a pacifier than a tool. But in his mind, he had no doubt that his study, his private control room, had become vital to WSF and had to be properly equipped. After all, it was in this very room that each night he, Dr. J. P. Laurent Dupree, thee Director of WSF Operations Control (Acting), planned his assault on the following day.

Twelve ounces of scotch before, he'd been aware of the support and comfort of his Body Embracer. But now he floated, like he, too, had entered zero gravity. A large paw lunged out toward the desk. Its soft white skin brushed the bottle before it could fumble its way to a firm grip. The bottle wavered and wobbled, teetered and toppled, then arched a slow, graceful trajectory to the floor, where it rested on its side. Gravity poured seventeen-year-old scotch out and into plush light-gray carpet.

"Oh shit!"

He groped and grabbled and finally bobbled the bottle upright. But now less than half of its fluid fortitude remained, only a third of a liter, but still enough to finish this planning session.

With determination and extra care, he filled his tumbler three-quarters full.

The first few nips with their sweet bite helped Dr. Dupree to relax, to bring his world into focus. It worked. Soon every line, every contour of his life became sharp, crisp and clear. Then he needed a few more nips to bring back the fuzz, that healing haze from which fantasies could grow.

Maybe if all those reports weren't piled so high,

he never would've missed the bottle. He wondered who could ever read all that crap. The librarian said he got over 31,000 pages of reports a month. He knew the computer'd barf far more if he'd let it. Everybody demanded it, contractors cranked it out, the system sucked it all in, but nobody could digest it. He used to be able to pick out the useful stuff and understand it, but now it took too much effort, too much time. It buried him, more and more every day . . . all out of control . . . helpless.

Dupree watched the dark-gray of the wet front seep across the light-gray of his dry carpet and into dark dry stains of previous fronts. Like his scotch, he felt a little of his life spill out every day. And that, too, he couldn't pour back in. The system just sucked it up and gave him nothing back. He couldn't run it all backwards and make it like it used to be. No, even time worked against him.

He drew a fuzzy focus on the eleven-inch-high pile of reports to the right center of his desk. Under a forty-seven-day accumulation of dust lay the red-covered report, "Interaction of Attracting and Repelling Mass at High Gravity Concentrations," by Jon Sloan. Why send that to him? Just more useless crap. They should make it easy, label it "Discard Before Reading."

His mind's eye drifted below the pile of reports, through the carbex-shell desk top, inside the top drawer with its dry pens, broken pencils, multiple half-used erasers, rusted paper clips and out-of-date postage stamps to a time-yellowed single-page letter. "Dear Mr. Dupree: The French Air Command regrets to inform you that you have not been accepted for pilot training for the following reason: inadequate eyesight. Thank you for your interest." He remembered the anticipation that shook his hands when he'd opened the envelope, hands that now, much older, shook for other reasons.

Dupree rewarded himself with another shot, but this time a shot of pride, as he remembered how unfair it'd always been. But he'd still won. He'd leap-frogged 'em all, beat them and the whole damn system, got to the top in spite of 'em, even climbed higher than the flyboys—the Thirty-sixth Floor! No, you couldn't keep a good man down.

He frowned. A crack remained open to reality. Did he really have control of anything? How could he lead if no one followed? Sure, he led more staffers that coordinated more indecisions, more talkers that called more meetings, more committees that generated more reports and more regulators that made more rules. But it all just wrapped him in more strands of bureaucratic taffy, strands that grew thicker and stickier every day. To be sure, he fired out orders, but they fell like cannon balls into the ocean. Nothing ever happened, even his ripples died.

Dupree took a long pull on his liquid insight. He knew who did this to him—the flyboys. He had control up till '31, up to when they gave all the responsibility to station commanders, to those egotistical power grabbers. Now ground control didn't control anything. They just gave advice to the hotshots. But how come he now worked harder than ever? The flyboys used him like a wooden axle to hold up their overloaded cart, an axle whose fibers stretched and popped a little more every day. They wouldn't appreciate him till he broke. No, they'd just toss in another axle, and leave him to rot in the mud beside the road.

Dupree, an intelligent man, a reflective man, understood what lay before him. Alcohol would kill him. A self-image crept into Mind before Ego could force it out. Pickled veins in his cheeks and nose ballooned and exploded. His pickled liver shriveled into leather. And his pickled brain shrank to a pea inside his skull. But his nerves were shot—he had to pickle them every day just to stop the shaking. Yes, the peak had come and gone. Now he could do nothing but scream downward like a kamikaze pilot into the residue of his life.

Dupree caught himself. He forced a smile and made it radiate inward. Yes, not everything had turned bad. *Wayfarer 2* still progressed as desired, except for the two screwups by the crew. The system had even accommodated all his changes. But would it turn out like *Wayfarer 1*? He still couldn't understand it. He'd seen Ted go through hell and even felt sorry for him, the prick. Something happened that still no one talked about, something the system couldn't seem to fix with all its rules and regulations and casts of thousands.

Dupree's big paw, steady now, swung an empty glass toward his face. He paused. A quizzical look ripened on his features. Then he put the glass down and, with determination and full concentration, he reached out and gripped the bottle.

Yes, Dupree knew he'd done all he could before they wrestled control from him. Now Arrogant Ryder and Smartass Spencer made all the decisions. Well, all right—let those bastards figure it out!

22

Polarize

Light and warmth—basic human essentials. Jake soaked them in as he relaxed alone in the wardroom.

Well over a century before, sailors on warships used the term "wardroom" to refer to officers' living or eating quarters. Several astronauts on Skylab, America's first space station sixty-four years previous, had naval backgrounds and also called their eating area the wardroom. The name stuck.

The designers of *Wayfarer 2* located the wardroom at the forward tip of the module. A four-foot-high by seventeen-foot circular wall of food lockers surrounded a seven-foot circular white table. A clear plexan bubble covered the enclosure and gave the crew full view of the universe they penetrated.

But now, just ten hours after the burn started, Jake could see only one object in the heavens—the Sun—Good Old Reliable Sun. The aft end of his *Wayfarer 2* Alpha module obscured Earth, but even if he could've seen it Earth would've appeared as a disk shrunk to about the same size as the moon viewed from the ground. But Good Old Reliable Sun, off to the side and a slight bit forward, blazed away at its normal strength and size.

In fact, Good Old Reliable Sun continued to blaze away much like billions of other balls of hot gas in the universe. Its nuclear furnace, with its voracious appetite, devoured five million tons of mass every second and transformed it into energy. Like a chameleon, this energy changed "color" as it fled the furnace and struggled to the surface: x-rays changed into ultraviolet rays, then into visible rays— light that provided man with sight and warmth, security and cheer. Every second, for over billions of years, Good Old Reliable Sun flooded its energy into cold, dark, empty space.

It required but an infinitesimal amount of Sun's energy to fuel the evolution of man. And, at this one infinitesimal point in Sun's life, an infinitesimal portion of that energy pierced the plexan dome of *Wayfarer 2* and hit the back of Jake's neck and head and the light-blue cloth of his flight suit. It warmed his skin, soaked in and kindled a familiar internal warmth.

Rest had wiped Jake's mental slate clean. He felt loose, his total body relaxed and fresh. The Caution and Warning had remained silent all night, and the engines continued to perform without flaw, something he'd verified as soon as he awoke.

Through gold-mirrored sunglasses wrapped around his face, Jake saw his shadow stretch across the table's white, sun-drenched surface. He squeezed the soft accordionlike body of his orange juice container and took a long pull. Its frigid acid taste slid down his throat and revived his senses.

One by one, his crew half-strolled, half-hopped into the wardroom, snuggled down into their own turf around the table and, between yawns and stretches, began breakfast. Irwin bounded in last.

Throughout his career, Jake had spent many hours at wardroom tables and regarded it as one of the best settings to extract the candid thoughts of his crew. The descendent of a long line of kitchen-eaters, he felt at home nestled in its loose informality. Jake glanced around at his crew. Their sun-saturated torsos, also wrapped in light-blue flight suits and gold-mirrored sunglasses, contrasted with the black emptiness outside the plexan behind them.

Jake turned his mirrors toward Irwin. "Find anything?"

"Nope. After you left, I compared all commands issued by CT 7000 last night with what we observed in our simulations. It all matched."

Ada looked too relaxed to issue an "I-told-you-so." She just nodded and smiled.

Boris held up a dark-green pill equal in size to the tip segment of his little finger. He turned it over and inspected it several times, like a golfer looking for nicks in his ball. "Why do we still have to take this damn calcium blocker? We're not in zero gravity any more."

"True, but one-fifth gravity doesn't put enough stress on your bones to prevent some calcium loss," said Faye. "However, you always have the other option—a short burst of exercise in the body loader. It actually does a better job. All you have to do is put high stress on your bones for ten or fifteen minutes every day and you'll have no problem with calcium loss. The pill is really intended for bed-rest patients, not us."

"I'll take the pill. It's over quicker. You sure those're my only choices?"

"Only ones," said Faye. "Sorry."

"Bon appetit!" said Speed. "Better toss that little beauty down like a good lad because, without calcium in your bones, we'll have to tote you home in a bucket. And all you'll be able to do is just quiver around in there like a jellyfish with eyes."

The red, round, ripe tomato of the previous night had unripened a few shades toward green. With the face, head and body movements of a man with a live snake wiggling in his throat, Boris swallowed his pill.

Speed's cackle led the chorus. "Great moves, Boris! Have you ever thought of being a stunt man in porno films?"

"I've never seen anyone attack a pill quite like that, Boris," said Faye.

"It's a new Russian technique," said Speed. "You keep the pill fixed in space and wiggle your body up around it. It was developed by that world famous cosmonaut, Nod Gudunov."

Boris returned to intermediate pink. "OK, smartass, since you're bringing up dumb names, why don't you tell us how the hell you ever got the dumb name 'Speed'?"

Faye looked at Speed and chuckled again. "Yeah, Speed, let's hear it."

Speed snapped his face into its full-serious configuration, leaned forward and assumed his around-the-campfire-story-telling posture. "Well . . . when I was fourteen, I grew real fast. I went from short to tall in about a year. And I did most other things fast, too. Just my nature I guess. That was when older brother changed my nickname to 'Speed,' and it's stayed with me ever since."

Faye still looked puzzled. "Changed? What was your name before that?"

"Spud."

"Oh."

Five mirrored heads rocked side to side.

"Faye, am I still going to grow a couple of inches taller, like other flights, even while we're in one-fifth gravity?" asked Irwin.

"Nope. Probably only about an inch. But in the months of hibernation in zero gravity, you may gain up to three inches. Most of the growth'll still be in the regions between vertebrae in your backbone."

"Jaclyn got all excited the first time I called back from a mission and told her I was two inches taller," said Speed. "She went out and bought a new pair of high heels. Once we landed, gravity squeezed me right back down to my usual size. She got all ticked off, like it was my fault. When I got home, she looked down her nose at me and started calling me Prairie Pizza!"

This time Boris's laugh led the chorus. But his smile soon faded as he started careful inspection of another capsule, a Postlaunch Epigastric Distress Syndrome Inhibitor or, as referred to by the crews, a Sickness Inhibitor Capsule (SIC). "Faye, please tell me I don't have to down one of these things, too."

"The SICs are your choice," said Faye. "If you feel OK, forget 'em."

Boris glowed.

Faye continued. "One-fifth gravity's enough so that your system functions almost as it would in normal gravity, and most people don't experience space sickness. But if we were to more closely approximate zero gravity, your nervous system would receive such conflicting messages from your vestibular organs, eyes, muscles, circulatory system and other sensory signal sources that it'd tend to shut down your peristalsis and, as you know, could even cause reverse peristalsis."

"What?" squinted Boris.

Speed leaned forward. "More technically, what she means to say is that in zero gravity your gut grinds to a halt and you barf."

"Ohh . . . not at breakfast, Speed," said Irwin.

Jake shook his head. "Speed, go to your room."

"Or, if you stay here, imitate a sane person," added Faye.

Jake and his crew remained at breakfast for over two hours. They continued to bask in light, warmth and camaraderie. Both lunch and dinner came early and lasted late. Jake, like his crew, unwound and relaxed before he thought ahead.

Mission day three took on the same loose structure, except their meals and conversations grew shorter. Also, they shifted their sleep period so that their schedule coincided with the flight control team in Houston. Their bodies still demanded that they live on a twenty-four-hour clock even though, for them, Good Old Reliable Sun never set. But, by dinner, Jake noted how much the sun had crept toward the rear of their module and shrunk in size and strength.

"It'd make it a lot easier to plan if we knew what condition we'll find Ted and his crew in," said Irwin.

Faye perked up. "For now, we'll have to assume some or all of them were able to enter hibernation."

"That's right," said Jake. "That may not be the most likely situation, but it's the one that demands the most from us when we reach 'em. And we have no data that tell us for sure that that's not the case."

"All they require for hibernation is that their electrical power, environmental control and CT 7000 are still functional in at least one module," said Faye.

"If one module lost all of its propellant because of an engine failure, got separated from the other one and couldn't rendezvous with it again, whoever was in it would realize that they could be out there for years before rescue came," said Boris.

Faye nodded. "Right. They had only enough food for three months of high activity and would've concluded that hibernation was their only hope. If we reach 'em, it'll be best to just transfer them to our spacecraft, each in their own hiberpod, and bring them back without changing their state. That way, they'd use very little of our consumables. And, if any of them had a major injury, it'd be easier to treat back home."

"But if they were injured, could they still've started the hibernation?" asked Boris.

Faye nodded again. "Very easily. They had available a nearly automatic mode operated by CT 7000. All they had to do was enter their pod, self-insert the serum feed needle, hit the POWER ON and AUTO INITIATE switches, close the pod door and relax. CT 7000 would've done the rest. They didn't even have to hit a vein with the needle, just get it under the skin and restrain it."

With the mention of self-insertion of a needle,

some of the color again disappeared from Boris's face. "Faye, even though I've tried some of the serum in my familiarization test, I still don't understand what it'd do to me."

"Sorry, Boris," said Faye. "I wish we'd had more time to cover it in training. The serum really has two components that're injected sequentially. Initially, a muscle relaxant is injected, and that takes you to the edge of sleep. Then comes the Hibernol, first at a relatively high concentration. Once the right respiration and heart rates are reached, the concentration is adjusted to maintain them. Also, since your body temperature is maintained at just a little above freezing, the serum contains a thinner so that the blood can still flow, if ever so slowly."

Boris persisted. "But what'll it really *do* to me?"

"Hibernol is a metabolic inhibitor. That is, it slows the rate of all reactions at the cellular level. In simple terms, it slows down your body clock. Your temperature'll drop approximately sixty degrees down to a minimum of thirty-seven degrees. Your heart rate'll decrease to approximately three beats per minute. And you'll breathe about once every two minutes. Your brain waves'll be greatly reduced in magnitude, but'll still be detectable."

"Boris, you're white!" said Speed. "All your blood must be hiding in your shoes!"

Boris ignored Speed. "But haven't there been accidents? What happens if I get too much Hibernol?"

Speed flashed a full grin at Boris and spoke before Faye could answer. "That's easy. Your metabolic rate drops to zero, but you don't die until they try to wake you up. A real Catch 22, as me ole Pappy used to say. All you know is that, when you do wake up, you find yourself dead."

Boris muttered to himself.

Ada came to life. "It's not possible to get too much Hibernol! The CT 7000 senses the respiration and heart rates and keeps them within acceptable bounds by adjusting the Hibernol feed rate. It's a feedback loop with many backups in the software."

Faye tried to beam a smile into Boris's face, but it appeared to have little effect. "Ada's right, Boris. Don't worry. It's true that, when they first started doing hibernation experiments on humans at the end of the last century, they did have a few . . . ahh . . . accidents. And, unfortunately, the accidents caused delays in our research and basic understanding of metabolic inhibitors. But now our system and procedures are well understood and reliable. Besides, I'll be there to make sure it all goes well, both when we initiate the process and when you wake up."

"Boris, you still look half a quart low," said Speed.

Boris glanced at Speed, then directed his question to Faye. "Are there any negative effects when you do wake up?"

Speed beat Faye again. "Oh, nothing that you haven't experienced before. Kinda like a liter-of-vodka hangover. Your mouth feels like the bottom of a bird cage, and even your hair hurts."

"Com'on, Speed," said Faye. "It isn't bad at all. When you first wake up, Boris, you'll feel numb, cold and a little groggy. And a lot of bacteria will've built up in your mouth. But you'll experience no pain. With heat, mild stimulant and a little mouthwash, you'll feel almost back to normal within eighteen hours."

Boris managed a weak smile.

"Jake, what condition do you really think we'll find Ted and his crew in?" asked Irwin.

Jake paused. Humor faded from their faces as they turned toward him. "No way to know for sure. I hope for the best, but know that we'd better be prepared for the worst. Personally, I think they met up with more than they could handle."

"And what about us?" asked Faye.

* * *

By mission day four they'd reached two milestones. Sun had crept half the distance to the aft end of their module. And Speed ran out of stories, although the bottom to his one-liner reservoir was nowhere in sight.

At breakfast, a bright red Boris bounced up and down at his position next to the table. "Faye, even though my brain waves will be almost zero when I hibernate, will I really still be alive?"

Faye laughed and nodded. "Of course!"

"Will I dream?"

"Good question," said Faye. "No sleeplike brain waves or rapid eye movements have ever been observed in someone in deep hibernation. They only show up when you enter and exit. But then, the brain's still not understood well enough to know. Even at extremely low voltages, we could still have thoughts."

In a casual soft voice, Ada added, "Soon we'll be able to connect a CT 20,000 series computer into the brain and spinal chord and replace most of the brain's functions, as well as detect its thoughts, even during hibernation."

"What?" Faye looked quizzical. "I don't think so. The brain has capabilities, even just its basic ones, that could never be replaced by a computer."

Whether through Faye's challenge or the low gravity, Ada managed to tower on her side of the table. Her words zipped out with the precision of a high-speed dot-matrix printer. "Never match? Even our CT 7000 that *controls* this mission has 373 trillion full words of working memory, approximately ten thousand times more than the number of neurons in the brain. And we've only started. In less than a decade the brain will look even more like child's play."

"Ada, that's naive." Faye also pushed upward to dominate her side of the table. "The neuron's not just a simple ON–OFF switch like a bit in one of your digital computers. It's the elite of the body's cells. Each neuron is connected to thousands of other neurons. Some in the cerebral cortex have over 200,000 connections. In fact, the brain has over 100 trillion neuronal connections."

Jake cocked his jaw to the side. Should he stop it? They'd both hit a nerve. Ada found religion in computers; Faye, in the human body. Better let it flow, or it'd only be worse later at a more critical point.

Ada sneered. "It's only a matter of time until the number of computer logic paths dwarf the number of neuronal connections, too, till we're limited not by a computer's memory or our ability to program it, but only by its ability to program itself. The brain's doomed to become a second class citizen."

All eyes swept back to the other side of the table to a wide-eyed Faye and waited for her return.

"Naive again! The essence of the brain is found in the nature of these connections, not just their number. They're not simple like a network in one of your electronic contraptions. Each connection has a synapse, a small gap about a millionth of an inch wide. An electrical signal's converted to a chemical one there, and then back into an electrical one again as it jumps the gap."

All eyes back to Ada . . .

"Cumbersome and inefficient. We'd never do it that way if we designed the brain."

Eyes to Faye . . .

"Inefficient and cumbersome? No! Complex and selective? Yes!" Faye's eyes narrowed. "That's what gives the brain its edge, gives us the richness of our thought. When a neuron fires an electrical signal out to a synapse, a chemical, a neurotransmitter, is released. It must link up with just the right receptor on the next neuron for the signal to flow. There are many different chemicals that serve as neurotransmitters, each with its own receptor. This chemical coding makes it a very selective process, gives human thought a staggering number of options. Each thought, each memory may involve the encoding of trillions of synapses."

Eyes to Ada . . .

"Sounds more random than selective, and certainly inefficient."

To Faye . . .

"Look, try to understand! Neurons are alive, computers are not. Each neuron doesn't spit out just a simple one or zero like one of your digital deviates, but each type of neuron has a different degree of responsiveness to the neurochemicals that impinge on it. The amount of information storage and transmission that this represents is astronomical, far above anything we could ever do with a computer."

To Ada . . .

"Just speculation. And I say it's not only inefficient, but it's slow. Most of CT 7000's calculations are done in parallel with one another, like the brain, but it does them much faster. It's rated at 730,000 Tera-operations per second, that's almost a billion billion per second. Its signals flow at the speed of light. That leaves the brain in the dust."

To Faye . . .

"For once you're right," Faye laughed. "That's about ten million times faster than signals flow in the brain, but it's also irrelevant. Whole fields of neurons will interact until they finally relax into a stable configuration just to form a single thought. The end result is what counts. The complexity and grandeur of thought, the ability to control our bodies, that's what's important."

To Ada . . .

Ada ratcheted another notch higher and shrugged her shoulders. "Grandeur? What's that? . . . Look! What you fail to recognize is that computers continue to grow in capability, and the brain is fixed in size. It's limited, bound to be surpassed."

Faye . . .

"No! What *you* fail to recognize is that the brain is not limited. A brain increases in capability as the richness of neuronal interactions and multiplicity connections increase. We're just now understanding how to make all this happen at an enhanced rate. We're developing biochemicals that help increase the permanence and complexity of neuronal connections, that accelerate and enhance the complexity of our thought. We used to be limited to stimulants, like caffeine, along with oxygen, glucose, other nutrients, and hormones, like vasopressin. Now we can use a wide variety of biochemicals, not to get high, but to increase our intelligence. The brain's telling us how to make itself smarter, and the whole thing's about to take off. With increased IQ, we're learning how to increase our IQ even further—human intelligence is about to experience exponential growth!"

Speed leaned forward and inserted a full grin into the volley. "Wish I thought of that before. I'd of had some of my Irish blend whiskey classified as a mind-enhancing biochemical and brought it with us."

Speed was ignored.

"More speculation. Besides, for decades we've had computers that learn, that even design other computers. Long ago we took the best the brain has to offer, the architecture of its connections, and formed neural networks. They too learn from experience and even form the basis of our CT 7000's learning sector."

Jake grew impatient. This could get worse, and he'd heard it all before. Better turn it off soon, if it doesn't happen on its own.

Faye beamed her anger straight into Ada's face. "No matter how many of those bit buckets you strap together, organize to think like a brain and glorify with a fancy name, it's still just a computer, just a creation of our minds. It can only learn and perform as we've coded it. It just pushes old logic around and reshapes it. Don't you understand? It can't create, but our brain can! Our brains can make intuitive leaps, those synaptic connections that weren't there before, to produce original thought, new ideas and fresh insights. That's the miracle of human thought."

Ada frowned. "Miracle? Now you're getting mystical. Computers can also learn, and always faster than humans."

Faye tried to move in for the kill. "Does a computer think? Is it conscious? Only the brain allows us to create, to be inspired, to detect meaning and purpose and beauty. It's taken millions of years to evolve and not likely to be surpassed in a few hundred by anything man-made. If you want to appreciate the works of the Creator, you don't have to look out to the edge of the universe or in at elementary particles. The human mind holds all the wonder one could ever want."

Ada snickered. "Who wants it?"

Before Faye could make a return, Jake leaned over the court, put up both hands and stopped the volley. "Look, it's hard to tell nowadays if we're trying to make computers think like humans or forcing humans to behave like computers. You're both right. In the extreme, neither one makes much sense. Fortunately, there's a reasonable middle ground. Accept it, and make use of it—minds and computers are fundamentally different but complementary—but only useful when working together, not separately."

Both players sank back and appeared grateful that Jake had called it a tie. And before either one could take another shot, Speed launched into his own lecture. "Jake's right. Let our minds make intuitive leaps, solve unpredictable problems and use their capacity for original thought only where they can be productive. And let computers control what's predictable, make calculations billions of times faster than we can, hold astronomical quantities of facts and direct our robots. But minds and computers shouldn't compete—make 'em cooperate!"

Jake and Speed both grinned at Faye, at Ada and then back and forth several times like fathers laying down the law to quarreling kids. Silence hung.

Then Speed snapped to full grin. "Game's over!"

All four laughed.

"Thanks for the education," said Jake. "No doubt about it. This's gonna be a fun trip." In a single hop, he dropped through the exit hatch in the floor, and Speed followed.

Faye waited for Ada, who was the last to leave. "Ada, I enjoyed our discussion."

Ada surprised Faye with a rare smile. "I did, too."

"When we can find some time together on this mission, let's talk again. I'd like to learn more about what computers can do to enhance human thought."

Ada's smile slid down and off her face. "*Enhance*? You didn't understand a thing I've told you. Computers will *replace* human thought!" With a lurch, Ada's body also dropped down and disappeared through the floor.

. . . has to be a way out! . . .

Ted tensed as he sensed his chamber. The drift of isolated memory packets toward openings had swollen into rivers that gushed outward, torrents of memories that rushed away toward distant chambers through mazes of twisted tunnels.

. . . I'm losing, Obscureaucrats are winning— my time's running out—have to escape! . . . maybe if I can just understand what Choke's done to me . . .

. . . Choke sees me just as a source of memory packets, of data . . . but now, even I'm starting to see everything as data, interesting but still just data . . . feel emotion for others only when I fuse with my own memories—but only then . . . can't feel fresh emotions, all just memories, concepts, oddities of the flesh . . . maybe now I'm like Choke, no more of emotion's drags and pulls . . . Eva and Willie, their love and joy, all those distractions that cloud data flow, free of it all! . . . since I don't feel emotion for others, I don't care—I just don't care . . .

Ted's awareness softened as he sensed memories continue to bleed from his chamber and disperse into something larger, dissipate into an organism with an insatiable capacity to absorb.

. . . but just the same something's happening to me, I'm being consumed by Choke . . . all my data controlled by random movements of Choke's Obscureaucrats . . . what'll Choke do with me? or with anyone else who comes? . . .

23

Snooze

Their thoughts drifted inward.

On days five and six, the crew of *Wayfarer 2* marked time. Speed checked and rechecked all the systems but could find no problems. Ada ran out of new ways to praise CT 7000 and finally monitored it in silence. Boris spent most of his hours at his navigation work station except when he and Jake discussed their future operations at the Wayfarers. Irwin scrutinized the engine operation and reviewed all the procedures yet to be employed. Faye prepared the hibernation pods and checked out their computer control. And Jake periodically touched base with each of them.

When they gathered for dinner on day six, no one wore sunglasses, but they did wear jackets. The inside temperature remained a constant seventy-three degrees, but the small size of the sun made it feel cooler.

Jake prepared his meal in silence, as did the others. He heated his frozen lobster thermidor with a thirty-five-second burst of microwaves and removed the plastic cover. A puff of steam invaded his nostrils, and he savored its aroma. Like most recent meals, he found himself absorbed in the sensual experience. In fact, as the flight had progressed, he found no real challenge for his intellect and his basal instincts wormed closer to the surface.

As he looked at Faye, one part of his mind observed another part but couldn't turn it off. Yes, she looks sexier today. Wonder what she'd be like? Could hide it, but Val would know. Couldn't hurt her like that. What we have's worth far more.

Speed broke the silence. "Faye, does our hibernation differ much from what's being developed for interstellar flight?"

"Nope. It's essentially the same. We operate at the lowest safe metabolic rate in both cases. You'd gain very little by driving it lower."

"Wish we didn't have to do it at all," said Boris. "What do we really gain?"

"Something you like, Boris," said Faye. "Propellant. If you figure the weight of the food, packaging and system support required, it comes out to a little over two pounds per day for each of us. That saves us about seven thousand pounds on this flight, assuming we recycle our water."

Boris stroked his face with his fingertips. "If we had to give up that much propellant, we'd still do the mission, but it'd take a lot longer."

Faye's eyes sparkled as she continued. "But there are other advantages, too. In hibernation our bodies'll suffer much less damage from radiation. And the loss of bone calcium'll be much slower. Actually, Speed, the development of hibernation would've occurred without its application to space flight. There're too many surgical procedures that depend on it. And it slows not only aging and the effects of injuries, but also the spread of infection, cancer and other diseases."

"You sure it's been around long enough to be reliable?" asked Boris.

"Hibernol was first synthesized right after the turn of the century. The breakthrough came when the hibernation trigger was isolated from the blood of hibernating woodchucks, then synthesized from basic organic building blocks and fully tested on rhesus monkeys. In 2007 it was first used on a human. Since then it's been refined and is now a highly reliable drug."

Boris scrutinized Faye through narrowed eyes. "And the stimulant to come out of it is just as reliable?"

"More so. There's a wide range of stimulants that can be used. And even if we do nothing but cut off the Hibernol feed, you'll still come out of it. We use stimulants only to have better control over the arousal phase."

Speed jerked to attention and rubbed his hands together. "Arousal phase. I've heard of that!"

Faye scowled. "You know what I mean, Speed."

Three heads made small sympathy wags, and Ada remained impassive. On the first few days of flight, Speed's humor would've cascaded. Today it made but a small blip on an otherwise somber mood.

By the evening of day eight, the tail of their module shadowed Good Old Reliable Sun. Fall arrived, and with it, the promise of a colder darkness yet to come. Under artificial light, the sleeve of Jake's light blue flight jacket looked dull, no longer vibrant. The skin on the back of his hand'd lost its tone. And the ham on the end of his fork took on a listless brown. The flavor still came alive, yet somehow it seemed separate and apart from the object he put into his mouth. In silence he listened to the conversation.

"I wonder if Ted's crew felt the same as we do once they lost the sun?" asked Faye of no one in particular. No one responded. "Better question yet, how did they feel once they got all the way out to the Wayfarers?"

"From the look on Ted's face, I'd say he wasn't too happy," said Irwin.

"If gravity gradient rips our modules apart, none of us are gonna look too happy either," said Boris.

"But after that, once he was back in zero gravity, he felt something else," said Faye.

Boris arched his back and spoke with conviction. "It was just the shock of breaking his arm and hitting his head. What else could've happened to him?"

"Nothing," said Irwin with a shrug of his shoulders. "Nothing else was there to do anything to him."

"Right," said Ada, who picked up Boris's forceful tone. "Everything we saw was caused by his injuries."

Speed lobbed his grenade into the conversation. "Who are you all trying to convince—yourselves?" He sounded authoritative, not like the joker they had taken at face value.

No one brought the subject up again.

. . . tunnel after tunnel, chamber after chamber . . . explored thousands of 'em, followed my memory packets from one to the next and on again, and still can't make any sense of it . . . don't get discouraged . . .

. . . I'm being absorbed by Choke, by something with potential capabilities far greater than I ever could imagine—unbounded and interconnected information systems, a consciousness and data storage of colossal proportions, a megamind . . . the Ultimate? . . . no way to know, yet . . .

. . . and Choke has a powerful ability to observe, one that I have too, when I can tap into Choke's senses, one that's so easy and so natural . . . Choke uses the universal language of images—they define and detail it all . . . numbers and figures and equations aren't needed—they're just messy middle men, just that bulky bookkeeping required by mental midgets . . .

. . . and Choke exists right on top of my old world . . . never could sense it before, like man before he could sense the sea of radio waves or cosmic rays that he bathes in every day . . . never touch except at black holes like Wayfarer's . . .

. . . Choke oughta be a storehouse of knowledge . . . think of the possibilities! . . . of all the advanced species in the universe that've traveled in space, that've joined the cosmic club . . .

. . . and Choke has a unique advantage . . . in my old world all knowledge and culture gets erased every time the universe sucks itself back into the fireball of a big bang . . . but not Choke!—Choke's permanent, Choke might get twisted and distorted, but it'll never collapse and lose its stored data, never have to start over again from scratch . . . the data it's collected must approach infinity, and once I learn to tap into it, I'll be immortal and learn forever!—the ultimate graduate student . . .

. . . how could Choke happen? . . . did the Obscureaucrats make Choke; or Choke, the Obscureaucrats? . . . given enough time, anything but the impossible can happen . . .

. . . oh yes, Choke's gotta be a near-infinite storehouse of culture and knowledge—and soon I'll find a way in! . . .

On mission day nine, the crew of *Wayfarer 2* returned to their stations to watch the last event that separated them from hibernation—engine shutdown.

Boris made one last entry into his keyboard and watched the numbers flash on his display. "All the past three updates to our relative state vector have produced negligible change to shutdown time. It's still at 17:43.37, less than one minute away."

"Good," said Jake.

They each watched the countdown on their own displays. At zero, the engine dropped into its low thrust mode for five seconds, then shut off.

At first, the silence sounded like a fresh noise. They waited, and they listened. It persisted. The background hum had become like the purr of a cat, a steady sign of vitality, of life. Now they heard only its absence. Nothing.

Their gravity from acceleration also vanished. Now, like most every other body in the universe, only gravity of distant masses balanced their acceleration. They fell. And they felt nothing. Relative to Sun, they moved away at one-half percent the speed of light. And still they felt nothing.

Jake relaxed and gripped the edge of the table with just his fingertips to stabilize his body. He laughed to himself. It felt like the table beat with its own heart! When he pressed harder, it stopped; but when he relaxed, it started. The ole ballistocardiographic effect, he thought. One jaw breaker of a word for something so simple. Blood pulsed through his arteries and fingertips, jiggled his body just a little and yielded the sensation that it was the table, not he, that owned the heart.

But other than his own heartbeat, Jake felt nothing. And he heard nothing. He glanced around at his crew and saw sober looks of awareness as they searched each other's faces. Yes, what you see is what you get, all your tools, right here and up front—each other.

Jake completed the change of attitude of the modules for the coast phase. The engines now pointed in the direction they would next fire to brake their speed at the Wayfarers, 292 days away. Then he rejoined his crew in the wardroom. Their somber mood persisted as they stared at Good Old Reliable Sun. The familiar bright ball hung at high noon, but it looked less than one-third its normal size and one-tenth the brightness they'd taken for granted all their lives.

"Looks like Son of Sun," said Speed.

"Has everyone finished their systems checks?" asked Jake.

With their eyes fixed on the Sun, they each nodded affirmative.

"Seen any anomalies?" asked Jake.

No one responded. Jake had already reviewed CT 7000's Anomaly Log and found it blank.

"If it looks dim now, what'll it look like when we wake up?" asked Faye.

"Almost like another star," said Speed. "It'll be a hundred times smaller, and its intensity will be ten thousand times less. But at least it'll still be the brightest star in the sky. And no need to sweat it."

"It's one thing to talk about it," said Faye. "But it's another thing to experience it."

"Like the first time I ever looked back at Earth," said Boris.

"Sort of . . ." said Faye. "But that gave a feeling of awe. This feels more like a dark day that's only going to get worse."

Speed pushed off the floor, shot to the top of the plexan dome in the center of their vision and shouted back. "Anyone want to send a last message home before the transmitters drop into low power?"

Silent stone faces answered him.

"I just finished my Christmas message to Jaclyn," Speed continued. "Had to tell her how to operate the surprise tree I got for her."

"What kind of tree did you get her?" asked Faye.

"A Holo Tree."

"A what?"

"You know, one of those holographic Christmas trees that International Holography has been advertising."

"You didn't!"

"Sure did. Since I won't be there to help her with a tree this Christmas, or next, I got her a holographic one. Have it all set. All she's gotta do is throw the switch and *zap!*—instant Christmas tree, decorations, lights and all—the whole enchilada! Yep, a puff or two of pine scent, a few canned carols, a couple holographic presents, and she's got it—instant Christmas. No fuss, no muss, no bother. And it's even better when it's time to take the tree down. Just flip the switch again and *zap!*—she'll pop that sucker right outta there in nothin' flat!"

Faye put her hand over her closed eyes as she shook her head.

"Love that Christmas spirit, Speed," said Jake as he glided over to the wardroom remote CT 7000 terminal. "Nothing but a pure romantic."

"Is it time, Jake?" asked Boris.

"Yep. Meteoroid shield's comin' closed."

Jake entered his commands, and a meteoroid shield crept over their plexan dome, one identical to that already in place on the Beta module, a shield that would stop meteoroids from pitting the plexan while they slept.

The sun disappeared.

Speed yawned. "Nap time."

"Irwin, you're first," said Faye. Irwin looked at his checklist and nodded.

Jake had selected Irwin to lead the way and set a good example for entry into hibernation. Irwin had complete faith in their procedures and Faye's ability to execute them. To Irwin, his ten-month sleep was but another step in a larger procedure.

Like a mother duck, Faye led her brood single file from the wardroom into the central tunnel of their module. Boris brought up the rear. They floated past the food storage volume, command center, science laboratory, observation room, airlock, maintenance and repair complex, exercise facility, entertainment room and lavatory.

"In case anyone still has to use the bathroom, do it now," said Faye. "However, the kidney and intestinal stimulants you took yesterday should've long since done their work."

"Listen to your mother, kids," said Speed. "Better take a quick wiz now because you're not going to get another chance till we're a lot farther down the road."

They continued past the sleep compartments and into the hibernation chamber. It nestled at the bottom of the module's habitable core, inside the ring of propellant storage tanks and over the nuclear-ion engine, where the crew would be well protected from bursts of high-energy solar radiation.

The hibernation chamber, a circular room just high enough to house the hibernation pods upright against the wall like vertical columns, resembled a group mausoleum. Each of the six pod openings mounted flush against the circular wall, and a three-by-seven-foot, clear plexan-bubble door covered each opening. Electronic controls and displays ornated the area between each door where indicators glowed red in the chamber's soft light. In an identical chamber in the Beta module, six similar but dormant pods waited.

Faye called up the hibernation prep procedures using a CT 7000 remote terminal on the console at the center of the chamber. Irwin looked over her shoulder while the rest of the crew floated on either side of his pod door.

"We're all set to go," said Faye. "Let's get you hooked up."

Without hesitation, Irwin floated into his pod and held out his left arm. With the ease she'd close the buttons on a shirt, Faye inserted the feed needle into a vein and secured it to his skin.

"Here's your EEG cap," said Faye. "The electrolytes are ready. Just put it on and pull it snug."

"Got it."

"All electrodes show good contact," said Faye, who'd moved to the console keyboard.

"Ready to close the door," said Irwin.

"Wait! You surprise me, Irwin. First time I ever saw you leave a step out of a procedure. Here's your rectal thermometer."

"I was hoping you'd forget it."

"Nice try, Irwin," said Speed. "But don't feel picked on. People keep suggesting things like that to me all the time."

"OK, got it."

With set jaw and tight lips, Irwin stared straight ahead. Faye glanced at his face, then slowed down the pace of her movements, floated eye to eye with him and smiled as she spoke. His face relaxed. "Irwin, this'll be no different than your familiarization tests. You should be asleep in ten minutes, although initially it won't be deep, just the REM stage. That is, you'll be treated to a few vivid dreams before the Hibernol depresses your brain activity. You'll reach a stable state in about thirty-six hours."

"Will you stay awake and make sure that we really do stabilize?" asked Boris.

"Sure will," said Faye. "And don't worry. It'll be just like a night's sleep. You leave your dreams on this end and pick 'em up on the other when the stimulant takes hold. You won't feel at all like ten months've gone by."

Faye gave Irwin's arm a light pat, closed the pod door and depressed the AUTO INITIATE switch. Irwin had already closed his eyes. She floated to the center console, where she called up his display.

"I've never had the chance to watch this before, even during our tests," said Jake.

"Me neither," said Speed.

They waited.

"Look at his heart rate," said Faye. "He's already gone from eighty-five down to sixty-two. The relaxant is having its effect."

"He looks like he's already asleep," said Speed.

"It's only light so far," said Faye. "Just REM."

Jake studied Irwin's face. "Yeah, and you can see the movement of his eyes under his lids. They're really bouncing around. His dream must be a real mind-blower."

"The Hibernol should show its effects soon," said Faye.

Irwin's eyes remained closed as he yawned. Then, as if he'd bitten into an apple and found half a worm, he stuck out his lips and tongue, retched and gagged.

Boris pushed away from the pod. "What the hell's wrong?"

Faye turned her radiant shine on Boris. "He's fine. He doesn't even know he's doing it. It's just the natural reaction to an opiatelike substance. It'll stop soon."

They floated in silence above Irwin. Within minutes his features faded toward a placid, tranquil state, settled toward a calm like a pool's surface once the last swimmer's left.

Faye returned to the display. "Heart rate at 42, respiration at 6 per minute and temperature at 94.7. And all're decreasing. The EEG shows he is entering slow-wave sleep. His frontal cortex activity is subsiding."

"What's that mean?" asked Boris.

"The higher brain functions are affected first. That is, the parts of your brain responsible for complex thought and logic are suppressed before those parts responsible for your basic instincts."

They continued to watch as Irwin's vital signs crept toward zero. After a few more minutes, Speed grew impatient. He swept his hand toward the serene figure. "Ta-daaaa . . . one Rip van Winkle. Who's next?"

"You are," said Faye.

"You should've started him yesterday if you want him asleep at the same time as the rest of us," said Boris.

"Get your fanny over here, Speed," commanded Faye through a wide grin.

Faye started Speed down the same restful road as Irwin. Ada, Boris and Jake would soon follow. The road sloped downward for a good piece, leveled out, then hung just above Absolute Tranquillity. Faye, who'd trained to complete the procedure on herself, would monitor them until they each coasted well onto the flat. Then she'd follow.

* * *

Jake watched the blurred image of Faye's hand withdraw from the handle of his pod door. Although the curved plexan distorted the dim light, he could make out an arc of four sets of two green lights and a single set of two red lights around the distant edge of the chamber. Up close, on the left side of his own pod, two yellow lights glared. They stretched and danced as he moved his head from side to side. He froze his lungs, then his whole body, but his ears couldn't detect any sound. He placed his fingertips against the hard sides of the pod, but he couldn't feel any vibration. The air felt cold, as cold as his body would be in thirty-six hours.

Faye's outline moved toward him again. Her arm reached to his left. The snap of the depressed switch jolted his ears and fingertips. The two yellow lights bobbed and weaved, then flared, before they turned green.

Cold serum began its flow up his left arm. But he felt no pain, no discomfort, just a relaxation and a looseness . . . at ease and limp, calm, composed and remote. Yes, that's it—remote. He always could put his mind outside himself and look back, always could remain detached and cool, objective and analytical.

For sure, his good friend, Self-Control, never failed him.

For sure, Self-Control always kept IT submerged, always held IT under.

For sure, Self-Control never let IT get to the surface, never let IT distort reason and action, never let IT take command—never.

Never? Well, just that one time as a kid, but just that once. He'd forgotten all about it. And, after all, he was just a kid. Every kid gets a good scare now and then. Right? Sure! You need a good scare now and then so you can learn how to control IT. Just part of being a kid. Right? Of course.

Deep sleep pulled Jake further under. Logic and reason, superficial containers of primitive instinct, submerged first.

Yep, I was just a kid. Twelve? Certainly no more. First holographic movie I ever saw. A dumb story. Made it through most of it before . . .

Yep, a dumb jungle story, really dumb. All that blackness with all that depth—something to fear? . . . No. OK, just a little fear. Force IT down. But I see 'em—yellow eyes . . . seem real! That big black head. Tongue flicks and body shines, a strong body. Yellow eyes locked on me. Must have a small brain. All instinct. IT doesn't care. Does what IT must to survive. Force IT down!

Can't . . . IT slides at me, glides at me—fast, thick and strong. Right at me! Jaws open. Huge jaws. Foul smell, dead smell. Left arm. Fangs hit. Pain. Cold venom. Real pain! It's REAL! Fangs in me. Venom in me. Jaws grip me and shake me and shake me and shake and shake and . . .

. . . at last . . . it's over, movie's over.

Walk home alone. It's over. Safe. Almost there. It's over. Feet light. Love these moccasins. Tight. Thin soles. Cold asphalt comes right through 'em. Legs strong. Full of spring. Can outrun anybody . . . or anything. Asphalt black. No light. All so black. Just a sliver of a moon. Just see edges of road. Just see dark clumps. Black bushes. Stay out here in center of road, away from black clumps, from black forces . . . away from Wayfarers—away from IT!

Something moved to left. Something's in there. Stop. Freeze. Don't move. Don't draw attention. IT must hear my heart. IT glides. Can't be! Only a movie. Walk fast. Still with me. Stop. Anything there? . . . OK to breathe again? . . . No. IT slides—I hear IT. IT glistens—I see IT. IT's there!

Jog. Road slopes down. Looks OK ahead. But IT's still there. Run.

IT can't move this fast. Then what? Yellow eyes. White fangs. Keeps up with me. Like a black leopard, gonna spring on me as IT did on Ted. Tear head open —let blood seep out . . . claw lungs open—let air hiss out . . . rip neck open—let warm life pump out. Run!

Can't be. Only fear. Control IT.

RUN! Legs like pistons. Road steeper. Screamin' downhill. And IT's still in there. Right with me. And on right, too. Everything's comin' awake in there. On both sides. Road narrows. Steeper. Chute leads straight down . . . down into black hole—into IT!

RUN! Run . . . run . . . run . . . run . . . run . . . run . . . run . . .

V

CONDEMN

For maximum human contribution—
accept the whole human.

24

Create

Ideas, like wild horses, stampeded into Jon Sloan's mind.

A familiar surge of life flowed from his brain, rippled excitement into his throat and tingled and warmed his body. He closed his eyes and herded each thought, each concept into mental corrals. He couldn't let any of them escape, become free to roam on their own—they might just never return. His hand remained frozen. The pencil it held couldn't scribble near fast enough, as useful as oil paints at the finish line. Let all of them buck and charge around first. Let them sort themselves out. Let them quiet down. Then start the tedious roundup. Then put each one into its proper stall. Then start the documentation that just might help transfer some of the beauty and energy of these untamed thoroughbreds to another mind.

Jon had experienced similar roundups many times before. The capture, taming and admiration of each new idea held the moments for which he lived; most of the remainder of his work—the explanation to the skeptical and bored—held all the attraction of the cleanup of the stalls.

He preferred to work at home. Each time Jon told the department secretary at the university he'd be at an "informal office," he laughed to himself. A two-place, one-third-painted, wooden kitchen table and matching chair established the tone of his informal office decor. Jon termed this centerpiece of his selection of fine furniture as "mature," although his younger sister, who lacked his keen eye for value, described it as "ancient, exhausted junk." And, at just the right angle and distance from the table to be both functional and coordinated, Jon'd positioned his brick and board bookcase. As a unit, this whole elegant ensemble was positioned between the water heater and dust-covered wooden stairs that led up to the first floor. The contour of the room's adjustable, mobile light distribution system carried the flow of line and form from one functional area into another. It consisted of a bulb that hung at the end of an extension cord, which then executed a few graceful loops around the nail above Jon's head before it arced onto a smooth trajectory toward the wall outlet by the distant washer. Decorator items that carried the central motif throughout included scribbled notes hung at odd angles from almost all open areas, the rusted cover of the water heater control box, the cobweb-draped wooden studs of the open wall and the gray and yellow mattress folded with finesse and flair under the stairwell.

Jon's office at Darmont University held all the modern electronic aids and oozed with style, but his informal office at home satisfied all of his basic wants and needs. It had warmth, light and just enough room. But above all, it had the real essentials—peace and quiet! Once entrenched, Jon couldn't be raided by the distractions of lectures, meetings, phones, visitors or chattering colleagues, those thieves that the practical world accepted, and even promoted, thieves that broke the rush of thought from one concept to the next, and, in many-a-place and at many-a-time, reduced brilliance to mediocrity. In his informal office Jon communed with his creative drive, gave it free rein and compiled the results with care and precision.

Jon's sister never understood how he could spend seven straight hours down there among the spiders, bugs, dust and mold, yet come back upstairs refreshed and happy. She wanted to move, to find a place that had a separate upstairs room for his informal office. Yes, that'd be nice, but Jon felt certain he couldn't find another apartment compatible with the income of his research assistant's salary plus WSF lecturing fees and the cost of her undergraduate degree. Sure the apartment came with seventy-year-old dust and technology, but it also came with yesterday's prices. Now that both their parents were gone, Jon'd taken on the responsibility for her education, a natural thing to do. He placed spiders, bugs, dust, mold and everything else a distant second. What he loved most, his sister and his research, would both flourish.

He glanced at the spider web between the studs. The strands wove tighter as his eye moved toward the center where the Spider, his good buddy of two weeks, with his big, black, bulbous body, waited with infinite patience. Jon smiled as he wondered if Spider's construction resembled anything he'd constructed in his own mind—negative gravitational potentials, inverse space curvature, compressional magnetic filaments, or space connections? Yes, all possible with the old quantum and super string theories, but could he show it made any sense with current theories? Maybe . . .

"It sounds like fun. How did you ever arrive at it?"

Jon saw the twinkle in Howie's one good eye. Even the black patch over his other eye seemed to radiate enthusiasm. Once again Howie'd given Jon an invitation to lay out his thoughts, examine and see how to improve them. Howie'd been Jon's thesis advisor up to the spring before last, when Jon earned his Ph.D. in astrophysics. And, despite an age difference of fifty-seven years, they'd become close friends. Jon had come to love these sessions, for Howie always zeroed in on Jon's positive results, showed him how to improve them and pointed out what needed to be discarded. Together they would always forge something of value.

Jon flashed his quick smile. "I was trying to get a better definition of the requirements for a closed universe. So I went back to the basic equations for gravity."

"And?" Howie's eye opened wide above his own smile of anticipation.

"I couldn't get a solution to my equations unless I let symmetry exist. That is, if I accept the obvious physical fact of mass that attracts itself, I also have to accept the possibility of mass that repels itself."

By this time, the discussion with most serious-minded researchers would've ended. But Howie, one of the rare kind, continued. "I've asked myself that before, but I never pursued it."

"By experience, we've become so used to mass that attracts itself that we find it hard to picture anything else. A hundred years ago people couldn't picture what it'd be like to float in zero gravity either. Now people accept it as normally as accelerations in a car. Mass that repels itself is just as easy to picture, once you get over the mental block."

Howie's eye narrowed. His stiff white goatee thrust outward and bobbed up and down as he spoke. "Can't you motivate it better than that?"

"Sure can. First, consider two of the five fundamental forces in nature, the electric and the gravitational forces. They're similar. Both're effective over long ranges and fall off as one over the square of the distance from their sources. Electric charges can be positive or negative. Electric forces can either attract or repel. Why not the same dual nature for gravity?"

"Anything else?"

"The symmetry in the equations themselves. I'll

get to that in a minute. But first, try to picture what it'd be like if mass repelled itself rather than attracted."

Howie patted the pockets of his sport coat, a loose tweed with leather patches on its elbows and a black stain under its vest pocket, where his elderly pen had lost its bladder control back in '25. He found his pipe in the right pocket and patted around again for his lighter. Howie, one of the few specimens left who found some odd pleasure in turning leaves into smoke with his mouth, waved his pipe toward Jon. "OK then, tell me what'd it be like."

"Different, very different. It's obvious that matter would spread out, tend to be uniform. It wouldn't concentrate itself in planets or stars or galaxies. The production of heavy elements couldn't occur. Life as we know it couldn't evolve. There'd only be an extremely tenuous gas spread throughout the whole universe. If this mass-repelling universe equaled the mass and current volume of our mass-attracting universe, there'd only be about four hydrogen ions in every cubic meter. Pretty thin."

Howie found his lighter on his desk. "How'd you even define the limits to this mass-repelling universe?"

"Good point. Our current concept of universe includes all the mass and radiation that's spread outward since the big bang. The matter of our mass-attracting universe was all compressed together at one point and exploded about twenty-one billion years ago. The edge of the expansion is the edge of our knowable universe. It's meaningless to speculate about what's beyond it. In a mass-repelling universe, the edge can't be so defined. Its mass would tend to spread out forever, or until it ran into another like universe adjacent to it, if that spatial concept even has meaning. Also, since I have no idea what its history's been, if it exists at all, I have no way to define its extent. Its limits, like the idea itself, can be nothing but speculation."

Through the swirl of smoke around Howie's head, Jon detected a smirk. However, the twinkle of good humor in his eye remained. "What can you say about a mass-repelling universe at all then?"

"We can say something about the general nature of its local properties and how it would interact with our universe."

"OK."

"First, it would spread itself around and into everything in our universe."

"That's clear. It could not be stopped."

"Second, since the gas in a mass-repelling universe would be so diffuse, the electrons and nucleus of each atom would be separated. That is, they would be fully ionized and electric effects could be important."

"No different than most of our universe."

"Third, the two types of matter, mass-attracting and mass-repelling, have negligible interaction. The two universes could coexist in the same space with hardly any interaction."

"You're using the old ploy. Come up with a theory that can't be proved or disproved by experiment, and you've given yourself a lifetime job. But, what do you mean by 'with hardly any interaction'?"

"When you solve the gravitational-wave equation by expanding in powers of the Rosealli Gravitational Constant, you find that there can be interaction between the two universes wherever gravity is exceptionally strong."

"Oh?" asked Howie as he patted his pockets again, now in a search for his pipe-cleaning tool. He carried the hunt to his top desk drawer.

"Yes, at black holes it would be possible for the phenomena of one universe to leak into the other."

"Leak?" Howie smiled as he spied the tool in his briefcase.

"For instance, the electric and magnetic fields in the mass-repelling universe could be measured and felt in our universe in the regions around black holes.

In general, the greater the gravitational strain in the fabric of space, the greater will be the interaction between the two universes."

Howie stood up and turned to Jon. As he pulled up his baggy pants and hooked their top front over his modest pot belly, tattered sneakers popped into view. His face beamed. "That's a neat concept. I don't yet know if it's got the wildest chance of having any validity. But it's interesting. Two universes on top of one another—one static, one dynamic."

"That's right." Jon knew Howie's mind had sped far out in front of their words, but they needed to be said anyway. "Once every big bang, every hundred billion years or so, our universe wipes its slate clean. All the stars, planets, worlds and civilizations tumble into the ultimate black hole—the big bang. It's just like dumping a computer memory. All developed information is lost, and we have to start all over again. But the mass-repelling universe just sits there, cycle after cycle."

"Jon, that's nifty! I see what you are leading up to. If information can be transferred from our universe to your mass-repelling universe through these leaks around black holes, the slate wouldn't be wiped clean at each big bang. Some of the information could leak out and be saved."

"Yep."

"But what could ever exist in your mass-repelling universe? It'd be just a thin gas of charged particles, electrons and protons."

"I can't be sure. But whatever it is, it's had an infinite time to evolve."

"That does open up the possibilities."

Jon smiled.

Howie remained quiet as he searched his desk for his pipe tobacco. He found it in the left pocket of his jacket. "OK, now let's see if all this daydreaming could have anything to do with the real world."

Jon's slight frame popped up to a standing position, and in three quick strides he reached the blackboard. He ignored the CompuThink Wall Slate terminal that lay next to the board under a thick layer of chalk dust. "It's clear that in the nonrelativistic treatment, all we have to do is reverse the sign of Newton's constant and use Green's function to derive the basic equations as before. Let me save time though and show how we have to alter the metric tensor in the more general case. We can derive all we need to from that. I've not been able to derive it yet starting with hyperstring theory, but I'm making headway at it."

Howie remained standing. He'd transitioned from cheerleader to examiner. A quiet intensity replaced the twinkle as he started to twist strands of his goatee. Time to get serious. "That sounds like a good place to start."

Jon's mind, quick and precise, manifested itself in a rapid stream of typewriterlike print that, equation by equation, marched across and conquered the blackboard.

In two hours and twenty minutes, Jon'd erased four wallfuls of equations and Howie'd burned three pipefuls of leaves. They ran out of concentration together.

"Let me think on this, Jon. Please see me tomorrow morning."

"Thanks for listening."

"Thank you. I've enjoyed it."

"Mornin'."

"Hi, Jon. I've got a proposal for you."

"Yes?"

"You've developed your ideas to the point that they could use a little objective criticism from a wider audience. I'd like you to give a seminar to the department."

"Sure. I guess it's inevitable."

"Swell. How about Friday three weeks from today? Do you have any more WSF lectures to give before then?"

"Nope. Haven't given any since I talked to Jake Ryder and his *Wayfarer 2* crew last fall. And I don't see any more on the immediate horizon."

"Good. Then you can give it your full attention. I'll set it up with Professor Prandelwoldter."

"Thanks. Who'll be there?"

"A couple dozen or so astrophysics grad students, Professor Prandelwoldter and his crew, Professor Dulles, myself, about a dozen physics students and some drifters. You should draw a full house."

"Probably so. Everybody loves to speculate about cosmology."

"Jon, this seminar is important to you. Your long-range future here rests with Professor Prandelwoldter. You should try to get him more on your side. As the new department chairman, he'll be the one who has to approve your promotion to faculty status, your tenure."

"Yeah, I've worried about that! How much longer will you be here?"

"Only about another two months. The position of professor emeritus is like a lame duck."

"It's criminal to make someone like you retire at eighty-five."

Howie beamed. "Sure is. Shucks, I'm just gettin' started."

. . . hung like so much frigid flesh in a meat locker . . . being part of Choke also has a downside . . .

. . . for all its data, Choke's not too sensitive . . . it's stored my total existence as short sterile stories, dissected my life and stored it as cold unrelated sanitary facts, catalogued it like automobile parts . . . acting together Choke's Obscureaucrats have no affinity for human values or emotions . . .

. . . and my data packets are always on the move—but Choke never seems to use 'em . . . just locates and classifies and organizes, then relocates and reclassifies and reorganizes, shuffles my data back and forth, forth and back . . . Choke's impotent, can't act or create, just shuffles and reshuffles without stop . . .

. . . Choke must've slipped into an evolutionary cul-de-sac and can't back out . . . should've learned to single out the new and noble with all this time and data, should've developed near-supreme judgment and values . . . but Choke can't seem to recognize any of my data of obvious worth and segregate it to special chambers, can't seem to separate the gems of genius from the droppings of dullards.

. . . Choke seems to increase in only one thing —quantity . . . will it ever gag or ever vomit? . . . does it have infinite volume in its digestive tract? . . . or somewhere on the backside of its universe is Choke dropping intellectual cow pies? . . .

. . . and now that I'm part of Choke, is all this to be my whole life—and my limits too? . . .

. . . will Choke take all my data—my life—and fold me into itself, blend me into its bland awareness, masticate me into its tasteless cud? . . . or will I remain a unique entity, something able to add value and improve us both? . . .

. . . will Choke keep me here for eternity? . . . or am I to be plucked from this potluck bin of souls and recycled? . . .

. . . is Choke like me—just another lower form of the Ultimate Intelligence? . . . or have I been dumped into some depository serviced by the Devil? . . .

. . . will I always be alone? . . . or are others coming? . . .

. . . will I become immortal with Choke? . . . or will I be terminated? . . .

. . . if terminated—what's next? . . .

25

Offer

It fell back into his hand. Too bad.

Jon flipped the pencil-size electronic scribe up again, and it fell back again. If only it was mass-repelling. That'd sure make this next hour go easier.

Jon stood next to the CompuThink Wall Slate terminal and watched his audience file in. Only three minutes before one o'clock and, as usual, the second half of the audience had just started to flood into the room. Howie'd already arrived and settled into his favorite spot, a plush comfortable chair at the end of the first row farthest from the door.

Two of Prandelwoldter's graduate students tried to wedge through the door at the same time. Jon studied them as they repeated the process. The shorter of the two displayed an ear-to-ear grin that looked as permanent as his solid mass of freckles and red hair—a surgical implant? The sole function of his frail body must've been just to hold up that humongous grin. Jon knew that Prandelwoldter loved it. The second graduate student resembled Cro-Magnon Man. His extra-long, powerful arms swung from rumpled openings in a dirty dark-blue T-shirt, with the backs of his hands always forward—obviously an experimentalist. Grinner toddled and

Knuckle Dragger lumbered to the seats in the middle of the second row. They remained standing.

At thirty seconds before one, with the room almost full, all conversation ceased. The atmosphere changed, as if someone had just poured a jar of piranha into the hot tub. Professor Ottis T. Prandelwoldter bounced and bristled through the door. He paused, then scowled as he scrutinized his domain.

Professor Prandelwoldter looked a bit out of place. He'd decorated his short, powerful body with a gray sharkskin, three-piece suit and yellow bow tie. The suit looked as if it could've been a perfect fit at some time in the past, sometime before his body shrunk two sizes. The bottom of the pants continued past his elevator shoes and scraped the floor. Underneath the sharkskin, a ball of dynamic energy charged forward at full speed, the only speed it knew. Although the path of the bunchy ball often appeared to vary at random, the contents of its wake remained predictable: racing and confused minds, elevated blood pressures, half-eaten meals and churning stomachs.

Professor Prandelwoldter charged toward the three open seats left for him in the center of the first row in front of Grinner and Knuckle Dragger. Close on his heels, like a shadow, came another of his students. Jon didn't recall that he'd ever seen the kid by himself. He just seemed to always grovel along a pace behind Prandelwoldter and nod affirmative like a bouncing doll with a spring for a neck. No doubt, thought Jon, the kid had to be seasick by the end of the day. Yep, this had to be the teacher's pet in first grade, the kid who carried the briefcase. And he always took Prandelwoldter's side, but then always got in his licks, too, like the little dog who uses his big brother's growl to yip at your feet, bite your pants, then pee on your ankle.

Professor Prandelwoldter remained standing and gave the room another dose of visual venom while Groveler took his place next to Grinner and

Knuckle Dragger. When Professor Prandelwoldter sat, they all sat.

Howie yawned, stood up, stretched and walked to the center of the room in front of Jon. At the squeak of his sneakers, eyes shifted his way. "Today Jon Sloan's going to share with us some of the really nifty work he's been doing. He's started to look at the possibilities, and consequences, of mass that repels itself rather than attracts. Or negative gravity, you might call it. This is far afield from what most of you are doing. But I urge you to give him your closest attention. He has done his work with imagination, care and precision. It's interesting not only in its own right, but it should make us all take a step back and open our minds to the many possibilities that we overlook daily, more by habit than by good reason. Jon's creativity is responsible for some grand concepts that only he is privileged to expound."

Professor Prandelwoldter jammed his elbows onto his knees, flexed his shoulders, shuffled his feet, pulverized his gum and fired a stare through the floor.

"Thank you, Howie. Let me motivate the theoretical treatment that I'll discuss in a minute. In setting up the basic equations for the description of a closed universe, I chose to use a treatment of gravity that assumed symmetry. That is, both attracting and repelling gravity are assumed to be possible. Then, as the observables are derived, we can go back and see if the assumption leads to something that we can immediately rule out by observation of the real world. This assumption was in part motivated by noting that two of the five fundamental forces in nature, gravity and . . ."

CLICK!

Jon's head jerked up toward the sound. Full Professor and Department Chairman Ottis T. Prandelwoldter aligned his conformal clippers on a second fingernail.

". . . gravity and electric, which're both long-range forces, are both . . ."

CLICK!

". . . are both effective over long ranges and fall off as one over the square of the distance from their . . ."

CLICK!

". . . from their sources. Electric charges can be positive or . . ."

CLICK!

". . . or negative."

Four down, six to go. Jon hoped Prandelwoldter wouldn't take off his shoes.

"So why not the same dual nature for . . ."

CLICK!

". . . for gravity?"

Grinner's grin enlarged. He crossed his legs, wrapped his foot behind his calf and gently rested one palm on the back of his other hand.

"When we look at the correspondence between the graviton and photon, we see that . . ."

CLICK!

". . . that the symmetry of . . ."

Groveler looked down and dragged the bottom third of his tie out from the inside of his pants. Jon suspected that it'd been tucked in there all day. He gaped at it for a split second . . . if he added a little water to that thing, he'd be well on his way to a whole meal.

". . . of the off-axis terms of the metric tensor are . . ."

CLICK!

". . . are equal but opposite in sign in the mass-attracting and mass-repelling universes, what I'll call the MA and MR universes from here on."

Groveler removed his glasses with the spotted lenses, rubbed them with his tie, achieved the uniform translucence of wax paper and returned the lenses to a position halfway down his faceless nose.

"The solution to the Schroedinger equation is obtained by expanding in powers of the Rosealli Gravitational Constant and keeping all terms up to second order. First order terms cancel."

CLICK!

Jon glanced at Howie. Oh-oh. Eyelids sagging over pupils. Must've been a good lunch. He's going under.

"The second order equations that result show that there can be interaction between the MR and MA universes wherever gravity is exceptionally strong. At black holes the electromagnetic fields from the MR universe could leak into these . . ."

CLICK!

". . . into these nodal points of our MA universe or isolated points of space connection and . . ."

Howie's goatee buried itself in his chest, which heaved at a relaxed peaceful pace.

". . . where the evolution would be open-ended, unlike our closed universe where the slate's wiped clean every . . ."

CLICK!

". . . every one hundred billion years or so by a big bang."

Muscles in Professor Prandelwoldter's neck twitched. Veins bulged. He'd run out of fingernails and patience simultaneously.

"Dr. Sloan." The voice came from the middle of the third row, a drifter from the physics department. "No one could argue with your general approach. I think it's simple, maybe elegant. But the question is, of course, does it have anything to do with reality? Can you devise an experiment to test it?"

Professor Prandelwoldter turned around, glared at Drifter and coiled.

Jon addressed Drifter. "Good point. Yes, our connections to the universe in which mass is repelling is . . ."

Professor Prandelwoldter exploded upward,

then bolted forward. Before any sound could escape, he jabbed his manicured index finger toward Jon while the pistons in his jaw built up a full head of steam. "I'll . . . I'll tell you what's repelling. This whole subject's repelling! It's one big fairy tale. You tell us that now we have to worry not only about an MA universe, but also an MR universe. It's all ridiculous daydreaming!"

Groveler snickered. Grinner grinned. Knuckle Dragger looked confused.

Jon felt stunned and sick. The aura of the moment evaporated in a snap, as quickly as if the bride'd vomited at the altar. But he had to defend himself. "Just because we can't immediately prove that something exists, we shouldn't be stopped from looking at the consequences that result if it does. Its importance . . ."

Prandelwoldter interrupted. "There are no observations to support any of this preposterous drivel. You . . ."

Jon continued. "Its importance . . ."

Prandelwoldter burst into full fury. How dare this postdoc try to talk while he, Full Professor and Department Chairman Ottis T. Prandelwoldter, was interrupting. "There are no observations to support anything you say!"

"Yes, none," added Groveler with a firm nod of the head.

Drifter stood up. Perhaps, since he was from another department, he felt he had nothing to lose. "Jon, you're right. All of the evidence we have is obviously biased. Since we haven't had any interaction with this other universe, the only thing we can know about is our own."

"What?" spit out Professor Prandelwoldter.

Drifter smiled. "Yes. Absent evidence is not evidence of absence. It's like all the stories we've heard about dolphins that help tired swimmers back to shore."

"What's that got to do with . . ."

"We've never gotten any reports back from all those swimmers who've been helped farther out to sea."

Even Knuckle Dragger chuckled.

Shook from his slumber by the commotion, Howie massaged his face with his hands and struggled to his feet. "Ah, ah, it looks like we have had a most lively discussion. Let us thank Dr. Sloan for a most informative seminar and call it a day."

Professor Prandelwoldter's sneer intensified as he bolted from the room.

. . . Choke feels all too familiar, like charging into a ten-ton marshmallow—yes, same feel as bureaucracy . . .

. . . also functions like something designed by committee . . .

. . . and grows like bureaucratic cancer: consumes data, gobbles up intellects, devours people and just gets bigger . . . cancer's most ghoulish form—neither operable nor terminal . . .

. . . does Choke also organize high talent to always function at their lowest common denominator? . . .

. . . or bungle into war and force souls with no argument to kill one another? . . .

. . . or nurture internal exploitations while choking off all external explorations? . . .

. . . Choke's existence makes no sense, but then, neither does man's toleration of his bureaucracies—fertile minds create, then become slaves to, organisms far inferior to themselves, rich minds continue to offer the awesome resource of their combined talents to something that chokes down their combined output to a trickle . . .

. . . but Choke's not one of man's bureaucracies, Choke's somehow evolved all on its own—addition after addition, eon after eon . . .

. . . is this thing, this Choke, the cosmic norm?

. . . are creativity and spirit and individual achievement only rare exceptions? . . .

. . . is Choke the Cosmic Parent of all Bureaucracy?! . . .

. . . all this makes me tired, and I haven't even expanded outside my own chamber . . . gotta stop trying to understand Choke . . . gotta understand what's happening to me! . . .

. . . but it's hard to remember much anymore . . . memory's gone, my images are just plain gone . . . what's my age? my brother's name? did I have one? was that Willie? or someone else? do I even care? . . . no, not really . . . emotions are gone, and memories are going—senility in reverse order . . .

. . . chamber's almost barren, few packets left . . . like a waterfall, no way to hold back the flow, futile . . . Choke's taken all my data, my memories and left me with just barren thought . . .

. . . what really is this chamber? . . . an entry hall?—seemed so at first . . . a home?—seemed so for a while . . . a hideaway?—certainly not! . . .

. . . face it—Choke's both predator and carnivore . . . its mental maggots have chewed me into billions and billions of bits, and now I'm nothing more than a live rat inside a snake . . . digestion near its end, and it's only a matter of time till Choke's juices distribute the rest of me throughout its flesh . . .

. . . I've really been dead all this time and didn't realize it . . . gulped in by this cosmic predator, just a step in some cosmic food chain . . . but Choke's not malicious, doesn't know emotion . . .

. . . sealed in Choke's eternal tomb, and soon there'll be no Self left, no Identity . . . just an array of cold facts to be forever diluted as they flow through this boundless arctic memory bank . . . could Choke ever know any other way? . . .

. . . but I still have awareness . . . maybe

Choke'll move me to another chamber, a full one
. . . I can still Think and Reason, still have Spirit,
can still Create . . . that's gotta be worth something! . . .

26

Flush

Jon Sloan's time had run out.

Professor Ottis T. Prandelwoldter considered himself a patient man. He'd given Sloan every possible chance to shape up. He offered him one spot after another on the team. Then he tried being a bit more forceful. Sometimes, if things don't fit, you have to use a bigger hammer. Still nothing. The only thing Sloan wanted to do was go off in the corner somewhere—and only God knows where, for he never could be found—and fill up paper with the dribblings of his daydreams. A nonproductive loner.

Professor Prandelwoldter sat in his elevated high-back chair and looked down over his raised desk at Sloan. Viewed against the unblemished, high-gloss, carbon composite grain of his desk top, Sloan didn't look all that impressive. In fact, he looked like a small, cold, wet rat as he perched on the edge of his small, hard, wooden chair, the only other chair in the room. Today's task would be much easier now that Howard had finally retired and gone.

Sloan dodged and squinted as he tried to look at Professor Prandelwoldter's face, which only partially blocked out the bright ball of sun that pierced through the window behind the desk. Yes, just the right time of day for this conversation. Professor

Prandelwoldter shuffled and reshuffled the stacks of computer printouts and exam papers on either side of his desk. Papers marked D— with bold, heavy strokes were displayed on top; the few with B— in faint, small print were hidden on the bottom. His pursed lips, furrowed brow and darting hands were at their officious best as Sloan waited an emotional eon for him to speak.

". . . ahh . . . Dr. Sloan . . . Let me remind you once again of the rules of the business we are in. The support which we receive for our computational facility, labs and observatory is all dependent upon a timely and consistent publication of research results. No pubs—no bucks!"

Even though he wore no bifocal glasses, Professor Prandelwoldter cocked his head back and looked down his nose, first at the computer printout on his desk and then again at Sloan. "We at Darmont have chosen to do first-class, in-depth, comprehensive research. It is the type that requires organization, sophisticated computational capabilities and a real team effort on the part of everyone involved. We attack the major problems of modern astrophysics with the best technology that exists in the world today. We will settle for nothing less!"

Jon squinted and squirmed.

"Last month I made my last suggestion to you. You may recall, although you have most likely dismissed it completely from your mind, that I offered you the opportunity to derive the perturbation terms for the second order extinction of NGC 58,813's Lyman Alpha line by aligned, dipolar, charged ice crystals moving across a magnetic field. I made it abundantly clear that that's all we want from you—nothing more, nothing less! And, in detail, I gave you all the appropriate rules and regulations that should guide your work.

"So far you have produced nothing. I have finally ordered one of *my* students to do it. This data is required to support one of the many inputs to the

NGC 58,813 MegaCalc Project. This part is the only one not completed and has therefore held up the programming of the entire project for the CT 9000. Until the program is run, we get no results. And with no results, we get no follow-on support. I consider your failure to follow the rules of participation that I've laid down for you as nothing but irresponsible."

"But I was working on . . ."

"I know what you were playing with." Prandelwoldter's bow tie bounced in rhythm with the finger he jabbed in and out of the sunlight. "I've told you before. Forget it. That's not what we want from you!" Then he leaned back, exhaled, flicked the inside of his hand toward Sloan as if he tossed him an invisible ball and let his hands drop to his desk with a thump. "You leave me no alternative but to deny your request for a faculty position here at Darmont. We have a limited number of positions available, and I have to give them to those who will contribute most to the department's research."

Dr. Sloan lost all color. "But . . . but how can I continue my research? . . . and . . . and support my sister?"

Professor Prandelwoldter had not wanted to make this unpleasant, but Sloan continued to force it. He was aware of the finger that he continued to jab toward Sloan but not of the sneer that consumed his face. "Forget *your* research. I don't care if you sell insurance in East Blotoville, North Dakota. Now you'll just have to go out and get a job, a real one, the kind that most everybody else has to tolerate."

The good stuff—almost all gone.

Choke probed and sampled as it continued to pick over the bones. All the meat—Facts, Data and Information—Choke had consumed. Only residue remained—Logic and Reason that related one fact to the next, Creativity that introduced new Logic and Expression, and Spirit that drove all thought and action with vitality and energy—nothing of meaning, nor nourishment to Choke, just waste to be discarded.

Choke sensed the time had come to make room, time to snare another intellect and drag its fresh meat into the lair. It zeroed the electrical voltage in Ted's chamber, one of its many depleted data buffers. And Ted's ability to think went to zero with it, excreted and flushed into a nonexistence from which there could be no retrieval.

The remnants of Son, Husband, Father, Friend, Commander, of Ted's human essence, that'd been ripped from one universe into another, ceased to exist in either.

Salvation could abide only in a third.

VI

CONFRONT

Noble or notorious, fulfilling or futile,
Man expands outward—as long as an
outward exists.

27

Arouse

0700 hours Houston time, Monday, August 30, 2038; 299 elapsed mission days on *Wayfarer 2*.

Two CT 7000 redundant timers issued electrical signals within 0.037 billionths of a second of one another. The signals changed to light pulses that traveled through fiber optics to the hibernation electronics assembly, and there, to electrical current that closed redundant Hibernol serum feed control valves, opened redundant arousal stimulant injection control valves and stimulated redundant heater controls.

By 0737 hours an EEG monitor indicated that the average voltage level in the brain of Commander Jake Ryder had doubled. Thought patterns, frozen in the icy slush of hibernation 290 days previous, thawed and inched forward.

. . . run . . . run . . . run . . . run . . . run . . . Glow ahead . . .

The road widened into a two-lane highway. A car, its door opened, waited alongside. Jake slid in. The engine kicked over, and he accelerated toward the glow.

A Drab Bomb, but it moves. IT hides in darkness. Have to reach light. Be there soon. Smokin' right

along. Ow! What're those? . . . Ow! More of 'em
. . . even out here—damn speed bumps!

Road narrowed back to a single lane as a sign
blared its message—STOP! Jake stopped. Below the
sign discreet letters whispered, "Backing up or moving forward will result in severe tire damage. Thank
you. Have a nice day."

Jake accelerated.

Screw 'em. Gotta get to that glow. Tires're
ripped off, but rims're still good. Press!

Road crumbled to cobblestone and turned up-
hill. Jake peered ahead as the light approached. Drab
Bomb clanged and bounced, then slogged to a stop as
road petered into a spongy path.

Bastards can't stop me!

Jake's feet sank into mush, a sticky gray mush
that blended upward into gray air.

Hardly breathe. Hardly see. Glue's up to my
knees. No taste, no character—just resistance. But
almost there. I won't be stopped!

The light sharpened to a single gray beam that
radiated a lone desk and chair. Jake trudged to a stop,
flinched and started to turn. But Hands came out of
the grayness, first a few, then hundreds.

Hey, Hands, get off me. Let me up!

But the hands held his body tight as they thrust
Out-Basket in his face. His eyes darted to his left—
empty paper, gray recycled paper that waited for his
words. To his right—a blank computer screen that
waited for his inputs.

Jake flexed his body and inched toward the computer. The invisible hands softened their grip on his
arms. His fingers rippled over the computer's keyboard. The screen yielded its menu.

Good. Maybe this damned digital devil's on my
side. But what procedure should I select? Yeah,
there's the one—Bureaucracy Override! Call it up.
Great! Just a simple set of equations. Need to input
only a few numbers. References me to page Z-13p of
appendix R 3.1D, update 61. Call it up. Got it!

Warmth filled Jake as a smile of anticipation spread over his face. His hands trembled. Then small discreet letters bloomed on dull screen:

This page intentionally left blank.

Jake's stomach heaved.

Stimulant continued to increase electrical activity in the brain of Jake Ryder. Horror faded. Reason gained upper hand. In the basement of his mind, lids slid over tops of pots from which his seamy dreams boiled. Now the covers could block the sinuous streams of black vapor that erupted from seething depths and turned gray as they welled upward. Now Rational Mind could expand into the void above, surge up and out to meet the warm and brilliant light that shafted in from the sane and sensible world above. Yes, from here on Reason would prevail, Rational Mind would monitor, organize, censor and control each and every thought, each and every action . . . except where a cover leaked.

Jake's feet sunk into grass, into the field alive with crickets and robins who broadcast with equal joy. Earth's rawness saturated his nostrils. He squinted ahead into the morning sun, first at a possum that scurried out of his path, then at Val who seemed to glide toward him over the field's blanket of yellow flowers. He reached for her hands.

VAL—LIFE!

Jake's hands squeezed.

"Jake, are you awake? Your EEG shows you are."

Faye? Already? Yellow indicators're off. Gotta get outta my pod. Help others. Get control. Lot to do. Hustle!

Jake pushed a few sounds through his vocal cords, through the viscous glue that clogged his throat. "Uh-uh. Hi."

"Hi, Jake. You're coming out of it just fine. Here, have some water. Take a lot. It helps your throat. You also need a couple of liters just to get rid of the toxins you've accumulated."

Water trickled down Jake's throat. Glue dissolved. Then he gulped the water down. "Thanks. How's the ship?"

"Good. No alarms, active or stored. Only some messages from Houston in the computer, waiting in cue."

"Great. Body feels stiff, like petrified wood."

"You'll feel better once you move around. Your heart rate, metabolic rate and brain activity are almost back to normal. And your color's good. Here, let's get your needle and electrodes off."

"Thanks. Good thing its zero g. Don't think I'd steam around too quick in normal gravity."

"Once you're moving, you'll come back rapidly."

Jake pushed his arms out with deliberation and extra care. His flesh felt like glass and any fast motion would cause it to shatter. "Is Speed up next?"

"Yep. His stimulant injection just started."

Jake removed his thermometer, eased out of his pod and floated to the computer console at the center of the chamber. Another fragile push moved him to the plexan door of Speed's pod.

"God, Faye! Did I look that . . . that dead?"

"Not really dead, but you did look just the same."

"Looks like something's had him stuffed and mounted. A wax mold of the real Speed. Just a lifeless bag of ivory-colored leather."

"Blood pressure's still low. Most of his blood's still concentrated in his vital organs. But within the hour he'll return to the old, fun-filled Speed we know and love. Com'on over here and watch the monitor. See, his EEG's picking up."

"Yeah, something's perkin' in there."

Choke slumbered.

As with every living creature, digestion sapped its strength. Choke directed all its energy inward to its electrical arteries, which transported packets of devoured data from sorting chambers to distant tentacles and their cells of electrical flesh. Every cell scrutinized each and every packet it received, anguished, then decided—save or discard.

Though each tentacle had created its own procedures, the net result of all decisions never varied: each cell either reproduced each packet it received, sent the reproductions on to numerous other cells and saved the original, or it reproduced each packet it received, sent the reproductions on to numerous other cells and discarded the original. Every second Choke's flesh made millions of decisions, passed on billions of packets and created millions of new cells.

As Choke slumbered, Choke grew.

And once all devoured data cleared Choke's arteries, Choke catnapped; once all reproduced data cleared, it awoke.

Choke flexed and stretched. Energy returned.

28

Crave

Quiet and pensive. Jake's mood mirrored his crew's as he glanced around the wardroom table. He tried to shake the last remnants of lethargy from his system as he composed himself and thought of what lay ahead. He'd emerged from hibernation into a dull, round, empty nowhereland. But time and stimulants brought well-ordered thought and, with it, intensity and purpose. But now the focus changed. Study, training, preparations, travel and warm-ups no longer mattered a bit. Game time—now only performance counted!

Jake measured himself. He felt ready. In fact, he'd never felt the level of mental energy that his rational mind now sought to control. With every thought and every suggestion, vivid images, as precise packets of data, snapped front and center and froze at attention before his mind's eye.

Jake studied his crew. They, too, looked ready.

After Irwin had regained full consciousness, Faye ran each of them through an automated body tissue, bones and fluids analysis. She'd detected no physical abnormalities. But they each shared the same mental hurdle. Although ten months had marched by, it seemed like only one long night's sleep. The length of their hair and fingernails gave some evidence of the actual passage of time. The view out the dome confirmed it.

"We'll take another look," said Jake. "Lights, zero." The wall glow faded.

As Jake's eyes adjusted to the blackness behind the plexan, a faint sea of bright points emerged. First hundreds appeared. Then thousands of stars bloomed and thickened. A fresh awareness burst forth in Jake's mind. For the first time in his life, Jake no longer felt confined to a single star. He'd stepped out and now moved within this three-dimensional sea, graduated from observer to participant. True, he'd made only a small tentative step, just a shuffle or stumble, but nonetheless a step, like all those first steps man'd made onto land, across mountains and oceans, and into air and space; he'd made that first step that must precede the strides between stars and galaxies; a step that'd lead to the matter-of-fact stellar travel that'd fill the billions of years left for man in his current universe; a step into those eons of man's time before gravity would again pull all matter and energy back to a point, squeeze it and spurt it into the next cycle.

"If anyone ever doubted the Sun is only another star, they should see it like this," said Faye. "The brightest star in the sky, but still just a point."

"Yep, no brighter than a night light," said Speed.

As a packet, a vivid image of a baby with Speed's face popped into Jake's mind and he chuckled to himself.

. . . next to his night light . . . rubbing a silk blanket against his cheek . . . sucking his thumb . . .

"It's about five times as bright as a full moon back on Earth."

Faye squinted into the gloom around their modules. "Good comparison, Speed. I can see sharp shadows from the truss on Beta, but it's nighttime for sure. And it's just a black and white world, no color. Kinda eerie."

"It'll stay like this and might even seem darker when we get closer to the Wayfarers," said Speed.

They continued to stare at the stars in silence until Irwin brought up the lights. The flight plan required they finish their breakfast.

Jake's coffee floated a foot from his eyes in its clear, accordionlike container. He peered into its blackness, then cupped his hands around it and let its warmth spread into his palms and fingers. It appeared friendly enough. He put its fingerlike spigot to his lips and nudged out some fluid. Warmth flowed into his mouth, down his throat and into his core. Its smell permeated his nose and consciousness, dredged up a single packet of memories.

. . . rich coffee aroma . . . perfume . . . sleep creases on Val's cheek . . . soft bathrobe and skin . . . gentle half-opened eyes . . . soft smile . . .

"When can we see the Wayfarers?" asked Faye.

"Won't see them for about another four days," Boris boomed in a relaxed deep voice. Hibernation had agreed with him. "That is, they can't be seen by eye until we're about two days away from them. I looked and couldn't even see them with the telescope."

"What's your last calculation on the time for the braking burn?" asked Jake.

"Ignition's about two hours from now, at 0107 on mission day 300. It'll last six days and 3.173 hours. We'll blend that burn right into the one for rendezvous with *Wayfarer 1*. We can set up for that once we get some radar tracking on either one of their modules."

"When will we be close enough for that?" asked Jake.

"In about five days, or about one day away from rendezvous."

Jake turned to Irwin. "Find anything in your last look at the systems?"

Irwin looked straight at Jake and spoke with

crisp precision. "Nope, nothing more than what you and I already discussed, the slightly high voltage on the B2 redundant power amplitron over here in this module. And nothing at all off nominal over in Beta." A packet of memories of warmth, of home, of morning's freshness spread outward with the bacon flavor on Jake's tongue. "Ada, computer system still clean, like we found it at our previous status check?"

"Sure is!" At home in her element, Ada's face wore the radiant glow of enthusiasm and confidence. "Looks as good as it did at its preflight checkout."

"Yep, boss, this's the best simulation we've had so far," said Speed.

"Let's keep it that way," said Jake. "Everybody at their stations by 2400. It'll give us each an hour to get squared away before the braking burn."

By an hour into the burn, the image of the long violet-red shaft from the Beta module and the buzz that vibrated throughout their own structure again crystallized and sunk downward in the back of Jake's mind. All systems remained nominal. Again, he had free time and he reviewed the medical observations he'd just transcribed.

The tumbling sensation he sometimes felt at the start of a burn had lasted only about thirty seconds this time. Interesting. And also mild compared to the start of reentry burns after other long missions. Jake felt like he'd tumbled head over heels, but in no certain direction. Must be just the same as they first noticed way back on Skylab, just a vestibular disturbance of some kind. His inner ear hadn't felt gravity for months, and it sent out signals that on other long flights his brain forgot how to interpret. But this time, hibernation had slipped ten months of zero gravity by his brain and made it appear like only weeks.

Jake turned down the intensity of his display and reflected. Yep, a perfect mission, shootin' right down the center of the pike. But why did he feel uneasy?

Systems and computers worked as advertised. And he and Boris understood every detail of the flight from the time they'd split into Alpha and Beta till they'd join up again. Yet, even though everything looked exactly in place, he felt something layin' out there over the next rise with a knife in its teeth, something that moved on silent feet . . . That's dumb! Lighten up, Ryder. Val always said watchin' all those late-night holovision horror flicks wasn't good. Get on with it.

Jake turned up his display and reviewed the system status again. Nothing had changed. He relaxed. His limp hand slipped into the inside pocket of his flight jacket, the spot reserved for the hard copy of Val's message that waited in computer memory when he awoke. He again pulled the message out, its paper dog-eared at the corners and worn at the folds. Like he held dried leaves, his fingertips finessed the paper open again.

A familiar warmth tingled over his skin as he read her words and her holovision image, which also waited in computer memory, surged forward in his mind as a single packet.

Ryder, you horny old buzzard, even after all these years she turns you on more than ever. Seems just a reach away. His fingertips refolded the message and slipped it back into the warmth of his inner pocket.

Choke's last meal, the first nourishment that it'd extracted from this smaller tentacle, the one called Wayfarer, tantalized Choke. The detail and complexity of the food called Man had made it a challenge to digest, for it necessitated a reproduction of data and growth of cells on scales never before encountered. But Choke had met the challenge, digested Man and, in the process, added and reproduced many new cells and enhanced the size of this and several other tentacles.

Man provided Choke with all the basic building

blocks required for its flesh, much like protein provided for Man himself. And the richness of Man's savory and succulent data now left Choke with a voracious appetite. Empty data buffers again settled and simmered. Electrical jaws flexed and their power surged.

Choke, a cosmic shark on the prowl, turned all its sensors up to full gain—time to find another meal!

29

Sever

"Looks like a miniature galaxy," said Faye, as she squinted through the eyepiece.

"In a way it is," said Boris. "The black hole at the center holds the Wayfarers together as they revolve, like the gravity of all the stars does in a galaxy."

Jake pressed the key at the central control console marked TV SOURCE—TELESCOPE. "Let's all take a look." The image of a white, flat cloud filled the wall screen.

"Looks like a huge plate," said Faye. "All the Wayfarer Objects are in the same plane."

Speed floated in front of the screen. Enthusiasm burbled out from his core like bubbles that boiled from water heated in a microwave. "Yeah. Most of these little Wayfarer jobber-do's must've been going around the black hole for millions of years. After banging into each other lots of times, they've finally agreed to go in the same direction—smarter than humans."

Boris's eyeballs did a slight roll. "At least that makes it easier for us to maneuver around them. Cuts down the chance of collision."

"Right," said Jake. "A break for us. What's the radar track on the *Wayfarer 1* modules show?"

Boris pressed the RADAR OVERLAY and TRAN-

SPONDER RETURN keys. Two red points appeared
within the white cloud on the screen, almost on top
of one another. "Although the power levels are way
down, both modules are still returning our radar signals."

"If their radar transponders are working, so
should their comm transmitters, and they should've
been able to return all our calls," said Jake.

"Unless . . ." said Boris.

"They're in hibernation," said Faye.

"Ahhh . . . yeah," said Boris.

They each stared at the screen in silence, except
for Boris who made a short series of entries into CT
7000. "We should have enough tracking data by now
to define their orbits."

CT 7000 replaced the telescope image with several lines, then labeled them. A red oval, flattened to
the shape of a cigar, it labeled WAYFARER 1; a large
black dot at one end of the red cigar, BLACK HOLE;
and a curved blue line that made a smooth connection to the other end of the cigar, WAYFARER 2 AP-
PROACH TRAJECTORY.

Speed let out a low lurid whistle. "Holy horse
hockey. Look at that baby! *Wayfarer 1*'s whippin'
back and forth in almost a straight line—largest yo-yo
in the galaxy. Orbit's really eccentric. What're its
parameters?"

Boris made additional keystrokes and numbers
popped up next to the cigar. "Both *Wayfarer 1* modules are in approximately the same 50-by-47,450-
mile orbit."

"You mean they go to within fifty miles of the
black hole, and then out to a distance almost a thousand times larger?" asked Faye.

Boris nodded. "Also, their orbit's almost fifteen
times longer than it is wide. One module is slightly
ahead of the other, and their orbital period is 21.73
hours."

"Why haven't either of the modules hit any of

the Wayfarers and been knocked into the same circular orbit with them?" asked Jake.

Boris called up the side view of the orbits of the modules and the Wayfarer Objects. Two straight lines appeared in the shape of an open jaw. A red line, labeled WAYFARER MODULES, formed the top jaw. A white line, labeled OBJECTS, which represented the flat cloud of Wayfarer Objects seen on edge, formed the bottom jaw. The large black dot, again labeled BLACK HOLE, rested at their intersection.

"See, that's the reason. They're not in the same plane as the Wayfarers," said Boris. "There's an angle of 37.3 degrees between them."

"No wonder they haven't been knocked around," said Jake. "They can only hit one of the Wayfarers when they're close to the black hole. And the Wayfarers must be small enough there, like sand, that the hits are only minor."

"But, eventually, they will hit enough of them and drop into the hole," said Boris.

Jake glanced at Speed who floated next to him in a rare state—speechless. Something'd turned off the energy to the microwave. Speed just smoldered and steamed. Jake grabbed his shoulder, rotated him as he floated in space so that they were face-to-face and jiggled him. "Speed?"

". . . wonder . . . I wonder what it'll be like to get that close to a black hole," Speed mumbled to himself before he looked at Jake. "Fifty miles? Just like we feared. We'll have to dive right into the bowels of that black beast!"

Numbers flashed on the console in front of Boris. "Looks like we'd have a force of twelve times gravity pulling our modules away from each other at their fifty-mile perigee, just like we calculated before."

"Damn," said Jake. "There's no way around it. I'd hoped we wouldn't have to split up. But we can't fight twelve g's."

"That's for sure," said Boris. "It's good we had

win and Ada start the checkout on Beta early. Now
ve're two hours ahead."

"Let's stay that way," said Jake. "Recalculate the
light plan so that we keep that two-hour pad in it
rom here on."

Boris returned to his keyboard, and a new time-
ine diffused onto his screen over the old. "There it is.
At 1430, an hour twenty from now, I'll go over to
Beta, help them complete the checkout and then
tay there. You and Speed go EVA and remove the
bridge at 1700. Tomorrow, mission day 307, at 0734
ve each start the burn for the final phase of the
rendezvous. We should join up with the first *Wayfarer 1* module by 0913."

"Good timing," said Jake. "That's when they'll
be farthest from the black hole. It should give us
enough time to check out both modules."

A placid Speed, full energy diverted to internal
hought, literally drifted into the conversation.
"Yeah. It should also give us enough time to really
study the situation—to decide if we really want to
follow them all the way down."

"Uhhh . . . com'on, ya little mother!"

"Let me get a hand on it too, Speed . . . uhhh
. . this last one's really tight . . . goin' to take both
hands."

"I've been on over a hundred EVAs, but none
like this," said Speed.

"Oh?"

"Here we are working our butts off in light that's
only a little brighter than a full moon—and that's it,
nothin' more. We'll never get back into daylight and
see what we're really doin'."

Jake looked back along 237 feet of bridge trusswork, back into blackness toward their Alpha module
where the glow in a single lighted window silhouetted Faye's head. "Yeah, some bright sun would be
nice, Speed. But this bridge couldn't care less how

much light there is. It always works the same. And this job's as straight forward as they make 'em."

"You're right. Let's show this locking clip who's boss. Together . . . pull! It's comin' . . . ahhh!" As the clip released, Speed's gloves slipped off its edge and he shot away into the dark void.

Jake's gloves held. "Good goin'. Beta's free."

Jake put the fingertips of his left hand on the window that contained Boris's round red face, wide eyes and white-tipped nose pressed up against the inside plexan. The heads of Ada and Irwin filled adjacent windows. He gripped the bridge with his right hand and gave a hard, steady push outward. Beta inched away. Boris, Ada and Irwin returned Jake's thumbs up with see-ya-after-lunch-type waves before they turned back inward to pick up their interrupted tasks.

Speed returned at almost the same velocity as he left. "Nice going, Hercules. Ya rrrreally got 'em rippin' away."

"Enough to do the job. Hustle. Let's collapse this bridge and get back inside."

Speed pulled himself hand over hand back toward the Alpha module. He stopped at the first joint and released the lock pin. "This whole frappin' operation is like something out of yesteryear."

"Right. Would've been automated if they'd had the time to do it. This's real grunt work."

"I knew ya brought me along for something besides housework."

"Yep, that's what I like—versatility."

Within fifteen minutes they reached Alpha.

"Doors are open, boss. Let 'er rip."

As a motor reeled in the carbon cord that ran the full length of the bridge through its center, the trusswork began a methodical collapse into the Alpha's storage pod. Inch by inch, the 237-foot structure grew shorter. Jake watched the pod start to swallow the last physical link between the two halves of his crew and weighed what they were doing.

The Split. Just one of thousands of procedures in the checklist. A mission requirement. Separate now or be torn apart later. But Jake still wondered. How much'd they really improved their chances of success, or survival? Will one half be better off without the other?

And in this module we have Jake, one-time hot-shot test pilot, now generalist, master of nothing, manager who feeds off the abilities of others; and his smartassed sidekick, Speed, superscientist steeped in useless theory; and lastly, Faye, female pill pusher and snooze specialist who doesn't know a redshift from a gearshift. You chose 'em, Ryder. You live with 'em—ya could die with 'em.

But over in that module we have Boris, tough-as-a-brass-bear Boris, best navigator on or off Earth—essential! Without precise navigation close to the black hole, especially in this yo-yo-type orbit, you make just one slip and in you go. Blaze for an instant and disappear forever. And no one knows the CT 7000 better than Ada, nor procedures better than Irwin. Mistakes in either area, and it could be over just as quick.

Is that the right slant? Jake smiled. Maybe not.

And in this module we have Jake, experienced space commander and sage leader, endowed with courage and infallible judgment; and that wonder who wallows in wit and wisdom, Speed, the ideal combination of brilliant scientist, sharp pilot and operational crewman; and lastly, Faye, that physician who dispenses keen human insight with only a minimum of observations and data.

But over in that module we have Boris, boring boorish Boris, the navigator who couldn't steer his palms to his buns without a full set of equations; and Ada, a callous computer queen hooked on digital dope; and lastly, Irwin, just a human robot who, without procedures, is as useful as a locomotive without tracks.

The pod swallowed the last section of bridge with the same precision and ease as the first.

Not even a burp. Which slant's right? Maybe a little of both. But how much of each applies here?

"Button up the doors, and let's go get some sleep. Tomorrow'll be here before we know it."

"You bet your big, bright, beautiful bippy, boss."

Jake winced. Maybe the first slant's more correct. "And the day's goin' to be a big one, Speed."

"Yep, a real biggy!"

30

Whisper

Hey, arm, what are you doing out there?

Even in zero gravity, Jake usually slept straight through the night—but not tonight.

In the blackness of his sleep compartment, he opened his eyes wide. He let them rove in their sockets, being careful not to move his head. No, no one here.

But Jake sensed a faint neural alarm, like eyes were riveted to the back of his skull. Impossible. Only a wall covered with pad and pillow behind him.

No, maybe it felt more like the stare from a crowd that one picks up out of the corner of his eye. But when the crowd's examined, phantom looker's never there. Impossible. No one could be there in this compartment with him.

Jake detected only the faint outline of his right arm suspended in front of him like that of a marionette. In the middle of the night, one or the other arm would sometimes work itself out from under his chest restraint and float free. If allowed to wake up slowly, he'd instinctively pull it back before he woke up enough to record its wanderings. But tonight something pulled him up from the depths of his sleep. Something zipped him in an express elevator from subbasement to top floor with no stops in between. Something! It wouldn't step forward, nor would it go away. Sneaky and sly, it just clung to him and stayed out of view.

Maybe it's a sound. Jake cocked his head to one side, locked his eyes and listened. Whispers! Someone or something. He turned his auditory gain up to maximum sensitivity. Each year the technician who tested his hearing asked the same question, "Doesn't the squeal of grass growing bother you?" If any sound existed, he'd hear it.

Yes, it had to be a sound.

And Jake did hear it, a soft and wily sound, a cunning sound, a cagey sound. He couldn't make out any words, or tone, or direction, or . . . But he heard it!

He felt poised at the entrance of a vast empty chamber, a chamber that echoed each creak from his shoes, each breath from his lungs.

Or could it be Faye? No, more likely Speed. Yeah, Speed. Like that time the deep voice boomed slow distinct words down and all around them: "This is God speaking!" Jake could still see Val's wide-open eyes. They must've looked at each other for a whole five seconds before they realized the voice didn't come from heaven but from Speed who shouted down their chimney. A first-rate gotcha. Must've laughed for an hour. Could he be up to something again? No, not here, not now. Even Speed has his limits.

Jake continued to fill his mind with counterfeit thought, to hold his real thoughts under and force himself back to sleep. But the pounding in his chest and ears distracted him.

And he still sensed something, something like one of those invisible infrared dots on your forehead from a laser sight of a high-powered rifle . . . or that snake coiled in the dark corner . . . or even those standard Hollywood Indians that peek down from behind every boulder in the pass.

Jake knew for sure he could talk himself out of it.

Forget it, Ryder, you need your sleep. But I'm a target of something or someone. Naw, you're just keyed up over tomorrow. But I'm not that way. I always plan it, then forget it. I never worry. So don't now—to hell with it—forget it!

Yet deep within his mind he heard that sound, that sly, cunning and wily sound.

Choke focused the detection antennae on its Wayfarer tentacle at their highest sensitivity. It waited, and it waited. Eventually, faint but readable signals appeared. Aroused, Choke reached out, probed, then sampled the aroma. Electrical saliva seeped into Choke's data buffers. Yes, the aroma resembled the last meal—delicious!

But food's distance also aroused a frustration within Choke, just way too far away for acquisition. But would it be forever? Choke sampled and waited, then sampled and waited again. With each whiff, the aroma grew just a little stronger.

Choke's drenched data buffers gnashed and churned. Empty chambers deep within its innards growled. No doubt about it—another feast headed its way!

31

Press

Tuesday, September 7, 2038, mission day 307.

At 0703 hours CST Klaus Hofmeister sat straight but relaxed in his firm high-back chair. He'd already been at work for two hours. His hands rested in loose lumps on top of his seventy-year-old oak desk. In these days when government issue meant either paper or plexan, Klaus felt proud of his possession, and his skills at bartering and midnight requisitioning to get it. Its massive structure and sturdy frame attracted him—something durable and dependable, something rare. An array of micro-nicks and chips covered its fine wood grain, but his hand had polished them into its satin finish where they gleamed like merit badges of performance. Yes, this hunk of wood had substance and character, qualities to be respected and honored.

Klaus looked at Dr. Dupree who sat on the edge of the adjacent chair. One large Dupree hand rolled itself into a tight ball in his lap while fingers of the other drummed a fierce but irregular beat on the satin finish under Klaus's nose. The heavy drummer hand jerked and thumped and banged with all the coordination of a tap-dancing sumo wrestler. Klaus leaned back.

"Klaus, I'll tell you just once again! The *Wayfarer*

1 orbit's a disaster. This tracking data changes the whole picture. We have to order them to stop and wait, wait for our analysis and commands."

"Nope. There's no way we can help them any more than we have already. There's no need to change our mode of operation."

"The orbit's too eccentric, too sensitive to error. If their navigation, guidance or control aren't perfect, they could end in the center of that thing and blow the whole mission. We never gave them rules for this type of thing."

"You're right. It'll be tricky. But they sent this data to us over one and one-half days ago. Right this minute they're probably pulling alongside one of the *Wayfarer 1* modules. And they're not going to sit still for a day and a half and wait for our instructions."

"They should."

"Why? All we have to contribute now is ignorance. And if I know them, waiting is not even a consideration."

"It should be. We've got far more navigation and computing capabilities than they."

"So what? They've got all they need to do the job."

Dupree's hands began a slow dry wash of one another. He slipped into the twilight of his resistance. "They couldn't have thought of everything."

"We can't operate that way. It'd be slower than playing chess through the old nonelectronic mail."

Dupree mumbled. "They should wait . . . we've got so much more data . . . we should be in control." His lips fluttered.

"But we don't have the data that's most useful—the what's happening there and now. We've given them all the help we can. We've sent the latest updates to the total onboard electronics data file, even detailed descriptions of the spacecraft structural modifications, optics-drive speed changes, remnants of the military radiation active-protection system and the latest test data on their nuclear power system. They have all that's relevant and far more."

"But . . ."

Klaus studied Dr. Dupree with patience, understanding and a twinge of sympathy. But just a twinge. Over recent months Dupree resembled a gaffed fish that flopped and wiggled in the bottom of the boat. Now he only burned energy, only did further harm to himself, only accelerated his own end. A picture of futility. A man who sensed his time was up.

These Wayfarer missions, even more than the space station and planetary missions, had forced a change. And Dupree couldn't adapt. Control had been his water, his means of motion, his source of life. He inhaled it and swam in it out of habit, out of emotional dependence. The bottle had proven not to be an adequate substitute, as had become obvious to those around him. Once gaffed and dragged into this new world, his dependence proved to be too deep, too finely woven into his nature to be extracted. After all, he controlled! He didn't assist, or help, or aid, or contribute, or do any of those mealymouthed things that, to him, meant only second best. If he couldn't be captain, he'd take his ball and go home. But this time he had a real problem. He no longer owned the ball.

Three days previous Dr. Daro told Klaus he had selected a permanent director of operations control —Klaus. It'd become clear that Dr. Dupree's "knowledge, experience and control expertise" could more appropriately be utilized in a staff position in the WSF Director of Documentation Regulation.

"Laurent, we got up early so we could watch the data come in and listen to their communications. The day's still young. Let's go do it. Who knows. We might actually think of something more that could help them, something useful that we should send up."

Dupree's face went blank, his color gone. Vitality evaporated. He slumped back, let out a long sigh and stared straight ahead.

Klaus once heard eyes described as windows to the soul. If so, something inside Dupree had just pulled the shades.

"Status, Speed."

"All systems good, no anomalies. Propellant's one percent above redline for nominal rendezvous and return. We're 3,700 feet away and closing at 21 feet per second. Should be there by 0913."

Faye pushed her face against the window. "I can't see which module we're coming up on . . . Ted's or his crew's."

Jake released his fingers from the hand controllers and pulled his face against the window. "Right, can't tell yet."

"Radar shows Boris just reached station-keeping distance," said Speed.

"Yeah, see him," said Jake. "He's just got the searchlight on it. Let's ask him."

As Jake reached for the transmit key on his personal comm, Boris's voice exploded from the speaker. Primed and ready for attack, Boris spit out words in an emphatic staccato. "The *Wayfarer 1* module is in the free drift mode but not tumbling. A major fracture is located at the bridge-spacecraft interface on the bridge side. The deformation pattern indicates that the stress was primarily longitudinal, but there was also a positive torque component in the Y-Z plane. The fracture initiated in the A4 strut and sequentially propagated through the remaining struts in the plus-Y direction at successively greater values of X."

Faye's eyes squinted and her mouth puckered. "What?"

"I think he said something ripped the hell out of that sucker," said Speed.

"Oh."

"Which module is it, Boris?" asked Jake.

"It's Beta, Ted's module."

"We're coming up on the opposite side of Boris,"

said Jake. "We'll dock at the plus-Z radial port, you take minus Z. As planned, we'll open our hatch and go in and find Ted. Keep yours closed until we give the OK."

"Right, Jake," said Boris. "We're dockin' now."

"We're twenty-seven minutes before apogee," said Speed. "Only eleven and a half hours to perigee."

Jake slid their module into position alongside Ted's *Wayfarer 1* module and Boris's *Wayfarer 2* module docked to it. He examined both. What a contrast! Except for shape, they didn't look like the same spacecraft. His searchlight glistened off polished silver and black surfaces of *Wayfarer 2.* But the dull gray pitted surface of *Wayfarer 1* diffused and absorbed his light. It looked like it'd been blasted by a cosmic sand storm. Maybe not too far from the truth, he thought. At perigee—it all happens at perigee. Must see lots of erosion as it smashes through the sand-sized Wayfarers. And it'll do it over and over again until it drops in.

Shafts of light streamed from *Wayfarer 2.* Nothing came from *Wayfarer 1.* A uniform gray curtain covered each of *1*'s windows and hid its contents, wouldn't let any of its darkness leak out. Except for the shreds of the bridge, Ted's module looked intact. But Jake also felt its gray and lifeless character, like Speed before he came out of hibernation. Is life also buried deep within its core?

Jake lined up on *Wayfarer 1*'s radial docking port and commanded closure speed. To his accelerated mind, they crept forward in slow motion. They hit with the familiar mellow thud and locked up tight.

Jake paused a few seconds to let his mind and body go limp. OK, so far so good. This docking's just as good as hundreds of others. But I feel something different, something hostile. We've knocked on Ted's door, and we're not welcome, not wanted. We don't belong, don't . . . bullshit—*press*!

"Data umbilical's mated," said Speed, as he

called up a display at his console. "Let's see what shape his module's in." He scrolled through several displays. "All systems are intact except for communications and power. Every transmitter's failed, as we knew, but every damn one of them is literally burned up! And they in turn've shorted out the total electrical system. Emergency power is still going to the atmosphere control and the radar transponder. At least the pressure's normal. The hull's tight."

"What's the status of the hibernation chamber?" asked Faye.

"Can't tell. No readouts from it without main power," said Speed.

Faye pushed away from the window. "Let's get in there and find Ted."

"We'll safe our systems first, then head for the airlock," said Jake. "And let's hustle. We gotta be undocked before perigee."

"Right, boss. If we don't undock, the black hole'll pull us apart like a steaming fresh croissant!"

32

Inter

"Everybody wins a prize," said Speed, as he passed out oxygen-intercom masks. He strapped his own carbex filament-wound oxygen bottle behind his hip. "They're each good for an hour twenty, but we may not even need them once inside."

"Take your thermal jackets and gloves," said Jake. "No power means no heat." That could also be true of Ted's hibernation pod, he thought, unless the pod's emergency power still worked.

Jake cracked open the valve on their airlock's outside hatch. Air flowed out and into the common volume between their module and Ted's that they created by their docking. As he waited for its pressure to build up and equal their own, the lull in activity left Jake's mind in idle. Memories flowed forward in bursts.

. . . valves and chambers and heart . . . life, Val—wide smile, blue eyes . . . blue pool, deep water . . . Command Post, sun, Hans, Vodkorn Blitz, newspaper . . . nuclear . . . Ryder! What the hell are you doing? Keep your mind on the job. Helluva time to let it wander.

But Jake didn't feel like it really wandered. It felt more like it was pulled, like all those random visions and thoughts were pulled. What should he do next?

Why couldn't he remember? Didn't he get enough sleep? Oh yeah, that's it, the airlock procedures on the computer checklist on his cuff: when pressure difference is less than 0.07 psi, open *Wayfarer 2* hatch; enter airlock and check pressure difference to *Wayfarer 1;* when less than 0.07 psi, open *Wayfarer 1* hatch. OK, now I'm back on track. What got me so distracted?

Jake hit a switch and the *Wayfarer 2* hatch popped off its seal and swept open. "Second delta P's good." He commanded the *Wayfarer 1* hatch open. No movement. No sound. He hit the switch a second time. Nothing. He pulled on the handle for manual operation. No movement. "Speed, give me a hand."

"More grunt work—my specialty."

The hatch cracked off its seal. They pushed. Faye joined them. The hatch jerked and grated open.

Jake floated forward, then halted as he hit a wall of arctic air. The cold stripped heat from his clothing and bit into his skin. His hand swung to his clothing heater control and snapped it up to maximum.

Speed studied the gas analyzer display in the wall next to the hatch. "Air's minus 43—colder than a witch's wazoo. But the oxygen level's good, and there're no toxic gases."

Jake swung his mask away. The shaft of light from his module illuminated an arm-length cloud of fog as it tumbled away from his face. He'd braced for the bite of cold on his cheeks but not for the invasion of his nostrils.

Foul! Not just stale. Ted? . . . probably not. Just spoiled food. It must've rotted while the module was still warm but without power. Yeah, spoiled food, that's gotta be it!

Jake replaced his mask, took a deep breath and cleaned his lungs.

They turned their backs to the airlock and aimed their spotlights down the corridor to the main tunnel. The dark cavern sucked in their light and returned only cold blackness. They nudged forward.

Jake's fingertips glided over handrails as he led the parade into the main tunnel, then toward the hibernation chamber. They inched their way along the full length of the tunnel that led to the chamber entrance. What little structure he saw and felt matched that in their own module. But there all similarity stopped. Something heavy and grim surrounded him, enveloped him, bore into him. He felt like he'd returned in the middle of the night, returned to the darkened but familiar structure of his house, to the home that used to hold warmth and cheer and light, only to find all life annihilated and the mortician busy at his trade.

"Tough to tell where we are in this tunnel with only these handheld lights," said Faye.

"Or even which direction we're going," said Speed.

Jake's light swept over the chamber entrance. "Got it. Over here."

Jake and Speed pulled open the hatch. The parade poured into the chamber. Their lights jerked from one hibernation pod to the next. A wave of disappointment and frustration mounted with the sight of each empty pod. It crested and broke as their lights hovered on the last one.

Jake's hope drained into the cold. "Damn! Hoped it'd be different."

Speed expelled a long sigh but said nothing.

"The odds of finding him alive anywhere else in this cold are next to zero," said Faye.

"Yeah," said Jake. "But just the same, we've gotta find him. Gotta find out what went wrong."

"The command center," said Speed. "That's where we last saw him on holovision."

"Right," said Jake.

In silence they snaked their way back into the main tunnel. Again, Jake felt it. The darkness held something, hid something. In Jake's mind, a black dread firmed its hold. IT confined and suffocated. He forced IT down, out of his thoughts, below the surface where IT belonged . . . but IT seeped back up, dark and foul and vile.

Jake's light ducked into and out of the entertainment room. It seemed not to belong in this module, not to fit, to be as out of place as a baby's rattle in the hangman's hand.

The parade accelerated. They glided past the exercise facility and airlock, past the maintenance and repair complex where their lights flicked by, then back over Ted's EVA suit. Its decapitated form hovered, motionless, a lifeless skin without its human contents to give it strength and motion and meaning.

Jake paused, put a finger under one side of his mask and forced it from his face. Half a breath—too much! Rancid, putrid, stronger than before. Gonna gag. Source ahead?

They swept by the observatory room and science laboratory, reached the entrance to the command center and slowed to a stop.

Jake took stock. His total body shivered. He couldn't control it. Cold had overrun his outer defense of clothing, even with its electrical heat, then wormed its way right to his core. But through his shivers he felt sweat that'd soaked into the cloth on his chest and back and pooled on his forehead. He held his breath and listened.

Quiet. Dead quiet. Absolute nothing, except for his pulse.

He moved his hand back toward his mask. The cloth over his shoulder scraped and grated in his ear. A foulness rushed in next to his finger. He recognized it—that same stench that once burst forth from that rodent hole he'd poisoned three weeks before. He held his breath and withdrew his finger. The foulness hovered there, trapped between his face and mask. He paused and waited. Finally, he had no choice. He inhaled. Decayed and decomposed, the stench of death flooded into his lungs.

Time's up. Open it.

They pulled. The hatch swung. He pushed forward.

Three shafts of light darted over walls, windows, floor, controls, displays and empty crew stations. Nothing. Nothing except that gray film that covered every surface, that film that'd locked out their light, that film that had to have a source. But . . . maybe Ted wasn't there. Maybe he went back to the other module. Maybe he might still be . . .

Jake felt a nudge on his right shoulder, soft and slow and gentle. He rotated his wrist and light, his head, then his vision.

FACE-TO-FACE!

NO! Not real—dreams only! World always takes care of these things, somehow. Death's never more than just a few tears, a few stories, a few pictures, a few forms, a few changes, a few . . .

Face-to-Face, it hovered, swelled and puffed and black. Tiny cracks in its coarsened leather exposed rivulets of lemon ice. Green covered one cheek— bestowed on Face the same dignity it would on month-old bread. Jake's vision slid to black crystals that sparkled on one ear and adjacent forehead, to the site where a hemisphere of blood shimmered like Jell-o over a year ago.

Jake's skin tightened. His viscera heaved. He locked his throat and forced his vision away, away and down into the comfort of darkness.

But Face commanded his eyes to return, to return to the yellow orbs that stared out from sockets pulled back toward brain center, to the orbs that once held all that pain and fear. What was it from?

Black purple lips pulled back to expose its teeth, a yellow oral ring that this thing once used to give its owner food and energy and life. But now it only grins —grins that goddamn frozen-in Grisly Grin. Grin'll never stop. Never!

He stared. Jake-to-Ted, Commander-to-Commander, Face-to-Face, Life-to-Death. As a branding iron, Face seared and scorched his brain as it floated forward.

The rigid bloated body below Face, frozen in the posture of zero gravity sleep, looked as if it rested in an armchair. Face's body drifted and rotated in a slow forward roll with a life of its own. Outward-stretched arms glided forward; bent knees, away.

THEODORE W. LUDENDORFF—COMMANDER, WAYFARER 1. The patch on the flight suit, the suit that strained to contain its distended and frozen contents, provided the only acceptable link to the human that once pulled this soft cloth over its warm skin.

Three lights continued to flick over the rigid torso, then purify themselves in random dances on mechanical structure.

Faye's voice, as a faint audio signal entrained in the torrent of visual signals, penetrated Jake's mind. "Must've not dropped below freezing for several weeks after he died."

Jake broke his stare, became aware of the others. "What got him?"

"Concussion?" asked Speed.

Faye paused as she ran her light from head to toe. "Can't tell."

"We'll probably never know," said Speed.

"If there's a way to determine what happened, we have to do it," said Jake.

"What's that mean?" asked Speed. "We have no way to get him back home with us."

"We can't learn much from direct examination now," said Faye. "The only other thing we can do is obtain some tissue samples for analysis."

Speed's light turned on Faye. "No. You don't . . . oh, no."

"Afraid so," said Faye.

Jake felt another wave of nausea. "Wish I could argue with you."

"Let's get on with it," said Faye. "Only way to

get it done is just to do it. I've got all the equipment I need. Jake, you steady him. Speed, hold our lights."

Jake let Faye take control. All of the recommendations on her were right, he thought. "She never fails to get tough when her time comes. She knows that's gotta be done, how to do it and always has the strength to push on through." But why's it so hard for me just to help, just to hold on to this cloth wrapper on this frozen mannequin? I'm not squeamish. This cloth, its color and weave and feel—it's exactly the same as mine! You were smart, Ted—am I any better? What's your secret? What's out here? What're you telling me? What're you screaming at me? WHAT GOT YOU?!

"Got all I need," said Faye.

Jake forced his hands open, tried to relax his muscles, tried to stop his shaking. "Good."

"What now?" asked Speed.

"Can't leave him like this," said Jake.

"Yeah, he could bump around in here for years to come," said Speed.

"Deserves more dignity," said Jake.

"Sure does," said Speed. "Deserves at least a burial. And there's only one place available."

"Yeah, and it shouldn't take much propellant," said Jake. "We're still close to apogee."

"You mean . . . send this module and him down into the hole?" asked Faye.

"It'd be no different than cremation," said Speed, "and then a burial in ground, sea or space. In several billion years, every one of our molecules is going to be squeezed into the same point—Ted's just going to beat us to there."

Jake paused. His mind raced from one alternative to the next and back through the list again. "That's it. It's the best we can do for him."

Jake, the last one out, pushed the hatch closed. He turned his back on the command center, pulsed the handrail with his fingertips and drifted away.

Wayfarer 1 Commander Theodore Ludendorff remained in the blackness seated at his commander's control station. A single tight strap fixed him in place, held him secure in his position of respect and authority.

Jake studied the displays at his commander's control station. "Boris, can you see my nav and guidance solutions on your displays?"

"Yeah, I got 'em. They match mine. All looks good."

"OK. Thanks. Let me run through our status and plan. Back at 0946, we were at apogee. In eight minutes, at 1225, you'll undock. At 1230, I'll start the first burn that'll put Ted and us on a trajectory into the hole. At engine cutoff, I'll undock and start the second burn that'll raise our perigee back to fifty miles."

"OK," said Boris. "What then?"

"Then we decide when and how to go after the rest of Ted's crew."

"Jake, let me give you a summary of what we found out about *Wayfarer 1* over the hard-line hookup while you were inside. I'll give you the details later."

"Shoot, Boris."

"Just as when we first looked at it, all the comm transmitters are burned out and the electrical system's shorted. But the computer also has a problem, one that keeps us from getting to their propellant. Its memory's gone, even the fixed memory. Ada says there's no way *that* could happen . . . but it did. Just like someone dumped and zeroed it, every shred of data from their computer's gone!"

At 1230.000 hours the auto sequencer commanded ignition.

"Perigee's coming down," said Speed. "There's twenty-five miles . . . 15 . . . 5 . . . 4 . . . 3 . . . 2 . . . 1 . . . cutoff—right on. Let's undock, swap ends and burn this baby again!"

"In work." Jake released the docking latches and began a slow drift away from *Wayfarer 1*. But his mind penetrated the gray-covered windows, focused on Ted who hovered in darkness at his controls and returned to Face—to Face as it surged forward, to Face with its Grotesque Grisly Grin, to Face that pulled and tugged on him. In only six hours, Face would plummet in and be shredded, compressed and squeezed into the ultimate darkness and take its secret with it.

"Com'on, boss. Let's get turned around and light the fire. Hightail it. Hit the road. We're headed right for the center of that hell hole!"

Frustration . . . or more anger? Hard to tell, and probably academic, for Choke felt them both in large measure.

The electromagnetic signals characteristic of data had reached a peak, then faded and disappeared. Choke found patience, never one of its virtues, forced upon it. It switched its sensors back to wide search, set their sensitivities to maximum and waited as energy continued to crackle and ripple along its digestive tract.

In time, the signals at its Wayfarer tentacle reappeared. And as they strengthened, Choke returned its detection to narrow beam and focused. The signals came from two adjacent enclosures. Choke studied them. Yes, just like the enclosures that brought the last delicacies of data, these would offer no resistance. Choke could again penetrate the skin and extract and devour data with the ease and gusto a tiger would tear open a baby's tender belly and gorge itself on sweet innards.

Though still too far away for acquisition, Choke sensed that soon it could start the dinner ritual, soon it could sample the aroma of each individual delicacy, soon it could select its first dish, soon it could dig in—and soon it could devour!

VII

SURVIVE

*Calculations, procedures and bookkeeping
—remnants, sometimes even reservations,
but never replacements for original
thought.*

33

Decide

Alive—it felt cool, fresh and alive.

Lettuce snapped and cracked and ripped under pressure from her fingers. Cold water bounced from its crisp leaves and bathed her hands and wrists. She pulled off another leaf, broke it and heard it snap above the water's steady hypnotic splatter. Each new leaf enhanced the clean garden aroma that saturated her nose and lungs. Chilly green, her sink's stark white and an expanse of hard-blue September sky filled her eyes, soothed her mind. She halted all thought, opened herself up and devoured the sensuous flood. An internal void absorbed it all.

Eva Ludendorff had come to enjoy life's small pleasures. The larger ones still escaped her, even though Ted had been gone for almost three years.

She glanced at her watch, then called out through the screen. "Willie, get away from that car! Bring in the box of groceries like I asked you to and eat your lunch. You've only got twenty minutes left. CompuLearn begins again at one."

From the depths of the garage came a soft sigh of defeat. "OK, Mom. Be right there." Minutes passed, but the black cavern refused to surrender Willie.

Eva shook her head. If he'd only spend as much time with his schoolwork as that car. Never should've let him trade away the Electro-Turbo. Its engine sure went out quick. Bullet's engine is too powerful . . . yet he's still always findin' ways to make it go even faster.

Eva had built up just about enough mental energy to unloose her come-or-get-grounded scream when a dynamo sprung from the darkness, a dynamo with wide-opened eyes and pimples on top, a flurry of elbows, knees, scabs and grease-stained cloth in the middle and feet that bulged through holes in one-month-old running shoes on the bottom. The dynamo tore around the corner of the house and bounded up the back stairs.

"Where's the groceries?"

"Oh, yeah."

At only a slight reduction in speed, the dynamo sprung up the stairs a second time. With his tongue in the corner of his mouth, a firm requirement for any level of concentration, Willie set the box of groceries on the counter. Using his fingers as a rake, he made several passes through his hair. A short inspection of his hands revealed that a double pass across the back of his pants ought to do the trick. Eva couldn't really get mad at him. She knew it came naturally. It was exactly how Willie remembered his Dad would've done it.

"What's for lunch?"

"BLT's. Almost ready. Two OK?"

"Ah . . . three, Mom?"

"Wash up first."

"But I . . ."

"Do it."

A moment later Willie returned. Water glistened off the grease on the back of his hands.

"Won't do, Willie."

"But I only eat with the insides."

"Again, Willie!"

Two flicks in time later, he returned. "Hey, Mom, isn't today when Mr. Ryder's supposed to get to Dad's module?"

The tomato slipped from her fingers. It smacked the counter with a dull plop. "Yes . . . it is." She searched Willie's eyes and wondered if he thought Ted was alive. Sometimes Willie would start to talk about him, but then he'd stop in the middle of a sentence and sink into silence. What was he thinking? What was he keeping to himself?

Willie started on the second half of his first sandwich. Eva finished making the second one and started on the third as she studied her son. Better hurry or he'll eat right up to my fingertips. Does he really remember Ted, or is Ted just a stale swarm of stories and holographs to him? Memories get rigid and hollow as we pull 'em along day after day, month after month. Three years is a long time to Willie. Could he really remember his father—the man? The fire in his eyes that melted into love and compassion in a flash? The strength in his hands when he held you? Or his softness? His humor? His . . .

"Hope Dad's OK. Wonder where he . . . ahh, where he . . ."

"Willie, help me put the groceries away before you go to your work station."

"OK. Should I throw out the box?"

Eva stared at the mute box, as if she was about to pass sentence. For months she'd been tempted to box up all of Ted's things and put them in storage. The box stared back. Open and empty and ready, it radiated its repulsive suggestion.

"No, put it in the back room for now, with the others."

A tear seeped out the corner of her eye and ran down a dark circle of skin. Without sound, it fell from her cheek to the floor, its essence reduced from grief to just water and salt.

She'd come to envy those who saw their loved one catapulted from warm, pink life to cold, black death in only hours or days. Then the dam could burst. Then tears could flood out, again and again, until the reservoir ran dry. Then the lucky ones could pick up the pieces and move on. But for her, the spike of pain never came. Sobs never healed. Instead, uncertain grief allowed her no more than a steady trickle, a runoff. The dam never broke. The reservoir always stayed full. Life just continued on, a steady abrasion of nerves and soul.

But maybe today would be the day. Maybe today she'd find out what to do with those boxes, those damned empty boxes—all those disgusting obscene boxes!

Choke reached out and focused. And it sensed.

Yes, soon Choke would again experience the pleasure of consumption, as well as the drudgery of digestion. And, as it did before every meal, Choke also perceived that this time it should be a little more selective, a little more organized than at its last orgy of eating. What food should it consume? And in what order? And which tentacles should be nourished most by data nutriments and allowed to grow?

Choke weighed the importance of these questions, and being the product of eons of continuous enhancements, marshaled an awesome capability to derive their answers. Sophisticated and complex, Choke's democratic decision process started with its Central Thought Processor, which immediately selected a Representative Thought Processor from each of its tentacles to coordinate and recommend a total strategy, a set of tactics and the corresponding procedures for an optimized acquisition and distribution of data nutriments, to develop—The Plan.

In turn, each representative delegated tasks to the groups that made up its own tentacle. Each Group, of course, delegated tasks to each of its Divisions, that in turn delegated to each of their Sections, that in turn delegated to each of their individual Cells. Cells could delegate to no other thought processors, so they each developed their own unique contributions to The Plan. Despite the trillions upon trillions upon trillions of unique cells that processed thought, each one of which had its own unique requirements, goals and constraints, the total process uncovered a certain uniformity as each Cell's thoughts were combined, coordinated, optimized and passed back up line.

Every Section recommended that they receive the very choice nutriments.

Every Division recommended that they receive all of the choice nutriments.

Every Group recommended that they receive all of the nutriments.

And every Representative reached immediate, unanimous agreement with one another on the first half of their assignment:

THE PLAN

1.0 Data Acquisition

> Eat as much as you can, as fast as you can!

However, Representatives could find no consensus on section 2.0, Data Distribution, although they continued to discuss and deliberate, review and evaluate, appraise and assess and, of course, consider and coordinate.

But, armed with its Data Acquisition Plan, Choke reached out again, sharpened its focus and probed inside each enclosure. It cracked the lid off each dish and, one by one, sampled its aroma.

Each a feast!

Choke took several more laps around the six dishes, lifted their lids each time, but always returned to its favorite. At this distance, Choke could only smell its next meal. But, as Food dropped inward, Choke sensed that Food not only accelerated, but this time it headed straight for its plate!

Hunger flared. The cosmic shark turned ravenous. Electrical energy rippled through empty data buffers and crackled through acquisition circuits.

Mmmmmmm . . . soon . . . yes, very soon, the banquet would begin!

Jake concentrated. Neurons fired. Internal control of their order and linkage defined his thoughts. Yet now, for brief periods, commands entered his brain from an external source. The mental confusion he'd experienced in the morning returned. And now it seemed stronger, almost as if something else guided his thoughts. At certain times and whenever his mind paused, it wandered. As soon as forward motion of his train of thought slowed, random ideas and memories surfaced and tried to force his thoughts off track. Yet, once under way, thoughts still rolled along with speed and precision.

The CT 7000 menu display summarized their choices:

1. RETURN TO EARTH
2. RAISE PERIGEE
3. RENDEZVOUS WITH WF 1-ALPHA

Jake's hands hovered over the keyboard. His fingers made idle circles on its keys. What should it be? 1, 2 or 3? Ignore the *Wayfarer 1* Alpha module and start home, raise their height of closest approach to the black hole and wait, or link up with Alpha and the rest of Ted's crew now?

"Run, or ahh . . . ahh . . . wait or go after 'em," said Jake, as he fought for control of his own thoughts and words. "What do you think?"

"We're here now," said Speed. "May as well press on. We don't know for sure that the rest of 'em are like Ted."

"And we've no right to assume they are," said Faye.

"We . . . we . . . we all feel the same," said Jake, as he wrestled again for control. "There's a small chance that one or more of 'em may still be alive. We have to go after 'em. Our only real choice is do we do it now, or do we raise our perigee and wait?"

"Perigee is at 8:37, about six hours from now," said Speed. "We got time. But on the other hand, waiting another half-day shouldn't change their status any, and then we could join up far away from the black hole."

Jake concentrated on the production of each word. "Ma . . . ma . . . ma . . . maybe. Wha . . . wha . . . what's the radar look like?"

"Looks kind of strange," said Speed. "I can see Old Buddy Boris, the *Wayfarer 1* modules and the disk of the Wayfarers on radar, but the black hole's just an open void. That little beauty just sucks up all our radar signals and gives nothing back."

Jake loosened his foot restraints and floated to one of the windows that lined the outside wall. His eyes soon adjusted to the low intensity scene. Soft light from the speck-sized sun behind their module reflected off the swarm of Wayfarers. Faint but sharp, their image filled his window. "Beautiful. Wish we had time to just watch it. Have to wait. Hope data recorders are doing it justice. Looks like a small version of Saturn's rings, but there's no planet. And the rings go almost all the way to the center." At last, Jake seemed to have gained control of his thoughts.

"Ye . . . ye . . . yeah . . . almost, but not quite," said Speed. "Lo . . . lo . . . look at the opening at the center. All I can see is an occasional flash. But there's a tiny point there that holds this whole thing together, that's made powder out of everything close to it."

"It's hard to believe that something you can't see, that's so tiny, can be so strong," said Faye. "Don't you wish you could go inside it and find out what's there?"

"Oh . . . oh . . . only in mmm . . . ma . . . ma . . . my mind," said Speed. "I want to keep my pink, tiny, tender, brittle, little body far away from it!"

Jake studied the black cavity at the center. His gut twinged. An indistinct fear oozed up and tugged at him. "If we go after Alpha now, we'll just skim it by only fifty miles at perigee."

"Yeah, perigee," said Speed. "I was once told a way to remember that perigee's the lowest point in an orbit—it's where things perish."

"Gr . . . gr . . . gra . . . great to know that, Speed," said Faye. "Gr . . . great reassurance. It already looks to me like we're headed straight down into the center of it."

"Faye, why are you stuttering?" asked Speed. "Ya must be nippin' at the bottle. Where're ya hiding it?"

"Ya . . . yo . . . yu . . . you're . . . na . . . na . . . no better."

"I've had the same trouble," said Jake. "Maybe we're just tired."

"Maybe," said Speed.

Faye nodded. "Ma . . . ma . . . ma . . . maybe."

"Let's decide," said Jake. "If we're going to make the rendezvous, we've got a lot of procedures to hustle through. Can either of you think of a reason why we shouldn't wait and do it next orbit?"

They each pressed their face against a window. No one spoke.

Jake reviewed their spacecraft status as he tried to answer his own question. Their systems, navigation and guidance programs, propellant quantity relative to redline and measured gravity gradient all looked nominal. He could see no technical reason not to go after 'em now. But as Jake stared again at the dark chasm, that dark unseen eye at the center of the rotating plate that filled his window, his thoughts thinned, then evaporated. The logic of nerve endings, of ganglia, as a cold black gelatinous mass, surged upward, flooded outward and suffocated. But Jake clung to his reason and logic as he clawed back to the surface—think . . . *Think*!

But something grabbed him, pulled him back

down, wrenched him under and held him tight at the bottom, locked him down in cold, dark mire and slime. IT pulled on him with the same strong, cold force that IT pulled on Grisly Grin. IT pulled on them both and would have them both. Yet, the force from the black hypnotic eye, sickening and disgusting, also repulsed him. Escape IT? Run? . . . Yes, run . . . run . . . RUN!

Attraction or repulsion, which force would dominate, which would win?

Gut sensed. And Gut decided. Now Rational Mind had to justify.

Jake paused as Rational Mind paraded out duty and responsibility. Everybody'd done all they could to get 'em there as soon as possible. Main mission objective—measure what's there. It just had to be done now. Discipline and procedures streamed into the parade—*Press*!

Jake pushed off the window and flew to the keyboard. His mind clamped onto its goal and locked out all other thought. "Let's stop screwing around and go after 'em." His fingers stabbed at the keyboard. "Three, enter." The screen filled with rendezvous parameters, burn times and procedures. "Speed, Faye, check the systems. I'll set us up for the burn."

Jake pressed the transmit key on his comm unit. "Boris, we can see no reason not to go after 'em now. We've set up for the rendezvous. Do the same, unless you can see something we don't."

Boris jerked his head up from his display, paused with a quizzical look on his face, then grabbed his comm control. "No . . . no . . . no . . . nope. Can't see a reason not to, Jake. Never any doubt. We've been set up to do it since we undocked from Beta."

"What do you think they've been doing all this time?" asked Ada.

Boris concentrated. His words seemed a little hard to get started. But, no problem. Once they got rolling, they came out just fine. "Pra . . . pra . . . prob . . . probably that candyass Speed. Damn scientists can't ever make up their minds. It's straight forward, even easy with our nav and guidance programs."

"Exactly right, Boris," said Ada. "It's all straight forward. Just stick to the procedures in our CT 7000, and let it solve any new problems that come up."

"Don't think we'll need anything new," said Irwin. "We got all the procedures we could ever need, and then some."

A smile slashed across Boris's tomato face as he struggled with his words, maybe even his thoughts. Sure, he sensed a small problem with himself, but he had no time for that now. "Ba . . . ba . . . be . . . be . . . besides, we'll be the first to navigate *that* close to a black hole and live to tell about it. There aren't many firsts left in the space biz, but that's one of 'em. And it'll be one helluva ride. When we skim the hole at only fifty miles, we'll be doing 225 thousand miles an hour and swing around it in only a couple seconds."

"That's one sharp corner," said Ada.

The slash in the tomato held its smile. "Ya . . . ya . . . yeah. It'll be a little like bouncing off a wall."

"But we'll be zero gravity all the way and should hardly feel a thing," said Ada.

The slash in the tomato widened. "True. Ba . . . ba . . . but, once we've done it, we'll have a record!"

34

Fall

Gravity won—always has, always will.

For but an instant, the tennis ball strained at the top of its arc, then fell. Not much of a throw, not much of a challenge, but Hans still responded. Habit and duty filled in for enthusiasm. He sauntered after it, let it bounce once on the dry grass, then plucked it out of the air without leaving the ground. He stopped, glanced at Val and trudged back as if his body had doubled in weight. As he flopped down at Val's feet, he let the saliva-laden ball slip from his teeth and again studied the two-by-four one foot in front of his paws. Grayed with weather, its ends curled and split, it'd settled into the dirt; he no longer dug it up nor carried it about. His body went limp, chin settled to the ground and large black orbs rolled up to stare at Val.

Val looked at her companion, nodded and sat on the grass next to him. She stroked the fur on the back of his head and neck. His tail flopped twice, then lay still. She tried a light scratch behind his ears. No movement. "I know, old buddy, for some reason I feel the same today, too."

In silence they watched the isolated thunderstorm cell tower, then move toward them and slide in front of the late-afternoon sun. Brightness and warmth dissolved. A cold wind came from their backs and gusted toward the darkness. Packets within the cell, pregnant with hot humid air, boiled and churned upward.

"What ya say, Hans, time for dinner? Let's go in."

Val rose and clapped her hands on her knees. "Hey, big guy. I've got a steak bone from last night—for you!"

Hans forced his body up. His blank eyes scanned the ground as they ambled toward the house.

"You wish I had two bones? So do I."

The four Wayfarer spacecraft strained at their invisible leashes. At 9:46 A.M., they each'd reached apogee where outward motion ceased. They paused. Their orbital velocity slowed to only 237 miles per hour. Yet, even at over 47,000 miles from the black point, it reached out and clung to them.

Hole pulled. They fell.

At first they only crept, but as they drew closer, their leashes tightened and they dropped with ever greater speed, ever greater acceleration. At 40,000 miles, they fell at over 3,100 miles per hour. By 30,000 miles, they exceeded 5,500 miles per hour. And still, as they plummeted in smooth silence, their captor seized them with an ever tighter grip.

Close to apogee, one of the new spacecraft had pushed on one of the old and given it just a slight nudge over an invisible ledge. The old spacecraft, with its sole occupant at the controls, now edged away from the other three and plunged on a path that led into the center of the hole. For this spacecraft and its commander, their captor's strength would build without bound.

Both of the new spacecraft now drew up on the second old one that remained.

"We're five miles out," said Speed. "Be docked in no time."

Faye looked into the binoculars. "This one looks different."

Speed turned away from the radar display and peered through the telescope. "Yep. It still has the bridge hooked up, and it's rotating like the minute hand of a clock, only twice as fast."

"But it also seems to glow," said Faye.

"You're right," said Speed. "Looks like the emergency lights are on." He turned back to his display. "Two point three miles out."

"Close enough," said Jake. "I'm flyin' it from here." He slipped the fingers of his right hand onto the rotation controller, those of his left onto the translation controller. The CONTROL MODE status light changed from AUTO to MANUAL.

Speed looked into the telescope again. "Except for the lights, the outside looks the same as Ted's module."

Jake pressed the transmit key on the rotation controller and looked toward the holovision cameras. "Boris, I'm going to dock first. We'll make a quick check on its status. Then we'll undock and wait till after perigee to dock again and go inside."

Jake glanced at the holovision display and saw the round red head of Boris that surrounded his O-shaped lips. "Oh . . . oh . . . oh . . . OK."

Jake sized up the task before him. It challenged him more than a normal docking. His target not only rotated but, with the bridge that hung off one side, it wobbled. He lined up on the oscillating center line and started to move in. Something jerked his eyes, his attention, his mind to the windows. That familiar gray coating obscured the inside. But with the soft illumination of the emergency lights that spilled out, the windows looked frosted, partially transparent. Only diffuse shapes and shadows escaped.

"Ya got a tough job this time, boss."

"Na . . . na . . . na . . . no sweat, Speed-eroo." In an instant Jake's mental confusion returned and he again fought for his words. "I'll . . . I'll grease it right in there, like always."

The exchange with Speed provided only a temporary tonic as he stared at the frosted panes. Maybe the lights meant people were home . . . people unlike Ted. But then he felt it again. Damn! Here he was, a grown man. And he'd just gone through all that. What could be worse?

But IT hung there, silent, sly and secret. IT commanded attention, yet IT hid. IT gathered and strengthened itself somewhere out there, behind that frost, maybe beyond. IT felt heavy, oppressive yet electric.

Jake pulled reason back to the surface. He fought to ignore IT, forget IT, concentrate and get the job done.

Danger! DANGER!

Words blasted him, not from his lips, not from his mind, but from the primordial watchman in his gut. Ice slid down the core of his spine from cortex to coccyx. His skin grew frigid and tight. Rigid tension diffused into arteries, muscles and flesh. Each squeeze of his heart hammered his chest, surged blood by his throat, up to his temple and brain. Hands wrung controls that'd grown slippery with sweat.

Com'on, Ryder, relax! Piece of cake. He forced looseness into his body, forced something back down under, something that only welled up again. Screw it. *Press!*

"Lookin' good, Jake baby," said Speed.

"Ga . . . ga . . . got . . . gotta make this fast," said Jake. "Once I draw a bead on the center line, I gotta drive it in before I lose it. Brace. It'll be a jolt."

Jake waited and sensed speeds and distances . . . now!

He rammed his left hand forward on the translation controller. Jets fired. They accelerated.

Alignment—perfect. Speed—extreme. They crashed.

Like gravity flicked on, every lose item in the module, including its three occupants, flew forward.

Jake's shoulder and back smashed into a window. Just as he tried to inhale, to recover the air jolted from his lungs, Speed's head rammed into his stomach. Together they tumbled away from the window.

"That's what I like about you, Jake. You've got that delicate touch, a finesse, a real feel for the fragile. Boss, hands down, you've just won the much-coveted Decoration of the Dainty Docker! When we get back, I'm . . . I'm . . ."

Jake wheezed in a shallow breath and looked up. Speed's eyes fixed on Faye. Her face, contorted by a blend of sorrow and horror, drifted away from a window. Jake pulled himself over and looked out.

The two docked modules now rotated together locked window-to-window. Jake studied the one opposite his. Some of the frost had been removed by random wipes, rubs and scratches. In slow motion, objects floated and churned in the opposite command center. He peered into the jumble, as if he watched a parade of sea life through a porthole in a tank. A checklist . . . pen . . . food container . . . leather hand . . . flight suit arm . . . shoulder . . . Face!—swelled and puffed and black and cracked and grinning and . . .

Nausea rippled up into his throat. Face drifted from view. He stared into a dance of the macabre, a dance of human debris, blackened and bloated and frozen. Grisly grins and yellow orbs twirled and tumbled, rigid limbs and trunks bumped and bounced, purple lips and yellow teeth . . .

"How many are there?" asked Speed.

"Da . . . da . . . da . . . don't know yet. I see at least three, maybe more," said Jake.

"Counted 'em twice," said Faye. "There're five."

Jake backed away from the window. All good people—and all dead! He wanted to take happiness, to take Life back home, not more pain and more hurt. No one left to tell them what happened—to stop them from looking like that!

"What got 'em?" asked Speed. "And what got Ted?"

Jake and Speed looked at each other, then at Faye.

"May not know until we get back, till the tissue samples are analyzed," said Faye.

"But what do we do now?" asked Speed.

"You mean if the same thing happens to us?" asked Jake.

"But what's that?" asked Faye.

"Don't know," said Speed.

"Don't you sometimes feel different?" asked Speed.

"Yeah, I do," said Faye. "Can't seem to think straight, feel confused, like a hundred people are talking to me at the same time."

Speed nodded. "It's like some yahoo's got a thousand fish hooks in my brain, and he yanks on the lines whenever he wants some kicks."

Faye nodded.

"Gotta figure it out," said Speed.

Jake pressed his comm button. "Boris, Ada, Irwin. We've docked with Alpha, and it's just as we feared. Looks like the rest of the crew's in the same condition as Ted."

"Th . . . th . . . that's too bad," said Boris over their speaker. His voice softened. "W . . . we . . . we feared the same . . . nevertheless, it's just too bad."

"Something got them, Boris," said Jake. "But we don't know what. How do you folks feel over there?"

"W . . . w . . . w . . . we're all OK here!" said Boris's voice.

"You don't sound OK," said Speed. "Does it sometimes feel like something's tugging on your brain with invisible meat hooks?"

"Invisible ma . . . ma . . . meat hooks?" asked Boris. "Maybe something hooked into your brain and olled it belly up, Speed, but we're all OK over here. Ahh . . . Speed, how many years've you felt this way?"

"Boris, I'm serious," said Speed. "I know how it sounds, but we feel something."

"We really do," said Faye. "Please, keep your eyes and mind open."

"They're right, Boris," said Jake. "Watch your-selves. We'll talk to you after perigee."

"T . . . t . . . ta . . . talk to you then," said Boris. "Thanks for the warning."

Jake felt it, too, just like Speed and Faye. But what'd it have to do with anything in the real world? Later he and the others, in moments of relaxation, could discuss it and examine it. But they couldn't mess with it now. They had to undock and ride out perigee first.

"Jake, maybe we can find a way to test for it," said Speed. "We've got a lot of sensors recording data, but they're all designed to operate unmanned with no readouts. If only we had a way to tap into some of it."

"And the time," said Jake.

Like a few frames from a movie . . . its nose buried in the runway . . . its tail thrust high in the air . . . its body enveloped in a fog of shame . . . RT7 flicked on and off the viewing screen of Jake's mind. Right, procedures. Can't ignore 'em this time. Can't start wingin' it now—methodical procedures come first!

"Le . . . le . . . le . . . let's g . . . g . . . get . . . undocked!" said Jake. Yet something again lurked in there with him, indistinct but real. IT let him pry up ITs corners and peak under ITs edges. Not enough. He had to rip off ITs cover, expose IT, examine IT, defeat IT! . . . but later.

Speed called up the undocking procedures on their displays. "Airlock vent's open."

Jake entered a command. "I'll get steps three through seven, Speed. Power goin' to dead face." No,

IT couldn't be seen or measured. And real was real. Nothing else existed!

"Speed, I'm not goin' to ATTITUDE HOLD. We'll get some rates when we come off, but we'll save some gas. No need to stop their rotation, bridge and all."

"Sounds good, Boss."

Face!—it exploded forward again with its grisly grin and eyes of pain. And he felt something command his thoughts. IT's real! Gotta get IT before IT gets us. Gotta deal with IT—intuition, hunch, suspicion, fear, panic, whatever—drag IT out, examine IT, understand IT, control IT . . . but we gotta undock first!

Jake punched the PROCEED key on his keyboard. The top line of his display changed to DOCKING LATCH POWER—ENABLE.

He punched PROCEED again, but this time the top line remained unchanged. He pulsed the key several more times. Seconds ticked by. The top line flickered, went blank and finally changed to DOCKING LATCHES—UNLATCH.

He punched PROCEED once more. Again, nothing. He hammered the key. Still nothing!

CT 7000 continued to follow commands, but not those from the human at the keyboard to release the fingers that held two spacecraft together; rather it followed new and stronger commands from outside.

Jake swung around to the EMERGENCY ACTION panel and entered the same command through a switch that bypassed the computer. Again, nothing. The spacecraft's electrical current, already high, showed no change.

"Ne . . . ne . . . ne . . . neither wa . . . wa . . . wa . . . works," said Jake. "Computer's na . . . na . . . not listening, and the switch must have a short. Neither gets power to the latches."

"Gotta get separated or get ripped apart at perigee!" said Speed.

A seed of pain grew at the core of Jake's mind. Subtle and isolated at first, now it strengthened and

welled. A pain not imagined but real, a pain that
robed and prodded and poked—RIGHT INSIDE
HIS SKULL!

With their leashes reeled in to less than 10,000
miles, the twelve human forms—six fresh and six
drained—plunged at over 14,000 miles per hour.
They penetrated ever deeper into foreign turf, and
till they accelerated.

Somewhere, signals exceeded limits. Choke
flexed as it made an instinctive decision. Time to put
the first half of The Plan into action—Data Acquisition.

Acquisition power surged to maximum. Six
chamber doors slid open.

35

Conform

Perfect—again his work came out perfect.

Boris examined his display and smiled. Exact knowledge blended with precise control. He loved it. For no matter which technique he used, machine integration or second order perturbation, his calculations of their perigee came out to be exactly 47.973013 miles, over two miles lower than the perigee established by *Wayfarer 1*.

Thus, Boris would be the first human to "successfully" navigate close to a black hole—and to within less than fifty miles! Even the environment around the hole had cooperated. Radar showed nothing but small dust along their flight path. Evasive maneuvers were not required. He would establish this milestone as he did everything else—with absolute precision.

His smile broadened. Boris knew he had a double importance. Not only did he function as commander of the Beta module but, with his equations, he also controlled the motion of both *Wayfarer 2* modules. In true fact, it was he who determined their true success or failure—*Commander Twice Over*.

His heart and mind raced. This time he'd be able to revel in his victory even as it happened! But he had to calm down, to get back to something practical, to start another calculation, to . . . that's it. Wouldn't it

e a useful check to know the maximum force, the
um of the centrifugal and gravity gradient forces,
hat any part of the spacecraft would experience at
erigee? It seemed almost too simple to compute:
ist assume gravity gradient keeps the x axis lined up
vith local vertical, a speed of 225,326.013 miles per
our, a distance of . . . of . . . Boris had to start
ver. Speed, squared, over . . . over . . . ahh . . .

Jake's voice slipped from the speaker three feet
rom Boris's ear and blended into his thoughts. "Bo-
is, Ada, Irwin. We've docked with Alpha, and it's just
s we feared. Looks like . . ."

Too bad. They were good people. But Boris
lidn't really expect to find either Ted or his crew
live. And something got them? What's that sup-
osed to mean?

"Ada, Irwin, you feel OK?"

"I'm fine," said Ada, although her face looked
insure.

"Me, too," said Irwin.

"W . . . w . . . w . . . we're all OK here!"
aid Boris.

Oh-oh, they're gonna keep on chattering. Invisi-
le meat hooks? The pressure's getting to Speed.
)amn scientist can't take it. And it sounds like he's
lriven the rest of 'em over the hill too. Gotta cut off
his chitchat so we can get ready for perigee.

"T . . . t . . . ta . . . talk to you then," said
3oris. "Thanks for the warning."

He returned to his problem, to something so
imple that now had become so hard. Yes, his mind
lid seem different, even feeble at times. But in mo-
nents of stress, there could be but one course to
ollow—put faith in calculations! They always pro-
'ided the precision and rigor required to meet any
:hallenge. The spacecraft's navigation and control
:quations continued to do their job, but that
:entrifugal force problem needed some work. Let's
ee, was it speed over distance from hole quantity

squared times radius from CG? . . . or? . . . ah
. . . no . . . ahh . . .

Her brow began to arch.

So far her CT 7000 had exceeded even Ada'
expectations. It'd executed all commands withou
flaw, reanalyzed the priority of each program to im
prove its own architecture and executed the naviga
tion calculations with even greater accuracy that
specified by Boris.

As the flight progressed, happiness and satisfac
tion mounted within Ada. For it was she and her C'
7000 that performed at the very tip of this technolog
ical spear. In true fact, it was she with her electroni
colleague who functioned as the real brains, the rea
control of this mission—*Commander Intellectual.*

But now she and her colleague had a problem—
actually, many problems. It'd started with a solitar
error, the flip of a one to a zero deep in the memor
of the Systems Monitoring program. Then other pro
grams experienced random errors. They hung up a
their start. Some even started all on their own. An
now the problems snowballed into a crisis. Soon sh
wouldn't be able to even support Boris's simple
minded calculations. And, as if all that wasn'
enough, her own mind seemed different, even feebl
at times. But in moments of stress, there could be bu
one course to follow—put faith in the computer
Command the Problem Analysis and Correction pro
gram to analyze the errors, specify their commo
source, then replace the program causing the prob
lem. Yes, let CT 7000 do it, let it work on itself. C'
7000 always remained steady, dependable and coo
in a crisis, able to meet any challenge.

"Boris, hold up a minute. We have a small prob
lem. But it'll take only a minute to fix."

Muscles in Irwin's back, neck and fingers stiff
ened. He gawked at his display. For the first time i
the flight, he didn't know where to begin.

Up to this point, Irwin had gloated in quiet, savored his private reservoir of pride and confidence. The mission had gone well, all because of his procedures. He'd written the music; the others just played. Boris only steered the module. Ada and her electronic abacus only did the bookkeeping. In true fact, it was he, with the discipline of his procedures, accurate and comprehensive procedures he both designed and implemented, that held this mission together and made it work—*Commander De Facto.*

But now, what a change—what a whole barnyard of problems! Irwin had never seen so many malfunctions, even in a simulation. First, the comm and telemetry transmitters had locked themselves in high power, then the video. Now every system seemed sick. And most of it must've been caused by that damn digital deviate that Ada mothered. It spit out random commands in every direction. Yeah, the software regenerated itself all right—mutation gone berserk. And if all that wasn't enough, even his own mind felt different, even feeble at times. But in moments of stress, there could be but one way to act— follow the procedures! They provided the summation of all previous thought relevant to the problem, all the guidance required to meet any challenge. Yes, go at it logically, just take one problem at a time and follow the relevant procedure.

Irwin pulled up three separate malfunction procedures on his display. He ran his finger to the top of the first one: COMPUTER INPUT/OUTPUT ERROR.

But he just couldn't concentrate. The lights had just started flickin' on and off, not just in the command center, but all throughout their module. And the temperature had dropped. Every heater must've been turned off and the power fed into those gluttonous transmitters. And now the structure down in the bowels began vibratin' like hell, like electrical power pulsed every hydraulic pump.

Irwin again ran his finger to the top of the procedure. But the warning alarm screamed in his ears again, as if it too felt pain. Every time he punched it off—like now—the damn thing popped right back on again. Awful squeal!

Irwin took a deep breath, tried to relax, but the odor spread fear into him again—burning insulation! Big trouble now. Transmitters must've finally burned up.

"Ah . . . ah . . . ah . . . Ada. Fi . . . fi . . . fix your computer!"

Ada remained stupefied by the fireworks within the cascades of colored lights and video screens on her electronic altar. With her body fixed and her mouth opened, her eyes blinked and fluttered but couldn't keep up with the altar's fitful flashes.

Irwin returned to his own display, ran his finger back to the top of the first procedure, then looked again toward Ada. "Ada!"

Impossible, but it'd happened. Ada's computer malfunctioned! And it didn't cause just a little snag or glitch for Boris, but a catastrophe—he could no longer call up any navigation programs.

Boris grabbed a handhold, yanked, bolted through the air and crashed into the edge of Irwin's work station.

"H . . . h . . . ha . . . haven't you and Ada fixed the computer yet?"

"No. Got me locked out. Not listening to any of my commands."

"You m . . . m . . . must have a procedure that'll work."

"I don't! Must be a new kind of problem."

"Can't be. Loo . . . loo . . . loo . . . look again."

"Did."

"You must have procedures somewhere that'll bail us outta this mess, you always do." Boris knew for sure that Irwin had a procedure that would come to their rescue. He had one for everything—for every conceivable problem!

But now Boris could think of any of it no longer.
His head filled with pain, not just a mild or general
pain, but a pain that grew lusty and sharp and strong.

"B . . . b . . . b . . . but . . . OW!"

Pain, pointed pain, exploded inside Boris's skull.
A needle plunged deep into the core of his brain. He
tried to think, to push it aside.

"Le . . . le . . . le . . . let's look at the list of
procedures in the manual checklist and . . . ahh!"

The needle jerked and jabbed. His whole head
prickled as his hair stood out. His skin tightened, then
it crawled.

"Ne . . . ne . . . need Faye. Must be sick. Ja
. . . Jake!"

Boris looked at the holovision display. The images of Jake, Speed and Faye blurred, sharpened,
then faded into empty noise.

Sweat poured out through cold skin. Boris's ears
hummed. Something surrounded and enveloped
him, something he couldn't smell and couldn't see.
Some Enemy, with its invisible energy, engulfed
him, suffocated him and now stabbed into him.
Trapped and under attack, as helpless as a bird flap-
ping in liftoff thunder, he'd nowhere to hide. No
escape and no understanding—just pain—lots of
pain!

"Ir . . . Irwin, my head . . . it . . ." Pain exploded again, but this time it expanded. Needles behind his eyes danced and dug backwards.

Still conscious, life's images and thoughts
streaked by.

. . . *"Then quit! We're going back to Russia."*
Her eyes're flared with anger—again—she never gets
off this subject, I gotta escape . . . "You weighed
thirty pounds less when we got married!" Her face's
frenzied with hatred—again—and she never takes a
breath, I gotta escape . . . Houston, Fat Face Fred-
die's wet T-shirt party, Suzie . . . gray skies, Com-
rade Yurinev's cold eyes on me, telescopes on me, lip
readers on me, cameras on me, questions on me . . .

new book, exciting book, smooth and cool, even smells good . . . computer work station, n-body problem, peace, quiet . . .

Enemy pulled up images and thoughts at an ever greater rate and machine-gunned them out through his mind's eye. Boris, no longer able to relive each memory, turned spectator—STOP!

But Enemy could not be stopped. It pulled with a relentless pull, and Boris yielded. He watched Enemy approach and take him over, watched it dominate and leave him helpless, watched it freeze his mind to its light like a rabbit to headlights. Only one input from his senses remained strong enough to register the present in his awareness—total pain.

Enemy won. It always did.

Pain dissolved. Resistance dissolved. Identity dissolved.

Fragments of Boris divided over and over again. Sliced and shredded, separated and sorted, he spurted through to the other side. In time, the fragments would further melt and flow, then mix and diffuse.

Enemy, something far larger than any human or group of humans, absorbed the essence of this human called Boris, and with this new essence, it grew larger once more.

At last it stopped. Calm returned to Boris.

At last, the screams faded. The last, more animal than human, sounded final.

At last, muscles no longer jerked, skin no longer twitched. Blood oozed from open gashes on his face and head and from shreds of flesh that hung from his nails. Maybe Boris'd found peace.

At last, Irwin again felt his own body, rigid and cold and wet. Horror subsided. His mind unlocked.

At last, Irwin could let his muscles go limp. His right index finger, bent back and sore, released its pressure and came off the display. His left hand opened. A page from his malfunction procedures,

twisted and ripped and crushed, floated away. He
snatched it and straightened it out. With the computer down, his paper checklist held the only instructions he had left on how to proceed.

His blank stare met Ada's just as the first needle
of pain penetrated his skull.

Lucinda Marie Rote felt sharp pain run up the
backs of her legs. After five hours on high heels, store
to store, she'd about reached her limit. This store had
to be the last—this time she had no choice. They all
were about to close.

"May I help you?"

The salesgirl, in her mid-twenties, looked attractive, but she had one obvious defect—those large
gold pendants that dangled and jangled from her
neck and ears. They went out of fashion last winter.
Not even close to being in. Obsolete. It was obvious
that she didn't keep up.

"Yes, please. Do you have the new knit dress
with the high collar yet? The one with the sweeping
fold of material in front that folds around the neck
from the back?"

Lucinda withdrew a copy of *Paris Leads* from
her purse. She opened it to the second page of COM-
ING WINTER FASHIONS.

"Here, let me show you. Doesn't it look elegant?
I hope you have it."

She held out the magazine and pointed to the
page, the one wrinkled and smudged from the fingers that had pressed into it since early morning. She
knew that within a month it'd be in all the stores and
in CompuCatalog within two. She hoped they had it.
But if they didn't, she'd still get it one way or another, still be first.

She wished Irwin could see it on her. Too bad. By
the time he got back, it'd be already out of style.

At last, food came within reach!
Choke had waited a long time. Although it had

no patience, it also had no choice. And all that early
sniffing and probing had only magnified Choke's appetite, amplified its ravenous state. But now, without
a doubt, food at this site had again become rich and
plentiful.

Hors d'oeuvres arrived first. Choke hadn't ordered them, they just came. Waves of electricity
flooded into Choke from the two enclosures. Like a
neverending line of robowaiters, they carried data to
the table. Not much taste, but it still felt good going
down. Choke sent the masticated fragments to one of
three chambers—COMMUNICATIONS, TELEMETRY,
or VIDEO—to be further divided, digested and distributed.

Choke could extract only small nourishment
from the data's pattern of ones and zeros. Nevertheless, the famished Choke gulped in its pabulum. It
paused only long enough to reach out to the enclosures and turn up the strength of the sources.

But soon, another appetizer dropped within
reach. A little more complex and a little more tasty, it
required more work. Choke's electrical utensils
reached into the closest enclosure and probed the
Executive program, the central control for the CT
7000. From here it could reach every data morsel in
the entire electronic carcass. The muscles, tissue and
fat, still only ones and zeros, had a structure intricate
enough to hold a good flavor. Choke cleaned its plate
and looked up for more.

The entrée in the closest enclosure now fell
within range. Choke's hunger exploded. Its electrical
arms shot out, and its hands grabbed.

The harder the shell, the sweeter the meat. And
this first shell, the one called Boris, resisted. But
Choke smashed it open and ripped.

Right to the core, right to the richness of the
association cortex. Choke missed most of the flavor as
it tore and gulped. It lost delicate tangs of memories,
language and thought to its savage consumption.
Choke decimated cells, dentrites and synapses of mil-

ions and millions of neurons as it ingested its food. Circuits in the frontal, temporal, parietal and occipital lobes smoldered, never again to recover, never gain to yield their data.

Choke paused, its starvation sated, and brought ts voracious appetite under control. Now it took mall deliberate bites and savored each fragment. With a surgeon's patience and finesse, its electrical ingers probed, induced and squeezed. In fact, Choke used the brain of Boris itself to stimulate data elease. Sharp electrical fingers titillated the memory distribution center in the hippocampus. At site after ite, they sought preferred circuits and conditioned onfigurations, read the intricate structure of dendritic trees and molecular switches. Energy crackled over the cerebral cortex, the bark of Boris's brain. Millions and millions of galaxies throughout the cerebrum twinkled and sparkled. Neurons fired, neurotransmitters flowed and data rippled.

Choke consumed.

As Choke worked its way through sensory and motor neurons, down into the midbrain, flavor faded. Body control, sensations and emotions tasted bland. Choke sped into the core, the medulla, site of primitive survival. Nothing of flavor there. It slashed through the thimble-sized, tight tangle of neuron circuits, the ganglia, the warning system that'd failed Boris, and out into the spine. No flesh there. All gone. Done.

Choke retraced itself. Circuits sizzled. Cells seethed. It scraped the skeleton clean of every shred of data that remained.

Choke reached out to the next shell, the one called Irwin, and smashed it with ease. It offered a new flavor, a good flavor, a flavor full of intricate structure and detail. But in time the flavor became repetitious and predictable, bland and dull.

The last shell also smashed with ease, a bad sign. Sure enough, its flavor offered nothing new, too much like the hors d'oeuvres of ones and zeros. The most delectable of the three shells had already been consumed. Nevertheless, Choke again cleaned its plate.

In all, the three shells provided not a bad meal, but still, just your standard lunch-counter meal, predictable and easy to acquire. Yet Choke could never turn away this common food, for it provided the protein that fed its flesh, the basic building blocks that, by themselves, allowed Choke to grow without bound—the sustenance of thought controlled only by equations, procedures and computers.

Choke paused, then started to power down, to make ready for digestion, to rest. But it couldn't ignore fresh pangs of hunger that surged from its three still-empty chambers. Again, Choke bristled with energy. It lunged into the second enclosure.

Tough shells, all three rigid and rugged shells. Fate had saved the best for last!

36

Reach

Gotta undock!

Jake rammed both feet against his display and sprang. Bull's-eye!

His body shot through the center of the main tunnel opening and hit the opposite wall. He clawed at the handrail and accelerated. At the airlock, he grabbed a handrail and wrenched to a stop. Speed and Faye hammered into his back.

Jake flew at the airlock hatch, wrapped one hand around the MANUAL DOCKING LATCH RELEASE handle and tore off its safety lock with the other. With both feet planted on the adjacent wall, he yanked the handle toward him. A muffled thump vibrated structure. "Three more to go."

Speed grunted. Structure thumped. "Two."

Jake ripped the third handle toward him and turned toward Faye and Speed. Their four hands were wrapped around the last handle. It gave.

Jake paused to sense motion. "I don't think we're free yet!" He soared back into the main tunnel and accelerated. At the command center, he flew straight to the TRANSLATION HAND CONTROLLER, pulled it toward him, pulled his face against the window and focused on the frosted, scarred surface opposite him.

It hesitated, then crept away. The frozen remains behind the frost hung motionless, indifferent.

Jake relaxed as the separation between the two modules widened. "Good job, troops."

"None too soon!" said Speed. "We're almost at perigee."

"Let's see where the nav display says we are," said Jake. The navigation display appeared for three seconds, then the screen blanked. "Oh-oh. CT 7000's got a problem."

Speed inspected his handheld checklist. "It's 8:31, we're six minutes from perigee. We must be about 4,000 miles out and dropping at 24,000 miles per hour."

Jake glanced out the window. The frozen twin of their module, now over two hundred feet away, sped over the background disk of the Wayfarers. The outside world had shifted into fast time. The disk inched closer.

He peered ahead to where the Wayfarers became sand, dust, then disappeared into the black void. Within only six minutes, Jake, Speed and Faye would plummet a distance equal to that from the surface of the Earth to its core. The void's invisible force would multiply their speed over ninefold, snap them around and throw them back into the direction they'd come—if their navigation was correct.

The warning alarm's squeal shattered his gaze.

"Current overload on all transmitters," said Speed.

Jake joined Speed at the displays. "Yeah, we've traded problems. Transmitters are sick but computer and displays're back up."

"How could all the transmitters be overloaded at the same time?" asked Speed.

"Makes no sense," said Jake. "There're each independent."

Jake turned toward the hand on his shoulder and looked into Faye's wide eyes. "Smell it? Smoke!"

"Yeah. Gettin' stronger. Fire alarm's not work-

ng. Must be from the wiring insulation in the
rans . . ." Jake froze.

Blackness. All lights in the command center
went out. Jake saw only the faces of Faye and Speed
flicker green in light from the displays. He felt a rush
of cool air strip heat from his wet skin.

"The devil's dickin' with our damn computer,"
said Speed.

"I feel like a puppet," said Faye. "Something's
really jerking us around."

"Can't be!" said Jake. "Just a lot of problems in
different systems. Gotta get with it, clean it up—get
on our *procedures*!" He paused, let his eyes adjust,
then moved his face closer to the keyboard until he
felt the warmth of his reflected breath. His fingertips
examined each key as he entered his command. "I'll
get the Warning System Summary display up first,
see what's wrong, then the malfunction procedures."

The Warning System Summary display flicked
on, then all screens went black. The brightest light
now came from the holovision image that hung
soundless just behind them. They turned.

"Oh, God!" Faye's gasp trailed off into their
merged silence.

Paralyzed, Jake watched unseen Enemy attack
the image of Boris and the image tear at its head as if
it could rip out its pain. He watched animal response
dominate, reason and control disintegrate.

Hands clawed. Flesh yielded. Bone resisted.

"Boris!" Jake knew his shout never left their
module. All comm'd gone dead. Even if his voice
reached Boris, it could do no good. He couldn't help.
He could do nothing but watch the image scream in
silence, its frantic flails grind to a stop, then its lacer-
ated remains go limp. A shiver jolted his body. His
blood tried to flee, to crowd inward, to find somewhere deep within to hide.

"Like Ted," said Speed.

"Worse," said Faye.

"Something's in there," said Speed.

"Has to be," said Faye. "Couldn't do that from something internal."

A new cadence pounded in Jake's ears. Unlike his heart, thrusters on their own module's skin boomed at random. "No. Can't get diverted. Can't waste time. Gotta get our systems back up!"

The holovision image jumped. Its motion tracker shifted focus from Boris to Irwin. But the fresh image of horror persisted for only seconds, then collapsed to a point and disappeared. The only light that remained came from the faint blur of Wayfarers as they raced by the windows.

Jake started to speak. "Got to get CT 7000 up." He glanced at the Wayfarers. "Got to . . ." Waves of primordial terror exploded from ganglia of nerve cells at the base of his brain. They'd plunged farther into Enemy's stronghold, dropped deeper into its lair, penetrated ever closer to the hunger at the rear of the cave.

Still just waking up from hibernation? A nightmare or reality? He couldn't tell—both fused together like a smooth joint in cold steel. But no, he could tell, could feel IT—IT's real! IT's out there in the open. IT didn't hide but slithered straight at him. IT got Ted, got Boris, got Irwin and IT'd get Ada—just as IT'd stab inside their skulls and get them! No place to go. Nothing to stop IT. Procedures? NO! Something different and unpredicted. To hell with procedures and computers and checklists and all that crap. Got to stop IT. Keep it away . . . *think*!

Jake turned in the direction of Speed and Faye. "Got to figure out what's out there—and hold it off!"

"If it comes from outside and attacks the brain, it can only be electrical," said Faye.

"Yeah, electromagnetic waves," said Speed. "Microwaves, radio waves, or . . ."

"Right, fits, has to be." Jake grabbed Speed's elbow, sensed the heat from his face a hand's length away. "Got to find a way to keep the waves out, away from us!"

"Can't. Module's made of carbex and waves come right through."

Jake's spirit sank. "Yeah, designed that way."

The breath from Speed's words felt hot on Jake's skin. "If we can't keep it out, have to confuse it, so . . ."

Jake's spirit perked as his mind sped. "To distract t, divert it. It must have some intelligence, some guidance."

A third voice, a breath away, joined in. "But how do we get to it?"

A faint hope glimmered and flickered as it fought for survival in the turbulence of Jake's mind. 'Need to make our own waves, like the military RAPS."

"RAPS?" asked Faye.

"Radiation active-protection system," said Jake. "Need a RAPS like what's built into all the military spacecraft. And don't we have it, or at least part of it?"

"Yeah, the RAPS antennas are molded right into the module's skin," said Speed.

Hope strengthened. "And so are the electronics and computer nanochips."

"Easier to leave 'em in than take 'em out."

"What's missing?" asked Faye.

"If what Klaus sent is correct, only the switches that hook the RAPS lines to power," said Jake.

"Right," said Speed. "They're not molded in, so they took 'em out to save weight."

Hope took rational form. "We gotta find the RAPS, select the right mode of operation and hook it up to power."

"Let's do it, Jake. Let's . . ."

A fireball exploded outside the windows, like a lightning bolt struck the house next door. Violet-white light blasted in and seared a scene on Jake's retinas, an image of polished carbon and metal surfaces, of reflections off glass displays, the whites of Faye's eyes, Speed's sweat-soaked flight suit, the sneer on his face, his opened doors, his anger. The scene faded and dissolved into blackness, except for the violet-white streak that still glowed on the back of his eyes, still fired signals to his brain.

"Ted just went in!" said Speed.

Violet-white streak magnified and flared in Jake's mind. He saw it, Ted's module, stretched like wire, pulled longer and thinner, then compressed. Metal and plastic, ice and bone, Orbs and Grisly Grin —all cracked and crushed, flamed and flashed, then squeezed to a point. STOP! Push IT back under. Last chance . . . *think*! "Down in power distribution— RAPS! All we have to do is . . ."

Jake read mental gyros, again rammed feet against display and shot into blackness. Shoulders passed through main tunnel opening, lower back hit edge and pain shot through spine. Body clawed and kicked and accelerated. Head glanced off handrail, elbows bumped over walls and hands probed openings. One . . . two . . . three . . . four . . . damn, overshot!

Hands seized handrails, arms pulled and body flew back. Right opening—maintenance complex.

Corner of first equipment box brushed Jake's hands, then dug into ear and shoulder. Fingertips raced around cover and tore at latches. Arms stretched wide, hands grabbed opposite edges, shoulders flexed and yanked cover off.

Exposed panel glimmered warm red. Luminescent surfaces outlined each circuit breaker, each electronic switch. Faint clicks danced at random inside. Circuits responded and pulsed, controlled not by CT 7000, but by external command.

Jake's eyes flicked across panel. Mind searched . . . NUCLEAR COOLANT PUMP 1 . . . PUMP 2 . . . HEAT EXCHANGER 1 . . . EXCHANGER 2 . . . HIBERNATION PODS 1, 2, 3, others . . . no open slots. Every slot filled. No RAPS!

He pounced on the next box, ripped off its cover . . . full!

Next . . . same.

Next . . .

"Jake. This one!"

He lunged toward Speed's voice. Three dim red panels emerged from blackness. One outlined Speed's torso.

"Speed, reach up."

"Got ya. Jake, look there, two open slots—gotta be RAPS!"

"Rip off the panel."

"Won't tear. Just bends."

"Good enough, Speed. Just hold it up. Yeah, there . . . need to make RAPS connections to emergency power right there!"

"No wire."

"Hold it. Be right back."

Jake pushed off. Four panels glowed warm red from the direction he'd just come. He landed on the first. His fingers pried up the surface by switches marked HIBERNATION PODS 4, 5, 6. He bent it back and wrapped both hands around one pair of wires. He yanked—nothing. He yanked again—nothing. He yanked and yanked and yanked—nothing. Then he yanked one wire at a time—each one yielded.

Jake clutched the two wires with both hands as he glided toward Speed. Blood seeped from sliced flesh onto insulation.

"Comin' at ya."

Speed grabbed Jake's collar and pulled him down again. "Good thinkin'."

"Just long enough to reach."

"Jake, right there, right next to the breakers—RAPS backup manual controls."

"Right. Gotta select mode of operation first, but there's thousands of 'em."

"Which one could ever be effective on that thing out there?"

"I don't know, Speed, but we've gotta pick one that'll keep it away from us!"

"What's its nature? What could it want more than what's in our minds?"

"Maybe it's like everything we know on Earth."

"Like us, Jake? Everything human or human-made?"

"Yeah, and with the same instincts."

"And the same weakness!"

"Right!"

"That narrows it down, Jake."

"Sure does . . . down to one. There! It's set on EMM."

"But it could like the EMM so much that it'll burn out the transmitters . . . just like before."

"Not if we give it this, Speed. It's set for three minutes of EMM, then sustained ECM. Let's put the power to it."

"The old one-two—it's our best shot."

"Pull the panel up a bit more . . . good. Got it. One end on. Now just a few more twists of this little guy and . . . there. One wire hooked up, one to go."

Jake straightened the second wire and hooked one end to the open RAPS connector. He slid his hand to the other end and moved it toward the power line. His motion slowed, skin tingled and tightened, hair lifted off his neck and head as dull probes sharpened and thrust inward toward brain center. Jake's mind accelerated and body froze. His vision recorded the copper wire and silver power line, saw the copper-silver separation widen—then open to a chasm!

A fluid force washed over him, wrapped around him, permeated him and submerged him. It dissolved the glue of his discipline and made way for steel commands that now locked him in place.

Jake, no longer able to act, observed without passion, without fear. He watched copper and silver fade to gray, a light airy gray. He let commands focus his mind on a distant point, focus all his awareness on a dark dot of compact pain. Packets of thought and light streamed toward Dot as it danced and dodged.

Dot advanced and grew, pricked and pierced, lightened and brightened, burned and blazed—and extracted and consumed!

Mind functioned, perhaps for the last time. So this is what it's like to die. Time's up. It's here. My turn and my time. But do I want to die? Lose life? Lose Val? No, probably not. No, no thank you. Not today. Not just yet. Not ready. Too much to do. Too much VAL. Too much LIFE. No! HELL NO! Get back into real world . . . copper and silver chasm—close it! But arms're frozen—FORCE it!

Jake saw his hand move.

"Hey, ole buddy, ya look a tad tuckered."

He felt Speed's hand wrap around his, saw copper and silver join in a violet-white arc, heard its zap, smelled its smoke . . .

37

Choke

Choke hesitated.

This first shell, the one called Jake, presented a unique challenge. Choke'd smashed it once, but it yielded only enough to leak out a squib of its enticing aroma. Hunger flared! Never before did Choke have to smash a shell twice. Never! It needed more force. Choke paused, gathered its energy, focused and . . .

Flow . . . a flow of new hors d'oeuvres! Unrequested, Flow streamed from the second enclosure into Choke and down its gullet. Within but a swallow, Flow tasted familiar. Within three swallows, Flow's magnetism captured Choke. And within a dozen swallows, Flow's allure and appeal intensified into something more acceptable and more pleasant than anything Choke'd ever consumed, something bearing a brilliant message, something close, something intimate.

AGREEMENT—RESONANCE—HARMONY!

Choke released its electrical utensils and ignored the three unopened shells. The potential contents of any human mind, whether gifted or retarded, compassionate or malicious, faded to a distant second. The potential value of the shell's balanced diet could offer no competition to Flow's sumptuous string of narcotic delicacies. Nutrition lost to drug. Like an opiate, Flow brought Choke a comfort and a well-being it'd rarely known.

Choke opened wide, relaxed . . . and gobbled and gulped and gorged.

"You OK, Jake?"

"Yeah, think so. Let me tighten this connection."

"You went out on me there."

"I could hardly seem to move this wire. I . . . thanks."

"Think it's working?"

"Don't know, Speed. Have to wait. But I feel better. Headache's gone."

"Mine, too. Good sign."

"Hey, we got lights."

"Jake, you're a mess! Who's your tailor?"

"Listen, the jets aren't popping anymore. And . . . that's Faye."

They floated into the main tunnel, then toward Faye's voice.

"She's in the command center," said Jake.

They glided to where Faye worked at a display.

"What is it?" asked Jake.

"Computer. Good old CT 7000's back up. And all systems look good except for the burned out transmitters."

"Either the RAPS is doing its job, or you really know how to sweet talk a computer," said Speed.

"I vote for RAPS," said Faye.

"Any transmissions from Ada or Irwin?" asked Jake.

"No. It's possible they're OK, but I doubt it," said Faye.

Hurt flickered across Speed's face. "That's the way I read it, too."

"As soon as we get by perigee, we've gotta get to 'em," said Jake.

"Did the experiments record any data while all this has been goin' on?" asked Speed.

"Looks like all of 'em stayed up and running on

their own internal power," said Faye. "As they're programmed to do, they each acquired data, analyzed it and kept asking more questions. And, for some reason, whatever's out there completely ignored 'em."

Jake checked his watch. "Minute twenty to perigee. Let's strap in, just in case." He paused, waited for the other two to tighten their restraints, then dimmed the lights. "It'll be a sharp corner. We should be able to see the sky rotate. The heavy end of the module with the propellant will stay pointed at the hole and we oughta feel some centrifugal force."

He braced, waited and felt nothing . . . nothing . . . nothing . . . A soft force, a gentle force, plucked at him and nudged him against his straps. Structure groaned, soft and low like a distant foghorn, then force faded back into silence.

Speed looked disappointed. "You mean, that's it, dear? It's all over? We're through?"

"All I saw was the sky flip half a turn," said Faye.

"That's about all there is to it," said Jake. "We've turned the corner."

They floated to the windows.

"Can't see much except stars," said Faye. "No. There's some faint flashes."

"Yeah, I see 'em," said Speed. "Must be dust-sized Objects that drift into the hole like . . ."

Jake pressed his face against the window. "Look back and hold your head still. It's like watchin' the ground at liftoff. We're really moving out!"

Light from the Wayfarers reflected from Speed's eyes and teeth, from his grin. "Big hill, and at last we're on the way back up."

Faye's grin matched Speed's. "My headache's gone. How do you both feel?"

"Good," said Jake.

"Same here," said Speed. "You were pretty rocky for a while there, boss man. What happened?"

"Don't know. Like a bad dream, one I can't remember."

"From what I saw on your face, it's probably just
as well," said Speed.

Jake moved away from the window. "We need to
take a thorough look at all systems. You two start. I'm
going to check the RAPS. If it stays healthy, so do
we."

Within minutes Choke's empty buffers and digestive tract, devoid of real nourishment, issued
more pangs of hunger. But Flow could not be ignored. Instinct told Choke that a stronger Flow could
again subdue its hunger. Yes, turn Flow up to maximum, just like it had before. Choke opened wide,
gripped its electrical utensils and reached into the
enclosure.

That's when it happened—Flow changed!

In an instant, Flow carried sharp pits and thorns
that cut into Choke's mouth, ripped at its throat and
tore into the lining of its digestive tract. And its taste
turned obnoxious and offensive. Never before had
Choke consumed anything so painful and excruciat-
ing, anything so repulsive and repugnant.

DISSENSION—DISCORD—CONFLICT!

Choke spit Flow from its mouth and slammed
itself closed. But a retch forced Choke open just
enough to vomit the Flow that still offended its
chambers. Though Choke shut itself up tight again, it
couldn't stop the retches and heaves in its innards,
nor the trembles and shudders that rippled throughout its entire organism as it fought to accommodate
what Flow had already infiltrated its flesh.

As Choke's trauma slackened, it focused outside
just long enough to retract its utensils from the unopened shells that drifted outward. No shell, regardless of its contents, could be worth the shock. By
instinct, Choke could take but one and only action—
complete rejection.

Jake disliked cleanups, especially messy ones.
And this one required all his mental endurance.

They'd docked with their sister module and found Boris, Irwin and Ada in the condition they feared. Without much success, Jake tried to recouple his mind from his vision as he helped Faye run a wide range of tests. Speed located the unused RAPS transmitter and installed it in their own module as a backup. And at apogee, they gave the other half of their crew a gentle push that put them on a trajectory in pursuit of Ted. Then they rendezvoused for the second time with Ted's crew and also gave them a precise, and by now all-too-familiar, nudge toward the infinitesimal crypt.

Jake continued to stare in the direction of *Wayfarer 1* long after it'd faded into the stellar background. They were finished. At last! Ted, his five and Jake's three—all on their way there. But where? Nine gone, only three left. No, not a good score. Lucky it wasn't zero to twelve. They now had a whole potful of data, but he'd trade it all for the nine. Maybe to others back home, the data'll seem more important. Maybe it'll even stimulate the next step. Worth it? Jake had no way to know, but the human value he understood—nine large losses.

Nine fresh sorrows blossomed in Jake's mind, sorrows that bloomed like flowers, funeral flowers that in time would drift to the rear and fade into an abundant background of older flowers, but sorrows that could each surge forward again in response to their own unique mental triggers, explode with another pulse of pain, then withdraw to the rear and lie in wait again.

Acceleration felt good, and it seemed stronger. In fact, it'd climbed to two-thirds earth's gravity. Although their engine's thrust had remained the same, their mass, through loss of propellant, had decreased to only 37 percent of what it'd been at mission start.

Jake bounced on the balls of his feet to release the energy pent up in his legs, steadied himself on the edge of the wardroom table with his fingertips d looked directly overhead at the only star visible, ood Old Reliable Sun, a unique star that clung to eir destination—a tiny blue ball of dirt that in turn ung to all he knew and loved.

Jake's eyes dropped inside.

"You're a genius, boss man, a frappin' genius."

"Speed's right," said Faye. "What gave you the sight to think of the RAPS?"

Jake pressed his fingers and palms around his ot, cream-colored coffee and studied their faces. ou guys gave me all the hints, and Klaus'd sent all e right data. But actually, insight's more attitude an intelligence or hints or data."

Speed nodded. "You're so right, Jake. I don't now what got into me. You're not a genius!"

"Wish I understood what we were up against," id Faye.

"Any clues in what your examinations turned p?" asked Jake.

"Only thing noticeable by inspection is that eir brain tissue looked thermally altered by electri- al current, right down to the neurons."

"Ya mean . . . cooked?" asked Speed.

Faye giggled. "Oh boy. This's gonna be a long de home." She paused. "Jake? How'd you two come p with the right mode for the RAPS?"

"Again, no logic, just a hunch."

"We assumed that whatever kind of goliath's out ere acts just like any one of us, or like any human oliath we've ever created back home," said Speed. That's why we selected the EMM."

"EMM?"

Jake nodded. "Yeah, the Enhanced Mimic Mode. 's a unique operating mode that reproduces the coming signal, adds more detail to it, amplifies it nd then sends it right back toward the source at full trength."

"Following that, Jake programmed RAPS into he ECM, the Enhanced Contrarian Mode," said peed. "It's just like the EMM except the signal it

feeds back is opposite in every respect to what cam
in."

"Do you think this thing was really after ou
minds?" asked Faye.

"No way to know for sure . . . yet," said Jake

"What could this thing do if it ever reache
Earth and could feed there?" asked Speed.

"Hell of a thought," said Jake. "Maybe after ev
erybody back home studies the data, *Wayfarer 3* ca
figure out what's out here."

"*Wayfarer 3*?" asked Faye. "Think there'll b
one?"

Jake's eyes sharpened. "No doubt about it! Th
only questions are who and when."

"Just the same, it's going to be a tough sell whe
we get back," said Faye. "We've got a bit of explain
ing to do."

"Afraid you're right," said Jake. "No matte
what we say or what's found in the data, they'll tro
out the same old issues and beat us with 'em agai
It'll be tough to force out another step."

Speed's eyes ignited. He flexed his ankle
hopped onto the center of the table and swept h
hand outward. "My fellow members of the Federa
tion. Don't let these cosmic kooks keep pouring ou
money into *their* stellar sink holes." He wagged h
index finger down at Jake and Faye. "We have th
sober obligation to distribute our people's money t
where it'll do our people the most good—at home
We need to build more space stations, upgrade ou
Mars and lunar stations and establish stations on th
outer planets. We have to take care of our people a
home first!"

Speed shook his finger again at Jake and Faye a
he stepped forward. "And I warn you. If we fail t
rein in these frivolous fools who romp outward at th
fringe of our society, our proud nation will be force
to pull our support outta the Federation!"

Jake grimaced and glared up. "Speed!"

"Yeah?"

"How about pullin' your foot outta my cereal."

"Oooops." Speed flipped over backwards and landed in his original position on the floor.

Jake turned to the pantry for another bowl. "The world's not quite ready yet. Don't go into politics."

"Wish I could laugh, Speed, but you're not too far from the truth," said Faye.

"Actually, Jake's right," said Speed. "This program'll go on just like the others. The cynical press and their feeders will make a lot of negative noise. But, in a few years and a little farther down the road, we'll look at 'em all in the rearview mirror and see 'em as just a few more speed bumps, just a few more bumps in that neverending string of bumps we somehow always put in our own way—annoyances that slow our outward reach but never stop it."

Jake poured fresh cereal into his clean bowl. "And it won't be all that bad either when we get back. There'll also be a few politicians who'll go out on the limb to support *Wayfarer 3*, a few who'll take their eyes off their shoes and look down the road, a few who'll do what's right in the long run. And eventually, they'll win out—they have to."

"Have to?" asked Faye.

Speed bounced on his toes. "Yep. As long as people are alive, sooner or later it'll happen. Outward reach is a basic human drive." His bounces strengthened. "It's like a river—it just keeps on a comin'. Most people just stand on the bank and watch it. Others ride with it. Some even paddle ahead on it. And then there's always those who try to dam it up, to choke it down to a trickle or even bring it to a stop. But in time the river always builds, overruns their dams and washes 'em to the side."

Jake watched Speed's bounces heighten. "You're almost making sense, Speederoo. Like I said, it's only when and who."

"I'd love to be alive fifty years from now and see how far we've gotten," said Faye.

Jake beamed. "So would I. It'd sure make you forget the problems of our times!"

Speed's knees reached table height. "Well, boss man, there's one thing I sure won't let you forget when we get back."

Jake put his hand over his cereal and pulled the bowl closer. "What?"

"Our first RT7 flight . . ."

"Yeah?"

"I've got front seat!"

Epilogue

Next Please

The door slammed. He glanced down at the folded newspaper left in the empty seat to his right. A single word commanded his attention and pulled his mind forward in search of meaning.

UN Subcommittee Labels Wayfarer
An Economic And Moral Outrage

NEW YORK, February, 22, 2040—In a sharply worded release, the U.N. Agriculture and Space Subcommittee chairman today repeated demands that the World Space Federation suspend all Wayfarer 3 resource expenditure until U.N. General Assembly Special Resolution WF-3/40 is passed. "Before we bring WF-3/40 to the Assembly, we must carefully synthesize the findings of our own independent Wayfarer investigation, our review of the reports of three independent Wayfarer Commissions and our analyses of the two petitions to the World Court for indictments of key program participants," said Chairman Moshe Sakar. "Also at issue here is whether control of appropriations should reside only with a single world agency rather than with the more equitable distribution of a shared authority for all . . ."

"Wayfarer," a close and personal word, penetrated deep. But the other words skipped off the surface of his mind as flat, hard pebbles, all officia and authoritative words, but all cold and irrelevan words—especially now.

He positioned the paper on the floor, fixed hi stare on the invisible end of the runway over the horizon and slid the throttle forward. Rigid feature yielded to a smile as he accelerated. He finessed the stick back.

Forces, real and trusty and understood, lifted Willie off the ground for his initial solo.

A Note From the Author

dward Gibson's next novel—working title **Gifts of
xcellence**—*is coming soon. Although Dr. Gibson
as reluctant to supply an excerpt so far in advance
f final draft, he decided that discussing some of his
leas wouldn't be giving away that much of what the
ovel holds in store. . . .*

Let's build another you, or another me. What's
aat? You want to make a few alterations, a few im-
rovements? Sure . . . no problem!

From stones to steel, marble to microchips,
hatever the building blocks, we humans have al-
ays loved to build, always felt compelled to apply
very new engineering talent. But what should we
o now that we've just about acquired the inevitable
—the knowledge and skills to build one of us? There
an be no doubt that among us there will be a Few
hose arrogance exceeds their wisdom, whose com-
ulsion exceeds their restraint.

Will it happen?

The blueprints and step-by-step instructions to
uild another one of us can be found in a six-foot-long
aread, actually two helical strands of interwound
)NA less than one millionth of an inch wide. In con-
ept, it's simple. Nucleotides, the thread's building
locks, come in only four varieties. To build another
aread, all we have to do is select the right block and,
/ith the wonders of computers and automation, con-

nect it to the previous block about three billion time
in a row. Then we will have synthesized a nascen
human life.

But three billion in a row? That could be a bit c
a challenge, even for the Few. How could anyon
ever make all those choices?

With the basics of genetic engineering now un
derstood, we have set about to "map" the nucleo
tides in our DNA, to enter into computers the dat
that specifies the content of our chromosomes an
genes. This multi-billion-dollar Human Genome In
tiative has just started and picks up efficiency an
supporters as it goes. In the future many geneti
birth defects, including cystic fibrosis, sickle-cell ane
mia and Downs syndrome, will be detected and re
paired immediately after conception. And given th
DNA of a couple, the potential for defects can b
accurately assessed even before conception. Yes,
good argument can be made to even the prudent an
moral that the Initiative will be well worth the in
vestment.

But back to the Few.

In the past we have rarely been content to onl
patch and repair when we have the ability to d
more. Will the Few lead us down the same road i
genetic engineering: first replicate, then improv
and finally optimize? Of course we should strive t
eliminate birth defects. But wouldn't you also lik
your offspring to be a little taller, a little stronger, o
most certainly, a little smarter? And once we start t
"optimize" our physical and mental beings, wha
happens to our society's tolerance for perceived "im
perfections"—or even diversity? Given society'
trends today, should we be optimistic?

Ahhh . . . a little stronger you say? . . . a littl
smarter? What's that doctor's number again? Hey
why not unsurpassed excellence for all?

No! We all know that in the end moral men wil
prevail. Laws will be passed, regulations will be im
plemented, and thorough inspections of every

rthly genetic engineering facility will be per-
rmed. Good, we've put that danger to rest.

Hey, who's that over in the dark corner of space?
hy it's one of the Few . . . and he's at it again!

New laws create new outlaws. The Few will al-
ays surface. There'll always be those with the capa-
lity, motivation and seclusion to do what moral
en fear most. It's simply a basic rule of human na-
re—there'll always be at least one little kid smirk-
g in the back of the room.

To the Few, might confers right. They never feel
e burden to balance power with privilege, never
guish over where technical reasoning leaves off
d morals and wisdom begin, and never ponder if
NA came first, then intelligence, or intelligence
st, then DNA. They have more urgent matters to
tend to.

Ahh yes, the Few—so much to do. . . .

EDWARD GIBSON

ABOUT THE AUTHOR

DR. EDWARD GIBSON was selected as a scientist-astronomer by NASA in June 1965. He served as a member of the astronau[t] support crew and as a capcom for the *Apollo 12* lunar landing. Dr. Gibson was the scientist-pilot of *Skylab 3* (the third and final manned visit to the *Skylab* space station), the longes[t] American manned space flight in the history of space explora[-]tion to date. He is presently Space Operations Consultant for Booz, Allen and Hamilton, Inc. REACH is his first novel.